THE SIGN OF THREE

Advances in Semiotics
THOMAS A. SEBEOK, GENERAL EDITOR

THE SIGN OF THREE

Dupin, Holmes, Peirce

EDITED BY

Umberto Eco and Thomas A. Sebeok

INDIANA UNIVERSITY PRESS

Bloomington

Library of Congress Cataloging in Publication Data
Main entry under title:

The Sign of three.

(Advances in semiotics)
Bibliography: p. 221
1. Doyle, Arthur Conan, Sir, 1859–1930—Characters—
Sherlock Holmes. 2. Poe, Edgar Allan, 1809–1849—
Characters—Auguste Dupin. 3. Peirce, Charles S.
(Charles Sanders), 1839–1914. 4. Detective and mystery
stories—History and criticism. 5. Criminal investiga-
tion in literature. 6. Logic in literature. 7. Semiotics.
I. Eco, Umberto. II. Sebeok, Thomas Albert, 1920–
III. Series.
PR4624.S53   1984   823'.8   82–49207
ISBN 0–253–35235–5
1 2 3 4 5 87 86 85 84 83

CONTENTS

PREFACE

The editors agree that this book has not been "programmed," which is to say, it did not result from rule and case, from, in a word, deduction. Peirce taught that it is not absolutely true that every event is "determined by causes according to law," as, for example, "if a man and his antipode sneeze at the same instant, [t]hat is merely what we call coincidence" (1.406). Consider the following peculiar sequence of events:

(1) In 1978, Sebeok casually told Eco that he and Jean Umiker-Sebeok are studying the "method" of Sherlock Holmes in the light of Peirce's logic. Eco answered that he was just then writing a lecture (which he eventually delivered, in November of that year, at the second International Colloquium on Poetics, organized by the Department of French and Romance Philology, at Columbia University), comparing the use of abductive methodology in Voltaire's *Zadig* with that of Holmes. Since both the undersigned were already incurably addicted to Peirce, this seeming coincidence was less than confounding.

(2) Sebeok then remarked that he knew of an essay, on much the same topic, published some years earlier by Marcello Truzzi, a sociologist and evident Holmes buff, not especially known to be "into" semiotics. Truzzi, citing mainly Popper, not Peirce, was undoubtedly concerned with the problem of abduction or, in any case, with hypothetical-deductive methods.

(3) A few weeks later, Sebeok found out that the eminent Finnish logician, Jaakko Hintikka, had written two (at the time) unpublished papers on Sherlock Holmes and modern logic. Hintikka made no explicit reference to Peirce's abduction, but the problem was the same.

(4) During the same period, Eco read a paper, published in 1979, which one of his colleagues at the University of Bologna had been announcing for a year or more. This paper recounted the employment of conjectural models from Hippocrates and Thucydides, to their use by art experts in the nineteenth century. The author, historian Carlo Ginzburg, quoted, however, in his revealing footnotes, *Zadig,* Peirce, and even Sebeok. It goes without saying that Sherlock Holmes was a chief protagonist in this erudite study, side by side with Freud and Morelli.

(5) Next, Sebeok and Umiker-Sebeok published an early version of their study—after the former delivered it, in October 1978, as a lecture at Brown University, within the framework of a meeting devoted to "Methodology in Semiotics"—juxtaposing Peirce and Holmes; and Eco published his lecture on *Zadig.* The latter then organized, in 1979, a six-month seminar at the University of Bologna on Peirce and detective novels. At almost the same time, Sebeok—completely unaware of Eco's parallel teaching activity—offered a course, entitled "Semiotic Approaches to James Bond and Sherlock Holmes,"

for Indiana University's Comparative Literature Program; (he did, however, utilize Eco's 1965 study of narrative structures in Ian Fleming). Among the more palpable consequences of Eco's seminar was the paper by two of his collaborators, Bonfantini and Proni, now included in this book; and one of the results of Sebeok's course was his analysis, jointly with one of his students in the course, Harriet Margolis, on the semiotics of windows in Sherlock Holmes (first published in a 1982 issue of *Poetics Today*). While all this was going on, Eco was pursuing researches into the history of semiotics, and ran across the Aristotelian theory of definition; his paper in this book is one outcome of these lines of investigation.

(6) In the meantime, Sebeok and Eco decided to put together these papers, and the Indiana University Press agreed, with much enthusiasm, to join them in this venture. During one of his fall courses at Yale University, Eco gave the collected manuscript materials to Nancy Harrowitz, who wrote a term paper for him on Peirce and Poe, for which Holmes's method, following a suggestion made in the paper of the Sebeoks, became an obviously compulsory term of reference.

(7) A further surprising fact came to light when Eco discovered that Gian Paolo Caprettini, at the University of Turin, had been conducting, for two years, a seminar on Peirce and Holmes. Caprettini is a well-known student of Peirce, but this was the first time that Eco and Caprettini spoke together about Holmes. This coincidence was at least worth following up, as a sequel of which Caprettini, too, was invited to collaborate in this book.

We are under the impression that, if we continued to fumble around, we might well have found other similar contributions. (Perhaps the spirit of history expressed in the *Zeitgeist* of our age is not a mere Hegelian specter!) But we had to abandon our quest, if for no other reason, for lack of time. Much to our regret, we also had to eliminate many other interesting materials dealing with the "method" of Holmes which did not take into account the logic of abduction (cf. our consolidated References in this book, and more generally, Ronald Burt De Waal's incomparable *World Bibliography of Sherlock Holmes and Dr. Watson,* 1974–). The secondary literature concerning Sherlock Holmes adds up to a truly awesome array of items, but we wished to concentrate on those relatively few and recent items that are pertinent to the history of abductive methodology. In the course of our researches, we both came to realize that every modern scholar interested in the logic of discovery has devoted at least a few lines, if not more, to Holmes. Saul Kripke, for example, wrote to Sebeok, on December 29, 1980, a letter which said, in part: "Actually I have one or two unpublished talks and a whole unpublished lecture series (my John Locke lectures at Oxford) on fictional discourse in empty names, in which Holmes might appear even more prominently" than in his earlier use of him in his "Semantical Considerations on Modal Logic," or the Addenda to his "Naming and Necessity." Many works are still tied to the idea that Holmes's method hovered somewhere midway between deduction and induction. The idea of hypothesis or abduction is mentioned, if at all, only glancingly.

Obviously, not all the contributions to this book come to the same conclusions. The editors do not wish to confront the differences in approach here, but to leave it to the reader to evaluate and use them, each according to his own interest.

The title of this book was meant to reverberate in two directions. There is the obvious referral (*renvoi*) to Doyle's novel-length chronicle, "The Sign of the Four," or "The Sign of Four," which first appeared in *Lippincott's* magazine, later in book form, in 1819. Then there was our driving compulsion to send our readers back to the funhouse of rampant triplicities, such as are discussed in Sebeok's introductory three-card monte.

At the present time, the logic of scientific discovery—the phrase will, of course, be recognized as closely associated with Karl R. Popper—has become a burning topic of focal concern for the theory of knowledge, pursued not only by Popper himself, but by his colleague, the late Imre Lakatos, and by Popper's erstwhile disciple, later his most ferocious critic, Paul K. Feyerabend, among many others. Popper's controversial picture of science as a matter of "conjectures and refutations"—he holds, among other ideas, that induction is mythical, the scientific quest for certainty impossible, and all knowledge forever fallible—was substantially anticipated by Peirce, whom Popper, incidentally, regards as "one of the greatest philosophers of all time," although falsification as one logical technique among others was by no means unknown even in the Middle Ages. Critics of Popper, such as T.S. Kuhn and Anthony O'Hear, disagree with Popper on some of these fundamental issues. We are convinced that a semiotic approach to abduction can throw a new light on this venerable and continuing debate. We hope that this collection of essays will be of interest to the host of fans of Sherlock Holmes, but that it will be read, as well, by votaries of both the *Prior Analytics* (on the syllogism), and the *Posterior Analytics* (which deals with the conditions of scientific knowledge). Naturally, we also expect to fascinate some of those concerned among the ever-growing worldwide group of habitués of Peirce. We are but two of them. In a modest way, however, we think the book will also be important for epistemology and the philosophy of science.

Umberto Eco
University of Bologna

Thomas A. Sebeok
Indiana University

Abbreviations in the Text

The titles of the Sherlock Holmes stories are
abbreviated according to the key given in Tracy 1977:xix.

THE SIGN OF THREE

CHAPTER ONE

Thomas A. Sebeok

One, Two, Three
Spells U B E R T Y

(IN LIEU OF AN INTRODUCTION)

IT IS A FAIR bet that while C.S. Peirce specialists have all at least thumbed through Arthur Conan Doyle's Sherlock Holmes chronicles, the mass of Holmes aficionados have never even heard of Peirce. A key question addressed, explicitly or implicitly, by most of the contributors to this volume, is whether any juxtapositions of the American polymath with the great English detective—the former a person real enough, and the possessor, moreover, as William James registered in 1895, of "a name of mysterious greatness," the latter a mythical figure, to be sure, yet who, as Leslie Fiedler has noted, "can never die"—are likely to vent esperable uberty? Esperable uberty? Etymological intuition assures us that *esperable,* a coinage—perhaps by Peirce himself, yet not to be found in any modern dictionary—must mean "expected" or "hoped for." *Uberty,* a vocable that has all but vanished from modern English, was first attested, from 1412, in an obscure work by the "Monk of Bury," John Lydgate's *Two Merchants;* it appears to be equivalent to "rich growth, fruitfulness, fertility; copiousness, abundance," or, roughly, what Italians used to call *ubertà.*

In a long letter Peirce penned, early in the fall of 1913, to Frederick Adams Wood, M.D., an MIT lecturer in biology, he explained that it should be one of the two principal aims of logicians to educe the possible and esperable uberty, or "value in productiveness," of the three canonical types of reasoning, to wit: deduction, induction, and abduction (the latter term alternatively baptized retroduction or hypothetic inference). It is the uberty, that is, the fruitfulness, of this last type of reasoning that, he tells us, increases, while its security, or approach to certainty, minifies. He spells out the differences, which he claims to

1

have "always" (since the 1860s) recognized: first, *deduction*, "which depends on our confidence in our ability to analyze the meaning of the signs in or by which we think"; second, *induction*, "which depends upon our confidence that a run of one kind of experience will not be changed or cease without some indication before it ceases"; and, third, *abduction*, "which depends on our hope, sooner or later, to guess at the conditions under which a given kind of phenomenon will present itself" (8.384–388). Progressing from primity, through secundity, to tertiality, the relationship of security to uberty is an inverse one, which means, plainly, that as the certainty of any guess plummets, its heuristic merit soars correspondingly.

"Magic numbers and persuasive sounds," in Congreve's measured phrase, especially *three* and numbers divisible by it, tormented some of the more brilliant Victorians, and haunt some of us still. This is indeed a strangely obsessive eccentricity, shared, for one, by Nikola Tesla (1856–1943), the Serb who laid much of the foundation for the electrified civilization of the twentieth century. When Tesla started to walk around the block where his laboratory was situated, he felt compelled to circumambulate it three times; and when he dined at the Waldorf-Astoria Hotel, he used 18, or $[(3 + 3) \times 3]$, spotless linen napkins to wipe his already sparkling silver and crystal tableware clean of germs, imaginary or otherwise. The great application of the numerological style of thinking has long—since at least Pythagoras—been for categorization and list-making. Pietro Bongo, in his *De numerorum mysteria* (1618), and, before him, Cornelius Agrippa, in his *De occulta philosophia* (written in 1510, published in 1531), pursued the magic of triads with manic determination, beginning with the highest meaning of *three*, namely, the triliteral name of God in His own language, Hebrew, through the Christian Trinity of Father, Son, and Holy Ghost, to triplicities rampant in every imaginable aspect of the world scheme of the times (an enchantment that lingers in today's zodiacal signs of the Houses used in casting a horoscope; Butler 1970:68).

Conan Doyle incorporated numbers in eight of his Holmes story titles. The ordinal of two, the cardinals four, five, and six each occur only once: "The Second Stain," "The Sign of (the) Four," "The Five Orange Pips," "The Six Napoleons." *Three* is mentioned no less than three times or, by stretching an occult principle, four: "The Three Gables," "The Three Garridebs," "The Three Students," and perhaps "The Missing Three-Quarter." Moreover, the Chevalier C. Auguste Dupin, that "very inferior fellow," is the central figure in three (out of four, or five, if "Thou Art the Man" is counted among them) of Edgar Allan Poe's triptych tales of detection: "The Murders in the Rue Morgue,"

"The Mystery of Marie Rogêt," and "The Purloined Letter," together dubbed by Jacques Derrida (1975) Poe's "Dupin Trilogy," and read by Jacques Lacan (1966:11–61) in terms of a set of repeated psychoanalytic structures of *"trois temps, ordonnant trois regards, supportés par trois sujets . . . ,"* constituting a tracery like this (p. 48):

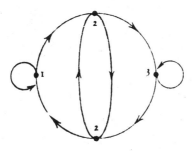

Indeed, as Derrida points out (p. 108), *"Les locutions 'trio', 'triangles', 'triangle intersubjectif' surviennents très fréquemment . . . ,"* in a reticulate *Wiederholungszwang.* (Dupin, be it recalled, lived in a mansion at 33, Rue Dunôt, *"au troisième,"* Faubourg St. Germain. (On "Poe-etics" according to Lacan and Derrida, see further Johnson 1980, Ch. 7.)

Butler's (1970:94) study shows that, in Western intellectual history, "numerological thinking was used for broadly philosophical, cosmological and theological ends." Peirce's fondness for introducing trichotomous analyses and classifications is notorious, as he knew only too well, and in defense of which he issued, in 1910, this beguiling apologia:

> *The author's response to the anticipated suspicion that he attaches a superstitious or fanciful importance to the number three and forces divisions to a Procrustean bed of trichotomy.*
>
> I fully admit that there is a not uncommon craze for trichotomies. I do not know but the psychiatrists have provided a name for it. If not, they should . . . it might be called *triadomany.* I am not so afflicted; but I find myself obliged, for truth's sake, to make such a large number of trichotomies that I could not [but] wonder if my readers, especially those of them who are in the way of knowing how common the malady is, should suspect, or even opine, that I am a victim of it. . . . I have no marked predilection for trichotomies in general. (1.568–569)

This defense notwithstanding, how fanciful is it to be reminded here that a significant portion of Peirce's career in the service of the Coast and Geodetic Survey was pnt with *triangulating* parties along the coast of Maine and of the Gulf States, and that, in 1979, a geodetic triangulation station, aptly named the "C.S. Peirce Station," was installed in recognition of this biographical circumstance in the front yard of Arisbe (his home near Milford, Pennsylvania)?

By 1857, Peirce—following "Kant, the King of modern thought" (1.369), not to mention Hegel's thesis/antithesis/synthesis (cf., in general, Peirce's letter to Lady Welby, October 12, 1904, reproduced in Hardwick [1977:22-36], which contains a lengthy exposition of the three universal categories, with specific references to both Kant and Hegel), and Schiller's trio of three "impulses" (Sebeok 1981, Ch. 1)—with the genuine philosophical aim of seeking generality and understanding the world, was already deeply immersed in the decorum of threefold classifications. The most basic of his triadic ontological categories was the pronominal system of *It*—the material world of the senses, the ultimate object of cosmology; *Thou*—the world of mind, the object of psychology and neurology; and *I*—the abstract world, the concern of theology. These basic distinctions, familiar to Peirce scholarship, are most generally called, in reverse order, Firstness, Secondness, and Thirdness, which, in turn, yield an enormously long list of further interplaying triads, the best known among them including Sign, Object, Interpretant; Icon, Index, and Symbol; Quality, Reaction, and Representation; and, of course, Abduction, Induction, and Deduction. Some are discussed, and many are displayed, in Appendix I of Esposito's excellent study (1980; cf. Peirce 1982:xxvii–xxx) of the development of Peirce's theory of categories, but these matters are so complex that they deserve much further consideration. For example, consonant with current views of the emergence of Big Bang cosmology is Peirce's statement that "Mind is First, Matter is Second, Evolution is Third" (6.32)—roughly corresponding to as many modes of being: possibility, actuality, and law (1.23).

We can say essentially nothing about the existence of the universe prior to about 20 billion years ago, save that, when it began in a singularity—equivalent to Peirce's Firstness—when any two points in the observable universe were arbitrarily close together, and the density of matter was infinite, we were past possibility and already in the realm of actuality (alias Secondness). In the opening millisecond, the universe was filled with primordial quarks. These fundamental particles, the basic building blocks from which all elementary particles are constituted, can best be grasped as signs, for as we learn from the physics of our day, "Quarks had never been seen. . . . Most physicists today believe that quarks will never be seen . . ." (Pagels 1982:231). As the universal expansion proceeded, temperatures fell to around 12^{27}K, the simple natural law that obtained in the infancy of this Cosmos unfolded into the three interactions now known as gravitation, the electroweak force, and the strong (Hadronic) force that binds the particles of the nucleus in the atom. The evolution—Thirdness—of these three forces, in a single mathematical framework, as hoped for in the Grand Unified Theory, marks the appearance of Peirce's "law," which would explain the universal preference for matter over antimatter, as well as provide a solution for the so-called horizon problem (i.e., for the homogeneity of the universe) and the flatness problem (having to do with its mass density).

At the pith of matter there is an ocean full of mere signs—or, if you like, mathematical tricks. Quarks, which Nobel-laureate Murray Gell-Mann (and Yuval Ne'eman) discussed under the label "the eight-fold way," constitute a hadron family of octets, arranged in a distinctive feature matrix built out of three quarks that come in as many "flavors." They are possessed by a postulated symmetry which, for a semiotician, resembles nothing so much as Lotz's (1962:13) tinker-toy-like cuboid Turkish vowel system:

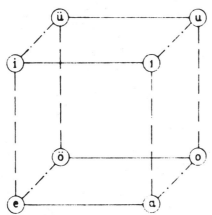

This graph projects eight phonemes in terms of three absolute binary oppositions. Comparably, the up, down, and strange quarks are denoted by u, d, and s, respectively (and so for the antiquarks $\bar{u}$, $\bar{d}$, and $\bar{s}$), with very simple rules for constructing the hadrons out of the quarks. The eightfold-way classification of hadrons for an octet would then look like the figure on the following page (6).

As for his religion, Peirce was early converted from unitarianism to trinitarianism, remaining within the Episcopalian framework. He had once written: "A Sign mediates between its *Object* and its *Meaning* . . . Object the father, sign the mother of meaning"—about which Fisch wittily commented: ". . . he might have added, of their son, the Interpretant" (Peirce 1982:xxxii).

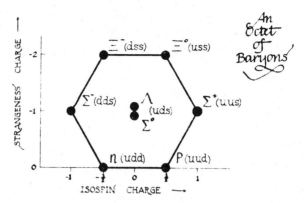

From *The Cosmic Code: Quantum Physics as the Language of Nature.* Copyright © 1982 by Heinz R. Pagels. By permission of Simon and Schuster, a division of Gulf & Western Corporation.

The radical triadicity of Freud, adumbrated recently by Larsen (1980) in specific comparison with that of Peirce, should, as Fisch (1982:128) has also urged, encourage other investigators to explore this seeming confluence of views in depth. Although Freud was probably wholly unaware of Peirce's *I, It,* and *Thou,* his 1923 tripartition of the mind into *Ego, Id,* and *Superego* (see esp. Freud 1961:19:19–39)—constituting the key concepts of psychopathology—remarkably resonates with Peirce's generative structure of semiosis. For instance, the notion of *Superego* uprears as the last of the great primal repressions out of his two earlier categories of primary and secondary repression. (Incidentally, Freud converged with Sherlock Holmes only in a novel, concocted by Nicholas Meyer, *The Seven Percent Solution,* and the film version, in collaboration with Herbert Ross.)

The title of this introductory essay, as many readers will already have recognized, echoes George Gamow's influential *One Two Three . . . Infinity* (1947). Gamow, the celebrated theorist who was the first to suggest the existence in hereditary information of the triplet code, was himself fascinated by tercets, as in the notorious letter, on the origin of chemical elements, published in the *Physical Review* (1948), the alleged authorship of which was given, jestingly, in this order, as Alpher, Bethe, and Gamow.

Peirce (rightly) held that nouns are substitutes for pronouns, not—contrary to the conventional view, and as codified in standard Western grammatical terminology—vice versa. Some of the implications of Peirce's fundamental triad for linguistics need the kind of expert attention the late John Lotz attempted (1976) in a structural analysis of this grammatical class. In this scarcely accessible paper, first published in Hungarian in 1967, Lotz demonstrated that there prevail, in fact, seven logically quite diverse possibilities among the three non-aggregate pronouns in question, only one of which, however, is viable for the language he was interested in. One relationship is triangular:

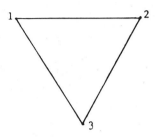

Three relationships form so-called T-structures:

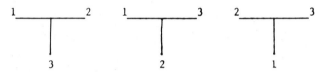

And three further relations are linear:

1	2	3
1	3	2
2	1	3

Ingram later (1978) examined the typological and universal characteristics of personal pronouns in general, claiming the existence (on the basis of 71 natural languages) of systems ranging from 4 to 15 persons, if singularity is fused with aggregation. According to Ingram, what he calls the English five-person system "is highly atypical" (ibid. 215), which, if true, would, at first blush, seem to require a thorough rethinking of Peirce's three fundamental conceptions and the immense edifice constructed upon that seemingly natural triangle. Thus, in the morphology of a language studied by one of us (Sebeok 1951) some thirty years ago, Aymara (as spoken in Bolivia), the number of grammatical persons has been determined as 3 × 3, each compacting coactions between one pair of possible interlocutors. Simplifying somewhat, the following forms can occur: first person is addresser included but addressee excluded; second person is addressee included but addresser excluded; third person is neither addresser nor addressee included; and fourth person is both addresser and addressee included. These, then, yield nine categories of possible interreaction: $1 \rightarrow 2$, $1 \rightarrow 3$, $2 \rightarrow 1$, $2 \rightarrow 3$, $3 \rightarrow 1$, $3 \rightarrow 2$, $3 \rightarrow 3$, $3 \rightarrow 4$, and $4 \rightarrow 3$. It is mind boggling to fantasy what the character of Peirce's metaphysic might have been had he been born a native speaker of a Jaqi language—a bizarre *Gedankenexperiment* for anyone who believes in the principle of linguistic relativity, or what the Swedish linguist Esaias Tegnér, in 1880, more forcefully called *språkets makt över tanken,* that is, "the power of language over thought."

Of course, for Peirce, each of the three elemental persons assumed the essence of one of the other two as the context shifted. He explained this in Ms. 917: "Though they cannot be expressed in terms of each other, yet they have a relation to each other, for THOU is an IT in which there is another I. I looks in, IT looks out, THOU co-mingles." (Another matter of interest to linguists, demanding early attention, but noted here only in passing, involves the uneasy and skewed association between the Jakobsonian dyadic principle, or binarism [e.g., Jakobson and Waugh 1979:20], *vs.* Peirce's a priori thesis of the indecomposability of triadic relations, namely, that the trisection of every field of discourse is unavoidably exhaustive, invariably yielding a trinity of mutually exclusive classes.)

Let us summarize and render concrete the foregoing by picturing Peirce's famous 1878 beanbag (2.623):

Deduction

Rule   All the beans from this bag are white.
Case   These beans are from this bag.
∴ *Result* These beans are white.

Induction

Case   These beans are from this bag.
Result These beans are white.
∴ *Rule* All the beans from this bag are white.

Abduction

Rule   All the beans from this bag are white.
Result These beans are white.
∴ *Case* These beans are from this bag.

It is important to repeat that these three figures are irreducible. "Hence, it is proved that every figure involves the principle of the first figure, but the second and third contain other principles besides" (2.807). In brief, an abduction enables us to formulate a general prediction, but with no warranty of a successful outcome; withal, abduction as a method of prognostication offers "the only possible hope of regulating our future conduct rationally" (2.270).

Note that every Argument, manifested, for example, as a Syllogism, is itself a sign, "whose interpretant represents its object as being an ulterior sign through a law, namely, the law that the passage from all such premisses to such conclusions tends to the truth" (2.263). Peirce calls any Argument a Symbolic Legisign. Each Argument is composed of three propositions: Case, Result, and Rule, in three permutations, respectively yielding the three figures displayed in the beanbag examples. But every Proposition is a sign as well, namely, one "connected with its object by an association of general ideas" (2.262), a Dicent Symbol which is necessarily a Legisign.

As both the Object and the Interpretant of any sign are perforce further signs, no wonder Peirce came to assert "that all this universe is perfused with signs," and to speculate "if it is not composed exclusively of signs" (see Sebeok 1977, passim). Even Fisch's allusion to Peirce's implied triadic family constellation of father, mother, and son—with subtle echoes of Milton's "The Childhood shows the man,/As morning shows the day," and Wordsworth's "The Child is father of the Man"—has found its anchoring in the life-science in Thom's sophisticated explanation of the genesis of signs: "Dans l'interaction 'Signifié—Signifiant' il est clair qu'entraîné par le flux universel, le Signifié émet, engendre le Signifiant en un buissonnement ramifiant ininterrompu. Mais le Signifiant réengendre le Signifié, chaque fois que nous interprétons le signe. Et comme le montre l'exemple des formes biologiques, le Signifiant (le descendant) peut redevenir le Signifié (le parent), il suffit pour cela du laps de temps d'une génération" (1980:264; Sebeok 1979:124).

Peirce, in a much discussed passage, answered the question "What is man" by categorizing him as a Symbol (7.583). As for the Universe, that he regarded as an Argument. He put forward, in a moving and memorable lecture series, delivered in the spring of 1903, the contention that the reality of Thirdness is "operative in Nature" (5.93), concluding: "The Universe as an argument is necessarily a great work of art, a great poem—for every fine argument is a poem and a symphony—just as every true poem is a sound argument. . . . The total effect is beyond our ken; but we can appreciate in some measure the resultant Quality of parts of the whole—which Qualities result from the combination of elementary Qualities that belong to the premisses" (5.119). Peirce followed this, in his next lecture, with a "series of assertions which will sound wild," and an orgy of further tripartitions, stupefying in their sweep, yet recognized by William James (1907:5) for what they were: "flashes of brilliant light relieved against Cimmerian darkness."

At the time of Poe's centenary, in 1911, Sir Arthur Conan Doyle presided at a celebratory dinner in London. It was he who passed on to Sherlock Holmes, among other facets of Dupin's qualities, that cunning ability, that bewitching semiotic illusion, to decode and disclose the profoundly private thoughts of others by reincarnating their unvoiced interior dialogues into verbal signs. He asked: "Where was the detective story until Poe breathed the breath of life into it?" (Symons 1978:170). In 1908, Peirce, referring to a remark of Poe's in "The Murders in the Rue Morgue" ("It appears to me that this mystery is considered insoluble for the very reason which should cause it to be regarded as easy of solution. I mean the outré character of its features.") said that "those problems that at first blush appear utterly insoluble receive, in that very circumstance . . . their smoothly-fitting keys" (6.460; see also Ch. 2 in this book). Where, then, we feel entitled to ask, were logic and physical science before Peirce instilled the law of liberty into them, that he called, in a coinage replete with uberty, the Play of Musement?

CHAPTER TWO

Thomas A. Sebeok and Jean Umiker-Sebeok

"You Know My Method":

A JUXTAPOSITION OF CHARLES S. PEIRCE AND SHERLOCK HOLMES[1]

"I never guess."
—Sherlock Holmes in *The Sign of Four*

But we must conquer the truth by guessing, or not at all.
—Charles S. Peirce, Ms. 692[2]

C.S. PEIRCE—CONSULTING DETECTIVE[3]

On Friday, June 20, 1879, Charles S. Peirce boarded the Fall River Line steamship *Bristol* in Boston, bound for New York, where he was to attend a conference the next day. Upon his arrival in New York, the following morning, he experienced what he describes as a "strange fuzzy sensation" in his head, which he attributed to the stale air of his stateroom. He hurriedly dressed and left the ship. In his haste to get some fresh air, he inadvertently left behind his overcoat and an expensive Tiffany lever watch which had been purchased for him by the U.S. government for his work with the Coast Survey. Soon realizing his oversight, Peirce rushed back to the boat only to find his things gone, at which point, faced with what he felt would be a "life-long professional disgrace" were he not able to restore the watch in as perfect condition as he had received it, he tells us that, having "then made all the colored waiters, no matter on what deck they belonged, come and stand up in a row . . . ,"

I went from one end of the row to the other, and talked a little to each one, in as *dégagé* a manner as I could, about whatever he could talk about with interest, but would least expect me to bring forward, hoping that I might seem such a fool that I should be able to detect some symptom of his being the thief. When I had gone through the row I turned and walked from them, though not away, and said to myself, "Not the least scintilla of light have I got to go upon." But thereupon my other self (for our communings are always in dialogues), said to me, "But you simply *must* put your finger on the man. No matter if you have no reason, you must say

11

Fig. 1. The *Bristol* (Fall River Line). From Hilton 1968:28.
Reproduced with the permission of Howell-North Books.

whom you will think to be the thief." I made a little loop in my walk, which
had not taken a minute, and as I turned toward them, all shadow of doubt
had vanished. There was no self-criticism. All that was out of place. (Peirce
1929:271)

Taking the suspect aside, Peirce was unable to persuade him, either
through reason, threat, or promise of fifty dollars, to return his belong-
ings to him. He then "ran down to the dock and was driven as fast as
the cabby could, to Pinkerton's." He was taken to see a Mr. Bangs, the
head of the New York branch of that famous detective agency, and
reports the following interview:

"Mr. Bangs, a negro on the Fall River boat, whose name is so-and-so (I
gave it) has stolen my watch, chain, and light overcoat. The watch is a
Charles Frodsham and here is its number. He will come off the boat at one
o'clock, and will immediately go to pawn the watch, for which he will get
fifty dollars. I wish you to have him shadowed, and as soon as he has the
pawn ticket, let him be arrested." Said Mr. Bangs, "What makes you think
he has stolen your watch?" "Why," said I, "I have no reason whatever for
thinking so; but I am entirely confident that it is so. Now if he should not
go to a pawn shop to get rid of the watch, as I am sure he will, that would
end the matter, and you need take no step. But I know he will. I have
given you the number of the watch, and here is my card. You will be quite
safe to arrest him." (1929:273)

A Pinkerton man was assigned to his case, but instructed to "act upon
his own inferences" rather than follow Peirce's surmises about who the

Fig. 2. Charles S. Peirce. (From the National Academy of Sciences, presumedly taken soon after Peirce's election to that institution, in 1877.)

culprit was. The detective, looking into the personal background of each Fall River waiter, began shadowing a man other than Peirce's suspect, and this proved to be a false lead.

When the detective thus came to a dead end in his investigation, Peirce returned to Mr. Bangs, and was advised by him to send postcards to all the pawnbrokers of Fall River, New York, and Boston, offering a reward for the recovery of his watch. The postcards were mailed out on June 23. The next day, Peirce and his Pinkerton agent recovered the watch from a New York lawyer, who directed them to the pawnbroker who had responded to his offer of a reward. The pawnbroker himself "described the person who pawned the watch so graphically that no doubt was possible that it had been 'my [i.e., Peirce's] man'" (1929:275).

Fig. 3. George H. Bangs, General Manager of Pinkerton's National
Detective Agency 1865–1881. From Horan 1967:28. Reproduced
with the permission of Pinkerton's, Inc.

Peirce and the detective then made their way to the suspect's lodgings, with the intention of also recovering the missing chain and overcoat. The detective was reluctant to enter the premises without a war-
rant, so Peirce, disgusted by the agent's ineptitude, went in alone,
confidently telling the agent that he would return in exactly twelve
minutes with his property. He then described the following sequence of
events:

I mounted the three flights and knocked at the door of the flat. A yellow
woman came; but another of about the same complexion was just behind

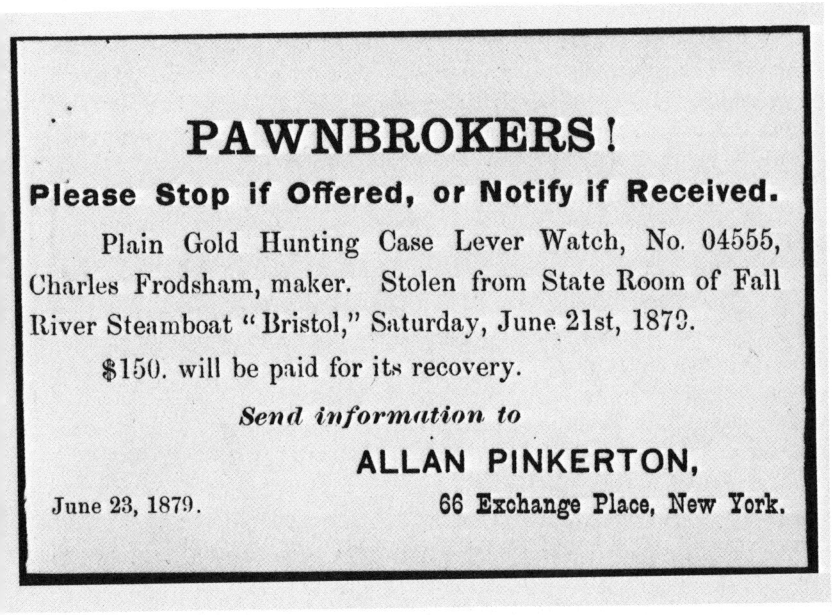

PAWNBROKERS!

Please Stop if Offered, or Notify if Received.

Plain Gold Hunting Case Lever Watch, No. 04555, Charles Frodsham, maker. Stolen from State Room of Fall River Steamboat "Bristol," Saturday, June 21st, 1879.

$150. will be paid for its recovery.

Send information to

ALLAN PINKERTON,

June 23, 1879.   66 Exchange Place, New York.

Fig. 4. An unused sample postcard offering a reward for the recovery of Peirce's watch. From the Coast and Geodetic Survey files in the National Archives.

her, without a hat. I walked in and said, "Your husband is now on his road to Sing Sing for stealing my watch. I learned that my chain and overcoat which he also stole are here and I am going to take them." Thereupon the two women raised a tremendous hullabaloo and threatened to send instantly for the police. I do not remember exactly what I said, I only know that I was entirely cool[4] and told them they were quite mistaken in thinking that they would send for the police, since it would only make matters worse for the man. For since I knew just where my watch and overcoat were, I should have them before the police arrived. . . . I saw no place in that room where the chain was likely to be, and walked through into another room. Little furniture was there beyond a double bed and a wooden trunk on the further side of the bed. I said, "Now my chain is at the bottom of that trunk under the clothes; and I am going to take it. . . ." I knelt down and fortunately found the trunk unlocked. Having thrown out all the clothes . . . I came upon . . . my chain. I at once attached it to my watch, and in doing so noticed that the second woman (who had worn no hat) had disappeared, notwithstanding the intense interest she had taken in my first proceedings. "Now," said I, "it only remains to find my light overcoat." . . . The woman spread her arms right and left and said, "You are welcome to look over the whole place." I said, "I am very much obliged to you,

Madam; for this very extraordinary alteration of the tone you took when I began on the trunk assures me that the coat is not here. . . ." So I left the flat and then remarked that there was another flat on the same landing.

Although I do not positively remember, I think it likely that I was convinced that the disappearance of the other woman was connected with the marked willingness that I should search for my overcoat through the flat from which I had emerged. I certainly got the idea that the other woman did not live far off. So to begin with I knocked at the door of that opposite flat. Two yellow or yellowish girls came. I looked over their shoulders and saw a quite respectable looking parlor with a nice piano. But upon the piano was a neat bundle of just the right size and shape to contain my overcoat. I said, "I have called because there is a bundle here belonging to me; oh, yes, I see it, and will just take it." So I gently pushed beyond them, took the bundle, opened it, and found my overcoat, which I put on. I descended to the street, and reached my detective about fifteen seconds before my twelve minutes had elapsed. (1929:275–277)

The next day, June 25, Peirce wrote to Superintendent Patterson that "The two negroes who stole the watch were today committed for trial. Everything had been recovered. The thief is the very man I suspected throughout contrary to the judgment of the detective."[5]

As noted in a later letter to his friend and disciple, the Harvard philosopher and psychologist William James (1842–1910), this story of detection was meant as an illustration of Peirce's "theory of why it is that people so often guess right." "This singular guessing instinct" (1929:281), or the inclination to entertain a hypothesis, more commonly referred to by Peirce as *Abduction*[6] or *Retroduction,* is described as a "singular salad . . . whose chief elements are its groundlessness, its ubiquity, and its trustworthiness" (Ms. 692). As to its ubiquity, Peirce writes:

Looking out my window this lovely spring morning I see an azalea in full bloom. No, no! I do not see that; though that is the only way I can describe what I see. *That* is a proposition, a sentence, a fact; but what I perceive is not proposition, sentence, fact, but only an image, which I make intelligible in part by means of a statement of fact. This statement is abstract; but what I see is concrete. I perform an abduction when I so much as express in a sentence anything I see. The truth is that the whole fabric of our knowledge is one matted felt of pure hypothesis confirmed and refined by induction. Not the smallest advance can be made in knowledge beyond the stage of vacant staring, without making an abduction at every step. (Ms. 692)

If all new knowledge depends on the formation of a hypothesis, there nevertheless "seems at first to be no room at all for the question of what supports it, since from an actual fact it only infers a *may-be* (*may-be* and *may-be* not). But there is a decided leaning to the affirmative side and the frequency with which that turns out to be an actual fact is . . . quite the most surprising of all the wonders of the universe" (8.238). Comparing our capacity for abduction with "a bird's musical and aeronautic powers; that is, it is to us, as those are to them, the loftiest of our merely instinctive powers" (1929:282),[7] Peirce notes that "re-troduction goes upon the hope that there is sufficient affinity between the reasoner's mind and nature to render guessing not altogether hope-less, provided each guess is checked by comparison with observation" (1.121).

> A given object presents an extraordinary combination of characters of which we should like to have an explanation. That there is any explanation of them is a pure assumption; and if there be, it is some one hidden fact which explains them; while there are, perhaps, a million other possible ways of explaining them, if they were not all, unfortunately, false. A man is found in the streets of New York stabbed in the back. The chief of police might open a directory and put his finger on any name and guess that that is the name of the murderer. How much would such a guess be worth? But the number of names in the directory does not approach the multitude of possible laws of attraction which could have accounted for Keppler's [*sic*] law of planetary motion and, in advance of verification by predications of perturbations etc., would have accounted for them to perfection. Newton, you will say, assumed that the law would be a simple one. But what was that but piling guess on guess? Surely, vastly more phenomena in nature are complex than simple. . . .[T]here is no warrant for doing more than putting [an abduction] as an interrogation. (Ms. 692)

Abduction, that is, retroduction—"a poor name," Peirce himself confessed—is, according to one of Peirce's later formulations, which would appear to owe much to the British philosopher George Berkeley (1685–1753), a means of communication between man and his Creator, a "Divine privilege" which must be cultivated (Eisele 1976, vol. III:206). For Peirce, "according to the doctrine of chances it would be practically impossible for any being, by pure chance to guess the cause of any phenomenon," and he therefore surmises that there can "be no reasonable doubt that man's mind, having been developed under the influence of the laws of nature, for that reason naturally thinks some-what after nature's pattern" (Peirce 1929:269). "It is evident," he writes, "that unless man had had some inward light tending to make his guesses . . . much more often true than they would be by mere chance, the human race would long ago have been extirpated for its utter incapacity in the struggles for existence . . ." (Ms. 692).

In addition to the principle that the human mind is, as a result of natural evolutionary processes, predisposed to guessing correctly about the world, Peirce proposes a second conjectural principle to partially explain the phenomenon of guessing, namely, that "we often derive from observation strong intimations of truth, without being able to specify what were the circumstances we had observed which conveyed those intimations" (1929:282). Peirce, to return to the story of the missing watch, was unable to determine on a conscious level which of the waiters of the Fall River boat was guilty. Holding himself "in as passive and receptive a state" (1929:281) as he could during his brief interview with each waiter, it was only when he forced himself to make what appeared to be a blind guess that he realized that in fact the crook had given off some unwitting index and that he himself had perceived this telltale sign in, as he put it, an "unself-conscious" manner, having made "a discrimination below the surface of consciousness, and not recognized as a real judgment, yet in very truth a genuine discrimination" (1929:280). The processes by which we form hunches about the world are, in Peirce's conception, dependent on perceptual judgments, which contain general elements such that universal propositions may be deduced from them. On the basis of his experimental work on the psychology of perception, conducted at The Johns Hopkins University with the well-known psychologist Joseph Jastrow (1863–1944), then his student (1929; 7.21–48), Peirce maintained that these perceptual judgments are "the result of a process, although of a process not sufficiently conscious to be controlled, or, to state it more truly, not controllable and therefore not fully conscious" (5.181).[8] The different elements of a hypothesis are in our minds before we are conscious of entertaining it, "but it is the idea of putting together what we had never before dreamed of putting together which flashes the new suggestion before our contemplation" (5.181). Peirce describes the formation of a hypothesis as "an act of *insight*," the "abductive suggestion" coming to us "like a flash" (5.181). The only difference between a perceptual judgment and an abductive inference is that the former, unlike the latter, is not subject to logical analysis.

> [A]bductive inference shades into perceptual judgment without any sharp line of demarcation between them; or, in other words, our first premisses, the perceptual judgments, are to be regarded as an extreme case of abductive inferences, from which they differ in being absolutely beyond criticism. (5.181; cf. 6.522, Ms. 316)

Abduction, or "the first step of scientific reasoning" (7.218),[9] and the "only kind of argument which starts a new idea" (2.97),[10] is an instinct which relies upon unconscious perception of connections between aspects of the world, or, to use another set of terms, subliminal communication of messages. It is also associated with, or rather produces, according to Peirce, a certain type of emotion, which sets it apart from either induction or deduction:

> Hypothesis substitutes, for a complicated tangle of predicates attached to one subject, a single conception. Now, there is a peculiar sensation belonging to the act of thinking that each of these predicates inheres in the subject. In hypothetic inference this complicated feeling so produced is replaced by a single feeling of greater intensity, that belonging to the act of thinking the hypothetic conclusion. Now, when our nervous system is excited in a complicated way, there being a relation between the elements of the excitation, the result is a single harmonious disturbance which I call an emotion. Thus, the various sounds made by the instruments of an orchestra strike upon the ear, and the result is a peculiar musical emotion, quite distinct from the sounds themselves. This emotion is essentially the same thing as in hypothetic inference, and every hypothetic inference involves the formation of such an emotion. We may say, therefore, that hypothesis produces the *sensuous* element of thought, and induction the *habitual* element. (2.643)

Hence the pronouncement of a certain confidence and conviction of correctness which Peirce makes in relation to his detective work.

SHERLOCK HOLMES—CONSULTING SEMIOTICIAN

Peirce's account of the method by which he recovered his stolen watch bears a striking resemblance to Dr. Watson's descriptions of Sherlock Holmes in action.[11] There are frequent allusions to Holmes as a foxhound (e.g., STUD, DANC, BRUC, and DEVI). For example, in BOSC, Watson writes:

> Sherlock Holmes was transformed when he was hot upon such a scent as this. Men who had only known the quiet thinker and logician of Baker Street would have failed to recognize him. His face flushed and darkened. His brows were drawn into two hard black lines, while his eyes shone out from beneath them with a steely glitter. His face was bent downward, his shoulders bowed, his lips compressed, and his veins stood out like whipcord in his long, ·sinewy neck. His nostrils seemed to dilate with a purely animal lust for the chase, and his mind was so absolutely concentrated upon the matter before him that a question or remark fell unheeded upon his ears, or, at the most, only provoked a quick, impatient snarl in reply.

Referring to this passage, Pierre Nordon comments: "Here we see a man transformed with all speed into a fox-hound before our very eyes, until he seems almost to have lost the power of speech and be reduced to expressing himself by sounds" (1966:217), heeding instead his instinctive, nonverbal powers of perception and abduction.

It is from such intuitive clue-gathering that Holmes is able to formulate his hypotheses, although he tends to subsume both the perceptual and the hypothetical processes under the rubric of "Observation," as in the following passage from the chapter entitled "The Science of Deduction" in SIGN, where Holmes and Watson are discussing a French detective named François le Villard:

> [Holmes]: "He possesses two out of three qualities necessary for the ideal detective. He has the power of observation and that of deduction. He is only wanting in knowledge. . . ."[12]
> [Watson]: ". . . But you spoke just now of observation and deduction. Surely the one to some extent implies the other."
> [Holmes]: "Why, hardly . . . For example, observation shows me that you have been to the Wigmore Street Post-Office this morning, but deduction lets me know that when there you dispatched a telegram."
> [Watson]: "Right! . . . But I confess that I don't see how you arrived at it."
> [Holmes]: "It is simplicity itself . . . so absurdly simple, that an explanation is superfluous; and yet it may serve to define the limits of observation and of deduction. Observation tells me that you have a little reddish mould adhering to your instep. Just opposite the Wigmore Street Office they have taken up the pavement and thrown up some earth, which lies in such a way that it is difficult to avoid treading in it in entering. The earth is of this peculiar reddish tint which is found, as far as I know, nowhere else in the neighborhood. So much is observation. The rest is deduction."
> [Watson]: "How, then, did you deduce the telegram?"
> [Holmes]: "Why, of course I knew that you had not written a letter, since I sat opposite to you all morning. I see also in your open desk there that you have a sheet of stamps and a thick bundle of postcards. What could you go into the post-office for, then, but to send a wire? Eliminate all other factors, and the one which remains must be the truth."

Watson then presents Holmes with an even more difficult task, and, when the detective again excels, asks him to explain his process of reasoning. "Ah," Holmes replies, "that is good luck. I could only say what was the balance of probability. I did not expect to be so accurate." When Watson then asks if "it was not mere guesswork" he says, "No, no: I never guess. It is a shocking habit—destructive to the logical faculty," and attributes his companion's surprise to the fact that "You do not follow my train of thought or observe the small facts upon which large inferences may depend."

Despite such disclaimers, Holmes's powers of observation, his "extraordinary genius for minutiae," as Watson puts it, and of deduction are in most cases built on a complicated series of what Peirce would have called guesses. In the preceding example, for instance, Holmes can only guess that Watson actually entered the post office, rather than having merely walked in front of it. Furthermore, Watson might have entered the post office to meet a friend rather than to conduct some business, and so forth.

That Holmes was convinced of the importance of studying details for successful detection is brought out in the following passage:

"You appeared to read a good deal upon her which was quite invisible to me," I remarked.

"Not invisible but unnoticed, Watson. You did not know where to look, and so you missed all that was important. I can never bring you to realize the importance of sleeves, the suggestiveness of thumb-nails, or the great issues that may hang from a boot-lace. Now, what did you gather from that woman's appearance? Describe it."

"Well, she had a slate-coloured, broad-brimmed straw hat, with a feather of a brickish red. Her jacket was black, with black beads sewn upon it, and a fringe of little black jet ornaments. Her dress was brown, rather darker than coffee colour, with a little purplish plush at the neck and sleeves. Her gloves were greyish, and were worn through at the right forefinger. Her boots I didn't observe. She had small, round, hanging gold ear-rings, and a general air of being fairly well to do, in a vulgar, comfortable, easy-going way."

Sherlock Holmes clapped his hands softly together and chuckled.

" 'Pon my word, Watson, you are coming along wonderfully. You have really done very well indeed. It is true that you have missed everything of importance, but you have hit upon the method, and you have a quick eye for colour. Never trust to general impressions, my boy, but concentrate yourself upon details. My first glance is always at a woman's sleeve. In a man it is perhaps better first to take the knee of the trouser. As you observe, this woman had plush upon her sleeves, which is a most useful material for showing traces. The double line a little above the wrist, where the typewritress presses against the table, was beautifully defined. The sewing-machine, of the hand type, leaves a similar mark, but only on the left arm, and on the side of it farthest from the thumb, instead of being right across the broadest part, as this was. I then glanced at her face, and, observing the dint of a pince-nez at either side of her nose, I ventured a remark upon short sight and typewriting, which seemed to surprise her."

"It surprised me."

"But, surely, it was obvious. I was then much surprised and interested on

glancing down to observe that, though the boots which she was wearing
were not unlike each other, they were really odd ones; the one having a
slightly decorated toe-cap, the other a plain one. One was buttoned only in
the two lower buttons out of five, and the other at the first, third, and fifth.
Now, when you see that a young lady, otherwise neatly dressed, has come
away from home with odd boots, half-buttoned, it is no great deduction to
say that she came away in a hurry."

"And what else?" I asked. . . .

"I noticed, in passing, that she had written a note before leaving home
but after being fully dressed. You observed that her right glove was torn at
the forefinger, but you did not apparently see that both glove and finger
were stained with violet ink. She had written in a hurry and dipped her pen
too deep. It must have been this morning, or the mark would not remain
clear upon the finger. All this is amusing, though rather elementary. . . ."
(CASE)

What makes Sherlock Holmes so successful at detection is not that he
never guesses but that he guesses so well. In fact, he unwittingly follows
Peirce's advice for selecting the best hypothesis (see 7.220–320).
Paraphrasing Peirce's discussion, we might say that the best hypothesis
is one that is simplest and most natural,[13] is the easiest and cheapest to
test, and yet will contribute to our understanding of the widest possible
range of facts. In the episode of the post office, Holmes's guesses about
Watson's actions are the most reasonable under the circumstances.

Furthermore, they enable him, with the minimum of logical baggage,
to reach a point from which he may, through further observation, test
some of the predictions drawn from his hypothesis and thus greatly
reduce the number of possible conclusions. In other words, Holmes not
only selects the simplest and most natural hypothesis, but also "breaks a
hypothesis up into its smallest logical components, and only risks one of
them at a time," the latter procedure being what Peirce describes as the
secret of the game of Twenty Questions (7.220; cf. 6.529).[14] Taking the
hypothesis that Watson entered the post office in order to conduct
some postal business, Holmes deduces (in Peirce's sense) that such
business would be either to send a letter, purchase stamps and/or
postcards, or send a telegram. He then systematically tests each of these
possibilities, quickly coming to what turned out to be the correct one.
When several explanations are possible, "one tries test after test until
one or other of them has a convincing amount of support" (BLAN).

As we have already noted, Peirce maintained that a hypothesis must
always be considered as a question, and, while all new knowledge
comes from surmises, these are useless without the test of inquiry.
Holmes, too, remarks, to Watson in SPEC, "how dangerous it always is

to reason from insufficient data." The detective also agrees with Peirce (2.635; 6.524; 7.202) that prejudices, or hypotheses which we are reluctant to submit to the test of induction, are a major stumbling block to successful reasoning. Holmes notes, for example, that "I make a point of never having any prejudices" (REIG; cf. ABBE, NAVA). Peirce's admiration for great figures in the history of science, such as Kepler, stems precisely from their extraordinary capacity for sustaining the guessing-testing-guessing chain.

It is on this point, concerning the maintenance of objectivity toward the facts of a case, that Holmes, much like Peirce in the story that opens this book, finds himself at odds with the official representatives of the police, or, in the case of Peirce, the Pinkerton professionals.[15] In BOSC, for example, Holmes attempts to point out some critical clues to the detective from Scotland Yard, Inspector Lestrade, who, as usual, cannot see the relationship between the details unearthed by Holmes and the crime being investigated. When he replies, "I am afraid that I am still a skeptic," Holmes answers calmly, "You work your own method, and I shall work mine." Holmes later describes this conversation to Watson as follows:

"By an examination of the ground I gained the trifling details which I gave to that imbecile Lestrade, as to the personality of the criminal."
"But how did you gain them?"
"You know my method. It is founded upon the observation of trifles."

What so often leads the police astray in the Holmes stories is that, early in the investigation of a crime, they tend to adopt the hypothesis which is most likely to account for a few outstanding facts, ignoring "trifles" and thereafter refusing to consider data that do not support their position. "There is nothing more deceptive than an obvious fact," says Holmes in BOSC. The police also make the "capital mistake" of theorizing before they have all the evidence (STUD). The result is that, "insensibly," they begin "to twist facts to suit theories, instead of theories to suit facts" (SCAN).[16] The mutual distrust that results from this major difference in methodology pervades the Holmes stories. In REIG, Watson remarks to a country official, Inspector Forrester, that "I have usually found that there was method in his [Holmes's] madness," to which the inspector replies, "Some folk might say there was madness in his method."[17]

We are not the first to point out the importance of guessing in Sherlock Holmes's method cf detection. Régis Messac, for example, speaking of Holmes's reading of Watson's mind in CARD (cf. the almost identical scene in some editions of RESI), notes that there are a million things that Watson might be thinking about when he is looking at the portrait of General Gordon or that of Henry Ward Beecher, and that Holmes is in fact guessing (1929:599). Messac is correct in pointing out that, although Holmes occasionally admits that a kind of instinct for guessing is involved in his work (e.g., he admits, in STUD, that his "curious gifts of instinct and observation" are due to a "kind of intuition"—a sentiment he echoes in SIGN and THOR), he nevertheless "affirms the reality of 'deduction' " (1929:601). Messac also argues that Holmes's deductions are not true deductions at all, nor are they inductions properly speaking, "but rather reasonings founded upon the observation of one particular fact and leading, through more or less complex circumventions, to another particular fact" (1929:602). And Nordon concludes that "it must be said that in practice he [Holmes] gets much more conclusive results from observation than from logical processes" (1966:245).

Marcello Truzzi, in a searching article (Ch. 3 in this book) on Holmes's method, anticipated our present work by pointing to the similarities between the detective's so-called deductions, or inductions, and Peirce's abductions, or conjectures. According to Peirce's system of logic, furthermore, Holmes's observations are themselves a form of abduction, and abduction is as legitimate a type of logical inference as either induction or deduction (Peirce 8.228). In fact, Peirce maintains that:

> Nothing has so much contributed to present chaotic or erroneous ideas of the logic of science as failure to distinguish the essentially different characters of different elements of scientific reasoning; and one of the worst of these confusions, as well as one of the commonest, consists in regarding abduction and induction taken together (often mixed also with deduction) as a simple argument. (8.228)[18]

Peirce admits that he himself, "in almost everything [he] printed before the beginning of this century . . . more or less mixed up Hypothesis and Induction" (8.227), and he traces the confusion of these two types of reasoning to logicians' too "narrow and formalistic a conception of inference (as necessarily having formulated judgments from its premises)" (2.228; cf. 5.590–604; Ms. 475; Ms. 1146).

Abduction and induction do, of course, "both lead to the acceptance of a hypothesis because observed facts are such as would necessarily or probably result as consequences of that hypothesis." But:

> Abduction makes its start from the facts, without, at the outset, having any particular theory in view, though it is motivated by the feeling that a theory

is needed to explain the surprising facts. Induction makes its start from a hypothesis which seems to recommend itself, without at the outset having any particular facts in view, though it feels the need of facts to support the theory. Abduction seeks a theory. Induction seeks for facts. In abduction the consideration of the facts suggests the hypothesis. In induction the study of the hypothesis suggests the experiments which bring to light the very facts to which the hypothesis had pointed. (7.218)

Taking an example which could have been drawn from one of Holmes's cases, Peirce provides the following demonstration of the difference between these two types of reasoning:

A certain anonymous writing is upon a torn piece of paper. It is suspected that the author is a certain person. His desk, to which only he has had access, is searched, and in it is found a piece of paper, the torn edge of which exactly fits, in all its irregularities, that of the paper in question. It is a fair hypothetic inference that the suspected man was actually the author. The ground of this inference evidently is that two torn pieces of paper are extremely unlikely to fit together by accident. Therefore, of a great number of inferences of this sort, but a very small proportion would be deceptive. The analogy of hypothesis with induction is so strong that some logicians have confounded them. Hypothesis has been called an induction of characters. A number of characters belonging to a certain class are found in a certain object; whence it is inferred that all the characters of that class belong to the object in question. This certainly involves the same principle as induction; yet in a modified form. In the first place, characters are not susceptible of simple enumeration like objects; in the next place, characters run in categories. When we make an hypothesis like that about the piece of paper, we only examine a single line of characters, or perhaps two or three, and we take no specimen at all of others. If the hypothesis were nothing but an induction, all that we should be justified in concluding, in the example above, would be that the two pieces of paper which matched in such irregularities as have been examined would be found to match in other, say slighter, irregularities. The inference from the shape of the paper to its ownership is precisely what distinguishes hypothesis from induction, and makes it a bolder and more perilous step. (2.632)

Holmes indirectly acknowledges the more dangerous nature of hypothesis when he advocates the use of "imagination" (RETI, SILV), "intuition" (SIGN), and "speculation" (HOUN). One must be willing to imagine what happened and act upon such surmise, and this takes one "into the region where we balance probabilities and choose the most likely" (HOUN).

Holmes was known to oscillate between the almost frenzied single-mindedness of the fox-hound on the trail of his quarry and a sort of lethargic reverie, a combination John G. Cawelti calls "stereotype vitalization" (1976:11,58), an imaginative synthesis of figure types I. I. Revzin dubbed "fusion," also with specific reference to detective fiction (1978:385–388). The device, in this context, of course, derives from Poe's ambiguous Dupin. Watson points out in the following passage that the latter type of activity was also important to Holmes's detection:

> My friend was an enthusiastic musician, being himself not only a very capable performer but a composer of no ordinary merit. All the afternoon he sat in the stalls wrapped in the most perfect happiness, gently waving his long, thin fingers in time to the music, while his gently smiling face and his languid, dreamy eyes were as unlike those of Holmes, the sleuthhound, Holmes the relentless, keen-witted, ready-handed criminal agent, as it was possible to conceive. In his singular character the dual nature alternately asserted itself, and his extreme exactness and astuteness represented, as I have often thought, the reaction against the poetic and contemplative mood which occasionally predominated in him. The swing of his nature took him from extreme languor to devouring energy; and, as I knew well, he was never so truly formidable as when, for days on end, he had been lounging in his armchair amid his improvisations and his blackletter editions. Then it was that the lust of the chase would suddenly come upon him, and that his brilliant reasoning power would rise to the level of intuition, until those who were unacquainted with his methods would look askance at him as on a man whose knowledge was not that of other mortals. When I saw him that afternoon so enwrapped in the music at St. James's Hall I felt that an evil time might be coming upon those whom he set himself to hunt down. (REDH)

Peirce has also commented on the relationship between such mental activities and more mundane practices. "There is," he writes, "a certain agreeable occupation of mind which . . . involves no purpose save that of casting aside all serious purpose" and which "I have sometimes been half-inclined to call . . . reverie with some qualification; but for a frame of mind so antipodal to vacancy and dreaminess such a designation would be too excruciating a misfit. In fact, it is Pure Play" (6.458). One type of Pure Play, "a lively exercise of one's powers" with "no rules, except this very law of liberty," he names Musement, and defines as a process by which the mind searches for "some connection" between two of the three Universes of Experience (viz., of Ideas, of Brute Actuality, and of Signs [6.455]), "with speculation concerning its cause" (6.458). Musement

> begins passively enough with drinking in the impression of some nook in one of the three Universes. But impression soon passes into attentive ob-

Fig. 5. Sherlock Holmes dreamily enjoying a concert in "The Red-Headed League." Illustration by Sidney Paget for *The Strand Magazine,* August, 1891.

servation, observation into musing, musing into a lively give and take of communion between self and self. If one's observations and reflections are allowed to specialize themselves too much, the Play will be converted into scientific study. . . . (6.459)

Crime, Peirce notes, is particularly suited to the application of Musement. Citing Dupin's remarks in Poe's "The Murders in the Rue Morgue" (to wit: "It appears to me that this mystery is considered insoluble for the very reason which should cause it to be regarded as easy of solution. I mean the outré character of its features"), Peirce remarks that "those problems that at first blush appear utterly insoluble receive, in that very circumstance . . . [t]heir smoothly-fitting keys. This particularly adapts them to the Play of Musement" (6.460; see Sebeok 1981.).[19]

We agree, but for different reasons, then, with Nordon's opinion that "As the creation of a doctor who had been soaked in the rationalist thought of the period,[20] the Holmesian cycle offers us for the first time the spectacle of a hero triumphing again and again by means of logic and scientific method. And the hero's prowess is as marvelous as the power of science, which many people hoped would lead to a material and spiritual improvement of the human condition, and Conan Doyle first among them" (1966:247).

DISEASE, CRIME, AND SEMIOTICS

The roots of semiotics are grounded in ancient medical treatises (Sebeok 1976:4,125f., 181f.; 1979: Ch. 1), illustrating Peirce's contention that "Speaking in a broad, rough way, it may be said that the sciences have grown out of the useful arts, or out of arts supposed to be useful." As astronomy has evolved out of astrology, and chemistry out of alchemy, so, too, "physiology, taking medicine as a halfway out of magic" (1.226). Peirce appears to have been well versed in the history and theory of medicine. His family considered him headed toward a career in chemistry and made available to him the medical library of his late Uncle Charles, who had been a physician (Fisch: personal communication). In at least one place (2.11*n*1), Peirce lists some of the books on the history of medicine which he had consulted. In 1933, in an interview with Henry S. Leonard (a graduate student in philosophy at Harvard who had been sent to Peirce's home in Milford, Pennsylvania, following the death of his widow, Juliette Peirce, to collect any remaining manuscripts), Peirce's last attending physician, G. Alto Pobe, claimed that

> Peirce knew more about medicine than I did. When I went to see him I would stay with him a half-hour to an hour at a time. It did you good to talk to him. When I arrived he would often tell me all of his symptoms and diagnose his illness. Then he would tell me the whole history of the medical treatment for this illness. Then he would tell me what should be prescribed for him now. He was never wrong. He said he had to ask me to write out the prescriptions since he did not have an M.D. degree. (In the notes of Max H. Fisch)

Peirce acknowledges that, concerning statistical problems relating to sampling and induction, "The medical men . . . deserve special mention for the reason that they have had since Galen a logical tradition of their own," and, "in their working against reasoning *'post hoc, ergo propter hoc'*," recognize, "however dimly," the rule of induction that states that "we must first decide for what character we propose to examine the sample, and only after that decision examine the sample" (1.95–97). Peirce recognizes, on the other hand, that medicine, that "materialistic profession" (8.58), has difficulty adhering to another maxim of induction, which requires that samples not be small ones:

It is by violating this maxim that figures are made to lie. Medical statistics in particular are usually contemptibly small, as well as open to the suspicion of being picked. I am speaking now of the statistics of reputable physicians. It is extremely difficult to collect numerous facts relating to any obscure point in medicine, and it is still more difficult to make it evident that those facts are a fair representation of the general run of events. This accounts for the slow progress of medical science notwithstanding the immense study which has been bestowed upon it and for the great errors which will often be received for centuries by physicians. Probably there is no branch of science which is so difficult in every point of view. It requires a really great mind to make a medical induction. This is too obvious to require proof. There are so many disturbing influences—personal idiosyncrasies, mixture of treatment, accidental and unknown influences, peculiarities of climate, race, and season,—that it is particularly essential that the facts should be very numerous and should be scrutinized with the eye of a lynx to detect deceptions. And yet it is peculiarly difficult to collect facts in medicine. One man's experience can seldom be of decisive weight, and no man can judge of matters beyond his personal knowledge in medicine, he must trust to the judgment of others. So that while a sample requires to be more extensive and more carefully taken in this science than in any other, in this more than in any other these requisites are difficult to fulfill.

Nothing, therefore, more pitiably manifests the looseness with which people in general reason than the readiness of nine persons out of ten to pronounce upon the merits of a medicine upon the most limited, the most inexact, and the most prejudiced experience which it is possible to call experience at all. Any old woman who has seen any amelioration of symptoms follow after the administration of a medicine in a dozen cases at all resembling one another, will not hesitate to pronounce it an infallible cure for any case resembling at all any one of the dozen. This is shocking. But what is worse still, treatment will be recommended even upon a hearsay acquaintance with one or two cases.

Observe, I pray you, the combination of fallacies involved in such a procedure. In the first place, no induction can, with propriety, be drawn unless a sample has been taken of some definite class. But these foolish creatures—who think that merely spending time in a sick-room has made Galens of them—are utterly unable to define the disease in question. Suppose it to be *diptheria* [*sic*] for instance. How do they know diptheria [*sic*] from sore throat? Their samples are in reality samples of no definite class at all.

In the second place, the number of their instances is scarcely sufficient for the simplest induction. In the third place the instances are very likely derived from hearsay. Now in addition to the inaccuracy which attaches to this kind of evidence, we are more likely to hear of extraordinary things relatively to their frequency than we are of ordinary ones. So that to take into account such instances is to take picked samples. In the fourth place, the predicate which belongs to all the instances in common is usually utterly vague. In the fifth place, a deduction is usually made respecting a case in hand without carefully considering whether it really comes under the class from which the sample was drawn. In the sixth place more is apt to be predicated of the case in hand than has been found of the previous instances. All these fallacies are combined in a sort of argument which one can scarcely go a week without hearing an instance of. (Ms. 696)[21]

To the extent that the character Sherlock Holmes himself practices the methods of medicine,[22] an element of art and magic is blended into the logic of scientific discovery that he pursues. In our opinion, this is what sets Holmes apart as a character from the more purely logical method of Edgar Allan Poe's detective Dupin.

It is by now well recognized that Conan Doyle, a practicing physician himself until the Holmes stories made him rich enough to give up his practice, patterned the character of Sherlock Holmes after his professor, Dr. Joseph Bell, of the Royal Infirmary of Edinburgh. Conan Doyle's partial use of a doctor as a model was, however, a conscious attempt to introduce a more rigorous scientific method into criminal detection than was used theretofore. Messac correctly notes that Doyle followed Bell regarding diagnosis extended to the entire personality and life of the patient, and that diagnosis "is never absolutely rigorous; it involves irresolutions, errors." Detection of crime, like medicine, is a sort of "pseudoscience" (1929:617).[23] Writing of the birth of STUD, Doyle wrote:

Gaboriau had rather attracted me by the neat dovetailing of his plots, and Poe's masterful detective, Chevalier Dupin, had from boyhood been one of my heroes. But could I bring an addition of my own? I thought of my old teacher Joe Bell, of his eagle face, of his curious ways, of his eerie trick of spotting details. If he were a detective he would surely reduce this fascinating but unorganized business to something near to an exact science. (1924:69)

Doyle was impressed by Bell's exceptional ability at diagnosis, "not only of disease, but of occupation and character." He was Bell's outpatient clerk, which meant that he had to "array his out-patients, make simple notes of their cases, and then show them in, one by one, to the large room in which Bell sat in state surrounded by his dressers and students" (1924:20). The young medical student then "had ample chance of studying his [Bell's] methods and of noticing that he often learned more of the patient by a few glances" (ibid.) than by Doyle's own series of questions preceding the interview with the doctor.

Occasionally the results were very dramatic, though there were times when he blundered. In one of his best cases he said to a civilian patient:

Fig. 6. An early portrait of Dr. Joseph Bell of Edinburgh, on whom Conan Doyle founded his character. Note the distinctive Holmesian profile. From Haycraft 1941:48.

"Well, my man, you've served in the army."
"Aye, sir."
"Not long discharged?"
"No, sir."
"A highland regiment?"
"Aye, sir."
"A non-com. officer?"
"Aye, sir."
"Stationed at Barbados?"
"Aye, sir."

"You see, gentlemen," he would explain, "the man was a respectful man, but did not remove his hat. They do not in the army, but he would have learned civilian ways had he been long discharged. He has an air of authority and he is obviously Scottish. As to Barbados, his complaint is elephantiasis, which is West Indian and not British."

To his audience of Watsons it all seemed quite miraculous until it was explained, and then it became simple enough. It is no wonder that after the study of such a character I used and amplified his methods when in later life I tried to build up a scientific detective who solved cases on his own merits and not though the folly of the criminal. (1924:20-21)

While the Barbados dialogue was the only example of Bell's skill in observation and deduction recorded by Doyle himself, several other accounts of Bell's remarkable performances, noted down by physicians who were medical students with Doyle at Edinburgh or friends of Dr. and Mrs. Bell, have been published and are reviewed by Trevor Hall (1978:80–83). William S. Baring-Gould has reproduced one of the lesser-known anecdotes (from the *Lancet*, of August 1, 1956):

A woman with a small child was shown in. Joe Bell said good morning to her and she said good morning in reply.

"What sort of crossing di' ye have fra' Burntisland?"
"It was guid."
"And had ye a guid walk up Inverleith Row?"
"Yes."
"And what did ye do with th' other wain?"
"I left him with my sister in Leith."
"And would ye still be working at the linoleum factory?"
"Yes, I am."

"You see, gentlemen, when she said good morning to me I noted her Fife accent, and, as you know, the nearest town in Fife is Burntisland. You notice the red clay on the edges of the soles of her shoes, and the only such clay within twenty miles of Edinburgh is the Botanical Gardens. Inverleith Row borders the gardens and is her nearest way here from Leith. You observed that the coat she carried over her arm is too big for the child who is with her, and therefore she set out from home with two children. Finally she has dermatitis on the fingers of the right hand which is peculiar to workers in the linoleum factory at Burntisland." (1967:vol. I,7)

Or consider the following report of an interview with Doyle, in June 1892, originally published in an article by a Mr. Harry How entitled "A Day with Dr. Conan Doyle," which appeared in the *Strand Magazine* in August of the same year, and was reprinted by Hall (1978:82–83):

[At Edinburgh] I met the man who suggested Sherlock Holmes to me . . . his intuitive powers were simply marvelous. Case No. 1 would step up. "I see," said Mr. Bell, "You're suffering from drink. You even carry a flask in the inside breast pocket of your coat." Another case would come forward. "Cobbler, I see." Then he would turn to the students, and point out to them that the inside of the knee of the man's trousers was worn. That was where the man had rested the lapstone—a peculiarity only found in cobblers.

Hall (1978:78) also notes that Doyle acknowledged his debt to Bell on the verso of the title page of *The Adventures of Sherlock Holmes* (1892), where he dedicates the book to his former teacher. Hall further reports that, in a letter of May 4, 1892, to Bell, Doyle explained:

It is most certainly to you that I owe Sherlock Holmes, and though in the stories I have the advantage of being able to place [the detective] in all sorts of dramatic positions, I do not think that his analytical work is in the least an exaggeration of some effects which I have seen you produce in the outpatient ward. Round the centre of deduction and inference and observation which I have heard you inculcate, I have tried to build up a man who pushed the thing as far as it would go—further occasionally—and I am so glad that the results satisfied you, who are the critic with the most right to be severe. (1978:78)

Certainly the following passage echoes to a startling degree some of the anecdotes involving Joseph Bell. Holmes and his brother Mycroft are seated together in the bow window (cf. Sebeok 1981: Ch. 3) of the Diogenes Club, when Mycroft says:

"To anyone who wishes to study mankind this is the spot. . . . Look at the magnificent types! Look at these two men who are coming towards us, for example."
"The billiard-marker and the other?"
"Precisely. What do you make of the other?"
The two men had stopped opposite the window. Some chalk marks over

Fig. 7. Portrait of Mycroft Holmes. Illustration by Sidney Paget for
"The Greek Interpreter," *The Strand Magazine*, September, 1893.

the waistcoat pocket were the only signs of billiards which I [Watson] could
see in one of them. The other was a very small, dark fellow, with his hat
pushed back and several packages under his arm.

"An old soldier, I perceive," said Sherlock.

"And very recently discharged," remarked the brother.

"Served in India, I see."

"And a non-commissioned officer."

"Royal Artillery, I fancy," said Sherlock.

"And a widower."

"But with a child."

"Children, my dear boy, children."

"Come," said I [i.e., Watson], laughing, "this is a little too much."

"Surely," answered Holmes, "it is not hard to see that a man with that bearing, expression of authority, and sun-baked skin is a soldier, is more than a private, and is not long from India."

"That he has not left the service long is shown by his still wearing his ammunition boots, as they are called," observed Mycroft.

"He had not the cavalry stride, yet he wore his hat on one side, as is shown by the lighter skin on that side of his brow. His weight is against his being a sapper. He is in the artillery."

"Then, of course, his complete mourning shows that he has lost someone very dear. The fact that he is doing his own shopping looks as though it were his wife. He has been buying things for children, you perceive. There is a rattle, which shows that one of them is very young. The wife probably died in childbed. The fact that he has a picture-book under his arm shows that there is another child to be thought of." (GREE)

Bell himself brings out the similarity between crime and disease in the following passage, written in 1893 and cited by Starrett (1971:25–26):

Try to learn the features of a disease or injury, gentlemen, as precisely as you know the features, the gait, the tricks of manner of your most intimate friend. Him, even in a crowd, you can recognize at once. It may be a crowd of men dressed all alike, and each having his full complement of eyes, nose, hair and limbs. In every essential they resemble one another; only in trifles do they differ—and yet, by knowing these trifles well, you make your recognition or your diagnosis with ease. *So it is with disease of mind or body or morals.*[24] Racial peculiarities, hereditary tricks of manner, accent, occupation or the want of it, education, environment of every kind, by their little trivial impressions gradually mould or carve the individual, and leave finger marks or chisel scores which the expert can detect. The great broad characteristics which at a glance can be recognized as indicative of heart disease or consumption, chronic drunkenness or long-continued loss of blood, are the common property of the veriest tyro in medicine, while to masters of their art there are myriads of signs eloquent and instructive, but which need the educated eye to discover. . . . *The importance of the infinitely little is incalculable.* Poison a well at Mecca with the cholera bacillus and the holy water which the pilgrims carry off in bottles will infect a continent. The rags of a victim of a plague will terrify every seaport in Christendom. [Emphasis ours]

This manner of viewing symptoms as distinctive features of the identity of a disease, which is then treated as a concrete entity, brings to mind a passage in one of Peirce's unpublished manuscripts (Ms. 316), where, explaining that "our knowledge of the majority of general conceptions comes about in a manner altogether analogous to our knowledge of an individual person," he criticizes the dictum of French physiologist

Claude Bernard (1813–1878) that "Disease is not an entity; it is nothing but an assemblage of symptoms." Peirce maintains that, rather than a physiological doctrine, it is one of false logic. "But in the light of the positive discoveries of Pasteur and Koch, considered in connection with the theories of Weissmann [sic], we see that, as far as zymotic [i.e., infectious] diseases are concerned, they are just as much a thing as the ocean is a thing . . . [An] assemblage of symptoms [is] not only an entity but necessarily a concrete thing. . . ." Had Bernard understood this, Peirce goes on to say, "he might have set himself to work very usefully to obtain some further acquaintance with that thing."

Sherlock Holmes does indeed practice what Bell preaches. He builds up to a "diagnosis," that is, an identification of a criminal pathology, through a series of minute perceptions, linked together by hypothesis, and he furthermore usually ends by treating a former case like an old familiar friend. Consider, for example, the following often-cited account of Holmes reading Watson's mind (on "thought-reading," cf. *n.*14):

Finding that Holmes was too absorbed for conversation, I had tossed aside the barren paper, and, leaning back in my chair, I fell into a brown study. Suddenly my companion's voice broke in upon my thoughts.

"You are right, Watson," said he. "It does seem a very preposterous way of settling a dispute."

"Most preposterous!" I exclaimed, and then, suddenly realizing how he had echoed the inmost thought of my soul, I sat up in my chair and stared at him in blank amazement.

"What is this, Holmes?" I cried. "This is beyond anything which I could have imagined. . . . I have been seated quietly in my chair, and what clues can I have given you?"

"You do yourself an injustice. The features are given to man as the means of which he shall express his emotions, and yours are faithful servants."

"Do you mean to say that you read my train of thoughts from my features?"

"Your features, and especially your eyes. Perhaps you cannot yourself recall how your reverie commenced?"

"No, I cannot."

"Then I will tell you. After throwing down your paper, which was the action which drew my attention to you, you sat for half a minute with a vacant expression. Then your eyes fixed themselves upon your newly framed picture of General Gordon, and I saw by the alteration in your face that a train of thought had been started. But it did not lead very far. Your eyes turned across to the unframed portrait of Henry Ward Beecher, which stands up upon the top of your books. You then glanced up at the wall, and

Fig. 8. . . . I fell into a brown study. Illustration by Sidney Paget for "The Cardboard Box," *The Strand Magazine*, January, 1893.

of course your meaning was obvious. You were thinking that if the portrait were framed it would just cover that bare space and correspond with Gordon's picture over there."

"You have followed me wonderfully!" I exclaimed.

"So far I could hardly have gone astray. But now your thoughts went back to Beecher, and you looked hard across as if you were studying the character in his features. Then your eyes ceased to pucker, but you continued to look across, and your face was thoughtful. You were recalling the incidents of Beecher's career. I was well aware that you could not do this without thinking of the mission which he undertook on behalf of the North at the time of the Civil War, for I remember you expressing your passionate indignation at the way in which he was received by the more turbulent of our people. You felt so strongly about it that I knew you could not think of Beecher without thinking of that also. When a moment later I saw your eyes wander away from the picture, I suspected that your mind had now turned to the Civil War, and when I observed that your lips set, your eyes sparkled, and your hands clinched, I was positive that you were indeed thinking of the gallantry which was shown by both sides in that desperate struggle. But then, again, your face grew sadder; you shook your head. You were dwelling upon the sadness and horror and useless waste of life. Your hand stole toward your own old wound, and a smile quivered on

your lips, which showed me that the ridiculous side of this method of settling international questions had forced itself upon your mind. At this point
I agreed with you that it was preposterous, and was glad to find that all my
deductions had been correct."

"Absolutely!" said I. "And now that you have explained it, I confess that
I am as amazed as before." (RESI; cf. CARD)

Testing a hypothesis as to the identity of a person through the collection of clues from that individual's physical appearance, speech patterns,
and the like always involves a certain amount of guessing, for which
reason Peirce calls it *abductory induction* (or, sometimes, *speculative mod-
eling*):

> But suppose that, while I am travelling upon a railway, somebody draws my
> attention to a man near us, and asks me whether he is not something allied
> to a catholic priest. I thereupon begin to run over in my mind the observ-
> able characteristics of ordinary catholic priests, in order to see what pro-
> portion of them this man displays. Characteristics are not capable of being
> counted or measured; their relative significance in reference to the ques-
> tion put can only be vaguely estimated. Indeed, the question itself admits
> of no precise answer. Nevertheless, if the man's style of dress,—boots,
> trousers, coat, and hat,—are such that are seen on the majority of Ameri-
> can catholic priests, if his movements are such as are characteristic of them,
> betraying a similar state of nerves, and if the expression of countenance,
> which results from a certain long discipline, is also characteristic of a priest,
> while there is a single circumstance very unlike a Roman priest, such as his
> wearing a masonic emblem, I may say he is not a priest, but he has been, or
> has been near becoming, a catholic priest. This sort of vague induction, I
> term an *abductory induction*. (Ms. 692;cf. 6.526)

And again, from priest to nun:

> Streetcars are famous *ateliers* for speculative modeling. Detained there,
> with no business to occupy him, one sets to scrutinizing the people oppo-
> site, and to working up biographies to fit them. I see a woman of forty. Her
> countenance is so sinister as scarcely to be matched among a thousand,
> almost to the border of insanity, yet with a grimace of amiability that few
> even of her sex are sufficiently trained to command:—along with it, those
> two ugly lines, right and left of the compressed lips, chronicling years of
> severe discipline. An expression of servility and hypocrisy there is, too
> abject for a domestic; while a certain low, yet not quite vulgar, kind of
> education is evinced, together with a taste in dress neither gross nor
> meretricious, but still by no means elevated, bespeak companionship with
> something superior, beyond any mere contact as of a maid with her mis-
> tress. The whole combination, although not striking at first glance, is seen

upon close inspection to be a very unusual one. Here our theory declares an explanation is called for; and I should not be long in guessing that the woman was an ex-nun. (7.196)

In the preceding examples, each question put to Peirce is itself an hypothesis, similar in some respects to the inference noted in an autobiographical passage from another Peirce paper, where he writes:

> I once landed at a seaport in a Turkish province; and, as I was walking up to the house which I was to visit, I met a man upon horseback, surrounded by four horsemen holding a canopy over his head. As the governor of the province was the only personage I could think of who could be so greatly honored, I inferred that this was he. This was an hypothesis. (2.625)

The above examples illustrate what Sherlock Holmes refers to as "reasoning backward" (cf. Peirce's *retro-duction*), a skill which, while similar in many respects to the type of thinking in which the common man engages in his everyday life, nevertheless requires a certain amount of specialized training:

> "In solving a problem of this sort, the grand thing is to be able to reason backward. That is a very useful accomplishment, and a very easy one, but people do not practice it much. In the everyday affairs of life it is more useful to reason forward, and so the other comes to be neglected. There are fifty who can reason synthetically for one who can reason analytically."
> "I confess," said I 4 460nWatson], "that I do not quite follow you."
> "I hardly expected that you would. Let me see if I can make it clearer. Most people, if you describe a train of events to them, will tell you what the result would be. They can put those events together in their minds, and argue from them that something will come to pass. There are few people, however, who, if you told them a result, would be able to evolve from their own inner consciousness what the steps were which led up to that result. This power is what I mean when I talk of reasoning backward, or analytically." (STUD)

Holmes, in fact, frequently remarks to Watson that he sees just what everyone else sees, only he has trained himself to apply his method in order to determine the full significance of his perceptions. For example, Watson is asked by Holmes to examine a hat in order to find a clue as to the identity of the gentleman who had worn it. "I can see nothing," is Watson's reply, to which Holmes responds, "On the contrary, Watson, you see everything. You fail, however, to reason from what you see. You are too timid in drawing your inferences" (BLUE). Or again, when Watson says, "You have evidently seen more in these rooms than was

Fig. 9. Sir Arthur Conan Doyle at his desk in Southsea, 1886, allegedly writing "A Study in Scarlet." From Nordon 1966: facing 36.

visible to me," Holmes replies, "No, but I fancy that I may have deduced a little more. I imagine that you saw all that I did" (SPEC).

Peirce himself distinguished between what he called *logica utens,* or a rudimentary sense of logic-in-use, which is a certain general method by which everyone acquires truth, without, however, being aware of doing so and without being able to specify in what that method consists, and a more sophisticated sense of logic, or *logica docens,* practiced by logicians and scientists (but also certain detectives and medical doctors), which is a logic which may be self-consciously taught and is therefore a theoretically developed method of discovering truth (Ms. 692; cf. Ransdell 1977:165). The scientist or logician does not, however, invent his *logica docens,* but rather studies and develops the natural logic he and everyone else already use in daily life. Sherlock Holmes would appear to share this view, judging from his speech to Watson, in which he remarks: "We would not dare to conceive the things which are really mere commonplaces of existence. . . . Depend upon it, there is nothing so unnatural as the commonplace" (IDEN). Holmes asserts, furthermore, that his methods are "but systematized common sense" (BLAN).

This is Holmes's description of the model he attempts to follow:

> The ideal reasoner . . . would, when he had once been shown a single fact in all its bearings, deduce from it not only the chain of events which led up to it but also the results which would follow from it. As Cuvier could correctly describe a whole animal by the contemplation of a single bone, so the observer who has thoroughly understood one link in a series of incidents should be able to accurately state all the other ones, both before and after. (FIVE).

There seems to be little doubt that the *logica docens* of Sherlock Holmes stems in large part from the scientific training of his creator, Conan Doyle. Doyle's teacher, Bell, in fact, had written that "Dr. Conan Doyle's education as a student of medicine taught him to observe, and his practise, both as a general practitioner and a specialist, has been a splendid training for a man such as he is, gifted with eyes, memory and imagination" (Bell 1893, cited in Nordon 1966:213). In particular, the controlling awareness exhibited by Holmes would appear to owe much to his dedication to chemistry.[25] While "the façade of chemical research, never very strong, became less and less well-maintained as time went on, until it collapsed entirely," Holmes's chemical corner served "to keep him in practical touch with an exact science where cause and effect, action and reaction, followed each other with a predictability beyond the power of the less precise 'science of detection' to achieve, however hard he might strive toward exactitude in his chosen profession" (Trevor Hall 1978:36–37). As Holmes proclaimed: "Like all other Arts, the Science of Deduction and Analysis is one which can only be acquired by long and patient study, nor is life long enough to allow any mortal to attain the highest possible perfection in it" (STUD).

Peirce himself had a life-long devotion to chemistry. In 1909, he wrote:

> I early became interested in a childish way in dynamics and physics and my father's brother being a chemist, I must have been about twelve years when I set up a chemical laboratory of my own and began to work through Leibig's hundred bottles of qualitative analysis and to make such things as vermillion both in the dry and the wet way and to repeat a great many well-known processes of chemistry. (Ms. 619)

Fig. 10. Holmes was . . . working hard over a chemical investigation. Illustration by Sidney Paget for "The Naval Treaty," *The
Strand Magazine,* October, 1893.

Chemistry was the profession for which Peirce was specially educated,
and it was "the science in which [he had] worked the most" and "whose
reasoning [he] most admire[d]" (Ms. 453; cf. Hardwick 1977:114).

For the person unschooled in theoretical logic, an exhibition of the
reasoning skills of an expert will, if he is unenlightened by the latter as
to the logical steps which he followed, appear to be very much like
magic. Nordon points out that "His deductions lead Holmes to make
revelations which appear almost magical" (1966:222). Dr. Watson is, as
everyone knows, constantly overwhelmed by the deductions of
Holmes. This effect is heightened by Holmes's "notable taste . . . for
theatrical arrangement and dramatic effects" (Starrett 1971:29), an inclination that he shares with Peirce, judging from the dramatic way in

which the latter related the story of the missing watch, as well as from the fact that he was reputed to have shown quite an interest in and talent for drama from boyhood on.[26]

"The stage lost a fine actor," writes Watson of Holmes, "even as science lost an acute reasoner, when he became a specialist in crime" (SCAN). To some extent, the dramatic way in which Holmes displays his logical operations is akin to the manner in which some physicians seek to impress their patients as to their seemingly magical powers of diagnosis, thereby developing a feeling of confidence on the part of the patient that will contribute to the healing process.[27]

Joseph Bell himself refers to this type of psychological manipulation as follows:

> The recognition [of disease] depends in great measure on the accurate and rapid appreciation of small points in which the disease differs from the healthy state. In fact, the student must be taught to observe. To interest him in this kind of work we teachers find it useful to show the student how much a trained use of observation can discover in ordinary matters such as the previous history, nationality and occupation of a patient. *The patient, too, is likely to be impressed by your ability to cure him in the future if he sees*

Fig. 11. 'I can never resist a touch of the dramatic'—returning the stolen papers to Phelps in "The Naval Treaty." Illustration by Sidney Paget for *The Strand Magazine*, November, 1893.

that you, at a glance, know much of his past. And the whole trick is much easier than it appears at first. (Trevor Hall 1978:83; emphasis ours).

Holmes frequently opens his initial interview with a prospective client with a stunning series of "deductions," much as Bell describes, and these "clever little deductions . . . often have nothing to do with the matter in hand, but impress the reader with a general sense of power. The same effect is gained by his offhand allusion to other cases" (1924:101–102).[28]

And who among us has not been intimidated by a related interview technique used on us by our own doctor, when he asks us a series of seemingly unrelated questions (e.g., Have you been smoking heavily lately? Does it hurt only at night? Has your mother ever suffered from headaches?), upon the termination of which he may suddenly announce his diagnosis, a pronouncement that appears to us, being unable to judge the significance of each separate clue, and hence the logicality of the sequence of questioning, as nothing short of numinous. If the physician has already guessed at a diagnosis, but has not announced it to the patient, the questions which he uses to test his hypothesis will appear to the patient almost as an exercise in extrasensory perception (e.g., You have this sensation only one and a half hours after eating, and it is accompanied by a throbbing pain in your right arm—Why yes, how did you know?).

While guessing is an important part of all logical operations, as Peirce taught us, the typical patient might be expected to lose confidence in his doctor were he to learn the amount of guesswork that goes into medical diagnosis and treatment, so that physicians are more or less obliged to cover up this aspect of their practice, much as Sherlock Holmes is in order to build up his reputation as a master detective. As in the example just discussed, physicians do so by so-to-speak mystifying the client through the intentional obfuscation of the reasoning process, making questions appear as deductions, by simply acting as if a diagnosis had been arrived at through deduction and induction, without a preceding abduction, or by appearing to understand our innermost thoughts and feelings without the intermediary of signs given off by the patient.

The importance of such tricks for Holmes's reputation is brought out in the following passage where the detective is interviewing a Mr. Jabez Wilson. Holmes announces his startlingly accurate conclusion as to Mr. Wilson's background and lifestyle, at which point Mr. Wilson "started up in his chair" and asked "How, in the name of good fortune, did you know all that Mr. Holmes?"

"How did you know for example, that I did manual labour? It's as true as gospel, for I began as a ship's carpenter."

"Your hands, my dear sir. Your right hand is quite a size larger than your left. You have worked with it, and the muscles are more developed."

"Well, the snuff, then, and the Freemasonry?"

"I won't insult your intelligence by telling you how I read that, especially

Fig. 12. Impressing the client from the start, a favorite Holmes gambit. Here he shatters Mr. Grant Munro's incognito in "The Yellow Face" by reading Munro's name on the lining of his hat. Illustration by Sidney Paget for *The Strand Magazine,* February, 1893.

as, rather against the strict rules of your order, you use an arc-and-compass breast pin."

"Ah, of course, I forgot that. But the writing?"

"What else can be indicated by that right cuff so very shiny for five inches, and the left one with the smooth patch near the elbow where you rest it upon the desk?"

"Well, but China?"

"The fish that you have tattooed immediately above your right wrist could only have been done in China. I have made a small study of tattoo marks and even contributed to the literature of the subject. That trick of staining the fishes' scales of a delicate pink is quite peculiar to China. When, in addition, I see a Chinese coin hanging from your watch-chain, the matter becomes even more simple."

Mr. Jabez Wilson laughed heavily. "Well, I never!" said he. "I thought at first that you had done something clever, but I see that there was nothing in it, after all."

"I begin to think, Watson," said Holmes, "that I made a mistake in explaining. '*Omne ignotum pro magnifico,*' you know, and my poor little reputation, such as it is, will suffer shipwreck if I am so candid." (REDH)

Or again, Holmes remarks that "I am afraid that I rather give myself away when I explain. . . . Results without causes are much more impressive" (STOC). Holmes is less than completely candid when he says to a client, "I am afraid that my explanation may disillusion you, but it has always been my habit to hide none of my methods, either from my friend Watson or from anyone who might take an intelligent interest in them" (REIG).[29]

THAUMATURGY IN FACT AND FICTION

The juxtaposition of the method of Charles Peirce, detective, with the method of Sherlock Holmes, semiotician, which began as a *jeu d'esprit,* ends by shedding unexpected light on both the historical figure and the fictional one. From the perspective of the great logician and polymath, Holmes's Science of Deduction and Analysis, set forth comprehensively in his "The Book of Life" (STUD), where the "writer claimed by a momentary expression, a twitch of a muscle or glance of an eye, to fathom a man's inmost thoughts," are seen as far from the "ineffable twaddle" or "rubbish" that Watson at first thought they were. The theories that Holmes expressed in the article, which appeared to his Boswell "so chimerical, are really extremely practical," and his projected one-volume textbook on the "whole art of detection" (ABBE), to which he had planned to "devote [his] declining years," assumes a contextual rationale in the history of ideas, based, partly as it is, partly as it might have been, on a "mixture of imagination and reality" (THOR) and the judicious exercise of speculation as "the scientific use of imagination" (HOUN).

Holmes was a brilliant physician to the body politic, the disease of which is crime. He speaks of his cases "with the air of a pathologist who presents a rare specimen" (CREE). Holmes was pleased that Watson had chosen to chronicle those incidents that gave room for deduction and logical synthesis. While he maintained (STUD) that "all life is a great chain, the nature of which is known whenever we are shown a single link of it," he also held that his conclusions from one to the other "were as infallible as so many propositions of Euclid. So startling would his results appear to the uninitiated that until they learned the processes by which he had arrived at them they might well consider him as a necromancer."

Peirce was, in his way, as great a necromancer as Holmes, and that is why his writings and the details of his biography keep us all spellbound. He was, according to Charles Morris's both weighty and accurate characterization (1971:337), "heir of the whole historical philosophical analysis of signs. . . ." Peirce represents the tallest peak so far in the mountain range that begins to rise in ancient Greece with the clinical semiotics of Hippocrates, is more fully as well as more explicitly developed by Galen (Sebeok 1979; Ch. 1), and continues with the physician Locke, whose *semiotiké* Peirce "distinctly weighed, and duly considered" and which surely afforded "another sort of Logick and Critick, than what we have been hitherto acquainted with" (Locke 1975:721).

It is one thing to proclaim—as we do—the continuity and cumulative effect of this panorama, extending from archaic medical diagnostics and prognostics to the modern expressions of a doctrine of signs by Peirce and beyond, on the part of such modern virtuosos as the Baltic biologist Jakob von Uexküll (1864–1944), and the French mathematician René Thom (born 1923). To document it is quite another. The proof will take at least one more generation of concentrated effort by teams of knowledgeable specialists in the labyrinthine history of the sign science (cf. Pelc 1977), only the barest outlines of which have hitherto been delineated by those few explorers who are equipped to follow upon the clues laid bare by Peirce, so far the boldest pioneer, or backwoodsman, in this high adventure.

NOTES

1. The authors acknowledge, with thanks, the helpful comments made by Martin Gardner, Christian Kloesel, Edward C. Moore, Joseph Ransdell, David Savan, and John Bennett Shaw, in response to a preliminary version of this paper. Our special thanks go to Max H. Fisch, himself a master detective, for his generous and invaluable assistance in tracking down correspondence and passages in Peirce's unpublished manuscripts which bear upon the issues discussed here, and for sharing with us some of his endlessly varied and fascinating store of Peirce-related information. Fisch's detailed comments on this piece are included in Sebeok 1981:17–21.

2. References to the *Collected Papers of Charles Sanders Peirce* (see Peirce 1965–66) are abbreviated in the customary way by volume and paragraph number. References to Peirce manuscripts include the catalogue number from Robin 1967.

3. Peirce's full account of the ensuing story of detection, written in 1907, was not published until 1929, in *The Hound and Horn*. In a letter to William James, July 16, 1907, Peirce writes that, following James's suggestion, he had reported, in an article which he had submitted to the *Atlantic Monthly* that June, the story of his losing his watch (see the notes of Fisch 1964:31, fn. 28, concerning correspondence between Peirce and others regarding this article). Bliss Perry, the editor of that magazine, rejected his paper. A much condensed version of it, with the narrative of the theft merely summarized in a footnote, appeared in 7.36–48.

4. Peirce's remarkable aplomb is given charming expression in a letter which he sent to Superintendent C. P. Patterson, of the Coast Survey, on June 24: "I have to report that I arrived here last Saturday and my watch, the property of the Survey, was stolen from me . . . at the instant of my arrival. I at once set to work to find it and was so happy as to succeed this afternoon, I strongly hope to capture the thief tomorrow morning before seven o'clock. . . ."

5. Discussing his role in the legal formalities involved, Peirce goes on to say that "I sent word to the District Attorney and hoped he would keep the prisoners as long as possible after which I don't see that we need to press it further, to do which I should have to give up the Paris expedition." In 1902, Peirce was to express much stronger views on the question of crime and its punishment: "[It] so burns in my heart that if I could, I would abolish almost all punishment of grown people, and all judicial approval or disapproval except of the court's own officers. Let public opinion have its approvals and disapprovals, until public opinion learns better. But as for public force, let it be restricted to doing what is necessary to the welfare of society. Punishment, severe punishment, the barbaric punishment of a prison cell, infinitely more cruel than death, is not in the least conducive to public or to private welfare. As for the criminal classes, I would extirpate them, not by the barbarous method which some of those monsters whom economics has evolved propose, but by keeping the criminals confined in relative luxury, making them useful, and preventing reproduction. It would be easy to convert them from a source of enormous expense, and perpetual injury to people, into self-supporting harmless wards of the state. The only expense would be that of losing our darling revenge upon them. As for sporadic criminals, defalcators, murderers, and the like, I would deport them to

an island, and leave them to govern themselves, and deal with one another. For trifling violations of order, trifling punishments might be retained" (2.164).

6. "Abduction is, after all, nothing but guessing," he wrote elsewhere (7.219; cf. Ms. 692). Compare Chomsky's explicatory remarks (1979:71) in relation to abduction, concerning "the philosopher to whom [he feels] closest": "Peirce argued that to account for the growth of knowledge, one must assume that 'man's mind has a natural adaptation to imagining correct theories of some kinds,' some principle of 'abduction' which 'puts a limit on admissible hypothesis,' a kind of 'instinct,' developed in the course of evolution. Peirce's ideas on abduction were rather vague, and his suggestion that biologically given structure plays a basic role in the selection of scientific hypotheses seems to have had very little influence. To my knowledge, almost no one has tried to develop these ideas further, although similar notions have been developed independently on various occasions. Peirce has had an enormous influence, but not for this particular reason." The standard monograph on this neglected aspect of Peirce's contribution to the philosophy of science is Fann's (1970) very brief, yet thorough, thesis (written in 1963), a noteworthy feature of which is an allusion to Sherlock Holmes; Fann's examples are drawn to "show that the method of science has much in common with the method of detectives" (ibid.:58). See further Walsh (1972).

7. Peirce maintained elsewhere that the ability of a newly hatched chick to pick up food, "choosing as it picks, and picking what it aims to pick," while "not reasoning, because it is not done deliberately," is nevertheless "in every respect but that . . . just like abductive inference," and he further traces the physical and social sciences back to the animal instincts for, respectively, getting food and reproduction (Ms. 692). Retroduction is a type of instinctive behavior two classic examples of which are the migration of robins and the hive-building of bees. Peirce called the seemingly intelligent behavior of the lower animals *il lume naturale,* which he considered indispensable to retroduction. (On the notion of "lumière naturelle," see Ayim 1974:43, fn. 4). Peirce spoke of rational, animal, and vegetable instinct; we concur with Ayim's view (ibid. 36) that all levels of instinctive activity "have this feature in common—the activity caters to the survival and well-being of the species as a whole by enabling species members to react appropriately to environmental conditions"; this holds, as well, for man-as-a-scientist. See further Norwood Russell Hanson's interesting observation (in Bernstein 1965:59) that "Often the thrust of Holmes' comment, 'Simple deduction my dear Watson,' is to the effect that the reasoning in question has proceeded from the previously accepted to what should be expected. But just as often the mathematician and the scientist will argue from the bottom of the page 'up.'" This is one of the things Peirce identifies as 'retroducing'. It proceeds from an unexpected anomaly to a premiss cluster, most parts of which are already accepted. Needless to point out, contrary to Hanson's attribution, Holmes never uttered the words cited; nor did Holmes ever say, "Elementary, my dear Watson."

8. For a detailed discussion of the experimental work on the psychology of perception, conducted by Peirce and Joseph Jastrow, which Peirce presents as evidence in support of his theory of guessing, see Peirce 1929 and 7.21–48.

9. Concerning scientific method, abduction is, according to Peirce, "merely preparatory" (7.218). The other "fundamentally different kinds of reasoning" in science are deduction and induction (see the discussion in 1.65–68, 2.96–97,

5.145, 7.97, 7.202–07). Briefly, the step of adopting a hypothesis or a proposition which would lead to the prediction of what appear to be surprising facts is called *abduction* (7.202). The step by which the necessary and probable experiential consequences of our hypothesis are traced out is called *deduction* (7.203). *Induction* is the name Peirce gives to the experimental testing of the hypothesis (7.206).

10. Peirce also calls abduction "Originary Argument" since it is, of the three forms of reasoning, the only one which starts a new idea (2.96) and, in fact, "Its only justification is that if we are ever to understand things at all, it must be in that way" (5.145). Similarly, "neither deduction nor induction can ever add the smallest item to the data of perception; and . . . mere percepts do not constitute any knowledge applicable to any practical or theoretical use. All that makes knowledge applicable comes to us *via* abduction" (Ms. 692).

11. There is, to our knowledge, no direct evidence that Peirce had read any of the Holmes stories, or that he had met Sir Arthur Conan Doyle. It is likely, however, that Peirce heard something of at least the early Holmes stories. The first story to appear in the United States "A Study in Scarlet," was published as early as 1888, by Ward, Lock, and in 1890 "The Sign of Four" appeared in *Lippincott's Magazine,* the major contemporaneous rival to the *Atlantic Monthly,* which we know Peirce did read (see fn. 3 above). In addition, there was already a vogue for Doyle in the United States by 1894, when the celebrated writer spent two months in this country giving a series of lectures and meeting his American compeers (Nordon 1966:39–40). Peirce had grown up in the company of writers of fiction and artists as well as scientists. In a letter to Victoria, Lady Welby, of January 31, 1908, he wrote, "But my father was a broad man and we were intimate with literary people too. William Story the sculptor, Longfellow, James Lowell, Charles Norton, Wendell Holmes, and occasionally Emerson, are among the figures of my earliest memories" (Hardwick 1977:113). As an adult, Peirce appears to have kept abreast of contemporaneous developments in the verbal arts, for he frequently mentions both European and American authors of his time in his reviews in *The Nation* (Ketner and Cook 1975). Edgar Allan Poe (1809–49), moreover, seems to have been one of Peirce's favorite writers, and is mentioned in 1.251, 6.460, Ms. 689, Ms. 1539. Judging from his references to Poe's "The Murders in the Rue Morgue," Peirce certainly had a taste for detective stories. Of course, it is generally recognized that the character Sherlock Holmes is partly modeled after Poe's Chevalier Dupin (e.g., Messac 1929:596–602, Nordon 1966:212ff., Hall 1978:76;cf. further below). Hitchings (1946:117), in his article on Holmes as a logician, makes the good point "that in contrast to Dupin, who is the brainchild of a mathematician and a poet, Sherlock Holmes, even at his most theoretical, is the offspring of a doctor's brain, and always has his feet firmly planted on the ground." Hitchings is, however, on the wrong track when he claims that "Most of Holmes's reasoning is causal," citing the detective's own remark that "reasoning from effect to cause is less frequent and thus more difficult than reasoning from cause to effect" (ibid.:115–16).

12. Watson notes that Holmes's knowledge of "sensational literature [is] immense" (STUD). Holmes in fact kept an up-to-date index of unusual and interesting criminal cases from around the world, to which he frequently referred in order to solve a new case by analogy with other, earlier ones, as, for example, in IDEN or NOBL. "I am able to guide myself by the thousands of other similar

cases which occur to my memory," he tells Watson in REDH. Peirce refers to analogy as a combination of abduction and induction (e.g., 1.65, 7.98).

13. "It is an old maxim of mine," states Holmes, "that when you have excluded the impossible, whatever remains, however improbable, must be the truth" (BERY; cf. SIGN, BLAN, BRUC). Cf. Peirce's maxim that "Facts cannot be explained by a hypothesis more extraordinary than these facts themselves; and of various hypotheses the least extraordinary must be adopted" (Ms. 696). See Gardner 1976:125, who describes this process as follows: "Like the scientist trying to solve a mystery of nature, Holmes first gathered all the evidence he could that was relevant to his problem. At times he performed experiments to obtain fresh data. He then surveyed the total evidence in the light of his vast knowledge of crime, and/or sciences relevant to crime, to arrive at the most probable hypothesis. Deductions were made from the hypothesis; then the theory was further tested against new evidence, revised if need be, until finally the truth emerged with a probability close to certainty."

14. Sebeok (1979, Ch. 5) discusses Peirce's reflections about guessing in the context of some children's games, on the one hand, and certain stage illusions, on the other. The Game of Twenty Questions is the full verbal equivalent to the Game of Hot and Cold, in which verbal cueing is minimal, as it is in the kindred "Game of Yes and No," so vividly pictured by Dickens (1843, Stave Three). Averbal cueing, unwittingly emitted, guides the performer in certain types of magic acts, where verbal cues are excluded altogether, to the object sought. This averbal communication, or feedback, also accounts for such seemingly "occult" phenomena as the movement of a Ouija board, table tipping, and automatic writing, and is the basis of several types of mentalist acts, variously known in the magic business as "muscle reading" or "thought-reading." In acts of this sort, "The spectator thinks he is being led by the magician, but actually the performer permits the *spectator to lead him* by unconscious muscular tensions" (Gardner 1957:109; cf. idem 1978:392–96, where further key references are given). The best mentalists are able to dispense with bodily contact altogether, finding what they are seeking merely by observing the reactions of spectators in the room; examples of this from Persi Diaconis and a performer who goes under the name of Kreskin are cited by Sebeok (ibid.). These cases bear an uncanny resemblance to Peirce's story (1929). Diaconis, besides being one of the most talented of contemporary magicians, is also among the foremost experts in the sophisticated statistical analysis of guessing and gambling strategies, and in applying novel techniques in parapsychological research (with hitherto totally negative results; see Diaconis 1978:136). Scheglov's observation (1976:63) about the growth of tension and excitement as Holmes's logical reasoning gradually "creeps up on the criminal and lifts a corner of the curtain (we have here much the same effect as in the children's game 'Cold or hot' in which the area for hunting narrows down and gets 'hotter and hotter')" should also be mentioned in this connection. Muscle reading, which reached its height of public popularity in the U.S., also became popular as a parlor game known as "Willing."

15. Two Holmes stories, by the way, feature detectives from the Pinkerton National Detective Agency: Young Leverton, who has a minor role in REDC and Birdy Edwards, alias John ("Jack") McMurdo, alias John ("Jack") Douglas, who was probably tossed overboard off St. Helena by the Moriarty gang (at the conclusion of VALL).

16. See the comment on this passage by Castañeda (1978:205), "that philosophers *in fieri* may benefit from the several methodological principles that Sherlock Holmes formulates and illustrates in his different adventures. . . ."

17. An interesting parallel is found in Voltaire's *Zadig* (Ch. 3), where Zadig's clever reading of clues causes him to be arrested, tried, and fined.

18. Peirce admits that he himself, "in almost everything [he] printed before the beginning of this century . . . more or less mixed up Hypothesis and Induction" (8.227). Concerning the history of the confusion of these two types of reasoning because logicians had too "narrow and formalistic a conception of inference (as necessarily having formulated judgments from its premisses)" (2.228), see also 5.590–604, Ms. 475, Ms. 1146.

19. Cf. Holmes's remarks that "I have already explained to you that what is out of the common is usually a guide rather than a hindrance" (STUD); "Singularity is almost invariably a clue" (BOSC); "The more *outré* and grotesque an incident is the more carefully it deserves to be examined, and the very point which appears to complicate a case is, when duly considered and scientifically handled, the one which is most likely to elucidate it" (HOUN); and "It is only the colourless, uneventful case which is hopeless" (SHOS).

20. In addition to his specialized medical training, Conan Doyle was caught up in the general enthusiasm for science in England of his day. By the middle of the nineteenth century, science had become a solid part of English thinking at all levels, and there was generally a "dominant tone of positivist rationality" (Messac 1929:612; cf. Nordon 1966:244). Conan Doyle himself reports that "It is to be remembered that these were the years when Huxley, Tyndall, Darwin, Herbert Spencer, and John Stuart Mill were our chief philosophers, and that even the man in the street felt the strong sweeping current of their thought . . ." (1924:26). Hitchings (1946:115) explicitly compares the logic of Holmes with that of Mill: Holmes's "habitual method of solving these difficult problems is by his own extended version of Mill's Method of Residues."

21. As Gould (1978:504) recently confirmed, "unconscious or dimly perceived finagling, doctoring, and massaging [of data] are rampant, endemic, and unavoidable in a profession that awards status and power for clean and unambiguous discovery." In brief, such manipulation of data may be a scientific norm. Cf. Gardner 1981:130.

22. Reviewing the large number of examples of medical diagnosis in Holmes stories (diseases of the heart and tropical diseases especially), Campbell (1935:13), himself a heart specialist, concludes that, medically speaking, "Watson seems to have been excellently informed." It is interesting to note that, while Watson successfully follows the logical method of diagnosis with regard to pathology of the body, he is singularly inept in transferring this method to the detection of crime, and provides an example of someone who is only incompletely versed in *logica docens* (see below).

23. Concerning the artistic side of medicine, Messac correctly notes that Conan Doyle followed Bell regarding diagnosis extended to the entire personality and life of the patient, and that diagnosis "n'a jamais une rigueur absolue; il comporte des flottements, des erreurs." Detection of crime, like medicine, is a sort of "pseudo-science" (1929:617) According to Thomas (1983.32), "medicine was changing into a technology based on genuine science" about 1937.

24. Holmes, like Peirce, was more interested in his method than in the par-

ticular subject matter to which it was applied. He and Watson, for example, discussed the way in which the latter has reported cases of the former, and Holmes criticizes Watson, saying "You have erred perhaps in attempting to put colour and life into each of your statements instead of confining yourself to the task of placing upon record that severe reasoning from cause to effect which is really the only notable feature about the thing." When, in response, Watson implies that Holmes's criticism is based on egotism, Holmes answers "No, it is not selfishness or conceit. . . . If I claim full justice for my art, it is because it is an impersonal thing—a thing beyond myself. Crime is common. Logic is rare. Therefore it is upon the logic rather than upon the crime that you should dwell. You have degraded what should have been a course of lectures into a series of tales" (COPP).

25. Describing Holmes's knowledge of various subject matters, Watson lists only one—chemistry—as "profound" (STUD). On Holmes as "a frustrated chemist," see Cooper 1976.

26. The Peirce family had for generations displayed an interest in the theater and opera, even entertaining performers in their home. While still a boy, Peirce is reported to have distinguished himself as an orator, both through the reading of such works as Poe's "The Raven" and as a member of his high school debating society. (Personal communication by Max H. Fisch.) As an undergraduate at Harvard, Peirce continued to cultivate an interest in elocution, rhetoric, and theatrical performance. He became a member, in his junior year, of the W.T.K. (Wen Tchang Koun, Chinese for 'hall of literary exercise'), which specialized in debates, orations, mock trials, and the reading of essays, poems, and plays. During his senior year, in 1858, he was a founding member of the O.K. Society of Harvard College, which pursued the elocutionary and oratorical arts in relation to literary works. (Christian Kloesel, personal communication; see also Kloesel 1979 concerning Peirce and the O.K. Society in particular.) As an adult, Peirce was known to have given readings of Shakespeare's "King Lear" to friends, at his older brother "Jem" 's house in Cambridge, and to fellow members of the Century Club, in New York. Peirce attended the theater and opera when in Paris, and his second wife, Juliette, was an actress. He and Juliette remained in contact with theatrical friends, such as Steele and Mary MacKaye, and even occasionally took part in amateur theatrical events, such as a performance of Legougé's "Medea," which Peirce had translated into English. (Personal communication by Max H. Fisch.)

27. Ritual trappings in clinical practice constitute the essential ingredient of the placebo effect, and are discussed in more detail in Sebeok 1979, Chs. 5 and 10. The placebo is thought to be efficacious because the patient believes that it will be, a belief that is bolstered by appropriate cueing on the part of the physician and other attendant personnel, as well as shaped by the context in which the placebo is administered. For a sound, popular account, by a surgeon, of the workings of the placebo effect by "healers", and the power of suggestion, including sometimes hypnosis, see Nolen 1974. Some psychologists, such as Scheibe (1978:872–75) employ the term 'acumen' for a mode of prediction exhibited by Holmes, constituting "an emphatic skill combined with analytic precision." Scheibe observes: "If one believes oneself to be at a disadvantage vis-à-vis the terrible but well-controlled powers of observation and inference of the . . . detective, . . . then one has in effect granted authority to a superior and has no hope of mastering events. . . . To the extent that the . . . detective is

considered by the public at large to possess special powers of penetration, the powers of acumen of these practitioners will be enhanced. Also, to the extent that any player is able to exploit the naiveté or credulity of the other player about innocence of intent, the second player is effectively under control of the first. This is the basic principle for the confidence game." See further Scheibe 1979.

28. Hall (1978:38) notes that Holmes's chemical experiments also "helped to mystify Watson" (cf. Nordon 1966:222).

29. A similar con game is played out between the author of a detective story and his audience, of course. Conan Doyle acknowledged this both indirectly, through the character of Sherlock Holmes, and directly, in his autobiography. Holmes, for instance, tells Watson that "It is one of those instances where the reasoner can produce an effect which seems remarkable to his neighbour, because the latter has missed the one little point which is the basis of the deduction. The same may be said, my dear fellow, for the effect of some of these little sketches of yours, which is entirely meretricious, depending as it does upon your retaining in your own hands some factors in the problem which are never imparted to the reader" (CROO). In his autobiography, Conan Doyle (1924:101), discussing the composition of a detective story, writes that "The first thing is to get your idea. Having got that key one's next task is to conceal it and lay emphasis upon everything which can make for a different explanation." Holmes himself enjoyed taunting official detectives by deliberately pointing out clues without indicating their significance (BOSC, CARD, SIGN, SILV).

CHAPTER THREE

Marcello Truzzi

Sherlock Holmes

APPLIED SOCIAL PSYCHOLOGIST[1]

SIR ARTHUR CONAN DOYLE (1859–1930), best remembered as the creator of the fictional detective Sherlock Holmes, would have preferred to be remembered for his many other works, especially his historical writings and his defense of spiritualism.[2] He even attempted to discontinue Holmes's adventures by having him nobly killed in FINA, which Doyle published in 1893, but he found the great demand of the public for their hero enough incentive to bring Holmes back to life in 1904 to continue the saga.[3] The image of Holmes is epitomizing the application of rationality and scientific method to human behavior is certainly a major factor in the detective's ability to capture the world's imagination.

THE REALITY AND RELEVANCE OF SHERLOCK HOLMES

In her remarkable survey of the history of the detective novel, Alma Elizabeth Murch has noted that:

> There are in literature certain characters who have come to possess a separate and unmistakable identity, whose names and personal qualities are familiar to thousands who may not have read any of the works in which they appear. Among these characters must be included Sherlock Holmes, who has acquired in the minds of countless readers of all nationalities the status of an actual human being, accepted by many in the early years of the twentieth century as a living contemporary, and still surviving fifty years later with all the glamour of an established and unassailable tradition, the most convincing, the most brilliant, the most congenial and well-loved of all detectives of fiction. (Murch 1958:167)

In all of English literature, it has been said that only three other fictional names equally familiar to the "man in the street" might be those of Romeo, Shylock, and Robinson Crusoe (Pearson 1943:86).

Although the Holmes saga consists of only sixty narratives[4] by Sir Arthur Conan Doyle,[5] which first appeared between 1887 and 1927,[6] the foothold Sherlock Holmes gained upon the popular imagination has seldom been equaled. The depth of his impact is nowhere better demonstrated than by "the belief, held for years by thousands, that he was an actual living human being—a circumstance that constitutes one of the most unusual chapters in literary history" (Haycraft 1941:57–58). Thus, in addition to countless letters from troubled would-be clients addressed to "Mr. Sherlock Holmes, 221-B Baker Street, London" (a nonexistent address, too) and many sent to him care of Scotland Yard, the announcement of Holmes's retirement to a bee-farm in a 1904 story brought two offers from would-be employees (one as a housekeeper, the other as beekeeper). Doyle received several letters from ladies who had been contemplating possible marriages with Holmes (Lamond 1931:54–55) and there was even a gentleman (one Stephen Sharp) who believed himself to be Holmes, and he made several attempts to visit Doyle from 1905 onward (reported by Nordon 1967:205).

Aside from those who naively believed the Holmes legend, however, and much more sociologically significant, has been the fact that the "legend of Holmes's reality has been swelled by other enthusiastic if more sophisticated readers who know well enough that their hero has never lived in flesh and blood, but who like to keep up the pretense that he did" (Haycraft 1941:58). More has probably been written *about* Holmes's character than any other creation in fiction, and it is remarkable that it is Holmes and not Sir Arthur Conan Doyle who has been the focus of so much attention. Thus, Holmes has been the subject for biographies,[7] encyclopedic works,[8] critical studies,[9] and numerous organizations honoring and studying the Holmes character exist all around the world.[10] Several movements have even been started to get a statue of Holmes erected near his alleged home on Baker Street.[11] As Christopher Morley has often been quoted as saying: "Never, never has so much been written by so many for so few."

Apart from the delightful games of the Sherlockians and their playful mythologies, however, the character of Sherlock Holmes and his exploits touch a deeper reality, for, as has been noted, "this legend fulfills a need beyond the realms of literature" (Nordon 1967:205). Though, as Pearson (1943:86) has observed, Holmes symbolizes the sportsman and hunter, a modern Galahad hot upon the scent of a bloody trail, the character of Holmes even more clearly epitomizes the attempted application of man's highest faculty—his rationality—in the solution of the problematic situations of everyday life. Most of the plots of the stories came from real life events found by Doyle among the newspaper stories of the 1890s (Nordon 1967:236), and remarkably few of the plots deal with bloody violence or murder. In fact, as Pratt (1955) has observed, in fully one-quarter of the stories no legal crime takes place at all. The essentially mundane character of most of the plots clearly demonstrates the observation that the "cycle may be said to be an epic of everyday events" (Nordon 1967:247). It is this everyday setting of the applications of Holmes's "science" and rationality that so astounds and gratifies the reader. And it is not so much the superior ability of Holmes to obtain remarkable insights and inferences from simple observations which so impresses the reader; it is the seeming reasonableness and obviousness of his "method" once it has been explained to the reader. One truly believes (at least while under the spell of the narrative) that Holmes's new applied science is possible for the diligent student of his "methods." As has been noted:

> The fictitious world to which Sherlock Holmes belonged, expected of him what the real world of the day expected of its scientists: more light and more justice. As a creation of a doctor who had been soaked in the rationalist thought of the period, the Holmesian cycle offers us for the first time the spectacle of a hero triumphing again and again by means of logic and scientific method. (Nordon 1967:247)

This fascination with the possibility of the mundane application of scientific methods to the interpersonal world has captured not only the imagination of the lay readers of the Holmes saga. It has had an appreciable effect upon criminologists and those concerned with the real life problems that parallel those fictionally encountered by Sherlock Holmes. Thus, a representative from the Marseilles Scientific Police Laboratories pointed out that "many of the methods invented by Conan Doyle are today in use in scientific laboratories" (Aston-Wolfe 1932:328); the Director of the Scientific Detective Laboratories and President of the Institute of Scientific Criminology has stated that "the writings of Conan Doyle have done more than any other one thing to stimulate active interest in the scientific and analytical investigation of crime" (May 1936:x); and, most recently, an expert on firearms has argued that Holmes should be called "Father of Scientific Crime Detection" (Berg 1970). Many famous criminologists, including Alphonse Bertillon and Edmond Locard, have credited Holmes as a teacher and source of ideas, and Holmes's techniques of observation and inference are still presented as a useful model for the criminal investigator (Hogan and Schwartz 1964).[12]

In addition to the very practical consequences of Sherlock Holmes's influence upon modern criminology, the reality of his "method" is even better shown through an understanding of his origins. In his autobiography, *Memories and Adventures* (1924), Doyle clearly states that the character of Holmes was patterned after his memories of his professor of surgery when Doyle was in medical school, Joseph Bell, M.D., F.R.C.S., Edinburgh, whom Doyle recalled as capable of the kind of observation and inference so characteristic of Holmes. Bell's remarkable ability is well exemplified by the anecdote related by Doyle and reproduced in chapter 2. It is likely, however, that Holmes was only partly patterned after Dr. Bell and is actually a composite of several persons.[13] Ultimately, though, "there is no doubt that the real Holmes was Conan Doyle himself" (Starrett 1960:102). As Michael and Mollie Hardwick have shown in their remarkable study *The Man Who Was Sherlock Holmes* (1964), the parallels in Doyle's life, including the successful solution of several real-life mysteries and Doyle's championing of justice (best seen in his obtaining the ultimate release and clearing of two men falsely convicted of murder, the celebrated cases of George Edalji and Oscar Slater),[14] clearly demonstrate the roots of Holmes's essential character and methods within his creator. Dr. Edmond Locard, Chief of the Surete Police Laboratories at Lyon, stated that "Conan Doyle was an absolutely astonishing scientific investigator," and the criminologist Albert Ullman took the position that "Conan Doyle was a greater criminologist than his creation Sherlock Holmes" (quoted in Anonymous 1959:69).

The important point being made here is that the successes of Dr. Bell and Sir Arthur Conan Doyle demonstrate the fact that the methods of scientific analysis exemplified and dramatized by Sherlock Holmes in his adventures have had their counterparts in the real world. As the well-known American detective William Burns put it: "I often have been asked if the principles outlined by Conan Doyle, in the Sherlock Holmes stories could be applied in real detective work, and my reply to this question is decidedly 'yes' " (Quoted in Anonymous 1959:68).

What, then exactly, is the "method" of Sherlock Holmes, and what are its limitations and implications for a modern applied social psychology? We turn now to an examination of Holmes's views of science, and of man and society, and to his prescriptions for the applications of the former to the latter as these are outlined in the canon.

THE METHOD OF SHERLOCK HOLMES

It is unfortunate that although Holmes's method is central to his character and universal attractiveness, there is no systematic statement of it to be found in the canon. It is also surprising to find that relatively little consideration has been given to his techniques of "deduction" in the massive bibliography of Sherlockiana. Most Sherlockians have been more concerned with their own application of Holmes's techniques to the clues available in the canon than upon an examination of the methods themselves. Therefore, we must turn to a search for the many but scattered statements about his method uttered by Holmes throughout his adventures.

Holmes's "Science of Deduction and Analysis"

It has often been stated that science is but refined common sense. With this Holmes would probably agree for he states that his own approach is a "simple art, which is but systematized common sense" (BLAN). But his view is not a simple or mechanical view of the process, for at another point he notes that a "mixture of imagination and reality . . . is the basis of my art" (THOR). Though Holmes stresses raw empiricism to a degree reminiscent of the archinductionist Francis Bacon, he does not neglect the importance of creative imagination. "It is, I admit, mere imagination," Holmes states, "but how often is imagination the mother of truth?" (VALL). "One's ideas must be as broad as nature if they are to interpret nature" (STUD), he notes, and "breadth of view . . . is one of the essentials of our profession. The interplay of ideas and the oblique uses of knowledge are often of extraordinary interest" (VALL).

Although Sir Arthur Conan Doyle was to become a major promoter of spiritualism, Holmes, in a true Comtean manner of positivism and scientific skepticism refuses to seriously entertain hypotheses of supernatural causation. Recognizing that "the devil's agents may be of flesh and blood," before considering the possibility that "we are dealing with forces outside the ordinary laws of Nature," he argues that "we are bound to exhaust all other hypotheses before falling back on this one" (HOUN). Holmes states of himself that "this Agency stands flatfooted upon the ground, and there it must remain. The world is big enough for us. No ghosts need apply" (SUSS).

Holmes's general philosophical assumptions about the universe are somewhat unclear. Although he apparently believed in a purposeful universe,[15] and hoped for the goodness of Providence,[16] he also expressed a more cynical view when he asked Watson: "But is not all life pathetic and futile? . . . we reach. We grasp. And what is left in our

hands at the end? A shadow. Or worse than a shadow—misery" (RETI).
This view of all knowledge as "shadows," aside from its depressive context here, is very much in keeping with the modern scientific and essentially pragmatic view of man as a creator of "cognitive maps" and
theoretical "realities" or "conjectures" rather than as discoverer of objective truths and laws.

Holmes also epitomizes the basically deterministic orientation of
most modern social science. As he remarked:

> The ideal reasoner . . . would, when he had once been shown a single fact
> in all its bearings, deduce from it not only all the chain of events which led
> up to it but also all the results which would follow from it. As Cuvier could
> correctly describe a whole animal by the contemplation of a single bone, so
> the observer who has thoroughly understood one link in a series of inci-
> dents should be able to accurately state all the other ones, both before and
> after (FIVE).

Or as Holmes put it in his seminal article "The Book of Life" (in a
magazine Dr. Watson unfortunately neglected to name):

> From a drop of water . . . a logician could infer the possibility of an Atlantic
> or a Niagra without having seen or heard of one or the other. So all life is a
> great chain, the nature of which is known whenever we are shown a single
> link of it. Like all other arts, the Science of Deduction and Analysis is one
> which can only be acquired by long and patient study, nor is life long
> enough to allow any mortal to attain the highest possible perfection in it
> (STUD).

This determinism was seen as present at all levels of life, but Holmes
clearly sides with sociology against many psychologists when he states
that

> while the individual man is an insoluble puzzle, in the aggregate he be-
> comes a mathematical certainty. You can, for example, never foretell what
> any one man will do, but you can say with precision what an average
> member will be up to. Individuals vary, but percentages remain constant
> (SIGN).[17]

As with all nomothetic sciences, emphasis is placed upon the search
for laws and recurrent events. Holmes is greatly impressed by regularities and repetitions in history, and in speaking of a crime to his
friend Inspector Gregson, Holmes echoes Ecclesiastes when he says:
"There is nothing new under the sun. It has all been done before"
(STUD). And on another occasion he says of his arch-enemy: "Every-

thing comes in circles, even Professor Moriarty" (VALL). Holmes seeks out generalizations and will ultimately settle only for universal propositions. As he put it: "I never make exceptions. An exception disproves the rule" (SIGN).

Central to Holmes's basic approach, however, is his concern with the empirical verification of his conjectures. His emphasis on induction—an emphasis more present in his words than in his actual practice, as we shall see—is based on a great fear of conceptual detachment from the "real" world of observable phenomena. "The temptation to form premature theories upon insufficient data is the bane of our profession," he tells Inspector MacDonald (VALL). For as Holmes says again and again:

It is a capital mistake to theorize before one has data. Insensibly one begins to twist facts to suit theories, instead of theories to suit facts (SCAN).

It is a capital mistake to theorize in advance of the facts (SECO).

It is a capital mistake to theorize before you have all the evidence (STUD).

. . . it is an error to argue in front of your data. You find yourself insensibly twisting them round to fit your theories (WIST).

how dangerous it always is to reason from insufficient data (SPEC).

Holmes insists upon the absolute necessity of observable facts. "Data! data! data!" he cried impatiently. "I can't make bricks without clay" (COPP). But he claims even more than this, for his posture is attemptedly atheoretical in an inductive manner remarkably reminiscent of the sort of posture taken today by some behavioristic followers of B.F. Skinner. But like the Skinnerians, Holmes is forced to assert at least provisional hypotheses or "hunches" about the world. Holmes may cry out "No, no: I never guess. It is a shocking habit—destructive to the logical faculty" (SIGN), but he is forced to acknowledge that "one forms provisional theories and waits for time and fuller knowledge to explode them. A bad habit . . . ; but human nature is weak" (SUSS). At base, Holmes puts his trust in the empirical world which he sees as the firm and ultimate arbiter. "I can discover facts, Watson, but I cannot change them" (THOR). And these facts must always be questioned for "it is as well to test everything" (REIG).

Holmes's Method

Holmes clearly subscribed to the general rule of the modern scientific community that since scientific knowledge is of its definition *public* knowledge (insofar as it must be inter-subjectively communicable), it should ideally be open to public scrutiny. Holmes generally makes no secret of his methods. "It has always been my habit to hide none of my methods either from my friend Watson or from anyone who might take an intelligent interest in them" (REIG). Holmes does occasionally fail to inform his astounded clients of his methods, especially in the early stages of his cases, for, as he put it: "I have found it wise to impress clients with a sense of power" (BLAN). Yet, he usually lets us in on his reasonings and points out that the method is basically quite unmysterious.

> It is not really difficult to construct a series of inferences, each dependent upon its predecessor and each simple in itself. If, after doing so, one simply knocks out all the central inferences and presents one's audience with the starting-point and the conclusion, one may produce a startling, though possibly a meretricious, effect (DANC).[18]

Holmes was very concerned with the clear presentation of his methods, so much so, in fact, that he complained of Watson's romanticizing his adventures: "Your fatal habit of looking at everything from the point of view of a story instead of as a scientific exercise has ruined what might have been an instructive and even classical series of demonstrations" (ABBE).[19] He even spoke of his plans to do the job properly himself: "I propose to devote my declining years to the composition of a textbook which shall focus the whole art of detection into one volume" (COPP).

In speaking of the "qualities necessary for the ideal detective," Holmes noted that they were: (1) knowledge, (2) the power of observation, and (3) the power of deduction (SIGN). We turn now to an examination of each of these.

The Detective's Need for Knowledge. As we have seen, Holmes stressed the interconnectedness of all elements of the universe in his deterministic view. He also recognized the complexities and sometimes surprising connections that might be found, for he noted that "for strange effects and extraordinary combinations we must go to life itself, which is always far more daring than any effort of the imagination" (REDH). Thus, the effective detective must be well informed about a vast spectrum of potentially relevant bits of information. Holmes's own storehouse of information was astounding. As we noted earlier, he placed a great emphasis on breadth of knowledge (VALL). Watson indicates that Holmes's mastery of the topics relevant to his profession (including chemistry, British law, anatomy, botany, geology, and especially the sensational literature) was remarkable (STUD). Yet, Watson also notes that Holmes's "ignorance was as remarkable as his knowledge" (STUD), for Holmes apparently knew practically nothing of literature, philosophy, astronomy, or politics (STUD).[20] Holmes explained his lack of concern with these areas as follows:

> You see . . . I consider that a man's brain originally is like a little empty attic, and you have to stock it with such furniture as you choose. A fool takes in all the lumber of every sort that he comes across, so that the knowledge which might be useful to him gets crowded out, or at best is jumbled up with a lot of other things, so that he has a difficulty in laying his hands upon it. Now the skillful workman is very careful indeed as to what he takes into his brain-attic. He will have nothing but the tools which may help him in doing his work, but of these he has a large assortment, and all in the most perfect order. It is a mistake to think that that little room has elastic walls and can distend to any extent. Depend upon it there comes a time when for every addition of knowledge you forget something that you knew before. It is of the highest importance, therefore, not to have useless facts elbowing out the useful ones (STUD).

Despite this avoidance of the irrelevant (based upon a view of memory with which most contemporary experts on cognitive processes would certainly disagree), Holmes still stocked a vast quantity of information in his memory that was not immediately useful; for as he stated on another occasion: "My mind is like a crowded box-room with packets of all sorts stowed away therein—so many that I may well have but a vague perception of what was there" (LION). What Holmes basically argued for was the need for specialization in the quest for knowledge so that one might gain the maximum in resources relevant to one's analytic needs. The argument is not primarily one for avoiding some areas of knowledge so much as it is for a commitment of one's limited resources to the most efficient ends. As Holmes stated in a somewhat different context: "Some facts should be suppressed, or at least a just sense of proportion should be observed in treating them" (SIGN). Thus, not all knowledge is equally useful, a viewpoint certainly the dominant motif in education (not only in the study of social psychology but in most areas) today.

The Detective's Need for Observation. Holmes emphasized the need for keen observation, for in detective work "genius is an infinite capacity for taking pains" (STUD).[21] Openness and receptivity to data is essential. "I make a point of never having any prejudices and of following docilely wherever fact may lead me" (REIG). Holmes was much aware of the need to control for subjective distortions even in relation to his clients. "It is of the first importance . . . not to allow your judgement to be biased by personal qualities. A client is to me a mere unit, a factor in

a problem. The emotional qualities are antagonistic to clear reasoning"
(SIGN).

His greatest emphasis, however, was upon "observing" what others
merely "see." Thus, though both Dr. Watson and Holmes had walked
the steps leading up from the hall to their room hundreds of times,
Holmes had "observed" that there were seventeen steps while Watson
had merely "seen" them (SCAN). As Holmes put it:

> The world is full of obvious things which nobody by any chance ever ob-
> serves (HOUN).

> There is nothing more deceptive than an obvious fact (BOSC).

> I have trained myself to notice what I see (BLAN).

Holmes's observation extended not only to observed facts and events
but also to their absence. Negative evidence is frequently regarded as
highly significant. Thus, when Inspector MacDonald asks Holmes if he
found anything compromising following Holmes's search through Professor Moriarty's papers, Holmes replied, "Absolutely nothing. That
was what amazed me" (VALL). Or, speaking of the absence of international activity following the theft of an important government document, Holmes noted: "Only one important thing has happened in three
days, and that is that nothing has happened" (SECO). But the classic
example is the often-quoted instance during Holmes's search for a missing racehorse wherein Inspector Gregory asks Holmes:

> "Is there any other point to which you would wish to draw my attention?"
> "To the curious incident of the dog in the night-time."
> "The dog did nothing in the night-time."
> "That was the curious incident," remarked Sherlock Holmes (SILV).

Throughout the canon, Holmes emphasizes the importance of what
to the less trained might appear to be trifles. But for Holmes, "there is
nothing so important as trifles" (TWIS), and "to a great mind . . . nothing
is little" (STUD).

> It has long been an axiom of mine that the little things are infinitely the
> most important (IDEN).

> You know my method. It is founded upon the observance of trifles (BOSC).

> Never trust to general impressions . . . but concentrate upon the details
> (IDEN).

Attention to minutiae is essential, for "as long as the criminal remains
upon two legs, so long must there be some identification, some abra-

sion, some trifling displacement which can be detected by the scientific searcher" (BLAC).

The Detective's Need for Deduction. Holmes has almost unlimited faith in the power of scientific analysis to obtain a reconstruction of human events, for, as he put it: "What one man can invent, another can discover" (DANC). For Holmes, "the grand thing is to be able to reason backwards" (STUD). Reasoning from a set of events to their consequences Holmes calls "synthetic" reasoning, whereas reasoning "backwards" from the results to their causes he calls "analytic" reasoning.

> There are fifty who can reason synthetically for one who can reason analytically .... There are few people ..., if you told them the result, would be able to evolve from their own inner consciousness what the steps were which led up to that result (STUD).

The first step Holmes suggests is basic examination and sifting out from the existing information the definite from the less definite data.

> The difficulty is to detach the framework of fact—of absolute, undeniable fact—from the embellishments of theorists and reporters. Then, having established ourselves upon this sound basis, it is our duty to see what inferences may be drawn, and which are the special points upon which the whole mystery turns (SILV).

> It is of the highest importance in the art of detection to be able to recognize out of a number of facts which are incidental and which vital (REIG).

Following a sorting of the facts for their reliability, Holmes recommends special inspection of the unique and unusual details present in the situation.

> The more *outré* and grotesque an incident is, the more carefully it deserves to be examined, and the very point which appears to complicate a case is, when duly considered and scientifically handled, the one which is most likely to elucidate it (HOUN).

> Singularity is almost invariably a clue. The more featureless and commonplace a crime is, the more difficult is it to bring home (BOSC).

> What is out of the common is usually a guide rather than a hindrance (STUD).

> It is only the colourless, uneventful case which is hopeless (SHOS).

Yet, Holmes notes that extreme uneventfulness may itself be a singular event which gives a clue to the mystery: "Depend upon it there is nothing so unnatural as the commonplace" (IDEN).

Holmes is careful in his evaluation of circumstantial evidence. It is not to be ignored for "circumstantial evidence is occasionally very convincing, as when you find a trout in the milk" (NOBL). But the investigator must be very cautious, since "circumstantial evidence is a very tricky thing . . . ; it may point very straight to one thing, but if you shift your own point of view a little, you may find it pointing in an equally uncompromising manner to something entirely different" (BOSC).

Although Holmes's greatest emphasis is upon the objective gathering of facts, he fully recognizes the heuristic value of imaginative reconstruction through role playing by the investigator.

> You'll get results . . . by always putting yourself in the other fellow's place, and thinking what you would do yourself. It takes some imagination but it pays (RETI).

> You know my methods in such cases . . . : I put myself in the man's place, and having first gauged his intelligence, I try to imagine how I should myself have proceeded under the same circumstances (MUSG).[22]

Holmes emphasizes the need for pursuing several possible lines of explanation any one of which takes account of the facts. Other hypotheses must always be entertained, and when considering an explanation, "you should never lose sight of the alternative" (BLAC).

> One should always look for a possible alternative and provide against it. It is the first rule of criminal investigation (BLAC).

> when you follow two separate chains of thought . . . you will find some point of intersection which should approximate the truth (LADY).

From this reconstruction of alternative explanations which fit the facts, one must move next into what might superficially appear to be guessing but is actually "the region where we balance probabilities and choose the most likely. It is the scientific use of the imagination, but we have always some material basis on which to start our speculations" (HOUN).

Holmes sees arrival at the truth in terms of setting hypotheses into competition with one another. But the weighing of the alternatives includes not only a comparison of them in terms of *probability*. Explanations must always be considered in terms of their *possibility*. The *possible*, however, is determined not only by the feasibility of the suggested events. It is also the remaining result of elimination of those alternative hypotheses perceived to be impossible. Holmes often repeats "the old axiom that when all other contingencies fail, whatever remains, however improbable, must be the truth" (BRUC).[23]

Though the analytic process described above is primarily an exercise in logic without direct recourse to the empirical world, Holmes next demanded the empirical validation of the resulting hypotheses in terms which closely approximate what is today called the *hypothetico-deductive* method.[24]

> I will give my process of thought . . . That process . . . starts upon the supposition that when you have eliminated all which is impossible, that whatever remains, however improbable, must be the truth. It may well be that several explanations remain, in which case one tries test after test until one or other of them has a convincing amount of support (BLAN).

> . . . when the original intellectual deduction is confirmed point by point by quite a number of independent accidents, then the subjective becomes objective and we can say confidently that we have reached our goal (SUSS).

Throughout Holmes's approach, logical (mostly deductive) and empirical (mostly inductive) considerations are in constant interrelation. The empirical restricts the theoretical, as in the case where Holmes states that "It *is* impossible as I state it, and therefore I must in some respect have stated it wrong (PRIO).

But empirical events must be interpreted in terms of established theoretical considerations. Thus, "when a fact appears to be opposed to a long train of deductions, it invariably proves to be capable of having some other interpretation (STUD). In a very real and practical sense, Holmes's method anticipated the contemporary emphasis in sociology upon the intertwining relationships between theory and research (cf. Merton 1957: 85–117).

The Application of Holmes's Method

Thus far, we have outlined Holmes's general approach to the problematic in social life. We turn now to a consideration of the limitations of that approach, especially as exemplified in Holmes's own applications of his method.

Holmes's Uses of Observation. Throughout the adventures, Holmes insists upon intensive familiarization of the investigator with his problem, for familiarity will bring clarification. He notes that "it is a mistake to confound strangeness with mystery" (STUD).[25] Familiarity is seen as generally reducing the problematic elements in an event. He even states that "as a rule . . . the more bizarre a thing is the less mysterious it proves to be" (REDH). Familiarization can also remove fear, for the unfamiliar leaves us room for imagination, and "where there is no imagination, there is no horror" (STUD).

Holmes attempted to familiarize himself with all possible observable details of life which might have a bearing upon his criminal cases. This familiarization was not just the result of passive observation but includes the active search for new details of meaning which might prove useful in the future. Thus, for example, Holmes was described as having at one time beaten a corpse to discern how bruises might be produced after death (STUD).

Holmes argued, as we have noted, that all human actions leave some traces from which the discerning investigator can deduce information. This emphasis on obtaining indirect data from sources through observation of physical traces constitutes an early recognition of the potential uses of what recently have been termed *unobtrusive measures*. (Webb, et al., 1966: 35). Again and again, Holmes concerns himself with the small details about those involved in his inquiries.

> I can never bring you to realize the importance of sleeves, the suggestiveness of thumbnails, or the great issues that may hang from a boot lace (IDEN).
>
> Always look at the hands first, . . . then cuffs, trouser-knees and boots (CREE).
>
> [T]here is no part of the body which varies so much as the human ear. Each ear is as a rule quite distinctive, and different from all other ones (CARD).
>
> It would be difficult to name any articles which afford a finer field for inference than a pair of glasses (GOLD).
>
> Pipes are occasionally of extraordinary interest. . . . Nothing has more individuality save, perhaps, watches and bootlaces (YELL).

Nor does Holmes restrict his observations to things seen or heard. The investigator should develop his sense of smell, too, for "there are seventy-five perfumes, which it is very necessary that a criminal expert should be able to distinguish from each other, and cases have more than once within my own experience depended upon their prompt recognition" (HOUN).

Possibly the most important and frequent among the traces carefully examined by Holmes is the footprint. Of it he says: "There is no branch of detective science which is so important and so much neglected as the art of tracing footprints" (STUD). Even the traces of bicycle tires are not left unconsidered by Holmes, who claims at one point that he can differentiate some forty-two different "tyre impressions" (PRIO).

Though Holmes's uses of the observable differences which he notes and conveys to the reader are often fantastic and hardly practicable in the "real world" outside the pages of the canon, the basic approach represented by these fictional narratives has startling parallels in the actual world of criminalistics and forensic medicine (e.g., cf. Stewart-Gordon 1961) where true cases of detection through subtle observation and inference are often far more startling than anything ever suggested by Sir Arthur Conan Doyle.

The Character of Holmes's Inferences. Although examples of Holmes's remarkable uses of inference abound in the Sherlockian literature, as with his basic method, little attention has been given to an examination of the logic of his applications (minor, largely noncritical and merely admiring studies would include those of Hart 1948, Schenck 1953, Mackenzie 1956, Ball 1958, and, especially, Hitchings 1946).

Careful examination of the sixty narratives that comprise the canon reveals at least 217 clearly described and discernible cases of inference (unobtrusive measurement) made by Holmes. Many of these are strung together in logical chains with Holmes gathering a great deal of information from a single object or event.[26] Thus, numerous instances appear in one story (at least thirty in STUD) with few or none (as in DYIN) in others.

Although Holmes often speaks of his *deductions,* these are actually quite rarely displayed in the canon. Nor are Holmes's most common inferences technically *inductions.* More exactly, Holmes consistently displays what C.S. Peirce has called *abductions.*[27] Following Peirce's distinctions, the differences between deduction, induction, and abduction can be seen as follows:

Deduction

Case	All serious knife wounds result in bleeding.
Result	This was a serious knife wound.
∴ *Rule*	There was bleeding.

Induction

Case	This was a serious knife wound.
Result	There was bleeding.
∴ *Rule*	All serious knife wounds result in bleeding.

Abduction

Rule	All serious knife wounds result in bleeding.
Result	There was bleeding.
∴ *Case*	This was a serious knife wound.

Abductions, like inductions, are not logically self-contained, as is the deduction, and they need to be externally validated. Peirce sometimes called abductions *hypotheses* (he also called them *presumptive inferences* at times), and in the modern sense, that is what the conclusion in the abduction represents: a conjecture about reality which needs to be validated through testing.

The great weakness in Holmes's applications of inference—at least as Watson related them to us—was Holmes's failure to test the hypotheses which he obtained through abduction. In most instances, Holmes simply treated the abducted inference as though it were logically valid. (Most of the parodies on Holmes are built upon this weakness in the narratives.) The simple fact is that the vast majority of Holmes's inferences just do not stand up to logical examination. He concludes correctly simply because the author of the stories allows it so.[28] Upon occasion, the abductive inferences are strung together in a long narrative series which the startled client (or Watson) confirms at each step. In a sense, this constitutes a degree of external corroboration of the hypotheses (especially where they are made about things correctly known to the listener, which is often the case). Nonetheless, in the vast majority of instances, the basic reasoning process described by Watson whereby Holmes astounds his listeners must, in the final analysis, be judged logically inadequate if not invalid.

Despite the logical inadequacies of Holmes's abductions, it must be noted that Holmes does actually hypothesis test (i.e., seek external validation) in at least twenty-eight instances (though not even all of these occasions are directly related to the minimum of 217 abductions found in the canon). Several of the stories include more than one case of hypothesis testing (SILV and STUD both evidence three such tests), but most of the narratives show no such attempts at external confirmation by Holmes. The best example of such testing by Holmes occurs in the story of Holmes's search for the missing race horse Silver Blaze. Postulating that the horse's leg was to be operated upon by an amateur to damage it, Holmes reasoned that the culprit would probably practice the operation beforehand to gain skill and assure success. Since sheep were nearby, Holmes further conjectured that the culprit might have practiced upon them. Inquiring about the sheep, Holmes learned that several of them had recently and inexplicably gone lame. The sheep's predicted lameness thus acted as a confirmation of Holmes's conjectures (SILV).

The reconstruction of Holmes's methods and the extraction of the fundamental ideas in his thought is necessarily incomplete. Holmes relates only bits and pieces to us through the narratives of Dr. Watson, and even these items are stated sparingly. Watson noted of Holmes that "he pushed to an extreme the axiom that the only safe plotter was he who plotted alone" (ILLU). And as Holmes put it:

I do not waste words or disclose my thoughts while a case is actually under consideration (BLAN).

I claim the right to work in my own way and give my results at my own time—complete, rather than in stages (VALL).

Despite these obstacles, we have seen that a general reconstruction is possible, and it reveals a systematic and consistent orientation.

HOLMES AND SOCIAL PSYCHOLOGY

Just as with his basic method, examination of the canon reveals a large number of statements and insights, many stated in near-propositional and testable form about many aspects of social and psychological reality. We turn now to a look at some of the observations.

Holmes on Character and Personality

Holmes brings the same skepticism which served him as a detective of crimes into his general orientation towards the social world. As is the case with most social psychologists who term themselves symbolic interactionists (cf. Stone and Farberman 1970), Holmes was much aware that people's definitions of their situations, their phenomenological perception of their worlds, rather than physical realities, may be the important factors which determine their actions. "What you do in this world is a matter of no consequence. . . . The question is what can you make people believe you have done" (STUD). Holmes's skepticism of appearances bordered upon the paranoic when it came to women. Holmes was especially cautious in his relations with women and found it nearly impossible to correctly assess their motives.

Women are never to be entirely trusted—not the best of them (SIGN).

[T]he motives of women are so inscrutable . . . Their most trivial action may mean volumes, or their most extraordinary conduct may depend upon a hairpin or a curling-tongs (SECO).

He showed special concern about the socially isolated female.

One of the most dangerous classes in the world . . . is the drifting and friendless woman. She is the most harmless, and often the most useful of mortals, but she is the inevitable inciter of crime in others. She is helpless. She is migratory. She has sufficient means to take her from country to country and from hotel to hotel. She is lost, as often as not, in a maze of obscure *pensions* and boarding houses. She is a stray chicken in a world of foxes. When she is gobbled up she is hardly missed (LADY).

Yet, Holmes was no misogynist (as is well seen in his admiration for Irene Adler who bested him in SCAN), and he placed great value on female intuition: "I have seen too much not to know that the impression of a woman may be more valuable than the conclusion of an anlytic reasoner" (TWIS).

Holmes mentions several generalizations about women which proved valuable to him in successfully analyzing his cases, but these were highly specific to their situations and probably would not stand up under rigorous investigation in other contexts.[29]

In attempting to read a subject's character and motives, Holmes used a variety of subtle indicators. The movement of the subject's eyes and body were carefully noted (such study of "body language" is today called *kinesics*): "I can read in a man's eye when it is his own skin that he is frightened for" (RESI). And, seeing a young lady client's motions on the street as she approached his apartment, he noted: "Oscillation upon the pavement always means an *affaire du coeur*" (IDEN).

Extensive examination was always given not only to the subject under investigation but also to those with whom he associated, including children and animals.

> I have frequently gained my first real insight into the character of parents by studying their children (COPP).

> I have serious thoughts of writing a small monograph upon the uses of dogs in the work of the detective. . . . A dog reflects the family life. Whoever saw a frisky dog in a gloomy family, or a sad dog in a happy one? Snarling people have snarling dogs, dangerous people have dangerous ones. And their passing moods may reflect the passing moods of others (CREE).[30]

Holmes suggested a number of interesting ideas about personality. Thus, he endorsed the idea of complementarity in mate selection: "You may have noticed how extremes call to each other, the spiritual to the animal, the cave-man to the angel" (ILLU).[31] He argued that excellence at chess was "one mark of a scheming mind" (RETI). He claimed that all the misers were jealous men (ibid.), and that "jealousy is a strong transformer of characters" (NOBL). Recognizing the importance of man's inferiorities, Holmes noted that "weakness in one limb is often compensated for by exceptional strength in the others" (TWIS). Regarding the appreciation of subtle variations by those with expertise, he noted that "to the man who loves art for its own sake, . . . it is frequently in its least important and lowliest manifestations that the keenest pleasure is to be derived" (COPP). And of a man's stubborn psychological inertia, he generalized that "a man always finds it hard to realize that he may have finally lost a woman's love, however badly he may have treated her" (MUSG). All these generalizations must remain questionable until empirically tested, but these maxims suggest interesting and potentially fruitful directions for future research.

Holmes as Criminologist

Thus far, we have been primarily concerned with Holmes's general orientation to the investigation and perception of the realities of social life. As a consulting detective, however, his primary concern was with legal and moral crimes. We turn now to examine his insights and observations into this more specialized domain.

Holmes on Justice and Deception. Holmes felt that his personal hardships were "trifling details" that "must never interfere with the investigation of a case" (HOUN). But he was far from the usual stereotype most people have of the daring hero. Though a brave man, Holmes did not ignore adversity, for he thought that "it is stupidity rather than courage to refuse to recognize danger when it is close upon you" (FINA). Far more contrary to the pure heroic image, however, was the fact that Holmes's activities sometimes ran counter to the law. As an unofficial investigator, he was not bound to the conventions of the police. He had little respect for the abilities of Scotland Yard's men and thought them generally "a bad lot" (though he did display respect for the abilities of the Yard's Inspector Tobias Gregson). He went even further in his disdain for other police, as when he noted that "local aid is always either worthless or biased" (BOSC). Holmes was well aware of the inadequacies of law enforcement and commented that "many men have been wrongfully hanged" (ibid.).

Holmes did apparently have a degree of faith in the ultimate victory of justice, as indicated in his statement that "violence does, in truth, recoil upon the violent, and the schemer falls into the pit which he digs for another" (SPEC). But Holmes sometimes finds it necessary to go outside the law to assure justice. Thus, he occasionally commits trespass, burglary, and unlawful detention. Of the most serious of these, burglary, he argues that it "is morally justifiable so long as our object is to take no articles save those which are used for an illegal purpose" (CHAS). He adopted this basically vigilante role because, as he put it: "I think that there are certain crimes which the law cannot touch, and which therefore, to some extent, justify private revenge" (ibid.).

Holmes also recognized that prison was not always an appropriate punishment for a crime, and that it might actually deter the process of reform. Thus, on at least fourteen occasions, Holmes actually allowed known felons to go free (Leavitt 1940:27), for as he said of one such man he released: "Send him to gaol now, and you make him a gaolbird for life" (BLUE).

Holmes was also not beyond deception if he felt it might suit the ends of justice. This went to rather extreme lengths when he attempted to trap "the worst man in London" by disguising himself as a plumber and becoming engaged to the villain's maid to obtain information (CHAS).[32] Holmes was aware of the need to obtain the full confidence of his informants, and this he sometimes did by passing himself off as one of them. Thus, on one occasion when he needed certain information, he disguised himself as a groom, explaining to Watson that "there is a wonderful sympathy and freemasonry among horsey men. Be one of them, and you will know all that there is to know" (SCAN).

On other occasions, Holmes faked illnesses, accidents, information, and even his own death. He often used the newspapers in a manipulative manner[33] and noted that "the press . . . . is a most valuable institution, if you only know how to use it" (SIXN).

Holmes on Crime. Sherlock Holmes was well aware of the fact that crime rates normally show only *reported* instances of law violation. Thus, in looking at the pleasant countryside through which he and Dr. Watson were moving by train, Holmes remarked to Watson:

> You look at these scattered houses, and you are impressed by their beauty. I look at them, and the only thought which comes to me is a feeling of their isolation, and of the impunity with which crime may be committed there . . . They always fill me with a certain horror. It is my belief . . . founded upon my experience, that the lowest and vilest alleys in London do not present a more dreadful record of sin than does the smiling and beautiful country-side . . . . [And] the reason is very obvious. The pressure of public opinion can do in the town what the law cannot accomplish. There is no lane so vile that the scream of a tortured child, or the thud of a drunkard's blow, does not beget sympathy and indignation among the neighbours, that a word of complaint can set it going, and there is but a step between the crime and the dock. But look at these lonely houses, each in its own fields, filled for the most part with poor ignorant folk who know little of the law. Think of the deeds of hellish cruelty, the hidden wickedness which may go on year in, year out, in such places, and none the wise (COPP).

As with his views on personality, Holmes offers us numerous maxims about crime and criminal investigation which the contemporary criminologist might well consider. Thus, Holmes claimed that there was a potential relationship between the unusual and the criminal, as when he pointed out that "there is but one step from the grotesque to the horrible" and "often the grotesque has deepened into the criminal" (WIST). Yet, he also warned us that we should not assume such a relationship to be automatic for "the strangest and most unique things are very often connected not with the larger but with the smaller crimes, and occasionally, indeed, where there is room for doubt whether any positive crime has been committed" (REDH). Holmes found two types of crime especially difficult to unravel. He found the "senseless" or motiveless crime the greatest challenge for the criminal investigator: "The most difficult crime to track is the one which is purposeless" (NAVA). But where a discernible motive is involved, the planned crime presents great difficulties for a detective also, for "where a crime is cooly premeditated, then the means of covering it are cooly premeditated also" (THOR). This realization of the hidden complexities potential within a planned crime led Holmes to be most suspicious in such cases, especially of suspects with seemingly solid alibis, for, he noted "only a man with a criminal enterprise desires to establish an alibi" (WIST). Finally, it might be noted that in addition to seeing these two types of crime as formidable, Holmes also recognized special difficulty with cases where the criminal was an M.D.: "When a doctor does go wrong he is the first of criminals. He has nerve and he has knowledge" (SPEC).

Canonical Errors and Anticipations. As might be expected, the adventures sometimes show Holmes stating scientifically erroneous ideas. These largely reflect the popular notions of his time. Thus, Holmes placed far too great an emphasis on heredity as a causative factor in the creation of criminals. He referred to an hereditary criminal strain in the blood of the arch-villain Professor Moriarty (FINA) and strongly stated his views when he said:

> There are some trees . . . which grow to a certain height and then suddenly develop some unsightly eccentricity. You will see it often in humans. I have a theory that the individual represents in his development the whole procession of his ancestors, and that such a sudden turn to good or evil stands for some strange influence which came into the life of his pedigree. The person becomes, as it were, the epitome of the history of his own family (EMPT).

Holmes also seems to share some of the stereotypes and prejudices of his Victorian world in regard to some minority groups. Thus, he displayed mild prejudice toward Negroes and Jews.[34]

He also had some unusual and false ideas about thought processes. We have already mentioned his view of memory as similar to an attic which can become over-crowded (STUD). He also showed a degree of misunderstanding of cognitive processes in the following statements:

To let the brain work without sufficient material is like racing an engine. It racks itself to pieces (DEVI).

[T]he faculties become refined when you starve them (MAZA).

Intense mental concentration has a curious way of blotting out what has passed (HOUN).

Despite such occasional lapses into the misinformation common to his historical period, Holmes managed to pioneer in the anticipation of several innovations in scientific crime detection. Since the science of ballistics was unknown to police prior to 1909 (cf. Baring-Gould 1967, II:349, fn. 51), Holmes's statement about a villain in a story first published in 1903 that "the bullets alone are enough to put his head in a noose" (EMPT) seems to show him to be a true pioneer in this field. Holmes was also an early advocate of the importance of both fingerprints (NORW), and the Bertillon system of measurement (NAVA).

Among the most interesting of his anticipations was his realization of the possibility of distinguishing and identifying different types of communications. He was able to spot identifying differences between a wide variety of printing types in newspapers and magazines, and he stated that "the detection of types is one of the most elementary branches of knowledge to the special expert of crime" (HOUN). And, more important, he early recognized that typewriters could be identified: "It is a curious thing . . . that a typewriter has really quite as much individuality as a man's handwriting. Unless they are quite new, no two of them write exactly alike. Some letters get more worn than others, and some wear only on one side" (IDEN). But most of all, Holmes strongly believed in the great knowledge which could be gained through the careful examination of handwritings (cf. Christie 1955 and Swanson 1962). Holmes not only pioneered in this study but went considerably beyond what most graphologists would yet claim for their science when he made the statements that "the deduction of a man's age from his writing is one which has been brought to a considerable accuracy by experts" (REIG), and that "a family mannerism can be traced in . . . two specimens of writing" (ibid.).

Finally, it should be noted that Holmes may have anticipated some of the devices of later psychoanalysis. Thus, it would appear that he saw the basis for tests of free-association, for in analyzing a coded message which contained seemingly extraneous and meaningless words, he noted of the writer: "He would naturally use the first words which came to his mind, and if there were so many which referred to sport among them, you may be tolerably sure that he is either an ardent shot or interested in breeding" (GLOR). Holmes also clearly understood the defense mechanism of projection when he stated of a villain: "It may only be his conscience. Knowing himself to be a traitor, he may have read the accusation in the other's eyes" (VALL). And at another point, when speaking of the subtle influences of music, he would seem to have closely paralleled the idea of archetypes within the collective unconscious as later developed by Carl G. Jung when he said: "There are vague memories in our souls of the misty centuries when the world was in its childhood" (STUD).

Holmes, then, shared many of the errors of the men of his time, but as we hope has been adequately shown in this essay, he also extended our view of man. Given the extraordinary popularity of the tales of his adventures—created for us through the genius of Sir Arthur Conan Doyle—for many criminologists who recognized the merits of the detective's methods, it is doubtful that Sherlock Holmes could have had a greater impact on the sciences of man had he actually lived.

NOTES

1. This article was especially prepared for Truzzi 1973:93–126. Copyright 1971 by Marcello Truzzi.

2. Doyle's major works aside from the Holmes stories include *The Captain of the "Polestar"* (1887); *The Mystery of the Cloomber* (1888); *Micah Clark* (1889); *The White Company* (1891); *Rodney Stone* (1896); *Sir Nigel* (1906); *The Lost World* (1912); *The British Campaigns in Europe* (1928); *The Great Boer War* (1900); and *History of Spiritualism* (1926). Re Doyle's role as a spiritualist, a sympathetic account can be found in Yellen 1965.

3. For a consideration of Holmes's more general perspective in relation to scientific method, see Kejci-Graf (1967).

4. The fully accepted Holmes legend appears in four full-length novels and fifty-six short stories. Though a great many editions of the works exist, the most recent and authoritative version of the tales is to be found in William S. Baring-Gould's beautifully edited and introduced *The Annotated Sherlock Holmes* in two volumes (1967).

In addition to the above works (called the "canon" or the "sacred writings" by Sherlockian scholars), Holmes is also believed to figure prominently in two other stories by Arthur Conan Doyle ("The Man With the Watches" and "The Lost Special") available as *The Sherlockian Doyle* (1968). There also was published a posthumously discovered manuscript which was at first thought to have been written by Sir Arthur Conan Doyle as "The Case of the Man Who Was Wanted" (1948). The authenticity of this piece has since been challenged with the result being general agreement that the story was actually written by a Mr. Arthur Whittaker, who had sold the story to Conan Doyle in 1913. For full details on this episode, see Brown 1969.

Within the sixty narratives comprising the canon, mentions are made of at least fifty-five other cases (for a listing see Starrett 1971:90–92). A minority of Sherlockians would therefore be inclined to include twelve other stories among the sacred writings which were written by Sir Arthur's son and official biographer, Adrian Conan Doyle and John Dickson Carr (1954).

In addition to the canon and its apocrypha plus some secondary references to Holmes by Doyle (most notably in several of his plays based on the stories), there is a vast literature based directly on the canon including over twenty-one plays, one Broadway musical, hundreds of radio and television productions, and at least 123 motion pictures. This is not to count the hundreds of books and articles dealing with Sherlockiana or the hundreds of pastiches and parodies of the canon, of which many of the best were anthologized by Ellery Queen (1944).

5. According to Sherlockians, of course, Doyle is not the author of the stories but merely an acquaintance of Holmes's associate, Dr. John Watson, who wrote (narrated) fifty-six of the sixty adventures in the canon. BLAN and LION were apparently written by Holmes himself, and MAZA and LAST were written by a person or persons unknown. Sherlockians have speculated about the authorship of these two narratives, suggesting everyone from Mrs. Mary Watson, Inspector Lestrade, a distant relative of Holmes called Dr. Verner, to Dr. Watson himself merely pretending to write in the third person. Even the rather extreme suggestion was made, first by the great Sherlockian scholar, Edgar W. Smith, that these two stories were written by Watson's friend Sir Arthur Conan Doyle. For full details on this controversy, see Baring-Gould 1967, II: 748–750.

For biographical works on Sir Arthur Conan Doyle, see Carr 1949; Nordon 1967; Pearson 1943; Lamond 1931; and M. and M. Hardwick 1964. See also Doyle's autobiography (1924). Re Doyle's writings, see H. Locke 1928; Nordon 1967: 347-351; and Carr 1949: 285-295.

6. The adventures themselves have been chronologized differently by numerous Sherlockians, but Baring-Gould (1967) sees them as spanning from 1874 to 1914. Far more controversially, in his biography of Holmes, Baring-Gould (1962) calculated Holmes's birth year as 1854 and placed his death in 1957. For other chronologies, see Bell 1932; Blackeney 1932; Christ 1947; Brend 1951; Zeisler 1953; Baring-Gould 1955; and Folsom 1964.

7. E.g., Baring-Gould 1967 and Brend 1951. For a biographical study of Dr. John Watson, see Roberts 1931.

8. E.g., Park 1962 and M. and M. Hardwick 1962. Many other reference volumes on the canon exist including Harrison 1958; Christ 1947; Bigelow 1959; Petersen 1956; Smith 1940; and Wolff 1952 and 1955.

9. Among the many excellent books and collections of Sherlockiana one must include Bell 1934; Starrett 1940 and 1971; Smith 1944; and Holroyd 1967. A wide variety of such studies appear in the numerous Sherlockian journals. In addition to the best known *The Baker Street Journal,* published in New York, and *The Sherlock Holmes Journal,* published in London, there are many newsletters and other privately printed publications produced by Sherlockian groups around the United States, including: *The Vermissa Herald,* the *Devon*

County Chronicle, Shades of Sherlock, and the annual Pontine Dossier. For an extensive critical bibliography, see Baring-Gould 1967, II:807–824.

10. The most well-known organization in the United States is the Baker Street Irregulars, born in 1933 in the "Bowling Green" column conducted by Christopher Morley in the *Saturday Review of Literature.* For a brief history of the B.S.I., see Starrett 1960:128–136. The B.S.I. has Scion Societies (chapters) all over the world including the Orient. Re the Sherlockian organizations see Baring-Gould 1967, I:37–42; and Starrett 1971:128–136.

11. Though these movements have failed thus far, numerous other memorials have been erected to Holmes's memory including plaques in Picadilly, at St. Bartholomew's Hospital, at the Rosslei Inn in Meiringen, Switzerland, and even at the Reichenbach Falls. For full information, see Baring-Gould 1967, I:43–46.

12. For a somewhat more critical view of Holmes as criminologist, see Anderson 1903.

13. Nordon (1967:214) has argued that Doyle's description of Bell is "too like Holmes to be true," and that the model for Holmes was "invented" by Doyle *a posteriori* to fit the image of a proper man of science. Pearson (1943) suggested that Holmes was largely patterned after one Dr. George Budd, Doyle's eccentric medical partner with whom he briefly practiced at Plymouth. More recently, it has been convincingly argued that Holmes was basically patterned after the private consulting detective Mr. Wendel Shere (Harrison 1971).

14. *The Spectator* said of him: "The fights that he made for victims of perverted justice will stand alongside Voltaire's championship of Jean Calas and Emile Zola's long struggle for Dreyfus" (quoted in Anonymous 1959:67).

15. " 'What is the meaning of it, Watson,' said Holmes solemnly as he laid down the paper. 'What object is served by this circle of misery and violence and fear? It must tend to some end or else our universe is ruled by chance, which is unthinkable. But what end? There is the great standing perennial problem to which human reason is as far from an answer as ever' " (CARD).

16. "Our highest assurance of the goodness of Providence seems to me to rest in the flowers. All other things, our powers, our desires, our food, are really necessary for our existence in this first instance. But this rose is an extra. Its smell and its colour are an embellishment of life, not a condition of it. It is only goodness which gives extras, and so I say again that we have much to hope from the flowers" (NAVA).

17. In this passage, Holmes indicates his agreement with Winwood Reade's *The Martyrdom of Man,* which Holmes actually misquotes. Cf. Crocker 1964.

18. Along similar lines, Holmes also stated that "every problem becomes very childish when once it is explained to you" (DANC), and "results without causes are much more impressive" (STOC).

19. Holmes stated the matter more strongly when he told Watson: "Crime is common. Logic is rare. Therefore it is upon logic rather than upon the crime that you should dwell. You have degraded what should have been a course of lectures into a series of tales" (COPP).

20. Holmes's many statements dealing with these very areas in other stories patently contradict Watson's early impressions of Holmes's astounding ignorance in these realms, and Holmes's statement to Watson that he was unaware of the basic Copernican Theory of the solar system is generally taken by most

Sherlockians to have been intended as a joke by Holmes which Watson failed to perceive. Cf. Baring-Gould 1967,1:154–157, fns. 30–44.

21. For an excellent review of Holmes's uses of observations and their implications for modern criminological investigation, see Hogan and Schwarts 1964.

22. Holmes believed that getting into the same environment could facilitate this process for he said: "I shall sit in that room and see its atmosphere bring me inspiration. I'm a believer in the *genius loci*" (VALL).

23. Also, cf. (SIGN) and (BERY).

24. The hypothetico-deductive method is by no means new, for it can even be seen in the works of the ancient Greek philosopher Parmenides. For an excellent modern statement on this approach to knowledge, see Popper 1968:215–250.

25. At another point, Holmes quotes Tacitus's Latin maxim that "everything unknown passes for something splendid" (REDH).

26. According to Ball (1958), this ability is epitomized by what Ball argues are Holmes's twenty-three deductions from a single scrap of paper in REIG.

27. For full clarification of Peirce on abduction, the reader is best referred to Cohen 1949:131–153; Feibleman 1946:116–132; Goudge 1950:195–199; and Buchler 1955:150–156. For an excellent brief survey of the general problems of induction, see Black 1967.

28. Noting the logical discrepancies in Holmes's reasoning, one Sherlockian has commented that Holmes's successful conclusions might be accounted for by the suggestion that Holmes had psychic powers of extrasensory perception (Reed 1970). Holmes's remarkable abilities actually approximate the reading of Watson's mind in CARD.

29. These include: "[T]here are few wives having any regard for their husbands who would let any man's spoken word stand between them and their husband's dead body" (VALL); "No woman would ever send a reply-paid telegram. She would have come" (WIST); and "When a woman thinks that her house is on fire, her instinct is at once to rush to the thing which she values most. . . . A married woman grabs at her baby—an unmarried one reaches for her jewel box" (SCAN).

30. Recent years have seen social psychologists interested in a similar approach, e.g., see Levinson 1966.

31. For a modern version of this idea, see Winch 1955.

32. Holmes commonly obtains information from servants, especially the investigated subjects' ex-employees, for Holmes noted that for information "there are no better instruments than discharged servants with a grievance" (WIST).

33. E.g., in BRUC Holmes planted a false notice in the "agony columns" to get the villain to reveal himself.

34. Holmes apparently accepted the common stereotype of Caucasians that black people have extraordinary body odor for on one occasion he tells the black bruiser Steve Dixie, "I don't like the smell of you," and on another he snidely referred to looking for his scent-bottle (3GAB). Holmes also seems to have accepted an anti-Semitic stereotype for he referred to a client in debt by saying that "He is in the hands of the Jews" (SHOS).

CHAPTER FOUR

Carlo Ginzburg

Clues: Morelli, Freud, and Sherlock Holmes[1]

God is hidden in details.
—G. Flaubert and A. Warburg

IN THE FOLLOWING pages I will try to show how, in the late nineteenth century, an epistemological model (or, if you like, a paradigm[2]) quietly emerged in the sphere of the social sciences. Examining this paradigm, which has still not received the attention it deserves, and which came into use without ever being spelled out as a theory, can perhaps help us to go beyond the sterile contrasting of "rationalism" and "irrationalism."

I

1. Between 1874 and 1876 a series of articles on Italian painting was published in the German art history journal *Zeitschrift für bildende Kunst*. They bore the signature of an unknown Russian scholar, Ivan Lermolieff, and the German translator was also unknown, one Johannes Schwarze. The articles proposed a new method for the correct attribution of old masters, which provoked much discussion and controversy among art historians. Several years later the author revealed himself as Giovanni Morelli, an Italian (both pseudonyms were adapted from his own name). The "Morelli method" is still referred to by art historians.[3]

Let us take a look at the method itself. Museums, Morelli said, are full of wrongly attributed paintings—indeed assigning them correctly is often very difficult, since often they are unsigned, or painted over, or in poor repair. So distinguishing copies from originals (though essential) is very hard. To do it, said Morelli, one should refrain from the usual concentration on the most obvious characteristics of the paintings, for these could most easily be imitated—Perugino's central figures with eyes characteristically raised to heaven, or the smile of Leonardo's

81

women, to take a couple of examples. Instead one should concentrate on minor details, especially those least significant in the style typical of the painter's own school: earlobes, fingernails, shapes of fingers and toes. So Morelli identified the ear (or whatever) peculiar to such masters as Botticelli and Cosmé Tura, such as would be found in originals but not in copies. Then, using this method, he made dozens of new attributions in some of the principal galleries of Europe. Some of them were sensational: the gallery in Dresden held a painting of a recumbent Venus believed to be a copy by Sassoferrato of a lost work by Titian, but Morelli identified it as one of the very few works definitely attributable to Giorgione.

Despite these achievements—and perhaps because of his almost arrogant assurance when presenting them—Morelli's method was much criticized. It was called mechanical, or crudely positivistic, and fell into disfavor.[4] (Though it seems likely that many who spoke disparagingly of it went on quietly using it in their own attributions.) We owe the recent revival of interest in his work to the art historian Edgar Wind, who suggests it is an example of a more modern approach to works of art, tending towards an appreciation of detail more than of the whole. Wind (1963:42–44) relates this attitude to the cult of the spontaneity of genius, so current in romantic circles.[5] But this is unconvincing. Morelli was not tackling problems at the level of aesthetics (indeed this was held against him), but at a more basic level, closer to philology.[6] The implications of his method lay elsewhere, and were much richer, though Wind did, as we shall see, come close to perceiving them.

> 2. Morelli's books look different from those of any other writer on art. They are sprinkled with illustrations of fingers and ears, careful records of the characteristic trifles by which an artist gives himself away, as a criminal might be spotted by a fingerprint . . . any art gallery studied by Morelli begins to resemble a rogues' gallery. . . . (Wind 1963:40–41)

This comparison was brilliantly developed by an Italian art historian, Enrico Castelnuovo (1968:782), who drew a parallel between Morelli's methods of classification and those attributed by Arthur Conan Doyle only a few years later to his fictional creation, Sherlock Holmes.[7] The art connoisseur and the detective may well be compared, each discovering, from clues unnoticed by others, the author in one case of a crime, in the other of a painting. Examples of Sherlock Holmes's skill at interpreting footprints, cigarette ash, and so on are countless and well known. But let us look at "The Cardboard Box" (1892) for an illustration of Castelnuovo's point: here Holmes is as it were "morellizing."

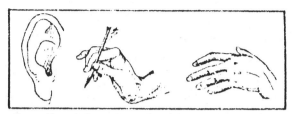

Ears and hands by Botticelli, from Morelli's *Italian painters* (1892).

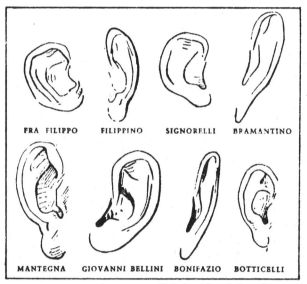

FRA FILIPPO   FILIPPINO   SIGNORELLI   BRAMANTINO

MANTEGNA   GIOVANNI BELLINI   BONIFAZIO   BOTTICELLI

Typical ears, from *Italian painters*.

The case starts with the arrival of two severed ears in a parcel sent to an innocent old lady. Here is the expert at work:

> [Holmes] was staring with singular intentness at the lady's profile. Surprise and satisfaction were both for an instant to be read upon his eager face, though when she glanced round to find out the cause of his silence he had become as demure as ever. I [Watson] stared hard myself at her flat grizzled hair, her trim cap, her little gilt ear-rings, her placid features, but I could see nothing which would account for my companion's evident excitement. (CARD)

Later on, Holmes explains to Watson (and to the reader) the lightning course of his thoughts:

As a medical man, you are aware, Watson, that there is no part of the human body which varies so much as the human ear. Each ear is as a rule quite distinctive, and differs from all other ones. In last year's *Anthropological Journal* you will find two short monographs from my pen upon the subject. I had, therefore, examined the ears in the box with the eyes of an expert, and had carefully noted their anatomical peculiarities. Imagine my surprise then, when, on looking at Miss Cushing, I perceived that her ear corresponded exactly with the female ear which I had just inspected. The matter was entirely beyond coincidence. There was the same shortening of the pinna, the same broad curve of the upper lobe, the same convolution of the inner cartilage. In all essentials it was the same ear.

Of course, I at once saw the enormous importance of the observation. It was evident that the victim was a blood relation, and probably a very close one. . . . (CARD)[8]

3. We shall shortly see the implications of this parallel.[9] Meanwhile, we may profit from another of Wind's helpful observations.

To some of Morelli's critics it has seemed odd "that personality should be found where personal effort is weakest." But on this point modern psychology would certainly support Morelli: our inadvertent little gestures reveal our character far more authentically than any formal posture that we may carefully prepare. (1963:40)

"Our inadvertent little gestures"—we can here without hesitation replace the general term "modern psychology" with the name of Sigmund Freud. Wind's comments on Morelli have indeed drawn the attention of scholars (Hauser, 1959; see also Spector 1969, Damisch 1970 and 1977, and Wollheim 1973) to a neglected passage in Freud's famous essay, "The Moses of Michelangelo" (1914). At the beginning of the second section Freud writes:

Long before I had any opportunity of hearing about psychoanalysis, I learned that a Russian art-connoisseur, Ivan Lermolieff, had caused a revolution in the art galleries of Europe by questioning the authorship of many pictures, showing how to distinguish copies from originals with certainty, and constructing hypothetical artists for those works of art whose former authorship had been discredited. He achieved this by insisting that attention should be diverted from the general impression and main features of a picture, and by laying stress on the significance of minor details, of things like the drawing of fingernails, of the lobe of an ear, of halos and such unconsidered trifles which the copyist neglects to imitate and yet which every artist executes in his own characteristic way. I was then greatly interested to learn that the Russian pseudonym concealed the identity of an

Italian physician called Morelli, who died in 1891. It seems to me that his method of inquiry is closely related to the technique of psychoanalysis. It, too, is accustomed to divine secret and concealed things from despised or unnoticed features, from the rubbish-heap, as it were, of our observations (*"auch diese ist gewöhnt, aus gering geschätzten oder nicht beachteten Zügen, aus dem Abhubdem 'refuse'—der Beobachtung, Geheimes und Verborgenes zu erraten"*). (n.d.:222)

"The Moses of Michelangelo" was first published anonymously: Freud acknowledged it only when he included it in his collected works. Some have supposed that Morelli's taste for concealing his authorship behind pseudonyms somehow also affected Freud; and several more or less plausible attempts have been made to explain the coincidence (see Kofman 1975:19, 27; Damisch 1917:70ff.; Wollheim 1973:210). In any case, there is no doubt that under the cloak of anonymity Freud declared, explicitly but also in a sense covertly, the considerable influence that Morelli had exercised on him long before his discovery of psychoanalysis (*"lange bevor ich etwas von der Psychoanalyse hören konnte . . ."*). To confine this influence to "The Moses of Michelangelo" essay alone, as some have done, or even just to the essays connected with art history[10] improperly reduces the significance of Freud's own comment, "It seems to me that his method of enquiry is closely related to the technique of psychoanalysis." In fact, the passage quoted above assures Giovanni Morelli of a special place in the history of psychoanalysis. We are dealing here with a documented connection, not merely a conjectured one as in many of the claims of "antecedents" or "precursors" of Freud; moreover, as we have said, Freud came across Morelli's writings before his work on psychoanalysis. Here we have an element which contributed directly to the crystallization of psychoanalysis, and not (as with the passage of the dream of J. Popper "Lynkeus" which was inserted in later editions of *The Interpretation of Dreams* [Freud])[11] just a coincidence noticed later on, after his discoveries.

4. Before we try to understand what Freud took from his readings of Morelli, we should clarify the precise timing of the encounter—or rather, from Freud's account, of the two encounters, "Long before I had any opportunity of hearing about psychoanalysis I learned that a Russian art-connoisseur, Ivan Lermolieff . . ."; "I was then greatly interested to learn that the Russian pseudonym concealed the identity of an Italian physician called Morelli. . . ."

The first of these can only be dated very roughly. It must have been before 1895 (when Freud and Breuer published their *Studies on Hys-*

teria); or 1896 (when Freud first used the term psychoanalysis; see Robert 1966); and after 1883, when Freud, in December, wrote his fiancée a long letter about his "discovery of art" during a visit to the Dresden Gallery. Before that he had had no interest in painting; now, he wrote, "I have thrown off my philistinism and begun to admire it."[12] It is hard to imagine that before this date Freud could have been attracted by the writings of an unknown art historian; but it is perfectly plausible that he should start reading them after this letter—especially as the first collected edition of Morelli's essays (Lermolieff 1880) contained those which dealt with the Italian old masters in the galleries of Munich, Dresden, and Berlin.

Freud's second encounter with Morelli's writings can be dated with more confidence, though still presumptively. Ivan Lermolieff's real name was made public for the first time on the title page of the English translation of the collection, which came out in 1883; later editions and translations, from 1891 when Morelli died, carried both name and pseudonym (Morelli 1883). A copy of one of these volumes could possibly have been seen by Freud earlier or later, but it was most likely in September 1898, browsing in a Milan bookshop, that he came upon Lermolieff's real identity. In Freud's library, which is preserved in London, there is a copy of Giovanni Morelli (Ivan Lermolieff)'s book, *Della pittura italiana. Studii storico critici—Le gallerie Borghese e Doria Pamphili in Roma* (Critical historical studies in Italian painting: The Borghese and Doria Pamphili Galleries in Rome), published in Milan in 1897. A note in the front records its acquisition: Milan 14 September (Trosman and Simmons 1973). Freud's only visit to Milan was in the autumn of 1898 (Jones 1953). At that time, moreover, Morelli's book would have a particular interest for Freud. He had been working for several months on lapses of memory—shortly before this, in Dalmatia, he had had the experience (later analyzed in *The Psychopathology of Everyday Life*) of being unable to recall the name of the painter of the Orvieto frescoes. Along with that painter, Signorelli, Botticelli, and Boltraffio, whose names kept substituting themselves, were mentioned in Morelli's book (Robert 1966; Morelli 1897:88–89, 159).

But what significance did Morelli's essays have for Freud, still a young man, still far from psychoanalysis? Freud himself tells us: the proposal of an interpretative method based on taking marginal and irrelevant details as revealing clues. Here details generally considered trivial and unimportant, "beneath notice," furnish the key to the highest achievements of human genius. The irony in this passage from Morelli must have delighted Freud:

My adversaries are pleased to call me someone who has no understanding of the spiritual content of a work of art, and who therefore gives particular importance to external details such as the form of the hands, the ear, and even, *horribile dictu* [how shocking], to such rude things as fingernails. (Morelli 1897:4)

Morelli could have made good use of the Vergilian tag so dear to Freud, which he chose as the epigraph for *The Interpretations of Dreams: Flectere si nequeo Superos, Acheronta movebo* (And if Heaven I cannot bend, then Hell shall be unleashed).[13] Furthermore, these marginal details were revealing, in Morelli's view, because in them the artist's subordination to cultural traditions gave way to a purely individual streak, details being repeated in a certain way "by force of habit, almost unconsciously" (Morelli 1897:71). Even more than the reference to the unconscious—not exceptional in this period[14]—what is striking here is the way that the innermost core of the artist's individuality is linked with elements beyond conscious control.

5. We have outlined an analogy between the methods of Morelli, of Holmes, and of Freud. We have mentioned the connection between Morelli and Holmes, and that between Morelli and Freud. The peculiar similarities between the activities of Holmes and Freud have been discussed by Steven Marcus (1976:x–xi).[15] Freud himself, by the way, told a patient (the "Wolf-Man") how interested he was in Sherlock Holmes's stories. When, however, in the spring of 1913, a colleague of his (T. Reik) suggested a parallel between the psychoanalytic method and Holmes's method, Freud replied expressing his admiration of Morelli's technique as a connoisseur. In all three cases tiny details provide the key to a deeper reality, inaccessible by other methods. These details may be symptoms, for Freud, or clues, for Holmes, or features of paintings, for Morelli (Gardiner 1971:146; Reik 1949:24).[16]

How do we explain the triple analogy? There is an obvious answer. Freud was a doctor; Morelli had a degree in medicine; Conan Doyle had been a doctor before settling down to write. In all three cases we can invoke the model of medical semiotics or symptomatology—the discipline which permits diagnosis, though the disease cannot be directly observed, on the basis of superficial symptoms or signs, often irrelevant to the eye of the layman, or even of Dr. Watson. (Incidentally, the Holmes-Watson pair, the sharp-eyed detective and the obtuse doctor, represents the splitting of a single character, one of the youthful Conan Doyle's professors, famous for his diagnostic ability.)[17] But it is not simply a matter of biographical coincidences. Toward the end of the nineteenth century (more precisely, in the decade 1870–1880), this "semiotic" approach, a paradigm or model based on the interpretation of clues, had become increasingly influential in the field of human sciences. Its roots, however, were far more ancient.

II

1. For thousands of years mankind lived by hunting. In the course of endless pursuits, hunters learned to reconstruct the appearance and movements of an unseen quarry through its tracks—prints in soft ground, snapped twigs, droppings, snagged hairs or feathers, smells, puddles, threads of saliva. They learned to sniff, to observe, to give meaning and context to the slightest trace. They learned to make complex calculations in an instant, in shadowy wood or treacherous clearing.

Successive generations of hunters enriched and passed on this inheritance of knowledge. We have no verbal evidence to set beside their rock paintings and artifacts, but we can turn perhaps to the folktale, which sometimes carries an echo—faint and distorted—of what those far-off hunters knew. Three brothers (runs a story from the Middle East told among Kirghiz, Tatars, Jews, Turks, and so on; Vesselofsky 1886:308–309) meet a man who has lost a camel (or sometimes it is a horse). At once they describe it to him: it's white, and blind in one eye;

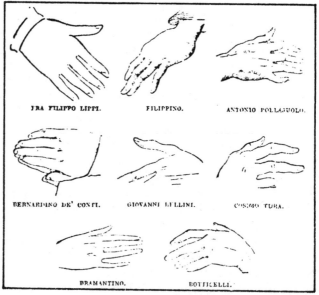

Typical hands, from *Italian painters*.

under the saddle it carries two skins, one full of oil, the other of wine. They must have seen it? No, they haven't seen it. So they're accused of theft and brought to be judged. The triumph of the brothers follows: they immediately show how from the barest traces they were able to reconstruct the appearance of an animal they had never set eyes on.

The three brothers, even if they are not described as hunters, are clearly carriers of the hunters' kind of knowledge. Its characteristic feature was that it permitted the leap from apparently insignificant facts, which could be observed, to a complex reality which—directly at least—could not. And these facts would be ordered by the observer in such a way as to provide a narrative sequence—at its simplest, "someone passed this way." Perhaps indeed the idea of a narrative, as opposed to spell or exorcism or invocation (Seppilli 1962), originated in a hunting society, from the experience of interpreting tracks. Obviously this is speculation, but it might be reinforced by the way that even now the language of deciphering tracks is based on figures of speech—the part for the whole, the cause for the effect—relating to the narrative pole of metonymy (as defined in a well-known essay by Jakobson in Jakobson and Halle 1956:55–87), strictly excluding the alternative pole of metaphor. The hunter could have been the first "to tell a story" because only hunters knew how to read a coherent sequence of events from the silent (even imperceptible) signs left by their prey.

This "deciphering" and "reading" of animals' tracks is metaphorical. But it is worth trying to understand it literally, as the verbal distillation of a historical process leading, though across a very long time-span, toward the invention of writing. The same connection is suggested in a Chinese tradition explaining the origins of writing, according to which it was invented by a high official who had remarked the footprints of a bird in a sandy riverbank (Cazade and Thomas 1977).[18] Or abandoning the realms of myth and hypothesis for that of documented history, there are undoubtedly striking analogies between the hunters' model we have been developing and the model implicit in the texts of Mesopotamian divination, which date from at least 3,000 years B.C. (Bottéro 1974). Both require minute examination of the real, however trivial, to uncover the traces of events which the observer cannot directly experience. Droppings, footprints, hairs, feathers, in the one case; animals' innards, drops of oil in water, stars, involuntary movements, in the other. It is true that the second group, unlike the first, could be extended indefinitely, since the Mesopotamian diviners read signs of the future in more or less anything. But to our eyes another difference matters more: the fact that divination pointed toward the future, while the hunters' deciphering pointed toward the actual past—

albeit occurring a few instants before. Yet in terms of understanding, the approach in each case was much alike; the intellectual stages— analysis, comparison, classification—identical, at least in theory. But only, of course, in theory: the social contexts were quite different. In particular, it has been observed that the invention of writing must have had a great effect on Mesopotamian divination (Bottéro 1974:154ff.). Mesopotamian gods had, besides other kingly prerogatives, the power of communication with their subjects through written messages—on stars, human bodies, everywhere—which the diviners had the task of deciphering. (This was an idea which in turn over thousands of years would flow into the image of "the book of nature.") And the identification and divination with the deciphering of characters divinely inscribed was reinforced in real life by the pictographic character of this early writing, "cuneiform"; it too, like divination, conveyed one thing through another (Bottéro 1974:157).[19]

The footprint, too, represents a real animal which has gone past. By comparison with the actuality of the footprint, the pictogram is already a huge advance toward intellectual abstraction. But the capacity for abstract thought implied by the introduction of the pictogram is in its turn small indeed beside that required for the transition to a phonetic script. In fact, pictographic and phonetic elements survived together in cuneiform writing, just as in the literature of the Mesopotamian diviners, gradual intensification of the tendency to generalize from their basic facts did not cancel out their tendency to infer cause from effect.[20] This also explains why the language of Mesopotamian divination was infiltrated by technical terms from the law codes, and also the presence in their texts of fragments relating to the study of physiognomy and of medical semiotics (Bottéro 1974:191–192).

So after a long detour we come back to medical semiotics. We find it in a whole constellation of disciplines (and anachronistic terms, of course) with a common character. It might be tempting to distinguish between "pseudosciences" like divination and physiognomy, and "sciences" like law and medicine, and to explain this bizarre contiguity by the great distance in space and time from the society that we have been discussing. But it would be a superficial explanation. There was a real common ground among these Mesopotamian forms of knowledge (if we omit divination through inspiration, which was based on ecstatic possession) (Bottéro 1974:89): an approach involving analysis of particular cases, constructed only through traces, symptoms, hints. Again, the Mesopotamian legal texts do not just list laws and ordinances, but discuss a body of actual cases (Bottéro 1974:172). In short, we can speak about a symptomatic or divinatory paradigm which could be oriented toward past or present or future, depending on the form of knowledge called upon. Toward future—that was divination proper; toward past, present and future—that was the medical science of symptoms, with its double character, diagnostic, explaining past and present, and prognostic, suggesting the likely future; and toward past—that was jurisprudence, or legal knowledge. But lurking behind this symptomatic or divinatory model one glimpses the gesture which is the oldest, perhaps, of the intellectual history of the human race: the hunter crouched in the mud, examining a quarry's tracks.

2. What we have said so far should explain why a Mesopotamian divination text might include how to diagnose an earlier head wound from a bilateral squint (Bottéro 1974:192); or more generally, the way in which there emerged historically a group of disciplines which all depended on the deciphering of various kinds of signs, from symptoms to writing. Passing on to the civilizations of ancient Greece, we find this group of disciplines changes considerably, with new lines of study developing, like history and philology, and with the newly acquired independence (in terms both of social context and of theoretical approach) of older disciplines like medicine. The body, speech, and history were all for the first time subjected to dispassionate investigation which from the start excluded the possibility of divine intervention. This decisive change characterized the culture of the Greek city-states, of which we of course are the heirs. It is less obvious that an important part of this change was played by a model which may be seen as based on symptoms or clues.[21] This is clearest in the case of Hippocratic medicine, which clarified its methods by analyzing the central concept of symptom (*sēmeîon*). Followers of Hippocrates argued that just by carefully observing and registering every symptom it was possible to establish precise "histories" of each disease, even though the disease as an entity would remain unattainable. This insistence on the circumstantial nature of medicine almost certainly stemmed from the distinction (expounded by the Pythagorean doctor, Alcmaeon) between the immediacy and certainty of divine knowledge, and the provisional, conjectural nature of human knowledge. If reality was not directly knowable, then by implication the conjectural paradigm which we have been describing was legitimate. In fact, according to the Greeks, various spheres of activity were based on it. Physicians, historians, politicians, potters, joiners, mariners, hunters, fishermen, and women in general were held, among others, to be adept in the vast areas of conjectural knowledge.[22] Such territory (significantly the domain of the goddess Metis, first wife of Jove, who represented divination by means of water) was marked off with words like "conjecture," "judge by the signs" (*tek-*

mor, tekmaîresthai). But this semiotic paradigm continued to be merely implicit; it was completely overshadowed by Plato's theory of knowledge, which held sway in more influential circles and had more prestige.[23]

3. Parts of Hippocratic writings have, on the whole, a defensive tone, suggesting that even in the fifth century B.C. the fallibility of doctors was already under attack (Vegetti 1965:143–144). That this battle is not over is presumably because relations between doctor and patient (especially the inability of the latter to check or control the skills of the former) have in some respects not changed since the time of Hippocrates. But what has changed over these 2,500 years is how the debate is conducted, along with changes in concepts like "rigor" and "science." Here of course the decisive shift is the emergence of a new scientific paradigm, based on (but outliving) Galilean physics. Even if modern physics finds it hard to define itself as Galilean (while not rejecting Galileo), the significance of Galileo for science in general, from both an epistemological and a symbolical point of view, remains undiminished (Feyerabend 1971:105ff., and 1975; Rossi 1977:149–150).

Now it is clear that none—not even medicine—of the disciplines which we have been describing as conjectural would meet the criteria of scientific inference essential to the Galilean approach. They were above all concerned with the qualitative, the individual case or situation or document *as individual*, which meant there was always an element of chance in their results: one need only think of the importance of conjecture (a word whose Latin origin lies in divination)[24] in medicine or philology, let alone in divination. Galilean science was altogether different; it could have taken over the scholastic saying "individuum est ineffabile" (we can say nothing about the individual). Using mathematics and the experimental method involved the need to measure and to repeat phenomena, whereas an individualizing approach made the latter impossible and allowed the former only in part. All of which explains why historians have never managed to work out a Galilean method. In the seventeenth century, on the contrary, the new growth of antiquarian methods among historians indicated indirectly the remote and long-hidden origins of history in the conjectural model. This fact about its source cannot be hidden, in spite of the ever-closer bonds linking it to the social sciences. History always remains a science of a very particular kind, irremediably based in the concrete. Historians cannot refrain from referring back (explicitly or by implication) to comparable series of phenomena; but their strategy for finding things out, as well as their expressive codes, is basically about particular cases, whether concerning individuals, or social groups, or whole societies. In this way history is like medicine, which uses disease classifications to analyze the specific illness of a particular patient. And the historian's knowledge, like the doctor's, is indirect, based on signs and scraps of evidence, conjectural.[25]

But the contrast I have suggested is an oversimplification. Among the "conjectural" disciplines one—philology, and particularly textual criticism—grew up to be, in some ways at least, atypical. Its objects were defined in the course of a drastic curtailing of what was seen to be relevant. This change within the discipline resulted from two significant points: the invention first of writing and then of printing. We know that textual criticism evolved after the first, with the writing down of the Homeric poems, and developed further after the second, when humanist scholars improved on the first hastily printed editions of the classics.[26] First the elements related to voice and gesture were discarded as redundant; later the characteristics of handwriting were similarly set aside. The result has been a progressive dematerialization, or refinement, of texts, a process in which the appeal of the original to our various senses has been purged away. A text needs to exist in physical form in order to survive; but its identity is not uniquely bound up in that physical form, nor in any one copy.[27] All this seems self-evident to us today, but it is not at all. Take, for example, the decisive role of the voice in oral literature, or of calligraphy in Chinese poetry, and it becomes clear that this very notion of a "text" is itself the result of a cultural choice whose significance is incalculable. And the example of China shows that the choice was not an inevitable consequence of printing replacing handwriting, since there the invention of the press did not sever the ties between literary text and calligraphy. (We shall see shortly that historical discussion of pictorial "texts" raises quite different problems.)

This thoroughly abstract notion of a text explains why textual criticism, even while remaining to a large degree divinatory, could (and during the nineteenth century did) emerge as rigorously scientific.[28] The radical decision to exclude all but the reproducible (in writing, or, after Gutenberg, in print) features of a text made it possible, even while dealing with individual examples,[29] to avoid the qualitative, that prime hazard of the humanities. It is surely significant that Galileo, while laying the foundations of modern natural science by a similarly drastic conceptual reduction, himself turned to philology. The traditional medieval comparison between world and book assumed that both lay open ready to be read. Galileo emphasized, however, that "we cannot hope to understand the philosophy written in this great book standing open before our eyes (and by this I mean the universe) unless we learn first to understand its language and to know the characters written there," that is, "triangles, circles, and other geometric figures" (Galilei 1965:38).[30] For the natural philosopher, as for the philologist, the text is an entity, deep and invisible, to be reconstructed through and beyond the available sense data: "figures, numbers and movements, but not smells or tastes or sounds that outside the living animal are, I believe, mere words" (Galilei 1965:264; see also Martinez 1974:160–169).

Galileo here set the natural sciences firmly on a path they never left, which tended to lead away from anthropocentrism and anthropomorphism. In the map of knowledge a gap emerged, which was bound to widen more and more. Certainly there could be no greater contrast than between the Galilean physicist, professionally deaf to sounds and forbidden to taste or smell, and the physician of the same period, who ventured his diagnosis after listening to a wheezy chest, or sniffing feces, or tasting urine.

4. One such physician was Giulio Mancini, from Siena, chief physician to Pope Urban VII. It does not seem that he knew Galileo well, but the two did probably meet, since they moved in the same circles in Rome, from the Papal Court to the Lincei Academy, and had common friends, from Federico Cesi to Giovanni Ciampoli to Giovanni Faber.[31] A vivid sketch of Mancini by Nicio Eritreo, alias Gian Vittorio Rossi, describes his atheism, his extraordinary diagnostic skill (detailed in words straight out of the divinatory texts), and his unscrupulous way of extorting paintings (about which his competence was notorious) from his customers (Eritreo 1692, II:79–82).[32] Mancini wrote a book called *Alcune considerazioni appartenenti alla pittura come di diletto di un gentilhuomo nobile e come introduttione a quello si deve dire* (Some considerations concerning painting as an amusement for a noble gentleman, and introducing what needs to be said), which had a wide circulation in manuscript (a critical edition of the whole text appeared in print for the first time about twenty-five years ago).[33] As its title says, it was aimed at noble amateurs rather than painters—at those dilettanti who in ever greater numbers flocked to the Pantheon for the exhibition of paintings old and new which was held every year, on March 19 (Haskell 1971:126 and 94ff.). Certainly, without this art-market, the part of Mancini's *Conversazioni,* which is probably the most original, devoted to the "recognition of paintings"—which sets out a method for identifying fakes, for telling originals from copies, and so on—would never have been written (Mancini 1956–57, I:133ff.). So the first attempt to establish connoisseurship, as it was to be called a century later, was made by a doctor famous for his brilliant diagnoses, who on visiting a patient "could divine" (*divinabat*) with one rapid glance the outcome of the

disease (Eritreo 1692, II:80–81).[34] We may surely see more than coincidence in this double skill, in his combination of the doctor's and the connoisseur's perceptions.

But before examining Mancini's views more closely, we should go into an assumption shared by him, the gentlemen he wrote for, and ourselves. It is an assumption not declared, since (wrongly) it is taken to be obvious: it is that between a canvas by Raphael and any copy of it (painted, engraved, or today, photographed) there is an ineradicable difference. The implications of this for the market—that a painting is by definition unique, impossible to repeat[35]—are plain, and they are connected with the emergence of the connoisseur. But the assumption arises from a cultural choice which must not be taken for granted, especially as a different one was made in the case of written texts. The pretended intrinsic features of painting and writing, respectively, are not relevant in this context. We have already seen how historical developments gradually stripped the written text of features not considered relevant. In the case of paintings this denuding has not taken place (so far at least). This is why we think that while manuscript or printed copies of *Orlando Furioso* can exactly reproduce the text Ariosto intended, a copy of a Raphael portrait never can.[36]

The differing status of the copy in painting and in literature explains why Mancini could not make use of the techniques of textual criticism when developing the methods of the connoisseur, though he was basically establishing an analogy between the act of painting and the act of writing (see a remark by Salerno in Mancini 1956–1957, II:xxiv, fn.55). But because he started with this analogy, he had to turn for help to other disciplines, which were still taking shape.

Mancini's first problem concerned the dating of paintings. To do this, he said, you had to acquire "a certain experience in recognizing the painting of particular periods, just as antiquarians and librarians have for scripts, so that they can tell when something was written" (Mancini 1956–1957, I:134).[37] The allusion to recognizing scripts almost certainly refers to the methods worked out in these same years by Leone Allacci, librarian at the Vatican for dating Greek and Latin manuscripts—methods which were taken up again and developed half a century later by Mabillon, the founder of paleography.[38] But "besides the common characteristics of the time," continues Mancini, "there are the characteristics peculiar to the individual," just as "we see among handwritings that they have their distinctive characteristics." So the analogy between writing and painting is made first at the general level (the period), and then renewed at the other end of the scale (the individual). For this range the proto-paleographic methods of an Allacci would not work. But there was in these years one solitary attempt to apply analysis to individual handwriting for a new purpose. Mancini, in his capacity as physician, quoting Hippocrates, said that it is possible to go back from "deeds" to soul's "impressions," which derive from individual bodies' "features." For this reason some fine intellects of our age have written arguing that it is possible to reveal a person's intellect and mind through that person's way of writing and through their handwriting. One of these "fine intellects" was in all probability Camillo Baldi, a doctor from Bologna, who included in his *Trattato come da una lettera missiva si conoscano la natura e qualità dello scrittore* (Treatise on how to tell from a letter the nature of its writer), a chapter which is probably the first European text on graphology. "What meanings"—the chapter heading runs—"may one read in the shaping of the letters" (*nella figura del carattere*). The word used here for "letter" is "character," meaning the shape of the letter as it is drawn with the pen on the paper (ibid.:107; Baldi 1622:17, 18ff.).[39]

In spite of his words of praise, Mancini was not interested in the claims of this burgeoning graphology to reconstruct writers' personalities by establishing their "characters" (in the psychological sense) from their "characters" (the shapes of their letters). (Yet again the origins of the double meaning may be traced back to an originally shared disciplinary context.) He was struck, however, by the preliminary assumption on which the new discipline was based, that is, the variety of different handwritings and the impossibility therefore of imitating them. By identifying the elements in painting which were equally impossible to imitate, he would achieve his aim of telling originals from fakes, the hand of the master from that of the copyist or the follower. Hence his advice to check each painting to see:

> whether the resolute hand of the master can be detected, especially where it would take much effort to sustain the imitation, as in hair, beards, or eyes. Curls and waves of hair, if they are reproduced exactly, will look too laborious, and if the copyist fails to get them right they will lack the perfection of the master's version. And these parts of a painting are like strokes of the pen and flourishes in handwriting, which need the master's sure and resolute touch. The same care should be taken to look for particularly bold or brilliant strokes, which the master throws off with an assurance that cannot be matched; for instance in the folds and glints of drapes, which may have more to do with the master's bold imagination than with the truth of how they actually hung. (Mancini 1956–1957:134)

So the parallel between painting and writing, which Mancini has already made in various contexts, is here given a new twist, and one

which previously had only been hinted at, in a work by the architect
Filarete (see section 6, below), which Mancini may not have known
(Averlino 1972, I:28).[40] The analogy is reinforced by the use of technical terms current in contemporary treatises on writing, like "boldness,"
"strokes," "flourishes."[41] Even the dwelling on speed has the same origin: with new bureaucratic developments an elegant cursive legal hand
needed also to be fast if it were to succeed in the copyists' market.[42] In
general, the stress Mancini placed on decorative features is evidence of
careful attention to the characteristics of hand-writing models prevalent
in Italy in the late sixteenth and early seventeenth centuries (Casamassima 1966:75–76). Studying how letters were formed led him to conclude that the master's touch could most confidently be identified in
parts of the painting which (1) were swiftly executed, and (2) tended
not to be close representations of the real thing (details of hair,
draperies whose folds had "more to do with the master's bold imagination than with the truth of how they actually hung"). We shall come
back to the rich implications of these two points, which Mancini and his
contemporaries were not yet in a position to develop.

5. "Characters" (*caratteri*). The same word occurs about 1620, in
either a literal or an analogical meaning, in the writings of the founder
of modern physics, on the one hand, and on the other, of the
originators respectively of paleography, graphology, and connoisseurship. Of course, it is only a metaphorical relationship that links the
insubstantial "characters" which Galileo with the eyes of the intellect[43]
saw in the book of nature, and those which Allacci, Baldi, or Mancini
deciphered on actual paper or parchment or canvas. But the use of
identical terms makes it all the more striking that the disciplines we
have assembled should be so diverse. Their scientific value (in the Galilean sense) varies too, declining swiftly from the "universal features" of
geometry, through the "common features of a period" detected in a
script, to the "specific individual features" of pictorial style, or even
handwriting.

This decreasing level of scientific content reinforces the argument
that the real difficulty in applying the Galilean model lay in the degree
to which a discipline was concerned with the individual. As the features
centered more and more on the individual, the more difficult it became
to construct a body of rigorously scientific knowledge. Of course, the
decision to ignore individual features would not of itself guarantee that
the methods of mathematics and physics indispensable to adopting the
Galilean model were actually going to be applied, but on the other hand
it would not exclude them altogether.

6. At this point, then, there were two possible approaches: to sac-

rifice understanding of the individual element in order to achieve a
more or less rigorous and more or less mathematical standard of
generalization; or to try to develop, however tentatively, an alternative
model based on an understanding of the individual which would (in
some way yet to be worked out) be scientific. The first approach was
that taken by the natural sciences, and only much later on by the so-
called human or social sciences. The reason is obvious. The likelihood
of obliterating individual features relates directly to the emotional distance of the observer. Filarete, in a page of his *Trattato di architettura*
(Treatise on Architecture, fifteenth century), after arguing that it is impossible to build two completely identical buildings, since whatever the
first impression there would always be differences of detail (just as
"Tatar snouts all look the same, or Ethiopian ones all are black, but
when you look more carefully they are all different as well as alike"),
goes on to admit that there are "some creatures which are so alike, as
with flies, ants, worms, frogs, and many fish, that they cannot be told
apart" (Averlino 1972:26–27). So for a European architect, the slight
differences between two (European) buildings were important, those
between Tatar or Ethiopian faces were not, and those between two
worms or two ants simply didn't exist. A Tatar architect, an Ethiopian
unversed in architecture, or an ant would rank things differently.
Knowledge based on making individualizing distinctions is always anthropocentric, ethnocentric, and liable to other specific bias. Of course
even animals or minerals or plants can be examined for their individual
properties, for instance in the context of divination;[44] especially with
cases that show abnormalities. (As is widely known, teratology was an
important part of divination.) But in the first decades of the seventeenth century, the influence of the Galilean model (even where not
direct) would lead toward study of the typical rather than the exceptional, toward a general understanding of the workings of nature rather
than divination. In April 1625 a calf with two heads was born near
Rome. The naturalists from the Lincei Academy took an interest. It was
the subject of a discussion in the Vatican Belvedere Gardens by a group
which included Giovanni Faber, the Academy's secretary, and Giovanni
Ciampoli (both, as we have noted, friends of Galileo), Mancini, Cardinal Agostino Vegio, and Pope Urban VIII. Their first question was
whether the two-headed calf should count as one animal or as two. For
the physicians, the feature distinguishing the individual was the brain;
for followers of Aristotle, the heart (Lynceo 1651:599ff.).[45] As Mancini
was the only physician present, we may assume that Faber's report of
the physicians' standpoint brings us the echo of his contribution. In
spite of his astrological interests,[46] Mancini considered the specific

character of the monster-birth with the object not of revealing the future, but of arriving at a more accurate definition of a normal individual who, insofar as he was a member of a species, could be rightly considered replicable. Mancini will have examined the anatomy of the two-headed calf with the same close attention he customarily gave to paintings. But that is where the analogy with the connoisseur must stop. To some extent a figure like Mancini represents the point of contact between the divinatory approach (in his activities as diagnostician and connoisseur), and the generalizing model (as anatomist and naturalist). But he also encapsulates the differences between them. Contrary to what it might seem, the dissection of the calf so precisely described by Faber, with the tiny incisions made so as to reveal the internal organs of the creature (Lynceo 1651:600–627),[47] was done with the aim of establishing not the "character" peculiar to that particular animal, but "the common character" (turning from history to natural history) of the species as a whole. It was a continuation and refinement of the tradition of natural history founded by Aristotle. Sight, symbolized by the sharp eye of the lynxes in the crest of Federico Cesi's Lincei Academy, was the central organ in these disciplines, which were not allowed the extrasensory eye of mathematics.[48]

7. These disciplines apparently included the human or social sciences (as we would define them today). This might have been expected, perhaps, if only because of their stubborn anthropocentrism, which we have already illustrated in the graphic quotation from Filarete. But there were attempts to apply the mathematical method even to the study of human phenomena (see, e.g., "Craig's Rules" 1964). It is not surprising that the first and most successful of these concerned political arithmetic, and took as its subject the most predetermined— biologically speaking—of human activities: birth, procreation, and death. This drastically exclusive focus permitted rigorous investigation; and at the same time satisfied the military or fiscal purposes of absolute states, whose interest, given the limits of their operations, was entirely in numbers. But if the patrons of the new science, statistics, were not interested in qualitative as opposed to quantitative factors, this did not mean that it was totally cut off from the world of what we have been calling the conjectural disciplines. Calculations concerning probability (as in the title of Bernoulli's classic *The Art of Conjecture* (*Ars Conjectandi,* 1713, posthumous), tried to give rigorous mathematical formulation to the same problems that had been tackled in a totally different way by divination.[49]

Still, the group of human sciences remained firmly anchored in the qualitative, though not without uneasiness, especially in the case of medicine. Although progress had been made, its methods still seemed uncertain, its results unpredictable. Such a text as *An Essay on the Certainty of Medicine* by the French ideologue Cabanis, which appeared at the end of the eighteenth century (Cabanis 1823), admitted this lack of rigor, while at the same time insisting that medicine was nevertheless scientific in its own way. There seem to be two basic reasons for medicine's lack of certainty. First, descriptions of particular diseases that were adequate for their theoretical classification were not necessarily adequate in practice, since a disease could present itself differently in each patient. Second, knowledge of a disease always remained indirect and conjectural; the secrets of the living body were always, by definition, out of reach. Once dead, of course, it could be dissected, but how did one make the leap from the corpse, irreversibly changed by death, to the characteristics of the living individual (Foucault 1973 and 1977b:192–193)? Recognizing this double difficulty inevitably meant admitting that even the efficacy of medical procedures could not be proved. Finally, the proper rigor of the natural sciences could never be achieved by medicine, because of its inability to quantify (except in some purely auxiliary aspects); the inability to quantify stemmed from the impossibility of eliminating the qualitative, the individual; and the impossibility of eliminating the individual resulted from the fact that the human eye is more sensitive to even slight differences between human beings than it is to differences between rocks or leaves. The discussions on "uncertainty" of medicine provided early formulations of what were to be the central epistemological problems in the human sciences.

8. Between the lines of Cabanis's book there shines an impatience which is not hard to understand. In spite of the more or less justified objections to its methods which could be made, medicine remained a science which received full social recognition. But not all the conjectural disciplines fared so well in this period. Some, like connoisseurship, of fairly recent origin, held an ambiguous position on the borders of the acknowledged disciplines. Others, more embedded in daily practice, were kept well outside. The ability to tell an unhealthy horse from the state of its hooves, a storm coming up from a shift in the wind, or unfriendly intentions from the shadow in someone's expression would certainly not be learned from treatises on the care of horses, or on weather, or on psychology. In each case these kinds of knowledge were richer than any written authority on the subject; they had been learned not from books but from listening, from doing, from watching; their subtleties could scarcely be given formal expression and they might not even be reducible to words; they were the heritage—partly common,

partly split—of men and women of any class. A fine common thread connected them; they were all born of experience, of the concrete and individual. That concrete quality was both the strength of this kind of knowledge and its limit; it could not make use of the powerful and terrible tool of abstraction (see also Ginzburg 1980).

From time to time attempts would be made to write down some part of this lore, locally rooted but without known origin or record or history,[50] to fit it into a straitjacket of terminological precision. This usually constricted and impoverished it. One need only think of the gulf separating the rigid and schematic treatises of physiognomy from its perceptive and flexible practice by a lover or a horse dealer or a cardplayer. It was perhaps only in medicine that the codifying and recording of conjectural lore produced a real enrichment; but the story of the relation between official and popular medicine has still to be written. In the course of the eighteenth century the situation changed. In a real cultural offensive the bourgeoisie appropriated more and more of the traditional lore of artisans and peasants, some of it conjectural, some not; they organized and recorded it, and at the same time intensified the massive process of cultural invasion which had already begun, though taking different forms and with different content, during the Counter Reformation. The symbol and crucial instrument of this offensive was, of course, the French *Encyclopédie*. But one would also have to analyze such small but revealing incidents as when a presumably astonished Winckelmann learned from an unnamed Roman mason that the mysterious unidentified little stone concealed in the hand of a statute discovered at Porto d'Anzio was "the stopper or cork of a little bottle."

The systematic collecting of such "little insights," as Winckelmann called them elsewhere,[51] was the basis of fresh formulations of ancient knowledge during the eighteenth and nineteenth centuries, from cookery to hydrology to veterinary science. To a growing number of readers, access to specific experience was increasingly had through the pages of books. The novel provided the bourgeoisie with a substitute, on a different level, for initiation rites, that is, for access to real experience altogether.[52] And indeed it was thanks to works of fiction that the conjectural paradigm in this period had a new and unexpected success.

9. In connection with the hypothetical origin of the conjectural among long-ago hunters, we have already told the story of the three brothers who, by interpreting a series of tracks, reconstruct the appearance of an animal they have never seen. This story made its European debut in a collection by Sercambi (Cerulli 1975).[53] It subsequently reappeared as the opening to a much larger collection of stories, pre-

sented as translations into Italian from Persian by an Armenian called
Christopher, which came out in Venice in the mid-sixteenth century
under the title *Peregrinaggio di tre giovani figliuoli del re di Serendippo*
(Travels of the three young sons of the king of Serendippo). This book
went through a number of editions and translations—first into German,
then, during the eighteenth-century fashion for things Oriental, into the
main European languages.[54] The success of this story of the sons of the
king of Serendippo led Horace Walpole in 1745 to coin the word
"serendipity," for the making of happy and unexpected discoveries "by
accidents and sagacity" (Hecksher 1974:130–131).[55] Some years before, Voltaire, in the third chapter of *Zadig,* reworked the first volume
of *Travels,* which he had read in the French translation. In his version
the camel of the original becomes a bitch and a horse, which Zadig is
able to describe in detail by deciphering their tracks. Accused of theft
and taken at once before the judges, Zadig proves his innocence by
recounting the mental process which had enabled him to describe the
animals he had never seen:

> I saw in the sand the tracks of an animal, and I judged without difficulty
> that it was a small dog. Long shallow furrows across mounds in the sand,
> between the pawprints, told me that it was a female with sagging teats, who
> had therefore recently given birth. . . .

In these lines and in those which follow, lies the embryo of the detective story. They inspired Poe and Gaboriau directly, and perhaps indirectly Conan Doyle.[56]

The extraordinary success of the detective story is well-known; we
shall return to some of the reasons for it. But for the moment it is
worth remarking that it is based on a cognitive model which is at once
very ancient and very new. We have already discussed its ancient roots.
For its modern elements we shall quote Cuvier's praise in 1834 for the
methods and successes of the new science of paleontology:

> Today, someone who sees the print of a cloven hoof can conclude that the
> animal which left the print was a ruminant, and this conclusion is as certain
> as any that can be made in physics or moral philosophy. This single track
> therefore tells the observer about the kind of teeth, the kind of jaws, the
> haunches, the shoulder, and the pelvis of the animal which has passed: it is
> more certain evidence than all Zadig's clues. (Messac 1929:34–35)

More certain perhaps, but of a very comparable kind. The name of
Zadig came to stand for so much that in 1880 Thomas Huxley, in a
series of lectures aimed at publicizing the discoveries of Darwin, de-

fined as "Zadig's method" the procedure common to history, archeology, geology, physical astronomy, and paleontology: that is, the making of retrospective predictions. These disciplines, being deeply concerned with historical development, could scarcely avoid falling back on the conjectural or divinatory model (Huxley indeed made explicit reference to divination directed toward the past),[57] and putting aside the Galilean paradigm. When causes cannot be repeated, there is no alternative but to infer them from their effects.

III .

1. This inquiry may be compared to following the threads in a piece of weaving. We have now reached the point where they can be seen to make a composite whole, a homogeneous and closely woven cloth. To check the coherence of the pattern we cast an eye along different lines. Vertically, this gives us the sequence Serendippo—Zadig—Poe—Gaboriau—Conan Doyle. Horizontally, the juxtaposition at the beginning of the eighteenth century by Dubos, the literary critic, in order of decreasing reliability, of medicine, connoisseurship, and identification through handwriting (Dubos 1729, II:362–365; quoted in part in Zerner 1978:215n.). Last, diagonally, passing from one historical context to another and behind Gaboriau's detective hero, Monsieur Lecoq, who restlessly ran along an "unknown territory, covered with snow," marked with the tracks of criminals like "a vast white page on which the people we are searching for have left not only footprints and traces of movement but also the prints of their innermost thoughts, the hopes and fears by which they are stirred" (Gaboriau 1877, I:44).[58] Those who stand out are the authors of treatises on physiognomy, Babylonian seers intent on reading the messages written in heaven and earth, and neolithic hunters.

The cloth is the paradigm which we have summoned up from way back, out of various contexts—hunting, divining, conjectural, or semiotic. These are obviously not synonyms, but alternative descriptions which nevertheless refer back to a common epistemological model, worked out for a number of disciplines, themselves often linked by borrowed methods or key words. Now between the eighteenth and the nineteenth century, with the emergence of the "human sciences," the constellation of conjectural disciplines changed profoundly: new stars were born, which (like phrenology)[59] were soon to fall, or which (like paleontology) would achieve great things, but above all it was medicine which confirmed its high social and scientific status. It became the reference point, explicit or by implication, of all the human sci-

ences. But what area of medicine? Around the middle of the eighteenth
century two alternatives became visible: the anatomical model, and the
semiotic. The metaphor of "the anatomy of the civil society," used in a
critical passage by Marx,[60] expresses the aspiration for a system of
knowledge, at a time when the last great system of philosophy—
Hegelianism—was already crumbling. But in spite of the great success
of Marxism, the human sciences ended up by more and more accepting
(with an important exception which we shall come to) the conjectural
paradigm of semiotics. And here we return to the Morelli-Freud-Conan
Doyle triad where we began.

2. So far we have been using the term conjectural paradigm (and its
variants) broadly. It is time to take it to pieces. It is one thing to analyze
footprints, stars, feces (animal or human), catarrhs, corneas, pulses,
snowcovered fields, or dropped cigarette ash, and another to analyze
writing or painting or speech. The distinction between nature (inani-
mate or living) and culture is fundamental, certainly much more important than the far more superficial and changeable distinctions between
disciplines. Morelli's idea was to trace out within a culturally determined sign-system the conventions of painting, signs which, like symptoms (and like most clues), were produced involuntarily. Not just that:
in these involuntary signs, in the "tiny details—a calligrapher would call
them flourishes" such as the "favorite words and phrases" which "most
people, whether talking or writing, make use of without meaning to and
without noticing that they do so"—Morelli located the most certain
clue to artistic identity (Morelli 1897:71).[61] Thus Morelli inherited
(even if indirectly)[62] and developed the methodological principles formulated so long before by his predecessor, Giulio Mancini. The time
when these principles finally came to fruition was perhaps not altogether at random. It coincided with the emergence of an increasingly
clear tendency for state power to impose a close-meshed net of control
on society, and once again the method that was used involved attributing identity through characteristics which were trivial and beyond conscious control.

3. Every society needs to distinguish its members, and the ways of
meeting this need vary with place and time (Lévi-Strauss, Claude, et al.
1977). There is, first of all, the name, but the more complex the society, the less satisfactorily a name can represent the individual's identity
without confusion. In Egypt during the Greco-Roman period, for instance, a man who came to a notary wanting to get married or to carry
out some financial transaction would have to set down not only his
name but also brief details of his appearance, including any scars or
other particular marks (Caldara 1924). But even so the chances of mis-

take or of fraudulent impersonation remained high. By comparison, a signature at the bottom of a contract was much better: at the end of the eighteenth century the abbot Lanzi, in a passage of his *Storia pittorica* (History of Painting), which discussed the methods of the connoisseur, maintained that the impossibility of imitating handwriting was intended by nature for the "security" of "civil society" (that is, bourgeois society. Lanzi 1968, I:15). Of course, even signatures could be faked; and above all, they provided no check on the illiterate. In spite of these shortcomings, European societies over centuries felt no need for more reliable or practical means of identification—not even when large-scale industrial development, the social and geographical mobility which it produced, and the rapid growth of vast urban concentrations had completely changed the fundamentals of the problem. In this kind of society it was child's play to cover one's tracks and reappear with a new identity—and not only in London or Paris. It was only in the last decades of the nineteenth century that new systems of identification—competing with each other—began to be put forward. This followed contemporary developments in class struggle: the setting up of an international workers' association, the repression of working-class opposition after the Paris Commune, and the changing pattern of crime.

In England from about 1720 onward (Thompson 1975), in the rest of Europe (with the Napoleonic code) a century or so later, the emergence of capitalist relations of production led to a transformation of the law, bringing it into line with new bourgeois concepts of property, and introducing a greater number of punishable offenses and punishment of more severity. Class struggle was increasingly brought within the range of criminality, and at the same time a new prison system was built up, based on longer sentences of imprisonment (Foucault 1977a). But prison produces criminals. In France the number of recidivists was rising steadily after 1870, and toward the end of the century was about half of all cases brought to trial (Perrot 1975, esp. p. 68). The problem of identifying old offenders, which developed in these years, was the bridgehead of a more or less conscious project to keep a complete and general check on the whole of society.

For this identification of old offenders it was necessary to show (1) that a person had previously been convicted, and (2) that the person in question was the same as the one previously convicted (Bertillon 1883; Locard 1909).[63] The first problem was resolved by the setting up of police files. The second was more difficult. The ancient punishments which had involved marking or mutilating an offender for life had been abolished. In Dumas's *The Three Musketeers,* the lily branded on Milady's shoulder had allowed D'Artagnan to recognize her as a

poisoner already punished in the past for her misdeeds, whereas in his
The Count of Monte Cristo, or in Hugo's *Les Miserables,* the escaped prisoners Edmond Dantes and Jean Valjean were able to reappear on the
social scene with false identities. These examples should convey the
hold which the old offender had on the nineteenth-century imagination.[64] The bourgeoisie required some identifying sign which would be
as indelible as those imposed under the Ancien Régime, but less blood-
thirsty and humiliating.

The idea of an immense photographic archive was at first rejected
because it posed such huge difficulties of classification: how could discrete elements be isolated in the continuum of images (see Bertillon
1883:10)? The path of quantification seemed easier and more rigorous.
From 1879 onward an employee at the prefecture of Paris, Alphonse
Bertillon, developed an anthropometric method—which he set out in
various writings (on Bertillon, see Lacassagne 1914; Locard 1914)—
based on careful measuring of physical details which were then combined on each person's card. Obviously a miscarriage of justice could
result (theoretically) from a mistake of a few millimeters; but there was
still a more serious defect in Bertillon's anthropometric system, the fact
that it was purely negative. It permitted the elimination of those whose
details on examination did not match up, but it could not prove that
two sets of identical details referred to the same person (Bertillon
1883:11). The elusive quality of individuality could not be shut out:
chased out through the door by quantification, it came back through the
window. So Bertillon proposed combining the anthropometric method
with what he called a "word-portrait," that is, a verbal description
analyzing discrete entities (nose, eyes, ears, and so on), which taken
together were supposed to reconstitute the image of the whole person,
and so to allow identification. The pages of ears presented by Bertillon[65] irresistibly recall the illustrations which accompanied writings by
the contemporary Morelli. There may not have been a direct connection, yet it is striking how Bertillon, also an expert on handwriting, took
as sure indices of forgery the idiosyncratic details which the forger
could not reproduce, sometimes replacing them with his own (Locard
1914:27).[66]

It is obvious that Bertillon's method was incredibly complicated. We
have already noted the difficulties posed by measurement. The word-
portrait made things still worse. What was the difference between a
protuberant hooked nose and a hooked protuberant nose? How did
you classify the exact shade of blue-green eyes?

A method of identification which made both the collection and the
classification of data much easier was put forward in 1888 by Galton, in

a memoir that was later revised and expanded (Galton 1892, which lists previous publications on the subject). This, of course, was based on fingerprints. As Galton himself quite properly admitted, he was not the first to suggest it.

The scientific analysis of fingerprints began in 1823 with a work by Purkyné, the founder of histology, called *Commentatio de examine physiologico organi visus et systematis cutanei* (Commentary on the physiological examination of the organs of sight and the skin system) (Purkyné 1948:29–56). He distinguished and described nine basic types of line in the skin, but argued that no two individuals ever had identical combinations in their fingerprints. The practical implications of this were ignored, though not the philosophical, which were taken up in a chapter called *"De cognitione organismi individualis in genere"* (On the general recognition of individual organisms) (ibid.:30–32). Knowledge of the individual was central to medical practice, he said, starting from diagnosis; symptoms took different forms in different individuals, and therefore equally required different treatment for their cure. Some modern writers, he said (without naming them), had defined practical medicine as "the art of individualizing" *(die Kunst des Individualisierens)* (ibid.:31). But it was the physiology of the individual that was really fundamental to this art. Here Purkyné, who as a youth had studied philosophy at Prague, echoed the most central themes of Leibniz's thought. The individual, "the being in every way determined *(ens omnimodo determinatum)*," has an identity which can be recognized in his every characteristic, even the most imperceptible and slightest. Neither circumstance nor outside influence are enough to explain it. It has to be supposed that there is an internal norm or "typus" which maintains the variety of each species within its limits: knowledge of this norm (as Purkyné prophetically affirmed) "would reveal the hidden understanding of individual nature" (ibid.:31–32). The mistake of physiognomy had been to subject individual variation to preconceptions and hasty conjectures: this had made it impossible till then to establish a scientific descriptive study of faces. Abandoning the study of palms to the "useless science" of chiromancy, Purkyné focused his own attention on something much less obvious: it was the lines on thumb and fingertips which provided him with the hidden proof of individuality.

Let us leave Europe for the moment and look at Asia. Unlike their European counterparts, and quite independently, Chinese and Japanese diviners had taken an interest in these scarcely visible lines which crisscross the skin of the hand. And in Bengal, as well as in China, there was a custom of imprinting letters and documents with a fingertip dipped in ink or tar (Galton 1892:24ff.): this was probably a consequence of knowledge derived from divinatory practice. Anyone who was used to deciphering mysterious messages in the veins of stone or wood, in the traces left by birds, or in the shell of a tortoise (Vander-meersch 1974:29ff; Gernet 1974:52ff.) would find it easy to see a kind of message in the print of a dirty finger. In 1860 Sir William Herschel, district commissioner of Hooghly in Bengal, came across this usage, common among local people, saw its usefulness, and thought to profit by it to improve the functioning of the British administration. (The theoretical aspects of the matter were of no interest; he had never heard of Purkyné's Latin discourse, which had lain unread for half a century.) But really, as Galton was to observe, there was a great need for some such means of identification; in India as in other British colonies the natives were illiterate, disputatious, wily, deceitful, and to the eyes of a European, all looked the same. In 1880 Herschel announced in *Nature* that after seventeen years of tests, fingerprints had been officially introduced in the district of Hooghly, and since then had been used for three years with the best possible results (Galton 1892:27–28).[67] The imperial administrators had taken over the Bengalis' conjectural knowledge and turned it against them.

Herschel's article served Galton as a starting point for a systematic reorganization of his thought on the whole subject. His research had been made possible by the convergence of three separate elements: the discoveries of a pure scientist, Purkyné; the concrete knowledge, tied in with everyday practice, of the Bengali populace; and the political and administrative acumen of Sir William Herschel, faithful servant of Her Britannic Majesty. Galton acknowledged the first and the third of these. He also tried to trace racial characteristics in fingerprints, but did not succeed. He hoped, however, to pursue his research among some Indian tribes, expecting to find among them "a more monkey-like pattern" (ibid.:17–18).

Galton not only made a crucial contribution to the analysis of fingerprints, he also, as we have said, saw the practical implications. In a very short time the new method was introduced in England, and thence gradually to the rest of the world (one of the last countries to give in to it was France). Thus every human being—as Galton boastfully observed, taking for himself the praise that had been bestowed on his rival, Bertillon, by a colleague in the French Ministry of the Interior—acquired an identity, was once and for all and beyond all doubt constituted an individual (ibid.:169; see also Foucault 1977b:158).

In this way, what to the British administrators had seemed an indistinguishable mass of Bengali faces (or "snouts," to recall Filarete's contemptuous words) now became a series of individuals each one marked by a biological specificity. This extraordinary extension of the notion of individuality happened because of the relationship of the state and its administrative and police forces. Every last inhabitant of the meanest hamlet of Europe or Asia thus became, thanks to fingerprints, possible to identify and check.

4. The same conjectural paradigm, in this case used to develop still more sophisticated controls over the individual in society, also holds the potential for understanding society. In a social structure of ever-increasing complexity like that of advanced capitalism, befogged by ideological murk, any claim to systematic knowledge appears as a flight of foolish fancy. To acknowledge this is not to abandon the idea of totality. On the contrary, the existence of a deep connection which explains superficial phenomena can be confirmed when it is acknowledged that direct knowledge of such a connection is impossible. Reality is opaque; but there are certain points—clues, symptoms—which allow us to decipher it.

This idea, which is at the heart of the conjectural or semiotic paradigm, has made itself a place in a wide range of intellectual contexts, most deeply affecting the human sciences. Minute graphic characteristics have been used to reconstruct cultural shifts and transformations (in direct line from Morelli, settling a debt owed by Mancini to Allacci almost three centuries earlier). The flowing robes of Florentine paintings in the fifteenth century, the linguistic innovations of Rabelais, the healing of the king's evil by French and English monarchs (to take a few of many possible examples) have each been taken as small but significant clues to more general phenomena: the outlook of a social class, or of a writer, or of an entire society.[68] The discipline of psychoanalysis, as we have seen, is based on the hypothesis that apparently negligible details can reveal deep and significant phenomena. Side by side with the decline of the systematic approach, the aphoristic one gathers strength—from Nietzsche to Adorno. Even the word aphoristic is revealing. (It is an indication, a symptom, a clue: there is no getting away from our paradigm.) *Aphorisms* was the title of a famous work by Hippocrates. In the seventeenth-century collections of "Political Aphorisms" began to appear.[69] Aphoristic literature is by definition an attempt to formulate opinions about man and society on the basis of symptoms, of clues; a humanity and a society that are diseased, in crisis. And even crisis is a medical term, dating from Hippocrates.[70] In literature too it can easily be shown that the greatest novel of our time— Marcel Proust's *À la recherche du temps perdu*—is a rigorous example of the application of this conjectural paradigm.[71]

5. Is rigor compatible with the conjectural paradigm? The quantita-

tive and anti-anthropocentric direction taken by the natural sciences since Galileo has posed an awkward dilemma for human sciences. Should they achieve significant results from a scientifically weak position, or should they put themselves in a strong scientific position but get meager results? Only linguistics has succeeded (during the course of this century) in escaping this dilemma, and so offers itself as a model for other disciplines, which to a greater or less extent they have followed.

The doubt creeps in, however, as to whether this kind of rigor is not perhaps both unattainable and undesirable, because of the form taken by the knowledge most closely bound up with everyday experience— or to be more precise, with every context in which the unique and irreplaceable character of its components seems critical to those involved. It was once said that falling in love meant overvaluing the tiny ways in which one woman, or one man, differed from others. This could, of course, be extended to works of art or to horses.[72] In such contexts the elastic rigor (to use a contradictory phrase) of the conjectural paradigm seems impossible to eliminate. It's a matter of kinds of knowledge which tend to be unspoken, whose rules, as we have said, do not easily lend themselves to being formally articulated or even spoken aloud. Nobody learns how to be a connoisseur or a diagnostician simply by applying the rules. With this kind of knowledge there are factors in play which cannot be measured—a whiff, a glance, an intuition. Until now we have carefully avoided this tricky word, intuition. But if it is going to be used, as another way of describing the instantaneous running through of the thought process, then we must make a distinction between *low* and *high* intuition.

Ancient Arab physiognomy was based on *firasa:* a complex notion which generally speaking meant the capacity to leap from the known to the unknown by inference (on the basis of clues).[73] The term was taken from the vocabulary of Sufi philosophy; it came to be used both for mystic intuition, and for the kinds of penetrating shrewdness which were attributed to the sons of the king of Serendippo.[74] In this second sense, *firasa* is neither more nor less than the organ of conjectural knowledge.[75]

This "low intuition" is rooted in the senses (though it goes beyond them)—and as such it has nothing to do with the extrasensory intuition of various nineteenth- and twentieth-century irrationalisms. It exists everywhere in the world, without geographic, historical, ethnic, gender, or class exception; and this means that it is very different from any form of "superior" knowledge restricted to an elite. It was the heritage of the Bengalis whom Sir William Herschel expropriated, of hunters, of mariners, of women. It forms a tight link between the human animal and other animal species.

NOTES

1. The original Italian text of this essay appeared in A. Gargani (ed.), *Crisi della ragione* (Torino: Einaudi, 1979) pp. 59–106. The author hopes to publish a revised and enlarged version in the near future.

2. For the meaning of "paradigm" see Kuhn 1962. Specifications and distinctions lately suggested by the same author (*Postscript* 1969 in Kuhn 1974:174ff.) are not part of my argument.

3. On Morelli, see first of all Wind 1963:32–51, and the sources he quotes. On Morelli's life, add Ginoulhiac 1940; for a re-examination of his method, Wollheim 1973; Zerner 1978; Previtali 1978. Unfortunately there is no general study of Morelli. It would be useful to analyze, besides his writings on art history, his early scientific education, his relationship with the German intellectual milieu, his friendship with the great Italian literary critic Francesco De Sanctis, his involvement in politics. (Morelli proposed De Sanctis for the chair of Italian literature in Zurich: see De Sanctis 1938). On Morelli's political involvement see passing references in Spini 1956. And for the European resonance of his work see his letter to Marco Minghetti from Basel, 22 June 1882: "Old Jacob Burckhardt, whom I visited last night, was extremely kind to me, and insisted on spending the whole evening with me. He is a very original man, both in his behavior and in his thinking; you, and especially Donna Laura, would like him. He talked about Lermolieff's book, as if he knew it by heart, and used to ask me a lot of questions—which flattered me a great deal. This morning I am going to meet him again . . ." (Biblioteca Comunale di Bologna, Archiginnasio, Carteggio Minghetti, XXIII, 54).

4. According to Longhi 1967:234, Morelli was "less great" than Cavalcaselle, "but important," suggesting however that his "materialist indications" rendered "his method shallow and useless from an aesthetic point of view." (On the implications of criticisms like this see Contini 1972:117.) The unfavorable comparison with Cavalcaselle has been suggested, for instance, by M. Fagiolo in Argan and Fagiolo 1974:97, 101.

5. Croce (1946:15) criticized Morelli's "sensualist appreciation of details taken out of their context."

6. See Longhi 1967:321: "Morelli either badly lacked the feeling of quality, or perverted it under the impulse of his connoisseurship . . . ," and even defined him "mean and lamentable."

7. Arnold Hauser (1959) makes a more general comparison between Freud's "detective" methods and Morelli's.

8. CARD first appeared in *The Strand Magazine* V (Jan.-June 1893). From Baring-Gould 1967:208, we learn that *The Strand* several months later published an unsigned article on the varieties of the human ear ("Ears: a chapter on," *Strand Magazine* VI, July-Dec. 1893). Baring-Gould thinks the author

likely to have been Conan Doyle, publishing Holmes's anthropological treatise on ears. But "Ears" followed an earlier article on "Hands," which was signed Beckles Wilson (*The Strand Magazine* V, Jan.-July 1893), and was presumably by the same writer. Nevertheless, the page illustrating possible shapes of ears does irresistibly recall illustrations in Morelli's work, which at least confirms that the notion was in common circulation during these years.

9. It is just possible that the parallel was more than a coincidence. An uncle of Conan Doyle's, Henry Doyle, painter and art critic, was made Director of the Dublin Art Gallery in 1869 (see Nordon 1964). In 1887 Morelli met Henry Doyle, and wrote about him to Sir Henry Layard: "What you say about the Dublin Gallery interests me very much, and all the more since in London I had the good fortune to meet with the splendid Mr. Doyle, who made the best possible impression on me. . . . Alas, rather than Doyles, what persons do you usually find in charge of galleries in Europe? (British Museum, Add. Ms. 38965, Layard Papers, vol. XXXV c. 120v). Doyle's acquaintance with the Morelli method is proved (though it could have been assumed in an art historian) by the 1890 *Catalogue of the Works of Art in the National Gallery of Ireland,* which he edited, and which made use of Kugler's manual, which was thoroughly re-worked by Layard in 1887 under the guidance of Morelli. The first English translation of Morelli appeared in 1883 (see bibliography, Richter 1960). The first Holmes story (STUD) was published in 1887. This does allow the possibility that Conan Doyle was, through his uncle, familiar with the Morelli method. But in any case such a supposition is not essential, since Morelli's writings were certainly not the only vehicle for these ideas.

10. The only exception is provided by Spector's fine essay, which excludes, however, the existence of any real relationship between Morelli's and Freud's method (1969:82–83).

11. Two late essays by Freud on his relationships with "Lynkeus" are mentioned in *The Interpretation of Dreams.*

12. See Gombrich 1966. It is curious that Gombrich does not here refer to Freud's passage on Morelli.

13. Freud's choice of Vergil's verse as a motto has been interpreted in various ways: see Schoenau 1968:61–73. The most convincing interpretation has been suggested by E. Simon: the meaning of the motto is that the hidden, invisible part of reality is no less significant than the visible one. On the possible political implications of Vergil's verse, already used by Lassalle, see the fine essay by Schorske (1980:181–207, particularly 200–203).

14. See Morelli's obituary by Richter (Morelli 1897:xviii): "those specific clues [discovered by Morelli] . . . which a master drops through habit and nearly unconsciously. . . ."

15. See also the bibliographical appendix to N. Meyer, *The Seven Percent Solution,* an undeservedly successful novel where Holmes and Freud appear together as characters.

16. For a distinction between symptoms and signs or clues, see Segre 1975:33; Sebeok 1976.

17. See Baring-Gould 1967:7 ("Two doctors and a detective: Sir Arthur Conan Doyle, John A. Watson MD, and Mr. Sherlock Holmes of Baker Street"), and after, on John Bell, the physician who inspired the character of Holmes. See also Doyle 1924:25–26, 74–75.

18. See also Étiemble (1973), where he argues, convincingly if paradoxically,

that humans learned first to read and then to write. On this subject more generally, see Benjamin 1955, especially the chapter on the mimetic faculty.

19. On the links between writing and divination in China, see Grenet 1963, especially 33–38.

20. The reference is to the kind of inference which Peirce defined as presumptive or "abductive," distinguishing it from simple induction. Bottéro on the other hand (1974:89) stresses the deductive elements in Mesopotamian divination. This definition oversimplifies (to the point of distorting it) the complicated trajectory which Bottéro himself reconstructs so well. The simplification seems to result from a narrow and one-sided definition of "science," belied however, by his significant analogy between divination and medicine, a discipline with almost no deductive character. The parallel suggested here between the two tendencies in Mesopotamian divination and the mixed character of cuneiform writing stems from some of Bottéro's observations.

21. See Diller 1932:14–42, especially 20ff. His opposition between analogical and semiotic approach must be corrected, interpreting the latter as an "empirical use" of analogy: see Melandri 1968:25ff. According to Vernant 1974:19, "political, historical, medical, philosophical and scientific progress implies a break with an attitude based on divination." In this passage Vernant seems to identify divination with inspired divination: but see p. 11, on the difficulty of explaining the coexistence, even in Greece, of both inspired and analytical divination. An implicit depreciation of Hippocratic symptomatology is suggested on p. 24 (see however Melandri 1968:251, and above all Vernant and Détienne 1978).

22. See Vegetti 1965:22–23. Alcmaeon's fragment is edited in Timpanaro Cardini 1958, I:146ff.

23. On all this see the rich study by Détienne and Vernant (1978). In the original French edition, the divinatory characteristics of Metis are discussed (pp. 104ff.), but see also, for the connections between the various types of knowledge listed here and divination, pp. 145–149 (mariners), and pp. 270ff.; on medicine, see from p. 297; on relations between the followers of Hippocrates and Thucydides, see Vegetti and Diller 1932:22–23. The links between medicine and historiography can be explored the other way round; see the studies on "autopsy" recorded by Momigliano (1975:45). The presence of women in the domain of Metis is discussed in Détienne and Vernant 1978, French edition: 20 and 267, and will be taken up in the final version of this work.

24. The *coniector* was a priestly soothsayer or diviner. Here and elsewhere I draw on Timpanaro 1976, though so to speak turning it inside out. Very briefly, Timpanaro thinks psychoanalysis is too close to magic to be acceptable; while I am suggesting that not only psychoanalysis but most of the so-called human or social sciences are rooted in a divinatory approach to the construction of knowledge (see the last section of this article). The individualizing tendency of magic, and the individualizing character of the two sciences of medicine and philology were pointed out by Timpanaro in *The Freudian Slip*.

25. There is a memorable passage on the "probable" (i.e., not certain) character of historical knowledge in Bloch 1953. Its indirect nature, relying on traces or clues, is stressed by Pomian (1975:935–952), who recalls implicitly Bloch's insistence on the importance of the critical method developed by the Benedictine congregation of St. Maure. Pomian's essay, rich in insights, ends

with a brief discussion of the differences between history and science: they do not include the more or less individualizing approach to knowledge (1975:951–952). On the connection between medicine and historical knowledge see Foucault 1977; but for another point of view see Granger 1967:206ff. My insistence on the individualizing character of historical knowledge has a doubtful ring to it, because too often it goes with the attempt to identify historical knowledge with empathy, or the equating of history with art, and so on. Of course, these pages are written with an altogether different intention.

26. On the repercussions of the invention of writing, see Goody and Watt 1962–63, and 1977. See also Havelock 1973. For the history of textual criticism after the invention of the printing press, see Kenney 1974.

27. The distinction between *espressione* and *estrinsecazione* suggested by Croce catches, even if in mystified terms, the historical process of dematerialization of the concept of text which I tried to sketch here. The extension of that distinction (obvious from Croce's point of view) to Art, with a capital A, seems to me untenable.

28. See Timpanaro (1963:1), who suggests that a discipline which before the nineteenth century was more an "art" than a "science," insofar as it was based on conjectures (*emendatio*), became more scientific through the development of *recensio*.

29. See Bidez's aphorism quoted in Timpanaro 1976.

30. See Garin 1961:451–464, where he discusses the interpretation of this and other passages from Galileo from a point of view close to mine here.

31. On Cesi and Ciampoli, see below; on Faber, see Galilei 1935, XIII:207.

32. Like Rossi, Naude too called Mancini a thoroughgoing atheist ("grand et parfait Athée") (Pintard 1943, I:261–262).

33. Mancini 1956–1957. The importance of Mancini as a "connoisseur" is stressed by Mahon (1947:279ff.). Hess 1968 is full of good references but too reductive in his conclusions.

34. On p. 82 he tells how, not long before, a diagnosis by Mancini which proved to be correct (the patient was Pope Urban VIII) was called second sight or prophecy (*seu vaticinatio, seu praedictio*).

35. Engravings obviously pose a different problem from paintings. Generally speaking, one tendency today is away from the unique work of art ("multiples" are an obvious example); but there are other tendencies too, which confirm the importance of the unrepeatable (of performances, not of works, as with "body art" and "land art").

36. All this relies of course on Benjamin (1969), who, however, only discusses works of figurative art. Their uniqueness—with a special insistence on paintings—is opposed to the reproducibility of literary texts by Gilson 1958:93 and especially 95–96. (I owe this reference to Renato Turci.) But Gilson treats it as an intrinsic difference, not a historical one, as I try to suggest. A case like that of the painter De Chirico "faking" his own works, shows how today's belief in the absolutely unique character of a given work of art tends to elbow aside the idea of the artist's own biological individuality.

37. At the end of the quotation I have replaced "pittura," "painted," with "scrittura," "written," as required by the context.

38. Here are my reasons for suggesting Allacci. In another passage, like the one quoted here, Mancini refers to "librarians, particularly at the Vatican," able

to date ancient manuscripts, both Greek and Latin (1956–57, I:106). Neither of these passages figures in the brief version, known as the *Discorso sulla pittura,* which Mancini finished before 13 November 1619 (ibid.:xxx; the text of *Discorso,* 29lff.; the part on "recognizing" paintings 327–330). Allacci was appointed "scriptor" at the Vatican in the middle of 1619 (Odier 1973:129; recent studies on Allacci are listed on 128–131). In Rome at this time there was no one except Allacci skilled in Latin and Greek manuscripts as Mancini describes. On the importance of Allacci's ideas on Paleography see Casamassima 1964:532, which also mentions the Allacci-Mabillon link, though it promises further reference in a sequel which never appeared. In the collection of Allacci's letters in the Vatican Library there is no indication of contact with Mancini, but they were undoubtedly part of the same intellectual circle, as their respective friendships with G.V. Rossi show (see Pintard 1943). For the friendship between Allacci and Maffeo Barberini before he became pope (Urban VIII, whose librarian Allacci then became), see Mercati 1952:26, n.1. Mancini, as I have said, was Urban's chief physician.

39. On Baldi, who wrote also some treatises on physiognomies and divination, see Tronti 1963, who ends quoting with approval the despising remark by Moréri: "on peut bien le mettre dans le catalogue de ceux qui ont écrit sur des sujets de néant." In his *Discorso sulla pittura* written before November 13, 1619 (see note 38), Mancini said: "the individual features of handwriting have been discussed by a noble spirit. In a small booklet widely read nowadays, he has tried to demonstrate and analyse the causes of these features, connecting the ways of writing to the complexion and habits of the writer: a rare and fine book, but a bit too short" 1956–57:306–307. (I have replaced "astratta" (abstract) with "astretta" (short) on the basis of ms. 1698 (60) of the University Library of Bologna, c. 34 r. The identification with Baldi suggested above meets two difficulties: (1) the first printed edition of Baldi's *Trattato* appeared at Carpi in 1622 (therefore in 1619 or so it could not have been "widely read"); (2) in his *Discorso* Mancini speaks of a "noble spirit," in his *Considerazioni* of "quick wits." Both difficulties, however, disappear when we read the printer's warning in the first edition of Baldi's *Trattato:* "The author of this small treatise did not want to publish it: but because a secretary printed it under his own name with many letters and writings of various authors, I decided that it was honorable to uncover the truth, reestablishing the true author's name." Mancini, therefore, saw first the "small booklet" printed by the "secretary" (I have not been able to identify him) and then Baldi's *Trattato,* which in any case circulated in a manuscript version, slightly different from the printed one (see Biblioteca Classense, Ravenna, ms. 142, which includes also other of Baldi's writings).

40. See generally pp. 25–28. The passage is referred to as presaging "the Morelli method" in Schlosser 1926, 11.4.

41. See for instance Scalzini (1585:20): "who becomes accustomed to write in this way, after a short time looses the quickness and natural boldness of his hand . . ."; Cresci (1622:84): ". . . you must not believe that those strokes, which they claim in their works to trace with a single stroke of the pen and many flourishes . . .", and so on.

42. Cf. Scalzini (1585:77–78): "If those fellows who write quietly, with their line and their varnish, should work for some Prince or Lord, who would need (as it happens) 40 or 50 long letters in four hours, how much time would they

take, by grace, for a job like this?" (the target of this polemical remark is provided by some unnamed "boastful masters," accused of teaching a slow and labored *cancelleresca*).

43. ". . . this great book, which Nature keeps open to everybody has eyes in his forehead as well as in his brain" (quoted and discussed in Raimondi 1974:23–24).

44. See Bottéro 1974:101, though he attributes the less frequent use in divination of the mineral or vegetable or even to some extent, animal, to their presumed "formal poverty" rather than, more simply, to an anthropocentric approach.

45. These pages are part of a section by Giovanni Faber, which is not clear from the title page. There is an excellent discussion of this volume, stressing its importance, by Raimondi (1974:25ff.).

46. Mancini (1956–1957, I:107) refers to a text by Francesco Giuntino on the horoscope of Dürer. (The editor of the *Considerazioni* II:60, n. 483, does not identify the text; but see Giuntino 1573:269v.)

47. It was Pope Urban himself who insisted that the illustrated account should be printed, Lynceo 1651:599. On the interest of this group in landscape painting see Cavina 1976:139–144.

48. See Raimondi's interesting essay (1974)—even if, following Whitehead, he tends to underrate the opposition between the two paradigms, the abstract-mathematical and the concrete-descriptive. On the contrast between Baconian and classical science, see Kuhn 1975.

49. On this subject, here scarcely touched on, see the very rich book by Hacking (1975). Also quite useful is Ferriani 1978.

50. Here I am taking up, though in a rather different sense, points considered by Foucault (1977b:167–169).

51. See Winckelmann 1954, II:316 (letter 30 April 1763 to G.L. Bianconi in Rome) and note on 498. "Little insights" are referred to in Winckelmann 1952, I:341.

52. This is true not only of novels about early life and development (*"Bildungsromanen"*). From this point of view the novel is the real successor to the fable. See Propp 1946.

53. On Sercambi see pp. 347ff. Cerulli's article on the origins and diffusion of the *Travels* must be integrated with what is known of the Eastern origins of the story, and its later indirect (through *Zadig*) outcome in the detective story.

54. Cerulli mentions translations into German, French, English (from the French), Danish (from the German). This list may be checked and perhaps extended, in a book which I have not been able to see (Remer 1965) which on pp. 184–190 lists editions and translations. (See Heckscher 1974:131, n. 46.)

55. This develops a point made in Heckscher 1967:245, n. 11. These two articles by Heckscher are extremely rich in ideas and references; they examine the origins of Aby Warburg's method from a point of view that is close to mine in this article. In a later version I plan to follow up the Leibnizian trail that Heckscher suggests.

56. See in general Messac 1929 (excellent though now a bit out-of-date). On the connection between the *Travels* and *Zadig* see pp. 17ff.; also pp. 211–212.

57. See Huxley 1881:128–148. (This was a lecture given the previous year. My attention was drawn to it by a reference in Messac 1929.) On p. 132 Huxley

explains that "even in the restricted sense of 'divination' it is obvious that the essence of the prophetic operation does not lie in its backward or forward relation to the course of time, but in the fact that it is the apprehension of that which lies out of the sphere of immediate knowledge; the seeing of that which to the natural sense of the seer is invisible." And see Gombrich 1969:35ff.

58. On p. 25 the "young theory" of the youthful Lecoq is contrasted with the "old practice" of the old detective Gévrol, "champion of the positivist police" (p. 20) who stops short at what he can see and therefore risks seeing nothing.

59. On the long-lived popular support for phrenology in England (when official science despised it) see Giustino 1975.

60. "My research reached the conclusion . . . that the anatomy of civil society must be sought in political economy" (Marx, Preface 1859 to *A Contribution to the Critique of Political Economy*).

61. Zerner (1978) argues on the basis of this passage that Morelli made distinctions at three levels: (a) the general characteristics of the school of painting, (b) the characteristic details of the individual painter, betrayed in hands, ears, etc., and (c) mannerisms unintentionally introduced. In fact (b) and (c) might combine, as with Morelli's point about the "exaggerated thumb of men's hands" which recurs in paintings by Titian, a "mistake" that a copyist would have avoided (1897:174).

62. Some echoes of the pages of Mancini discussed here may have reached Morelli through Baldinucci (1681:7–8) and Lanzi's history of Italian art (Lanzi 1968). As far as I know, Morelli never referred to Mancini's *Considerazioni.*

63. In 1885 the Waldeck-Rousseau law decreed prison for old offenders with a long record, and expulsion for those considered irredeemable. See Perrot 1975:68.

64. Branding was abolished in France in 1832. *The Count of Monte Cristo* dates from 1844, as does *The Three Musketeers* (both by Alexandre Dumas); Victor Hugo's *Les Misérables* from 1869. The list of convicts in the literature of this period could be extended both for France (Vautrin, et al.), and from English novels, especially Dickens.

65. Bertillon 1893b: xlviii: "But where the ear is most clearly superior for identification purposes is in cases where the court requires an assurance that a particular old photograph 'beyond doubt represents the person here before us' . . . there are no two identical ears and . . . if the ear corresponds that is a necessary and sufficient proof that the identity does too 'except in the case of twins.'" And see Bertillon 1893a (which accompanied the other work), plate 60b. For Bertillon's admiration of Sherlock Holmes, see Lacassin 1974, I:93 (which also quotes the passage on ears just quoted, in note 8).

66. Because of his skill as a handwriting expert Bertillon was called in during the Dreyfus case, to pronounce on the authenticity of the famous memorandum. Because his verdict definitely favored the case against Dreyfus, his career (so the biographies insist) suffered (Lacassagne 1914:4).

67. See the acknowledgment on p. 4. On pp. 26–27 he also refers to a precedent which never took practical form: a San Francisco photographer who had proposed facilitating identification of members of the Chinese community by the use of fingerprints.

68. The reference here is to Traube 1965—this point has been brought out by Campana (1967:1028); Warburg (1932) on the renaissance of ancient

paganism (the first essay dates from 1893); Spitzer 1910; Bloch 1973 (first published in 1924). The examples could be multiplied: see Agamben 1975:15 (Warburg and Spitzer are quoted, and Traube mentioned, on p. 10).

69. Besides Campanella's *Political Aphorisms,* which originally appeared in Latin as part of *Realis Philosophia* (De politica in aphorismos digesta), see Canini 1625 (see Bozza 1949:141–43, 151–52). And see entry "Aphorisme" in the *Dictionnaire Littré.*

70. Even if it was originally used in law; for a brief history of the term see Koselleck 1969.

71. The point will be further developed in the final version of this article.

72. Compare Stendhal's *Souvenirs d'égotisme* ed. (1948:51–52): "Victor [Jacquemont] strikes me as an exceptional man: recognizable as a connoisseur . . . . spots a fine horse in a four-month-old colt still unsteady on its legs" (Stendhal excuses himself for using the French word *connoisseur* in the sense it had acquired in English. See Zerner's remark [1978:215, n. 4] on the lack in French, even today, of an equivalent of the English word *connoisseurship.*)

73. See Mourad's rich and penetrating book (1939:1–2).

74. See the extraordinary adventure attributed to Al-Shafi'i (in the ninth century A.D. of the Christian calendar) in Mourad 1939:60–61, which looks like a Borges tale. The link between *firasa* and the deeds of the king of Serendippo's sons is raised, appropriately, by Messac (1929).

75. Mourad (1939:29) classifies the branches of physiognomy as follows from the treatise by Tashkopru Zadeh (A.D. 1560): (1) the lore of moles and blemishes, (2) chiromancy—the reading of hands, (3) scapulomancy—divination using shoulder blades, (4) divination through tracks, (5) genealogical lore involving examination of limbs and skin, (6) the art of finding the way in the desert, (7) water-divining, (8) the art of finding where metal lay (underground), (9) the art of foretelling rain, (10) prediction using events of the past and present, (11) prediction using the body's involuntary movements. From p. 15 on, Mourad is proposing a very interesting comparison, which will be followed up, between the Arab study of physiognomy and research on perceptions of individuality by the Gestalt psychologists.

CHAPTER FIVE

Massimo A. Bonfantini and Giampaolo Proni

To Guess or Not To Guess?

I. The Structure of the Investigation in *A Study in Scarlet*

Reconstructing the investigation conducted by Sherlock Holmes in STUD is not a simple matter for at least two reasons: In the first place, there is the *strategy of the text*. Conan Doyle does not furnish the reader with the same data as the detective possesses. These are revealed only at the end (like the reply to the telegram that Holmes sends as soon as he learns the site of the crime) as if they were trivialities, whereas in fact they are crucial to the solving of the case. In the second place, Holmes never lets us know at what point in the investigation he draws his conclusions or the purpose of certain of his actions or their outcome.

But what is of interest to us now is not a study of the narrative structures of the thriller but the *method* that is theorized in it. So we have reconstructed a schema of the fabula with all the components we are given in the course of the narrative, both what is known to the reader at the time and what he learns at the end. Not even this task is without difficulty. What Holmes observes is not what he infers from time to time. Further, while we know the chronological sequence of the observations and "experiments," we do not always know precisely at what point certain conclusions are drawn.

This schema is thus a *reconstruction*. At a few places it has been possible to pinpoint the stages of the investigation, at others it has been, because of the text, impossible to do. We shall point this out from time to time.

1. Holmes receives a letter from Gregson (one of the two Scotland

Yard detectives assigned to an investigation) asking for his help in connection with the murder of Enoch J. Drebber, found dead in an uninhabitated house in Lauriston Gardens.

2. In addition to his wealth of general knowledge (thorough and detailed), he *knows* that the evening before it had rained after a week without rain. On arrival at the address Holmes left the cab and did the last bit of road on foot. He thus *observes* the ruts of another cab left in the mud in front of the house where the crime had taken place. The narrow gauge of the wheels ensured that it was a cab. The imprints left by the horse's hoofs suggest that the animal had been left unattended.

From these data Holmes concludes that this cab had probably arrived during the night and been left unattended. At this point, probably, a vague hypothesis has already formed in his mind, that is, that the cab driver is in some way involved in the affair, unless the cab belonged to someone in the police. The text tells us nothing at this juncture. Holmes looks for other marks. He carefully *observes* the impressions on the pathway leading to the house, distinguishing among the others, half-covered and hence older, those of two men, one with square-toed boots and the other with elegant boots. The square-toed boots seem to belong to a young man because they bestride a puddle one meter twenty wide while the other boots skirt round it. From this he *concludes*, further, that the two men entered the house before anyone else (perhaps therefore during the night). One is tall and young and the other fashionably dressed.

3. Holmes meets Lestrade, the second man from Scotland Yard, and asks whether anyone arrived in a cab that morning. Lestrade says no. This *confirms* the hypothesis that the two men arrived at night in a cab and that one of them, presumably the one with the square-toed boots, was the cab driver, for where else could he have gone, having left the cab at night.

4. Holmes enters the house and sees the scene of the crime, with the corpse on view. It at once gives him further *confirmation:* the well-booted man is the victim. (From here it is a short step to imagining that the murderer is the cab driver, since the dead man can be neither.)

5. Holmes later *observes* several details, each of which prompts some hhpoth es:

(a) The dead man's face is agitated, as if by hatred or fear.

(b) His lips have a slightly sour smell. This may lead one to suppose that he had had poison forced upon him. Some similar cases make this plausible.

(c) On the wall the word "RACHE" has been scrawled in gothic characters in blood. Holmes at once *concludes* that this is the German word for revenge but that it is a trick to divert the investigations, because a real German would use roman characters for capital letters.

(d) A ring is found on the victim. *This leads him to imagine* that the object may have served to remind the victim of a dead or distant woman. (Holmes further knows at once, without the text telling us why, that that ring was *forgotten* by the murderer and not left deliberately.)

(e) On the floor there are traces of blood but no trace of struggle. From this Holmes *concludes* that the blood belonged to the murderer. Since he knows that full-blooded men are often liable to bleed under the influence of strong emotion, he conjectures that the murderer is a robust and florid person.

6. At this point Sherlock Holmes closely examines the whole room with a magnifying glass and tape measure.

(a) He *observes* the impressions of the square-toed boots and measures the paces and their number. From this he *infers* (by means of calculations he knows) the height of the man, *establishes* that he walked up and down the room several times and in great agitation, for his strides got longer and longer.

(b) He *observes* a heap of ash on the floor and from certain characteristics *establishes* that it is Trichinopoly cigar ash.

(c) He *observes* that the writing on the wall had been scratched and from this *concludes* that the murderer has very long nails.

7. At this juncture, having left the site of the crime, Holmes sends off a telegram. The reader is not told then where or what the text is but he will know later that in it Holmes asks Cleveland (Drebber's home town) for information on his marriage. It is done to *test* the hypothesis that arose from the ring, that is, that an affair of the heart is involved. We are not told in the text when he gets the reply, but this definitely happens before stage 10 when Holmes orders a search for Jefferson Hope among the cab drivers of London. The reply in fact tells him that at one time Drebber had asked for police protection from his rival in love by the name of Jefferson Hope.

8. Sherlock Holmes goes to see John Rance, the constable who had discovered the body while walking his beat that night, and *questions* him. Here we have textual proof that Holmes is already thinking of the cab driver as responsible for the crime: indeed he asks Rance whether he had met anyone in the road coming out of the house where he had found the victim and, on learning that he had seen a drunkard, he asked him whether by chance he held a whip and whether he had seen a cab. Rance says no to both questions and describes the drunkard as tall and

muffled. This further *confirms* Holmes's hypothesis: the murderer returned to pick up the ring but had run into the police. So he pretended
to be drunk.

9. Holmes puts an advertisement in the newspaper in the name of
Watson stating that he had found a gold ring in the neighborhood of
Lauriston Gardens. He intends *by this trick to draw out* the murderer,
who cannot think that an ordinary citizen has been able to connect the
crime with the ring, which he must therefore have lost in the street. In
short, let us say that *the trick fails* because it is not the tall man who
turns up but an old woman, who takes the ring and manages to shake
off Holmes.

10. Holmes gets onto another track: he gets a group of urchins (the
famous "Baker Street irregulars") to look for a cab driver by the name
of Jefferson Hope, answering the description he has established. He has
already *concluded* that J.H. is the murderer and that, as a cab driver, he
had an excellent means of flushing out his victim in London. He further
presumes that J.H. has not given up cab driving, in order not to arouse
suspicion, a few days after the crime and that he has not changed his
name, because nobody in London knows him.

11. At this point there is a coup de scène: a new victim is discovered,
stabbed in the heart: it is Stargeson, Drebber's secretary, who had not
been traced. This murder too was "signed" RACHE. In the context of
the story this seems to shatter all the investigations. Actually, if examined closely, the coup de scène simply confirms all Holmes's hypotheses.

(a) A hotel page saw the murderer escape and *confirms* that the man
is tall and high-complexioned.

(b) A telegram in Stargeson's possession *confirms* that "J.H. is in
Europe." (We do not know who this is at this point in the story but
Holmes does.)

(c) A box containing two pills *confirms* the use (the attempted use this
time) of poison.

12. After the second murder the police investigations seem to be all
at sea, but the solution to the drama is at hand: Lestrade has hardly
finished reporting the second murder when a cab driver, called by
Holmes, comes to pick up some luggage: it is the murderer. The
reader, who as yet knows nothing of Jefferson Hope, is amazed and so
are the rest of the dramatis personae. Sherlock Holmes, following his
mysterious red thread, has arrived at *the final proof, which confirms all his
hypotheses.* J.H. confesses at once.

Some of the points one could make on this schema are: First, the
suspense is clearly a textual artifice. Once the reader knows all that
Holmes is supposed to know he has no difficulty in reaching his con-

clusions. Those who do not know, or do not remember, the text should bear in mind that the reader does not know right up to the end either the contents of the Cleveland telegram or the fact that the horse was unattended. The first detail is more important than the second. Once we know that the victim had been threatened by one Jefferson Hope, it is not difficult to connect this with the crime.

Second, we would emphasize (for this purpose we have put the various types of operations that weave the investigation in italics) the stages in Holmes's investigative process. He carries out several types of operations: on the one hand he *observes* and on the other he *concludes, infers, conjectures.* In short, he forms theories and then *finds* and *constructs facts that confirm* these theories.

Third, we see that Holmes operates on another pair of levels. On the one hand, he *collects data,* and on the other, he *sets stratagems in motion* in order to trap the culprit.

II. HOLMES COMPARED WITH PEIRCE

Reflecting on the three points of the schema, let us set aside the last, which is concerned with the operations designed to capture the criminal rather than with his exposure and identification. Instead, let us focus our attention on the second point: the structure of Holmes's investigative process. Anyone who knows Peirce's works will have no difficulty in discerning the perfect structural correspondence between the logic of investigation according to Holmes and the logic of the process of knowledge in general and of science in particular according to Peirce.

On rereading our outline summarizing the investigative operations carried out by Holmes in STUD, the reader familiar with Peirce will easily see how the three stages of the cognitive process weave, follow one another, and combine in it; for Peirce these embody the three kinds of argument: induction, abduction (or hypothesis), and deduction. In sum, Holmes starts by observing, recording, and matching up several observational data (induction); he then advances a hypothesis to account for or interpret the observed facts in order to identify *possible causes* of *resulting events* (*abduction*); he sets forth analytically the consequences necessarily inherent in the hypotheses postulated (*deduction*); he puts the hypotheses and the consequences deduced therefrom to the test of observation and, in the broad sense, "experiment" (*induction*). Thus the hypotheses, thought up and selected one after another, end by forming a network that converges on the identification of the fundamental hypothesis: the identity of the murderer.

The perfect correspondence between Holmes and Peirce in the *mode* of understanding the complex logical structure of the cognitive process does not mean per se a perfect identity of *method*. In fact, the correspondence would or should have seemed to Peirce (if we understand him rightly) as perfectly natural and almost a matter of course. In the second of the two anti-Cartesian essays of 1868, *Some Consequences of Four Incapacities,* Peirce undertakes to demonstrate that it is impossible for a human being to perform any mental action and, a fortiori, anything approaching a cognitive process, whether valid or invalid, *without resorting to the three obligate and obligant kinds of argument: induction, deduction, and abduction.* Thus, since for Peirce the interweaving of the three stages of inference constitute a common constant both in coping with the day-to-day practical problems of life and in investigations with a specialist direction and in scientific research proper, it is not to be wondered at that an attentive illustration of the procedures of police *detection* should show the presence of the three canonical kinds of inference.

In brief, the spirit of Peirce, if we interpret him rightly, would turn to the spirit of Holmes (or of Conan Doyle) and say:

"To discover that we know through the combination of three fundamental forms of inference is to take a necessary but not fully sufficient step toward the development of a scientific *method.* The three kinds of argument have been known and explained since the times of the Greeks. I have found them in Aristotle's *Organon.* And at least since Galileo there has been a general awareness that the method of science is hypothetic-deductive-experimental. Now, the scientific method, as I recognize it in the practice of scientists and as I commend it in my philosophical reflections, is linked to the tradition of Galileo, which it renders more specific, of broader scope and innovative. The refinements and enlargements of *induction* (by means of instruments and techniques of observation and experimentation) and of *deduction* (by means of the formalization of analytical logic and the advances of mathematics) are known, accepted, and universally recognized.

"But, above all, I stress the importance of the function of *abduction,* of hypothesis. By emphasizing, against the Cartesian tradition, that all our knowledge has a hypothetical basis, on the one hand I highlight its intrinsic fallibility but on the other I proclaim the need resolutely to put abduction in the control room of the cognitive process in general and above all in the scientific process, for it is only by means of hypotheses, new and bolder abductions, that we can discover new truths, however approximate and provisional; it is only by means of new hypotheses that we can widen our vision of the real and discover new avenues of experience, propose new material for the test bench of experimentation.

Now, with a close study of your method, such as you theorize it and practice it in your investigations, dear Holmes, I wonder whether your method tallies in its fundamental lines with mine or whether the possible divergences are such that we may both benefit by correcting each other's dogmatic one-sidedness."

III. ABDUCTION ACCORDING TO HOLMES

At this point let us get down to a closer analysis of the character traits of Holmes's investigation. First of all, Holmes could naturally claim, to his credit, an effective, highly aware, methodical, and systematic use of the three modes of inference. And *therefore* the use of a method that may rightly be called more "scientific" than that of his "official" colleagues. Holmes is doubtless more precise, more accurate, and more attentive in the phase of observation. He sees and records more things and he does not neglect (and this is a point on which he insists a great deal when explaining his method to Watson) the apparently minor details at the scene of the crime. He analyses and compares what is *implicit* in the various observational results. He combines and links consequentially, and bearing in mind several aspects of the problem, the various series of hypotheses that he gradually puts forward.

It is on this very issue, the understanding of the function of hypotheses, or abductions, in the process of discovery as a whole, that the Holmes-Peirce comparison must focus. One *convergence* leaps to mind immediately: for Holmes as for Peirce abductions, excogitations of hypotheses on the unknown causes of resulting facts are the key stage in a search.

Holmes is extremely explicit about this. In the last chapter of STUD he explains to Watson that the whole secret in solving police investigation problems lies in "reasoning backwards." He adds that this habit of inference is an accomplishment practised little by ordinary people because "in the everyday affairs of life it is more useful to reason forwards, and so the other comes to be neglected. . . . Most people, if you describe a train of events to them, will tell you what the result would be. . . . There are few people, however, who, if you told them a result, would be able to evolve from their own inner consciousness what the steps were that led up to that result." Further, discussing with Watson the overall sense of the investigation in STUD, in the very first pages of SIGN, Holmes states categorically: "The only point in the case which deserved mention was the curious analytical reasoning from effects to causes, by which I succeeded in unravelling it."

All this is beyond doubt as well as obvious. That a police investigation must get back to the causes, to the origins—and hence, to use the learned terms of Peirce and not Holmes, be based more than anything on *retroduction* or *abduction*—is as plain as a pikestaff. The question is whether the type of abductions involved in police investigation is identical to or similar to or quite different from the type of abductions involved in theoretical scientific investigation that presumably is closest to Peirce's heart. That there may be some difference between the two types of abduction might be supposed a priori—bearing in mind the different purposes of the two types of investigation. In police work the aim is to get back from a *particular* event to its *particular cause* whereas in scientific work the aim is to find a fundamental theoretical law of general application or (more often) to fit an anomalous fact into the applicability of a fundamental law by rearranging the "intermediate" laws.

If we now look at how Holmes proceeds, we see that he does not rely on universal or specific laws of criminology. He *relies* on well-tried *experimental laws:* he often resorts to the strong indexical codes that belong to the more observational, more taxonomic, more "semeiotic" sciences less imbued with theoretical sophistication and closer to common sense (to take up the useful distinction between types of science introduced in the central chapters of Duhem's *Théorie physique*). And the way Holmes draws on experience is very different from that proper to a "very theoretical science" like, to cite the example par excellence, physics, especially contemporary physics. His are more *precise observations* of spontaneously occurring facts than *experimental reconstructions* of selected and "purified," artificially prepared facts, in which the experiment is loaded with theory and is specifically designed in accordance with a starting hypothesis.

The abductions of Holmes are consistent with his "institutional" function and *therefore* of a different type from at least *some* of the abductions that (a) are characteristic of theoretical scientific research and thus (b) are central to the philosophical thought of Peirce. This thesis now begins to look fairly plausible. But it must be stated more clearly.

In brief, we may say that the individual hypotheses of Holmes, the individual steps in his complex retroductive "plot," fall into one or other of the following four classes:

(1) They rest on the strong indexical codes proper to certain experimental sciences or to certain well-tried and institutionalized sectors of experimental sciences, which, Watson tells us in the second chapter of STUD, are definitely among Holmes's assets (botany, geology, chemistry, anatomy; and we may add physiology and medical semeiotics).

(2) They rest on strong indexical codes belonging to special areas of knowledge and techniques of classification and identification worked on and recast by Holmes himself (as we are told in the first chapter of SIGN) in monographs on topics such as distinguishing between ash of various types of tobacco, tracing footsteps, and correlating the various crafts or trades with the corresponding characteristic deformities of the hands.

(3) They rest on vast and well-kept files of descriptive knowledge concerning the usages of everyday life.

(4) They rest on ordinary common sense or on common knowledge regarding the logic of actions.

One need only cite some examples from STUD. The hypothesis that the victim was poisoned clearly falls into class 1; the hypothesis regarding the murderer's boots, like the proverbial statement "the murderer was smoking a Trichinopoly cigar," obviously falls into class 2; the identification of the wheel gauge as belonging to a cab fits class 3; the suspicion regarding Jefferson Hope, knowing that the victim had already asked for protection from him and that J.H. had been the victim's rival in love, naturally falls into class 4.

All these abductions have two fairly striking characteristics: *simplicity* and *soundness*. They are all highly probable or at least highly plausible and absolutely "sensible"—according to common judgment and "normal" knowledge (in a broader and more socially consolidated meaning of the adjective than is attached to it by Kuhn (1962) in the expression "normal science").

All these abductions of Holmes patently lack any *great originality*. They lack hazard and creative risk-taking and hence, in a way, geniality. Likewise the analysis—the concatenation, the comparison and the combination of the single hypothetical steps whereby Holmes reaches the solution of his problems—is always simple and linear. Holmes is fully aware of it. He keeps telling Watson how *simple* and *elementary* his steps are, and also his overall procedure. Toward the end of the third chapter of STUD Holmes sums up, without modesty but with precision, his professional cast of mind, when he says: "They say that genius is an infinite capacity for taking pains. It's a very bad definition, but it does apply to detective work."

A detective is a riddle-solver, not an interpreter of "opaque" facts. His art of abduction must thus belong to *puzzle-solving*, not to *hermeneutics*. Puzzle-solving, like detective work, calls for keen observation and encyclopedic knowledge in order to have at one's fingertips *the finite and predetermined set of immediate and clue-fitting possible hypotheti-*

cal solutions. Then one needs training in logical calculation, coolness, and *patience* for comparing and selecting the hypotheses until one finds the line of interpretation supplying the only *solution that fits all the clues.*

The story DANC is not only a tribute by Conan Doyle to Poe of *The Gold Bug,* it means to suggest that the art of detection is very similar to decryptography, or rather includes decryptography. Conan Doyle-Holmes's thinking may be put like this: the codes of clues are almost as strong and regular in cause-and-effect connection as the codes of cipher languages in the conversion from "clear" into "cipher." In detection it is necessary to combine the known or available codes to identify the hidden event by crossing; in deciphering it is necessary, on the other hand, to test the various imaginable codes until we hit on the only one that enables us to read the text. But, seen closely, detection is a combinatorial puzzle-solving art that takes as its base-level, its launching platform, *the deciphering of data,* of which decryptography is nothing but a more "stylized" and exemplarily difficult extreme case.

Let us try to draw a conclusion: the style of Holmes's abductions may be summarized as a habit of rigor, which (1) obeys an *imperative* of simplicity and plausibility according to logical and empirical criteria firmly accepted by society and which (2) obeys a complementary *ban*—"never guess!" (as Holmes proclaims, for example, toward the end of the first chapter of SIGN). This ban involves rejecting not only unjustified hypotheses but also hypotheses justified by newly excogitated and not commonly accepted principles of explanation.

Holmes denies that he himself uses creative theoretical originality because his institutional task does not allow it: the guilt of an individual must be proved on the basis of well-tried interpretations, according to commonly accepted codes, of certain facts. It is not admissible to introduce bold new theoretical laws, because it would be too "risky." A bold theoretical hypothesis may trigger a fertile research program, but at the time it is put forward it is by definition arbitrary, and it would therefore be *arbitrary* to condemn a person on the strength of it, that is, on the strength of a hypothesis outside the scope of a commonly and publicly recognized and verified legality and uniformity.

IV. ABDUCTION ACCORDING TO PEIRCE

We would say that it is easy to understand how it is that Holmes and Peirce prize *opposite* aspects of abduction. Peirce prizes the intrinsically original, creative, and innovative character of abduction whereas Holmes wants abductions to conform as closely as possible to recognized codes and laws. Holmes says that risk must be avoided, that abduction must never be the outcome of guesswork. Peirce remembers that both in the sudden and unexpected decisions of everyday life and in opening up new paths of scientific discovery bold and risky abductions are needed: it is impossible to do without guesswork! The fact is that Holmes and Peirce have in mind two different types of abduction and two different functions of hypothesis. Two functions that in first approximation we may relate respectively to "normal" science and to "revolutionary" science, in Kuhn's (1962) sense.

A conscious and explicit theorization of the various types of abduction is probably not to be found in Peirce. However, on the basis of his own pointers, it is possible to outline a typology of the abductions that will serve to specify the terms of our discourse. Indeed, from Peirce's texts we learn that, while abductivity is present in all moments of psychic life, we nonetheless get the suggestion that there are different degrees of freedom and creativity in abductive "orience."

Abduction is present at its lowest level of creativity in sensation, we are told in *Some Consequences of Four Incapacities*. Peirce rejects the thesis that sensation is a first or immediate "impression of sense," showing that it is in reality a selective and unifying interpretation of several impressions exerted by the stimulus on various nerves and nerve centers. Hence sensation has the same logical form and fulfills the same function of simple predicate that is attributed to a thing in place of a complex predicate, that is, it fulfills the function of a hypothesis. The only difference is that the hypothesis of real judgment is based on rational arguments whereas the hypothesis of sensation "or natural mental sign" is from the rational point of view "arbitrary" since it is determined "by the constitution of our nature." "Hence the class of hypothetic inferences, which the arising of a sensation resembles, is that of reasoning from definition to definitum" (5.291).

Let us try to elucidate this important point in Peirce's thought by giving an example of reasoning from definition to definitum and by showing that sensation follows the same pattern. According to arbitrary but rigid conventions of the Italian language the term *scapolo* (bachelor) always means and must always and only be used to mean "person of male sex who has never been married." The expression in quotes is thus the obligate definition of the term *scapolo*. Accordingly it is clear that when on a given occasion I wish to say shortly of a certain individual that he is "a person of male sex who has never been married," I shall do well to subsume this meaning under the term *scapolo* instead of using a roundabout paraphrase. So, if I remember the linguistic rule, I can get back from the complexity of the definition to the definitum: thus the individual in question will be qualified by a simple predicate instead of a complex predicate. The pattern of the argument is as follows:

For all individuals,
  that a given individual is a *scapolo* necessarily means
  that that individual is a *person of male sex who has never been married;*
but Tom is a *person of male sex who has never been married;* so Tom is a
  scapolo.

In the case of sensation, because of the constitution of our nature, of the structure of our sensory apparatus and of our nervous system, a given sensation of color, let us say red, arises always and of necessity as the result of the impact of a series of impressions of a given type on the eye. Hence a sensation expressible in the terms "This is red" is always and of necessity the outcome of a series of sensory impressions expressible in the terms "This stimulates the optic nerve in successive moments in such-and-such a way, with such-and-such duration and such-and-such intensity." Thus, when sensory impressions of this type arise on any given particular occasion the organism is obliged to retrace the road from the impressions to the sensation in a manner determined by the constitution of our nature. In the transition from the impressions to the sensation we switch from what is expressible in a complex predicate to what is expressible in a simple predicate. The pattern of the inferential process is as follows:

For all actual entities,
  that a given entity is *red*
    necessarily involves
  that this entity *stimulates the optic nerve in successive moments in such-and-such a way, with such-and-such duration and such-and-such intensity;*
but this entity *stimulates the optic nerve in successive moments in such-and-such a way, with such-and-such duration and such-and-such intensity;* hence this entity is *red.*

At the opposite pole from these "low" abductions Peirce places significant scientific abductions, citing at several points and with particular satisfaction Kepler's hypothesis. The inference whereby Kepler reaches the hypothetical conclusion that the orbit of Mars is elliptic may be put schematically in the following terms:

For all bodies in motion,
  the fact that a given body moves by describing an elliptic orbit implies

that that body passes through given positions geometrically determined in such-and-such a way;
but Mars passes through given positions geometrically determined in
such-and-such a way;
hence Mars moves by describing an elliptic orbit.

This pattern reflects the typical form of abduction as reasoning from
consequent to antecedent. All abductions have this form. As we have
seen, the inferential process that gives rise to sensation and argument
from definition to definitum harks back to this form. Neither the onset
of a sensation (in our example the sensation *red*) nor the identification
of the definitum (in our example the term *scapolo*) shine as particularly
original or innovative conclusions. Quite the reverse, they are obvious,
repetitive, even obligate. By constrast, Kepler's inference, writes
Peirce, is an "eternal exemplar" (2.96). But in what respects? Perhaps
only because Kepler applied the canonical form of abduction? One
would hardly say so, if this form, always identical, can also give rise to
very banal conclusions. And yet, writes Peirce, "An Abduction is [. . .]
the only kind of argument which starts a new idea" (2.96). Where is the
creative magic of this form of inference? And is abduction always so
creative?

Let us try to unravel these problems a bit.

1. First of all, an abduction is an inference. That is to say, the last step
in an abductive argument consists in drawing a conclusion from two
premises. In this respect abduction is just as formal and mechanical as
deduction and induction: the way in which the conclusion is drawn is
rigidly governed by a rule. Also in this respect abduction is no more
original or inventive than deduction or induction. Nor do there seem to
be valid grounds for thinking that one or other of the inferences is
psychologically easier or harder than the other. When I have before me
two specifically appropriate premises, if I recognize them as such and
remember the specific inferential rule, I shall immediately be in a position to draw my conclusion—deductive, inductive, or abductive. In
other words, to use Peirce's terminology, it is just as mechanical or
automatic to derive the *rule* from the case and the result (induction) as
it is to derive the *result* from the rule and the case (deduction) or the
case from the rule and the result (abduction).

2. Nevertheless, the abductive conclusion formally, while proceeding
just as automatically as deduction from the premises, not only makes
plain the semantic content of the premises but generates a recomposi-
tion of the semantic content. Therefore abduction is "synthetic" and
innovative and, as such, also contains an element of risk, since the truth

value of the abductive conclusion is not normally *determined* by the validity of the premises (that is, the premises may be true and the conclusion false). Abduction consists in the attribution to the subject of the
investigation, identified in the premise expressing the "result," of the
characteristics expressed in the protasis or antecedent of the major
premise or rule. So it is readily understandable that both the element of
risk, in addition to that which may be contained in the premises, and
the degree of novelty of the abductive conclusion depend on the relationships between the two propositions (antecedent and consequent)
constituting the major premise.

In the case of Kepler's abduction the conclusion was risky because,
although it is true that an ellipse includes given positions geometrically
determined in such-and-such a way, it could not be assumed that those
positions would be included only and necessarily in an ellipse. Of
course, as Kepler increased the number of recorded positions and these
proved to be consistent with an ellipse, the risk of additional error in
the conclusion decreased, because the reciprcal implication between the
antecedent and the consequent of the major premise increased. If the
reciprocal implication between antecedent and consequent is *total,* that
is, when their relationship can be expressed in the terms *if and only if p,
then q,* or when there is a one-to-one relationship without exception
between what is expressed in the antecedent and what is expressed in
the consequent, or the antecedent is not given without the consequent
or the consequent without the antecedent—then the hypothesis is apparent: it expresses no additional risk and the conclusion of the abduction can be reached just as well, reversing the two propositions of the
major premise, by deduction. Abductions that give rise to sensation or
to a definitum are close to being of this degenerate kind.

3. If the degree of novelty of an abductive conclusion depends on the
tenor of the major premise, then clearly the inventiveness, discovery
potential, or creativity of abductive reasoning lies not in the inference
but in the *interpretation* of the datum or "result," which is regarded as a
particular occurrence of the typical consequence of a law or general
principle. In other words, the heuristic process that gives rise to abduction has the datum as its starting point. To account for or explain or
justify this datum I have to regard it as a consequence of a general
principle. When I have identified this general principle, the conclusion,
as an assertion of the antecedent applied to the subject of the investigation, follows mechanically. What I have to go and look for and track
down is thus the general principle or major premise. The choice of the
major premise, or more precisely of its protasis or antecedent, exercises
the whole creative imagination of the researcher, and it is here that we

have the root of the major or minor novelty of the abductive conclusion. Roughly, it may be said that the more unusual the mating of consequent and antecedent, or the more distant their semantic fields are
from one another, the more pregnant the abduction will be. We are
obviously not going to get very far with the observation (which serves
as the major premise) "all the beans in the sack are white" to account
for the presence of some white beans in a cupboard and then drawing
the conclusion that the white beans come from that sack. Here indeed
we are in the domain of the observational findings closest to the datum.

The major premise introduced by Kepler, by contrast, has a certain
audacity: it reflects the courage to try unbeaten paths, since confronted
by his observations, Kepler breaks with the traditional way of thinking
that wanted a planet's motion to be circular and seeks a curve that can
include all the points recorded. The originality of Kepler's hypothesis
must not, however, be overrated, because the law expressed by his
major premise is not a creative invention but rather the ingenious and
opportune *refurbishing* of a perfectly known principle. Kepler's originality lay in the selection of the suitable principle (from among the
many abstractly possible and *known*) to account for a consequence such
as that expressed in the finding of the "result." The principle was really
fairly near to hand, in the sense that it involved no semantic leap from
consequent to antecedent. More marked is the novelty of the abduction
when the major premise connects the result with one of its possible
remote and "unlikely" causes. And the novelty of the abduction is still
sharper and stronger when the principle expressed in the major premise
is a *new* theoretical law rather than a universally accepted scientific law.
In that case the abductive conclusion is "a new idea" in absolute terms:
it is not just the application of the general principle to the subject of
the investigation that is new, it is the principle that is new too. Hence
the conclusion was not even potentially included in the existing store of
knowledge. For an example of the latter type of abduction, which is the
most fertile in scientific research, one could usefully take the process of
reasoning with which Bohr interpreted the mystery of the gaps in the
lines of the hydrogen spectrum (cf. Bonfantini and Macciò 1977:88–
102).

V. Peirce beyond Peirce: Two Conclusions

1. Summarizing and simplifying the outcome of this discussion, we
would say that it is necessary to distinguish three principal types of
abduction, with three ascending degrees of originality and creativity:

Abduction Type One—the mediation law to use for inferring the case from the result is given in an obligant and automatic or semi-automatic way;

ABDUCTION TYPE TWO—the mediation law to use for inferring the case from the result is found by selection in the available encyclopedia;

ABDUCTION TYPE THREE—the mediation law to use for inferring the case from the result is developed de novo, *invented*. It is in this last type of abduction that real guesswork comes in.

2. What is the basis of guesswork? And how is it that guesses are so often right?

These questions Peirce answers with his theory of natural bent, biologically rooted and accumulated in man in the course of evolution: *lume naturale,* ever-increasingly modeled by the influence of the laws of nature and so more and more spontaneously likely, by secret affinity, to reflect the patterns of reality. This theory of Peirce's is hardly defensible scientifically in that it implies the biological inheritance of culturally acquired cultural characters, when even (at least in the present state of knowledge, *pace* Lysenko) the inheritance of physically acquired physical characters is scientifically unacceptable. Here Peirce actually comes close to the thesis of *influent philosophy*. In our view, it is necessary to transform Peirce's theory by putting the expression *lume culturale* in place of *lume naturale,* which in addition to being steeped in bad metaphysics is too generic in that it explains everything and nothing.

When men have to guess, they find themselves guided by systematic and complex visions of reality, philosophical conceptions, of which they are more or less distinctly aware but which anyway shape their cast of mind, their deep habits which determine the bearings of judgment. These philosophies synthesize and organize, by processes of generalization, analogy, and hierarchical ordering, the knowledge and cultural acquisitions deposited in the course of the centuries and derived from extensive social practices. So it is not to be wondered at that these philosophies possess (obviously in varying degree) their force of truth, including the capacity to inspire new and valid scientific hypotheses.[1]

NOTE

1. References consulted for this article include: Copi (1953), Eco (1976, 1980), Feibleman (1946), Hammett (1930, 1934), Haycraft (1941, 1946), Hoffman (1973), Millar (1969), Peirce (Mss. 475, 682, 689, 690, 1146, 1539), Poe (1927), Robin (1967), Scheglov (1975), Stout (1938), and Chapters 2, 3, and 10 in this book.

CHAPTER SIX

Gian Paolo Caprettini

Peirce, Holmes, Popper

I. The Detective Story as a Universe of Clues

No narration can stand without symptoms or clues. The text as a semantically homogeneous space does not exist for a number of reasons: the graduality through which the meaning of a novel is captured, the continuous reformulation of this meaning in the sequence of actions and in the progressive unveiling of the characters, the partiality and reticence of the narrator's eye. Together with its clearly shown and defined parts, we find in a text other elements which hide themselves in the background, from where they imperceptibly vibrate. Depending on different texts, the relation between "strong" and "weak" symptoms is subject to change. For this reason the aristocratic look of a character, in an epic narration, defines his social status up to the point of even anticipating his identity beyond any reasonable doubt (this identity will later on be more precisely outlined by other details). This could be true in the case of a harmonious description, where all elements combine (even though with different degrees of importance) in an unambiguous representation of a given character.

Things are very different, however, when we deal with descriptions in a detective story; in that case the heterogeneity of the various elements ought to be selectively and critically examined. It is necessary to choose an interpretative approach which foregrounds certain features of reality to the detriment of others; these will be bracketed and considered deviant, deceptive, or simply useless. It is quite simple, even for a less-than-competent reader, to isolate the superfluous details, those which are used to embellish the narration: for example, the accurate

135

description of a character who is possibly involved in the story as a victim or as a figure of secondary importance. In the same fashion some description of landscapes, in creating an atmosphere which fits the tragedy that happened or is going to happen, serve the same function. It is also relatively easy to distinguish an important remark from an accessory one in a given description. Let us analyze this passage: "My villa is situated upon the southern slope of the downs, commanding a great view of the Channel. At this point the coast-line is entirely of chalk cliffs, which can only be descended by a single, long, tortuous path, which is steep and slippery. At the bottom of the path lie a hundred yards of pebbles and shingle, even when the tide is at full. Here and there, however, there are curves and hollows which make splendid swimming-pools filled afresh with each flow" (LION).

Undoubtedly the reader's attention is caught by the detail of the *path* which creates a sudden spatial restriction, in opposition to the setting constituted by the cliff. We recognize here a typical descriptive mechanism, which is also related to stylistic devices. From an undefined portion of space, on which the narrator's eye looks with that movement called "panorama" in cinema, we suddenly pass to a "close-up"; and the elements, originally disguised in the background, are now designated "pertinent," that is, shown as significant and relevant. However, this syntactical or morphological privilege is still unmotivated from a semantic point of view; we sense the importance of the path, "steep and slippery," but we remain in the dark as to its use and fate. In reference to other descriptive details, such as "Here and there, however, there are curves and hollows which make splendid swimming-pools . . . ," they obviously have a merely ornamental function.

So the reader is compelled to play an active role, even if he can measure out the degree of his participation, interrupting his reading to reflect on the data already acquired, or instead letting the flow of events carry him on as far as possible. In light of U.Eco's suggestive theory of textual cooperation, as outlined in *The Role of the Reader* (1979), the reader's "passivity" appears to be a borderline case. Moreover, the mechanisms of the detective story work in relation to certain hypotheses (more or less spontaneous, more or less critically evaluated), to which readers are led to refer, according to the way in which the tale is presented to them. If the detective story can be defined as a tale which consists of the *production of symptoms,* then it is obvious that the reader, invited to decipher them, can never completely escape this pressure. On the contrary, reading implies continuous decisions in order to control the pressure of clues. Knowing that not everything is relevant in the presentation (already filtered) made by the narrator, the problem is that of separating the enigmatic and discrete discourse of symptoms from that of evidence (often a deafening one).

We have already seen a first series of examples in regard to which it does not seem too difficult to make a choice. A second series could be constituted by the traces the detective finds at the scene of a crime. They should ideally constitute a clearly defined *corpus,* which can be enriched by means of accumulation during the investigation (without giving rise to conflicts among the various detectives). Actually, even in the case of traces (that is, elements contiguous to the crime) we notice a difference, and often a conflict, between the several persons inspecting them. Sherlock Holmes often reproaches Watson because he does not see what he has in front of him. But this imperfection does not totally depend on Sherlock Holmes's intellectual superiority. Obviously we do not expect Watson to be able to emulate his partner in determining a man's height on the basis of the length of his steps, or in a detailed classification of some ashes. However, this information, even of the sort most inaccessible to the reader, is always available to the narrator, and yet he does not know how to derive any benefit out of it. "You have not observed. And yet you have seen" (SCAN). Somewhere else Holmes tells him: "You did not know where to look, and so you missed all that was important" (IDEN).

We shall go deeper in Sherlock Holmes's method further on, but we can anticipate Watson's difficulty, the same as that of the police detectives, in concentrating on details, on trifles, that is, in isolating symptomatic elements out of the setting in which they are apparently absorbed. Think of the dumbbell in VALL. It is Sherlock Holmes who decides to consider its absence as a symptom; from this decision a new interpretation will arise.

Therefore, the semiotic status of an observed fact is determined by hypotheses: the symptomatic value of a certain element of reality, its referential value, is derived from the decision—taken as a conjecture—to consider it as pertinent. For this reason we perceive an unceasing redefinition of the frames that structure and enclose an event. What was first considered as a clue of guilt (as in LION), Professor Murdoch's reticence to explain why he visited the Bellamys turns out to be a delicate and humanitarian deed; in this case the perception of his semiotic status was not wrong (it was indeed a symptom), but the inferential process that it triggers is overly hasty. On the contrary, a fact which is supposed to have no value as a clue (like the tempest at the beginning of LION) authorizes the later hypothesis that unusual animals have been transported into the waters of Sussex.

The traditional distinction between *sign* and *symptom,* based on artificiality, arbitrariness, and conventionality in the case of the former, and on naturality, non-arbitrariness, and motivation in the case of the latter, is not completely satisfying in regard to the texts under consideration here, at least if we hold it to be an ironclad distinction. The inherent difficulties of such an approach appear especially when dealing with cases of simulation, that is, voluntary production of symptoms. Think, for instance, of a footprint on a beach. Even if it appears as an evident case of a "natural sign," there is a chance that, under particular circumstances, it could be intentionally produced in order to lead any investigation astray. It depends upon the interpretative hypothesis, upon the detective's (motivated) choice to consider it as either a sign or as a symptom. For example, a footprint on a windowsill (VALL) has been made by the murderer in order to make everyone believe he escaped that way. Of course, simulation, being the creation of a surreptitious but not completely groundless reality, is based on the coherence and probability of the clue it produces. In the case of the above situation, its incongruities threaten to turn against the person who originally produced the false clue.

Holmes's simulation in order to unmask an old enemy instead works out perfectly (DYIN). This is, for various reasons, a very peculiar story: first, the simulator is the person who usually has an interpretative role (Holmes's disguises are frequent, but only in this particular case does his masking constitute the center of narration); second, simulation involves the narrator himself much more than in any other story. Not only does Watson ignore Holmes's attempt, but his ignorance is the necessary condition for ultimate success.

Here a typical feature of Conan Doyle's detective stories is missing, that of the narration based on a difference of glances: the difference between Holmes's and Watson's perception is amplified in the extreme, both qualitatively and chronologically. The usual confrontation between their different ways of observation is delayed until the final *coup de théâtre* when Watson realizes that he is the victim of the same deceit as is Culverton Smith, Holmes's prey. Even the usual hierarchy of characters, in relation to forms of knowledge, appears created in a very peculiar way when compared to the "typical" Conan Doyle story. According to this hierarchy, Holmes always hovers over Watson, but Watson does not necessarily hover over the reader. When the reader disposes of both the narrator's perceptual data and Holmes's observations, he can at least sense in which direction the inferential process must go. However, the identification between Watson and the reader, in the above-mentioned story, can be called into question. In fact we suspect—we must suspect—from his somewhat inconsistent behaviour, that Sherlock Holmes is simulating mortal illness. We can say that, given the *frame*, "ill person lying in bed, needs attention," the fact that Holmes prohibits his friend from getting close to the bed breaks the clever scene painted by the simulator.

The transmission of truth in a detective story is achieved through details, apparently trivial fragments, odd things on which our attention concentrates only with hesitation. In fact we are distracted by other details and, most of all, by the story's general aspects. The most revealing details are but those which break the frame, showing its incoherence. They are its "missing acts."

Therefore we can extend the concept of frame to the *false solution,* which is usually outlined by a policeman, or by Watson, or by Sherlock Holmes himself in a beginning phase. Obviously, in certain stories where Holmes narrates in the first person, the function of outlining a false solution is presumably filled by him (see Shklovskij 1925 for the pattern of "mystery story").

We find an effective example of the problem of coherence in a set of clues arranged for simulation in the world of the fairy tale. We chose for this purpose the tale called *The Wolf and the Seven Kids,* from the Grimm brothers' collection. The wolf tries twice to get into the house where the kid goats are locked in, waiting for the return of their mother. And twice he fails, because of an incomplete or incoherent act of simulation. The first time he is betrayed by his hoarse voice; the second time (after he softened his voice by chewing a piece of clay) by his black paw lying on the window. On the third attempt he is more careful; having whitened his paw with flour, he successfully deceives the kids, who open the door. Only one of them saves himself, hiding in the grandfather clock, almost as if he had suspected a snare, despite the wolf's skilled deceit. Therefore not even the *coherence* of a set of clues authorizes a trustful or inattentive attitude on the part of the investigator. In this fairy tale, the six kids "represent" the absentminded reader, one who easily believes in appearances; they incautiously consider as a *sign* what, on the contrary, should be also intended as a possible *symptom* of another reality. Therefore, if it is true that the process of reading a detective story implies the transformation of symptoms into signs, it is important that this decoding procedure be valid for a large enough number of cases. In other words, it must pass a sufficiently difficult falsification exam.

As we said, simulation can be not only the result of an act of concealment performed by the criminal or by the policeman who wants to unmask him, but it can also be the result of our hypotheses. It is up to our perception of things to consider a clue as sufficiently valid, changing its status from symptom to sign. The seventh kid is the one who is not satisfied with the coherence of the symptoms because he is afraid of not having gathered enough of them, that is, of not having a big enough *receptacle*. This is the role Holmes usually plays. The universe of the detective story shows both incomprehensible *discontinuities* —a worn-out, loose reality, where mysterious elements shine in isolation—and fictitious *continuities* —misleading evidence, wrong connections, inadequate hypotheses, seductive fictions, persuasive mistakes. On the one hand, this universe shows difficulties or gaps that come to be considered ridiculous; on the other hand, it seems to help our classificatory and interpretative work, but with only apparently univocal facts. For these reasons the detective has to fight the tendency to dissimulate important data, recognizing them in the uniformity of the setting or in the proliferation of nonpertinent elements; but he also has to fight the tendency, on the part of both himself and others, to simulate answers that ignore or cover up the questions, not blatant questions but decisive ones, in working toward the end of an investigation.

II. THE PARADIGM, THE RECEPTACLE, AND THE LIGHTHOUSE

Holmes's ideal is that investigation ought to be, or become, a science: the positivistic mind dreams of extending rational and checkable procedures to the domain of traces, symptoms, clues, that is, to the dominion of *individual* facts. By this definition we mean all those entities (or better: micro-entities) whose meaning does not seem to depend upon a relationship with a general law, but on the link with a certain portion of reality. The detective's duty is that of drawing a line to connect two points—the clue and the guilty party—but never according to a principle of constant regularities and connections. The art of detection would belong to the sphere of those *disciplines of clues and symptoms* which, as Carlo Ginzburg said (Ch. 4), persist in Western culture (even with the status of "minor" knowledge) up to the point of constituting a real *paradigm*. Its origins would be related to hunting and divination; curiously this has been recently—and independently—reformulated by René Thom (1972), who has established as fundamental pattern for the birth of stories that of *predation*. (The basic sense of this is that at the bottom anthropological "universals" are lying, hardly attainable even with highly elaborated tools.)

Is this the case of the emergence of a specific form of rationality? At first sight, the paradigm seems to be clearly opposed to the one we could call the "Galilean paradigm," to be considered as the idea of universalizing, abstracting, quantifying reason. While the scientific method, developed from Galileo on (as far as the modern age is concerned), has tended to eliminate the individual, identifying it with an extrinsic accidentality, with a superfluous and accessory aspect, the "circumstantial method" emphasizes the humblest details just because of their individualizing attitude. The aim of these two forms of knowledge is in the first case universality, and in the second singularity. In the first case a law, in the second an empirical fact.

However, suspicions arose about the legitimacy of an absolute opposition of the two paradigms: M. Vegetti (1978), for instance, called attention to the possible permanence of a style of rationality in methods which are apparently different; Ginzburg himself (even if in another sense) mentioned the necessity of disarticulating the paradigm during its creation.

In fact—to go back to Sherlock Holmes—some points have to be made, besides the explanation of some misunderstandings which are not only terminological in nature. Let us consider, for instance, Holmes's imprecision, when he says that the "faculties of deduction and logical synthesis" are his "special province" (COPP). The word "deduction" comes back in another passage, an important one toward a definition of Holmes's epistemology: among the essential qualities of an ideal policeman, Sherlock Holmes lists "power of observation," "of deduction," and "knowledge" (SIGN). But, as others have already stated, the inferential procedure of a detective for his hypothetical reconstructions cannot be correctly called "deduction." Régis Messac (1929), reminds us that deduction consists in reaching particular conclusions from general premises, whereas induction refers to the opposite process and that Holmes's reasonings are based on a particular fact and lead to another particular fact in ways of various length. M. Truzzi (Ch. 3) showed the resemblance between Conan Doyle's "deduction" and Peirce's "abduction," anticipating a thesis recently stated by the Sebeoks in their "Juxtaposition of Charles S. Peirce and Sherlock Holmes" (Ch. 2).

It is therefore obvious that Holmes's rationality has its center in an inferential form which is also a common one, but which was described for the first time by Charles S. Peirce. According to the American philosopher, one of the most dangerous confusions consists "in regarding abduction and induction taken together (often mixed also with deduction) as a simple argument" (7.218). Given that the detective always reflects beginning from the facts, a confrontation between abduction and induction is probably more remarkable (the term "deduction" being obviously improper). Induction is based on a comparative process. It is a comparison of homogeneous facts, samples of a certain class; from this comparison, it enunciates general properties. Abduction on the contrary is based on a single fact, which sometimes presents itself as an enigma, something unexplainable: at this point the observer postulates a hypothesis, that is, he puts an idea into reality by asking himself if it can be demonstrated. Facing mysterious cases, abduction can be so described: "x is extraordinary; however, if y would be true, x would not be extraordinary anymore; so, x is possibly true." According to Sherlock Holmes's words: "It is an old maxim of mine that when you have excluded the impossible, whatever remains, however improbable, must be the truth" (BERY).

Peirce insisted on induction's lack of originality, opposing to it the creative character of the hypotheses generated by abduction. This recalls the Holmesian motif of *imagination,* which even gifted policemen unfortunately lack: "Inspector Gregory, to whom the case has been committed, is an extremely competent officer. Were he but gifted with imagination he might rise to great heights in his profession" (SILV). The heuristic character of this power, which is not a vague one, is reconfirmed in the following passage: " 'See the value of imagination,' said Holmes. 'It is the one quality which Gregory lacks. We imagined what might have happened, acted upon the supposition and find ourselves justified. Let us proceed' " (ibid.).

On the other hand, every detective is necessarily obliged to formulate hypotheses; so we discover that the policeman's main fault can be more one of excess than of a lack of imagination. In this case Holmes opposes the *naturalness* of his reasoning to the *artificial* and *contorted* aspects of the policeman's mind: " 'The case has been an interesting one,' remarked Holmes. ' . . . because it serves to show very clearly how simple the explanation may be of an affair which at first sight seems to be almost inexplicable. Nothing could be more natural then the sequence of events as narrated by this lady, and nothing stranger than the result when viewed, for instance, by Mr. Lestrade, of Scotland Yard' " (NOBL).

Another interesting example comes from LION. A man is killed in an appalling and inexplicable way: "His back was covered with dark red lines, as though he had been terribly flogged by a thin wire scourge." On the means of the murder many doubts remain, even after Sherlock Holmes's examination of the corpse with a magnifying glass. The hypothesis of the policeman—in this case, Inspector Bardle—is a sort of *simple inference,* imaginative but unlikely. From the difference in the intensity of the signs, he is driven to think that "if a red-hot net of wire had been laid across the back, then these better marked points would represent where the meshes crossed each other" (ibid.). The flaw in such reasoning is rather obvious. It takes the form of an inference which is strictly functional to the explanation of a unique detail; it loses its likelihood as soon as it is related to the context (it is strictly "local"). On the contrary, the Holmesian abduction is an attempt to find both a natural and coherent explanation, that is "natural" inasmuch as it allows without any contradiction, omission, or forcing of things the set of elements constituting the whole of circumstantial evidence to be satisfied. Abduction cannot allow itself to be seduced by a resemblance: "*if* [italics mine] a red-hot net of wire had been laid across the back . . . ." This hypothesis is both lacking in imagination (because it is too "contiguous" to the circumstantial evidence) and at the same time much too imaginative (because not submitted to contextual bonds).

Thus we begin to understand that the problem of a correct inference cannot be separated from that of a right method of data collection and evaluation. To postulate a good hypothesis means to choose a fixable starting point (better still: a point of support). Holmes boasts many times to Watson that he never guesses: "I never guess" (SIGN). As a matter of fact, as Sebeok pointed out, the brilliant chain of reasonings with which Holmes amazes his friend (or other characters in his stories) is not totally without a certain margin of luck in intuition. But basically the success of these reconstructions avoids the arbitrary thanks to these two procedures: first of all, in choosing a quite solid point of support, secondly in progressively eliminating the hypotheses (still rather numerous) that are legitimized by the choice of that very point. The verification and exclusion of such hypotheses often means further research, which generates further narrative possibilities: "I have devised seven separate explanations, each of which would cover the facts as far as we know them. But which of these is correct can only be determined by the fresh information which we shall no doubt find waiting for us" (COPP).

In reference to the circle "hypotheses/facts/hypotheses," we could ask ourselves where the beginning actually is. This problem, no minor one, is one of the main themes of Karl Popper's (1972) epistemology in his critique of the neopositivism of the Vienna Circle. Popper is known for having substituted the method of *falsification* for that of *verification* as a yardstick of judgment of the scientificity of a given theory. No theory can be verified once and for all. On the other hand, a theory can be declared unsatisfactory or false when one of the propositions deriving from its general premises is contradicted during an experiment. This radical transformation in the problem of a scientific control comports various epistemological consequences, among others, a new way of considering the relationship between *facts* and *hypotheses*. With such a stress on falsification, that is, on the scientist's need to construct better and better theories capable of undergoing more and more difficult controls, the idea of the existence of facts that are able to speak a univocal language is strongly weakened. If this were the case, the problem of an absolute and complete verification of a theory would not seem so unresolvable. But "facts," even though they constitute nuclei of resistance which are able to oppose arbitrary hypothezation, do not constitute those atomic and univocal entities in which the positivistic tradition puts its faith, in order to support its scientific discoveries irrevocably. In Popper's interpretation of scientific work, things are stressed *a parte subiecti.* Therefore he asserts that the hypothesis (or expectation, or theory, or no matter what we may want to call it) precedes the observation, even if an observation that refutes a certain hypothesis can provoke a new (and therefore temporally anterior) hypothesis.

In a lecture published in *Objective Knowledge* (Popper 1972), we find the opposition between the theory of the lighthouse and that of the receptacle. The latter one, which corresponds to the empiricist tradition criticized by Popper, considers the human mind in terms of a receptacle in which the data of perceptual experience can be collected. The former, on the contrary, is based on the theory that every observation is preceded by a problem, an hypothesis. Our observations are therefore always selective and they suppose something like a selective principle. Holmes's thought, as I have elsewhere suggested and will continue to stress, takes place in terms of a complementarity between the *attic* (the receptacle) and the *magnifying glass* (the lighthouse) in LION.

III. BETWEEN ENIGMA AND MYSTERY

At certain points, Sherlock Holmes seems to set himself up as an apologist for the facts, against every sort of anticipation and priority on the part of hypotheses. We find him recommending a strict control over his own imagination: "The temptation to form premature theories upon insufficient data is the bane of our profession. I can see only two things for certain at present—a great brain in London, and a dead man in Sussex" (VALL). Elsewhere, Holmes seems absolutely integratable into the frame of Popper's epistemology: " 'I cannot think how I came to overlook it,' said the inspector with an expression of annoyance [referring to a match]. 'It was invisible, buried in the mud. I only saw it because I was looking for it' " (SILV). We could not find a more explicit statement on the primacy of the hypotheses or, in other words, of the fact that "an observation is a planned and prepared perception" (Popper). The next problem is now to verify if there is a real opposition between the above-mentioned attitudes.

After all, Holmes's steadfast resistance to the tendency to anticipate a solution is not the same as saying that the facts themselves, with their univocal language, impose the only plausible interpretation. In a universe where a principle of simulation has to be always suspected, univocal facts or irrefutable evidence do not exist: " 'Circumstantial evidence is a very tricky thing,' answered Holmes thoughtfully. 'It may seem to point very straight to one thing, but if you shift your own point of view a little, you may find it pointing in an equally uncompromising manner to something entirely different' " (BOSC). In fact, we should not forget that, in the realm of the detective story, *to qualify a given datum as a "fact" means to say that a symptom has been already and once and for all transformed into a sign.* But this becomes possible only in the final stage of the investigation, when all or some clues find a coherent and exhaustive position. Two limitations prevent the consideration of a symptom as a fact: the contextual bonds, which cast different lights on this, and the possibility of simulation, that is, of the intentional fabrication of "evidence." That is why even the most apparently reliable datum is "a very tricky thing."

Therefore the value of an event depends upon the *lighthouse* which lights it; it is the hypothesis which allows us to notice a *dissimulated* element of the setting (see the example of the match). Because the meaning of the already visible data depends upon their relationship with the still-invisible data, which can be discovered only through hypothesis, it seems right to conclude that Conan Doyle's epistemology is very far from that proposed by neopositivistic philosophy.

Holmes's anthropology, however, seems at least partially positivisitic: its general assumption is the uniformity of the species. This uniformity guarantees Holmes's certainty in reconstructing; that is, the possibility of giving an explanation thanks to "the knowledge of preexisting cases" (NOBL). This kind of statement has a tendency to move Holmes's method from a *local* level, dominated by variables, to a *global* one. We must remember that the supremacy of the local, which seems to be peculiar to a paradigm based on circumstantial evidence, does not imply an absolute exclusion of regularity. On the contrary, regularities constitute the medium of the abductive process, by permitting a connection between two particular facts. It is for instance thanks to regularity—"It is seldom that any man, unless he is very full-blooded, breaks out in his way through emotion" (STUD)—that Holmes can say to the incredulous policemen that the murderer in this story is a strong ruddy-faced man.

However, not all of the uniformities Holmes uses during his interpretations can claim the same degree of generality: according to Holmes, the hesitating attitude of a woman toward the doorbell "always means an *affaire de coeur*" (IDEN). Such daring generalizations are allowable only in a universe with a lasting anthropology and a well-defined typology of characters.

It is interesting to consider once more the local/global couple in order to compare Sherlock Holmes's and Watson's cognitive strategies. The fact that the second is constantly outclassed by the first should not obscure the fact that Watson's eye (so similar, from various points of view, to the policeman's eye) obeys certain rules and principles. For Holmes's partner, reality is characterized by a clear alternation between areas of likelihood and areas of mystery. When the reality of circumstantial evidence suggests by itself an explanation, "when the account is correct" because there is a likely reconstruction, Watson considers this as the end of the investigation, without any further inquiry to explain certain still-unsolved *details*. Proceeding in this manner, Inspector Bardle thinks it is a good point to arrest Professor Murdoch, despite the big gaps still to be filled in (as Holmes points out to him in LION), such as the mysterious words McPherson utters before dying. The Inspector's reasoning can be schematized as follows: insofar as there must be a murderer, and insofar as the only suspect is Murdoch an arrest is necessary . . . in order to avoid public criticism.

In contradistinction to the areas of likelihood, Watson is impotent in the area where the mystery starts, a thick and unfathomable one, because he cannot concentrate on those trifles which allow Holmes to solve the enigma. There seems to be a relation between these two aspects: the mystery is nothing else than a sudden change of a local situation into a global one. Holmes's and Watson's different strategies correspond to two different attitudes of the detective story reader. Inevitably the Watson-like reader ends up asking himself too many global questions, such as "who is guilty?", whereas for the Holmes-like reader it is more important to understand (at least in those stories where the solution is not suddenly told, as in RESI), what is the circumstantial evidence to be valorized, evidence which probably has already been valorized by Conan Doyle's hero.

With Holmes, the relationship between the local and the global is always a function of abductive reasoning: to solve the enigma, regularities have to be found. For Watson, either the local already has its own explanation—irrefutable evidence—or we get lost in an entropy of circumstantial evidence; in its darkness, the only possible actions are simple inferences, that is, unlikely and contradictory hypotheses. Therefore "small facts" are the key for the local/global relationship in Sherlock Holmes's strategy.

Their function is not only heuristic, but also corrective, obviously even Sherlock Holmes himself finds wrong solutions. In such cases, his superiority over the other method consists in not refusing the falsification of a hypothesis by some unexplained trifle. If the police can boast of a success, Holmes always maintains a professional honesty which is also a kind of scientific rigor. According to Popper's theories, Holmes does not refuse to scrutinize his own theories rigorously and he mistrusts the first positive confirmations of the hypotheses.

After examining the power of "deduction" (that is, abduction), and "the power of observation" (that is, observing what is invisible to many people), we shall now analyze the third quality of an ideal policeman, as expressed in SIGN: knowledge. For Watson, in the first of Conan Doyle's novels, one of the most curious and amazing things is the vastness, heterogeneity, and discontinuity of Sherlock Holmes's knowledge. He even writes down a list of his kinds of knowledge, but he fails both to find a unifying point and to discover their ultimate aim. Exceptionally good in certain fields, Holmes does not even try to hide his ignorance of certain supposedly universally known notions. One day Watson discovers that his friend ignores Copernican theory and the structure of the solar system (STUD). But he is even more surprised when Holmes justifies himself for his extreme specialization of knowledge: "a man's brain originally is like a little empty attic, and you have to stock it with such furniture as you choose. A fool takes in all the number of every sort that he comes across, so that the knowledge which might be useful to him gets crowded out, or at best is jumbled up with a lot of other things, so that he has difficulty in laying his hands upon it. Now the skillful workman is very careful indeed as to what he takes into his brain-attic. He will have nothing but the tools which may help him in doing his work, but of these he has a large assortment, and all in the most perfect order" (STUD). This ideal, however, is not easily attainable; later on, Holmes acknowledges the impossibility of a scientific systemization of his theories: "My mind is like a crowded box-room with packets of all sorts stowed away therein—so many that I may well have but a vague perception of what was there" (LION). Sometimes we see that Holmes acts in regard to his mind in the same way that he does in regard to external reality. In the above-quoted story he rummages in a room full of books, in his house, without knowing what he is really looking for: "I had known that there was something which might bear upon this matter. It was still vague, but at least I knew how I could make it clear" (ibid.).

Crime brings disorder. The traces of a crime bring confusion into the transparent (until then, anyway) sphere of reality; Holmes opposes to all this another kind of disorder, which partially reflects the first one. In

fact, the detective must adapt himself to his adversary, to the am-
biguities the latter created to mix things up and to generate confusion.
Let us consider this passage, by Detienne and Vernant (1978), mentally
substituting the word "detective" for the word "doctor": "To see our
way clear in this world of uncertain symptoms, the *detective* needs all the
resources of an intelligence as polymorphic as the adversary is pro-
teiform." Let us recall the importance of disguise in Conan Doyle's
stories. Besides, it is almost a *topos* that the guilty party should visit
Sherlock Holmes's house in disguise, after an enticement by the detective. Therefore many investigations end up right in Holmes's room, a
room whose external confusion indicates both that chaos which he will
bring back to order, and that attic full of objects of every kind which is
Sherlock Holmes's mind.

IV. ETHICS, LOGIC, AND THE MASK

We can easily compare Sherlock Holmes's inner space to an encyclopedia, not only for its variety and vastness of knowledge, but also for
the impossibility of having them all under control to the same degree,
from the mnemonic point of view: "I may well have but a vague perception of what was there" (LION). On the other hand, we know that
Holmes makes a great effort to keep them in order, an order which
allows him to limit the number of possible associative chains and to
come to a conclusion; for instance, to go back to the *Cyanea Capillata*
in order to explain McPherson's horrible death (ibid.). In this case,
memory too works as a mechanism which produces circumstantial evidence: the detective knows that he read "something on that, in a book"
(ibid.) whose title he cannot remember. This is enough for him to check
his room and find the book he vaguely remembered. As always,
Holmes finds what he is looking for because he knows where to look.

Let us go back to the concept of "encyclopedia," more semiotically, in
its relation with the "dictionary" (as postulated in Eco 1976). Whereas
an encyclopedia shows reality through the enumeration of the cultural
variables through which its objects are thought, a dictionary uses much
more powerful categorical filters and emphasizes the most abstract net-
works of knowledge. This is the difference between an "historical" and
an "ideal" competence of knowledge. Even if Conan Doyle's texts are
not detailed on this subject, we have the impression that Holmes dominates the notorious and proliferating vastness of his thought through
dictionary-type filters and divisions.

The exclusion of knowledge, however, which is not oriented toward
investigation is not Holmes's only precaution to keep his mind com-

pletely efficient. A second barrier, as rigid and insuperable as the first one, must be built up against the risk of passions and particularly of "softer passions." Of course, this is valid only in the case of a personal involvement. "They were admirable things for the observer—excellent for drawing the veil from men's motives and actions" (SCAN). Passion is therefore a shortcut to knowledge, a possible means of getting to the truth without the obstacle of simulation. It is a utopia of transparent signs which guarantee actual knowledge of and control over a universe of circumstantial evidence. But what is most valuable for the observer is dangerous for the thinker: "for the trained reasoner to admit such intrusions into his own delicate and finely adjusted temperament was to introduce a distracting factor which might throw a doubt upon all his mental results. Grit in a sensitive instrument, or a crack in one of his own high-power lenses, would not be more disturbing than a strong emotion in a nature such as his" (ibid.). We could suppose that emotional participation in somebody else's feelings could increase our knowledge (as supported by a certain philosophical current), but Holmes completely refuses this possibility. Feelings and passions are only the object of knowledge, and never its subject. Their "determinism," which helps interpretation by eliminating the masks, obscures the strategic ability of the researcher. Holmes's misogyny—sometimes interpreted as homosexual—has its basis in a theoretical need: if the detective wants his mind to be the mirror of that sequence of causes and effects which ended in a crime, he must get rid of every subjective element of nuisance. The logical purity of his reason should not be disturbed by feeling and pathos. The woman, who has the power of starting illogical (that is, passionate) mechanisms in man's mind, must be strictly excluded from the sphere of analytical and abductive reasoning.

This is proved *ex negativo* the only time Sherlock Holmes loses: it is to a woman—bound to remain for him *"the* woman" (ibid.)—that he suffers this letdown. To be honest, the story does not explicitly ascribe the failure to the intrusion of a passional element. Holmes's feelings that she could have awakened, are hidden under an impersonal formulation: "I only caught a glimpse of her at the moment, but she was a lovely woman, with a face that a man might die for" (ibid.). Should we suppose that the enunciator of these words is unconsciously implied in his enunciation? When he expresses regularities in the collective behavior, Holmes usually appears as a detached man: "When a woman thinks that her house is on fire, her instinct is at once to rush to the thing which she values the most" (ibid.). The enunciator is the exception who confirms the truth of his enunciations. And this exception is possible because as opposed to the common man, Holmes knows how to create inside himself a barrier between *pathos* and *logos,* thanks to which the first one never gets mixed up with the second one. This corresponds to the ideal of investigation as a science; that is, a form of knowledge whose validity does not depend upon the empirical features of the investigators.

It is worthwhile to note that in SCAN Sherlock Holmes is not in love, but there is at least one bit of circumstantial evidence from which we could suspect a weakening of his intellectual ability. The evening before the final *coup de théâtre,* a person—"a slim youth in an ulster" (ibid.)—says hello to Holmes near his house. He has a rather strange reaction: "Now, I wonder who the deuce that could have been" (ibid.).

It must be pointed out that Holmes had just told Watson that the Irene Adler case was solved, so that he does not begin any new investigation on that. However, this time he forgets his own rules: he disregards a trifle, the mysterious identity of the person who said hello to him, because he does not consider that pertinent to the case he is taking care of. This is a real transgression of the methodology he has successfully applied up to now: Holmes thinks that his receptacle already has all the necessary data. On another occasion, he would have thought of confronting the already-made hypothesis with the *new* (and unexplainable) *fact* which later emerged. Here he does not behave so differently from Watson or from the police: a premature end to the investigation, the refusal of taking into consideration a detail which spoils the harmony of the explanation, the underestimation of "small facts." Directing the lighthouse lamp onto this enigmatic greeting, that is, accepting it as pertinent, Holmes could still modify the dénouement of the story. Why does it not happen, why this time is Holmes won over by laziness? Because of a woman? Is it because Irene Adler's image gets into mechanisms which do not take into account her presence so that she is invisible to Sherlock Holmes's eyes?

The woman, however, fights the detective by his own means: to his masking she opposes her masking. But how many times Holmes, even at the beginning of this story, has been able to recognize the true identity of a person behind a masking! Here is Irene who acts according to all of Holmes's rules; slightly suspicious of the priest who entered her house, she overcomes the laziness which makes one forget the details, and decides to verify her suspicion, following Holmes under a male masking. The situation is reversed. For Holmes camouflage and metamorphosis are a real necessity: as a mythological hero who must put himself in somebody else's place in order to unmask their actions, he must simulate a false identity in order to move efficiently in a world of circumstantial evidence, fictions, and enigmas. The mask allows him to put into action (or to put more rapidly into action) channels of communication which otherwise would not work. In this case, he splits between the function of data-collector and data-processor, which takes place *in his house.* Only here Holmes can take the liberty of keeping his identity unchanged and transparent.

Irene Adler uses the same methods of Sherlock Holmes, and in doing so she unmasks him. Still, if she wins, it is because Holmes neglects to apply his own methods of knowledge. In the letter she leaves for him, she points this out, maybe with a touch of malice: "But, you know, I have been trained as an actress myself. Male costume is nothing new to me" (ibid.). In fact, Holmes forgot to apply his usual procedure. Let us recall one of Peirce's formulations: "x is extraordinary; however, if y would be true, x would not be extraordinary anymore; so x is possibly true." Here y is known; it would be enough to remember this fact. Therefore Holmes could have inferred as follows: "an unknown person says hello to me; Irene Adler is an actress, so she knows how to look like an unknown person; the person who said hello to me is possibly Irene Adler."

It is a part of the Holmes-hero status that he can be defeated only by a woman, and only once; both these features make Irene Adler *"the woman."* Therefore the woman represents a kind of taboo, a prohibited, excluded space. On the other hand, Dr. Watson represents the transparent and reliable space of complementarity; but this complementarity is necessary. We find here a fairly diffused literary *topos,* from the myth of Don Juan to Faust to Maupassant's tales. The couple servant/master is based on an inextricable connection, where oppositions and differences, functional divisions and alliances meet. Watson's need must be therefore understood in many respects: first of all, he makes possible a hierarchical articulation of knowledge, in which he obviously occupies the humblest position. On the other hand, there would be no right solution by Holmes without wrong ones by Watson: no good master looks as such if not confronted with a bad student. Many conversations between Holmes and Watson are reminiscent of a Socratic dialogue in which the student does not know how to proceed correctly without the continuous help and suggestions of the master, and has a tendency to put forth wrong opinions each time that he works by himself. We get to know, even if only partially, the right principles applied by Holmes just because of Watson's mistakes. Even Watson's blind stubbornness, his persisting in making the same mistakes, if functional in terms of the search for truth, because it allows a new control on the efficacy of the method.

Watson, even if prone to relapse and to be stubborn, is always submissive and always ready to accept his friend's corrections. This creates in a certain way a swinging back and forth of the space between the two characters. Their distance can range from a maximum extension, when they reason separately or when Holmes acts without telling his friend (who is obliged to stand still, passive, waiting for the other's action), to a minimum extension, represented by moments of a full cooperative agreement (to act, listen, wait together). In this second case, identity and agreement are so full as to make completely useless a physical distinction between the two. Therefore Holmes tells the prince who wants to speak privately to him: "You may say before this gentleman anything which you may say to me" (SCAN).

It is an ambiguous sentence. We see a highest expression of estimation, but at the same time, a malicious accent; none of Watson's virtues are enough to eliminate a suspicion of him as a wishy-washy man. Holmes knows Watson at least as well as he knows himself; he will never be surprised or disappointed. The hierarchical relation between the two is so solid as to allow the master every kind of manipulation of his servant. In DYIN, besides the angst of Holmes's illness, he must bear the bitterness of his insults: "after all, you are only a general practitioner with very limited experience and mediocre qualifications" (ibid.). Even if Watson looks hurt, the presumably ill person does not cease to show him how ignorant he is. In fact, we always find in the servant/master *topos* a certain form of sadism, even if a vague and softened one. But we can distinguish between two forms of this *topos*. In the first one, we see the possibility of an overturning of power relations (see *Don Quixote,* when Sancho emancipates himself from his master and takes advantage of his madness). In the second one, the hierarchical relation is not changed, but subordinated to a whole series of undertones, from cordiality and intimacy to an overbearing and complete exploitation of the partner.

From another point of view, Holmes and Watson do not appear in a relation of subordination and apparent complementarity, but in a relation of alternance and compensation. Watson's aspiration is to a quiet family ménage; when he decides to marry, his happiness and his home-centered interests constitute all his problems. Holmes does not look for a moral integration into the society he protects from crime: "Holmes, who loathed every form of society with his whole Bohemian soul, remained in our lodgings in Baker Street, buried among his old books, and alternating from week to week between cocaine and ambition, the drowsiness of the drug, and the fierce energy of his own keen nature. He was still, as ever, deeply attracted by the study of crime, and occupied his immense faculties and extraordinary powers of observation in following out those clues, and clearing up those mysteries which had been abandoned as hopeless by the official police" (SCAN).

But the features "Bohemian soul" and "every form of society," are not to be opposed conflictually, but are to be intended as complementary. Both characters represent a reconciliation of opposites: Holmes alternates an indomitable energy with periods of apathy, stressed by cocaine, and Watson alternates quiet family ménage and work to often dangerous adventures which keep him away from his daily world. But thanks to their duplicity they often have a reciprocal relation of harmony. When Holmes is apathetic, Watson is found to be active; and when Holmes puts his extraordinary ability into action, Watson is seduced to a slow, incapable, absentminded but always faithful disciple. Each is, in his own way, incapable of doing something on his own initiative: Holmes's relation with the world is always defined by a request ("a lack," according to Russian formalists). Holmes is always called to play a role of mender or transformer (to use cultural anthropologists jargon). He can—as can heroes, semigods, priests, shamans— overcome and eliminate contradictions in reality. He acts only when his ambition and his perspicacious nature are stimulated by some worthy fact. Watson too is pushed to act by a causality which is not inside him, and this causality is Holmes, symbolically represented in the beginning of SCAN. Watson walks along Baker Street and feels like seeing his old friend again. When he sees Holmes's silhouette passing over and over energetically behind the window of his room, any hesitation becomes impossible: "To me, who knew his every mood and habit, his attitude and manner told their own story. He was at work again" (ibid.). Here is Watson, involved in a new adventure, recalled to his function of narrator, that is, the role of passive witness of Holmes's activity.

The perfect knowledge he shows of his partner is remarkable. As to knowledge of attitude, Watson is on the same level of Holmes, balancing with that the rigid subordination which is established when we move on the investigative method's level. This probably recalls another of Sherlock Holmes's duplicities: his aim is not ethical but logical. To follow traces, to reveal enigmas, to explain mysteries: to bring back the chaos of clues to a world of signs. After this, his mission is over, and the police are the ones to enjoy the moral advantages of success. Holmes complains of that only to a certain extent. If he never gives himself up to jealousy, rivalry, narcissim, it is just because he knows that his power does not go beyond the sphere of *logos*. We can say—as in an admired sentence by Watson: "You would certainly have been burned, had you lived a few centuries ago" (SCAN)—that Holmes acts as a sorcerer or a diviner, in charge of unveiling some supposed mysteries. He is the oracle of ancient societies, showing everybody the truth. And his theoretical power ends where the practical one, that of justice, starts.

(TRANSLATED FROM ITALIAN BY ROBERTO CAGLIERO)

CHAPTER SEVEN

Jaakko Hintikka and Merrill B. Hintikka

Sherlock Holmes Confronts Modern Logic

TOWARD A THEORY OF INFORMATION-SEEKING THROUGH QUESTIONING

I. SHERLOCK HOLMES VS. PHILOSOPHERS ON DEDUCTION

If one looks at intelligent laymen's ideas about such concepts as deduction, inference, and logic, we find a curious contrast to the prevailing philosophical views. There used to be—and to some extent still is—a strong current of popular thinking which assigns to logic and logical inference an important role in gaining new information about virtually any subject matter. In contrast to such an opinion, Wittgenstein claimed in the *Tractatus* that all logical truths are tautological, and most philosophers have agreed with him. Even when some heretic philosopher has subsequently voiced doubts about Wittgenstein's conception, these verbal disagreements have seldom led to any serious attempts to spell out the precise sense in which deduction is supposed to yield new information. And even those happy few of us who have ventured further and have in fact defined concepts of deductive information have admitted that logical inference does not in some other valid sense increase our knowledge of empirical reality. What is more important, such recent theories of deductive information do not assign to it anything like the importance which the other line of thought ascribes to logic as a tool of obtaining nontrivial new information. Moreover, Wittgenstein's claim had little novelty about it. He was merely giving a deeper foundation to similar claims that had been made by his compatriots Ernst Mach and Moritz Schlick. And they were in turn part of a longer tradition which goes back at least to Descartes's criticisms of the value of syllogistic reasoning. It is hence correct to say that there is a veritable mainstream tradition of philosophers of logic who have denied the informativeness of logic and logical inference.

In contrast to their doctrine of the tautological nature of deductive reasoning there is the other type of view which was mentioned earlier and which we shall refer to as the Sherlock Holmes view on logic, deduction, and inference. Not surprisingly, the best description of these ideas of the great detective comes partly from that inimitable chronicler of the exploits of Sherlock Holmes, Dr. Watson, and partly from the great detective himself. It is indeed to Dr. Watson that we owe a summary of Sherlock's own article on his method, which is claimed to rest precisely on those reputedly useless procedures, deduction and inference.

> " . . . it attempted to show how much an observant man might learn by an accurate and systematic examination of all that came his way. . . . The reasoning was close and intense, but the deduction appeared . . . to be far fetched . . . Deceit, according to him, was an impossibility in the case of one trained to observation and analysis. His conclusions were as infallible as so many propositions of Euclid. So startling would his results appear to the uninitiated that until they learned the processes by which he had arrived at them they might well consider him a necromancer. 'From a drop of water,' said the writer [i.e., Sherlock Holmes], 'a logician could infer the possibility of an Atlantic or a Niagara without having seen or heard of one or the other. . . . All life is a great chain, the nature of which is known when even we are shown a single link of it. Like all other arts, the Science of Deduction and Analysis is one which can only be acquired by long and patient study. . . . ' " (STUD)

This illustrates a widespread view that deduction and logic are most useful in gaining substantial knowledge concerning the world and can indeed produce, in the mind of one trained in the "Science of Deduction and Analysis," completely unexpected results. Indeed, a little later Sherlock Holmes claims that "those rules of deduction laid down in that article of mine . . . are invaluable to me in practical work." Similar testimonies are easily forthcoming from the likes of Hercule Poirot and Nero Wolfe. This view represents an extreme contrast to the philosophers' idea of the value of logic in all information-gathering.

It seems to us that philosophers have far too casually dismissed the deductions of detectives as being either illegitimately so-called or else mere enthymemes, inferences from premises which have been only partially formulated. It is indeed true, we believe, that there is nothing in Holmes's "Science of Deduction and Analysis," which is in the last analysis incompatible with the philosophers' thesis that in one perfectly good sense of the word logical inferences are tautological. However, saying that leaves untouched the task of explaining those uses of logic—or is it "logic"?—which apparently yield new information. Collingwood was wrong in claiming the methods of a clever detective for his idealistic methodology of history and philosophy. But even apart from Collingwood, the Sherlock Holmes conception of deduction and logic presents an important challenge to philosophical logicians. Along with the task of reconciling somehow the surprising inferences of an acute detective with the philosophers' thesis of the tautological character of all logical deduction, we have in the arguments of Sherlock Holmes and his ilk an amusing and pedagogically handy source of application and illustrations. We believe that the very structure of "deduction" and "inference" in Sherlock Holmes's sense presents an important new task for philosophical logic. We cannot just take the familiar tools of contemporary philosophical logic and apply them to a new area. In order to understand the methods of a Sherlock Holmes and to discuss and to evaluate them rationally we need new conceptualizations. It is our purpose in this study to indicate what some of the relevant new concepts and results are that will enable us to do this. We believe that the resulting new theory in philosophical logic will soon have an abundance of other applications both in philosophy and outside of it that will look weightier than my perhaps somewhat seemingly frivolous references to Conan Doyle. Later, we shall try to indicate what some of these intra- and interdisciplinary applications might be.

II. MAKING TACIT INFORMATION EXPLICIT THROUGH QUESTIONING

The first observation we need here is pretty obvious, even though it later turns out to need major qualifications. What Sherlock is doing in his so-called deductions is not so much to draw explicit inferences from explicit premises. Often he is eliciting from an enormous mass of undigested background information the suitable additional premises, over and above what has perhaps been announced as such, from which the apparently surprising conclusion can be drawn by our familiar commonplace deductive logic. The schematic picture of the enterprise is therefore not this familiar proof-tree figure, where $p_1, p_2, \ldots, p_k$ are the requisite explicit premises and $c_1, \ldots, c_l$ the successive conclusions.

How are we to refine this schematic picture? The crucial part of the task of a Holmesian "logician," we are suggesting, is not so much to carry out logical deductions as *to elicit or to make explicit tacit informa-*

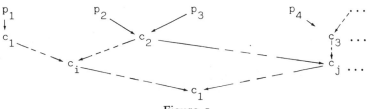

Figure 1

tion. This task is left unacknowledged in virtually all philosophical expositions of logical reasoning, of deductive heuristics, and of the methodology of logic and mathematics. For this neglect the excuse is sometimes offered that such processes of elucidation and explication cannot be systematized and subjected to rules. It may indeed be true that we are dealing here with problems which belong as much to heuristics as to logic or epistemology and also true that we cannot usually give effective rules for heuristic processes. It does not follow, however, that they cannot be rationally discussed and evaluated, given a suitable conceptual framework. It is the main purpose of this paper to sketch such a framework.

The key idea on which the framework is based is the notion of *question*. We shall consider the newly explicit (previously unacknowledged) premises as being answers to questions addressed to the tacit knower. The previously unacknowledged item of information is prompted to actuality by the question whose answer it is. In this sense, *the process of activating tacit knowledge is controlled by the questions which serve to elicit this information to actuality*. By studying these questions and the way they limit their answers we can in effect study the Holmesian "Science of Deduction." For example, one question can be better than another one in the sense that answers to the former will be more informative than answers to the latter. Our task of examining the actualization of tacit predeductive knowledge therefore becomes a part of a larger task of studying questions, answers, and their interrelations.

In other words, we can already see why a sharp theory of the question-answer relationship is absolutely vital for our enterprise. Our leading idea is to study certain types of information-gathering by thinking of the information as being obtained as answers to questions. The process can be controlled by choosing the questions appropriately. One cannot understand this control, however, without understanding how it is that a question determines its (full) answers, that is to say, without understanding the question-answer relationship.

III. THE STRUCTURE OF QUESTION-INFERENCE COMPLEXES

Thus we have to refine the schema in Fig. 1 by letting the premises p_1, p_2, to come about as answers to questions, answers which may be thought of as being based on tacit background information. However, this is not enough. It is not enough merely to think of each of the premises p_m as an answer to some question based on some tacit deeper premises m_1, m_2, . . . , somewhat like this:

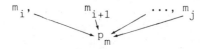

Figure 2

For one thing, the background information on the basis of which the relevant questions are answered may be impossible to capture by any finite (or countable) set of sentences of the language we are using. The content of one's information is specified by a set of sample-space points ("possible worlds"). There is no necessity that such a set is the set of models of any finite or countable set of sentences in a given language.

This already shows an advantage of the questioning model of information-gathering as compared with an inferential (deductive *or* inductive) model. An inference must be an inference from explicit sentences to an explicitly formulated conclusion, and they must all be formulated in some fixed language. There is no need that a question be answered on the basis of information that is specifiable in some given language even when both the question and its answer are formulated in that language. This gives the questioning model extra flexibility. It also shows that Fig. 2 is not the right way of making the schema in Fig. 1 more comprehensive in the way we want.

What we can explicitly indicate in our schema are only the different questions which prompt the appropriate premises as their answers. These answers are in the first place the premises p_1, p_2, . . . Hence the schema in Fig. 1 has to be replaced by something like this:

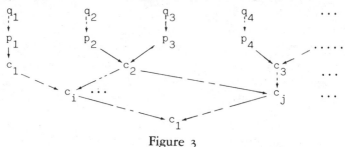

Figure 3

Here dotted lines indicate answers and solid lines inferences.

This is not yet a fully realistic picture. In 3, all questions are thought of as being answered on the sole basis of tacit background information. This is not realistic. The answers may be partly based on the inferential conclusions c_i. Hence any one part of Fig. 3 might have to be replaced by something like this:

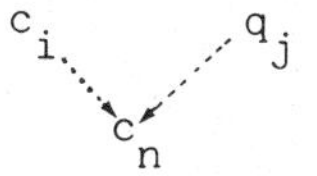

$$c_i \quad\quad q_j$$
$$c_n$$

Figure 4

In other words, answers to questions do not always precede (temporally or logically) deductive inferences. All these observations concerning the interplay of questions and inferences must of course be given a more explicit formulation later, in the same way as the rules of inference one is using must be formulated explicitly.

Several different points can meanwhile be raised by reference to our tentative schematic framework. One interesting conceptual link which we can now discuss within our framework is the connection between *memory* and *intelligence*. Eliciting tacit information by questioning can be viewed as one possible recall procedure. At the same time, it can be generalized so as to become a common model of several different kinds of information-gathering activities, deductive as well as inductive. This partially shared model for recall and intelligent inquiry may perhaps serve as an explication of a link between memory and intelligence.

For another thing, our general idea should not surprise any Sherlock Holmes fan. The *dénouement* of almost every successful story or novel in the Sherlock Holmes tradition can be paraphrased in the form of real or imaginary questions Holmes addressed to himself (or to the reader). In some cases, the great detective has to carry out an observation or even an experiment to answer the question. More frequently, all he has to do is to perform an *anamnesis* and recall certain items of information which he already had been given and which typically had been recorded in the story or novel for the use of the readers, too, or which are so elementary that any intelligent reader can be expected to know them. Take, for instance, the well-known incident of the dog in the night. Silver Blaze, the famous racehorse, had been stolen and his trainer had been found killed in the heath. Several suspects had cropped up, and all sorts of sundry information about the events of the fateful night had been recorded by the invaluable Dr. Watson. The import of Sherlock Holmes's famous comment on the "remarkable incident of the dog in the night" can be brought out by two questions: Did the trainer's watchdog in the stable bark when the horse was taken out by whoever stole it? The answer is known to be negative ("But the dog did not bark!" "*That* is the remarkable incident of the dog in the night.") Who is the only person a trained watchdog is likely not to bark at? His master, of course. Hence Sherlock Holmes's "deduction" of the role of the trainer.

Thus the role we have assigned to questioning in information-gathering is not unnatural in the context we have chosen to discuss it. Philosophers may nevertheless prefer to use as their paradigm the Socratic method of questioning or the process of scientific investigation, especially in a clinical context. We believe that these will be found to exhibit the same structural features as we are trying to discover in the Sherlock Holmes's "Science of Deduction."

IV. ON THE PRINCIPLE OF TOTAL EVIDENCE: BAYESIANISM

We can now also see one factor which has misled earlier analysts of human information-seeking, deductive as well as inductive. In the philosophy of empirical sciences this misleading assumption has been known as *the principle of total evidence.* Its role and its relative justification is seen best in theories which deal with scientific inferences in probabilistic terms as a series of steps of conditionalization. Such theories are sometimes called (somewhat inaccurately) Bayesian theories of scientific inference. Suppose we are given a prior probability distribution $P(x)$, and suppose that we have some background information e_0. Suppose we then obtain some new evidence e_1. What is the probability distribution which now represents our epistemic state? Clearly it is no longer $P(x)$ or even $P(x/e_1)$. It is $P(x/e_0 \& e_1)$. And here e_1 must really be thought of as codifying literally *all* one's pertinent information. Otherwise, our probabilistic treatment leads to paradoxes and mistakes, as can easily be shown.

This may be all right for small-scale applications, but it clearly tends to make Bayesian theories somewhat unrealistic models of actual large-scale scientific procedures. For in real-life applications it is very often literally impossible to contemplate actually or to write down *all* the potentially relevant information. There is in general no guarantee that this information can be codified in any one sentence (our "e_1") or a countable set of sentences of any one given language. Hence the need of imposing the requirement of total evidence is fairly generally acknowledged to be a weak point in Bayes-type probabilistic approaches to scientific inference.

This problem has been noted in the philosophy of science and has been discussed there to some extent. In our opinion, it is one of the most serious problems affecting Bayesian views of scientific inference.

It has not been pointed out, as far as we know, that there is a precisely analogous problem in the philosophy of deductive sciences. There, too, it has been assumed in studying inferential processes that all the relevant information has in some sense been already brought in and made instantly available. This is one of the oversimplifications involved in conceptualizing the situation depicted in Figs. 3 and 4 as if it were Fig. 1 or Fig. 2. It is a deductivist's version of the problem of total evidence. It is at least as desirable to develop means of dispensing with the deductivistic version of the principle of total evidence as it is to overcome its inductivistic version—which in the last analysis probably cannot be disentangled from each other. Even more importantly, we want to find means of discussing rationally and theorizing about those processes which serve to make our incomplete evidence (premises) more and more total. It seems to us that their study has been badly neglected by philosophers of logic, science, and knowledge.

V. THE ROLE OF OBSERVATIONS

In the spirit of these remarks, we can already see one important direction into which our observations can be extended beyond philosophical logic and philosophy of language. (This is one of the kinds of applications foreshadowed in our earlier remarks.) Not all of the items of background information need be thought of as having been there in the back of one's mind prior to our exercise. In other words, not all the questions that led to the premises p_i need be thought of as being addressed to oneself (i.e., to the logician in question). Some of the premises p_i and some of the intermediate conclusions c_n as depicted in Fig. 4 may be uncovered by suitable *observations* instead of having been part of one's background knowledge. However, the interesting thing is that *this does not change the picture* essentially. For we can still think of the premises p_i as having been elicited from a mass of merely potential knowledge by means of suitable questions. Only now some of them are questions put to nature in the form of pertinent observations. The different items of this potential knowledge need not be hidden somewhere in one's unconscious. They may simply be observable but so far unobserved facts. But this does not change the basic logical and methodological situation. We can still think of the new information (especially the premises p_i) as being obtained as answers to suitable questions. Observations actually made have to be chosen from a great many possible observations quite as much as actually used premises are selected from a wealth of collateral information. We can try to understand this choice of observations and the rest of their role in establishing certain conclusions by thinking of them as answers to questions put to nature. Then the relative virtues of different questions of this kind can be studied and assessed in the same way as the merits and demerits of questions which are calculated to tease out tacit information. It is in this way that the theory of information-seeking through questioning we are trying to develop becomes applicable beyond its first range of applications, namely, beyond the explication of tacit knowledge. Even though we cannot push the new applications very far in this paper, a few remarks are in order.

First, the Kantian metaphor of "putting questions to nature" receives in this way a less metaphoric explication, at least in one of its possible applications. The application we are giving to it is not merely metaphoric either, in that we can make many of the same concepts apply to observations as are applicable to questions and their answers. They include methodological concepts governing the choice of questions (including the choice observations or experiments), informational comparisons, and so forth.

Second, the dependence of observations on their theoretical background can now be discussed in a sharper manner than before. For instance, we have in recent years heard a lot of the theory-ladenness of observations. One can now see, however, that there is perhaps a sense in which we have a stronger reason to speak of the problem-ladenness or question-ladenness of observations. In our methodological model or perspective, an observation is always an answer to a question. This question-ladenness, of course, implies concept-ladenness. For an answer to a question normally has to be formulated in terms of the same concepts as the question was formulated in.

One can say more than this, however. Often, the correct way of expressing the content of one's observation is in the form of a conclusion which the imaginary bare observation allows us to draw, a conclusion which goes beyond the mere registration of one's sense-impression. This is precisely the kind of situation depicted in Fig. 4. The imaginary bare observation we can think of as one of the m_i's in the misleading Fig. 2, whereas the correct conceptualization of the actual observation is what we find in the schema in Fig. 4. What in Fig. 4 looks like an intermediate conclusion c_n in fact depends both on the question q_j to which it is an answer and on the interim conclusion c_i to which this question can be thought of as being conditional on.

One main reason for saying this is that the would-be chain of reasoning from the background information to the premises p_i and to the intermediate conclusions c_j can be completely unconscious. Again we can have classical illustrations among the most famous instance of Sher-lockianisms:

> " 'Dr. Watson, Mr. Sherlock Holmes,' said Stamford, introducing us.
> " 'How are you?' he said cordially, ... 'You have been in Afghanistan, I perceive.'
> " 'How on earth did you know that?' I asked in astonishment."

Later, Sherlock answers the question:

> " 'You appeared to be surprised when I told you, on our first meeting, that you had come from Afghanistan.'
> " 'You were told, no doubt.'
> " 'Nothing of the sort. I *knew* you came from Afghanistan. From long habit the train of thought ran so swiftly through my mind that I arrived at the conclusion without being conscious of intermediate steps. There were such steps, however. The train of reasoning ran, Here is a gentleman of a medical type, but with the air of a military man. Clearly an army doctor, then. He has just come from the tropics, for his face is dark, and that is not the natural tint of his skin, for his wrists are fair. He has undergone hard-ship and sickness, as his haggard face says clearly. His left arm has been injured. He holds it in a stiff and unnatural manner. Where in the tropics could an English army doctor have seen much hardship and got his arm wounded? Clearly in Afghanistan. The whole train of thought did not oc-cupy a second. . . . ' "
> " 'It is simple enough as you explain it,' I said, smiling." (STUD)

Several comments are in order here. First, one of the intermediate steps in Sherlock Holmes's rational reconstruction of his line of thought is literally obtained as an answer to the appropriate question. (Cf. "Where in the tropics . . . ?")

Second, contemporary psychology of perception confirms the appro-priateness of calling the "conclusion" n_j an *observation*. The question is whether the allegedly unconscious steps of reasoning are merely traversed so quickly as to escape active attention or whether they are sometimes truly inaccessible to conscious reflection and built right into one's unedited sense impressions. The answer we obtain from such psychologists as J.J. Gibson and David Katz affirms the latter alterna-tive. Perception, they tell us, means pickup of information, not pickup of unstructured sense-impressions, just as we have claimed.

This also vindicated Sherlock's habit of formulating his unconsciously reached conclusions as *perceiving that* statements, sometimes offered as equivalents to conclusions of deductions. For instance, concerning a deduction he had performed, Sherlock Holmes asks the faithful Dr. Watson: "So you actually were not able to *see* that that man was a sergeant of Marines?" (STUD). (Our italics.)

These observations already show something of the subtle interplay of observation and deduction which is characteristic of our model of information-seeking through questioning. In particular, they lead us to suspect that our Fig. 2 is oversimplified in still another important respect. There may not be any fundamental layer of starting points m_i at all. What happens in actually epistemic situations is double movement: downwards to ever richer conclusions and upwards toward more and more primitive data. There is no more reason to expect that the latter movement ever comes to a natural end than there is in the case of the former process.

In scientific contexts, too, the same structure is found. In an observational situation, much of the largely tacit background knowledge is taken for granted. This background knowledge corresponds to the m_i's of our schema in Fig. 2. What is actually registered as an observational statement is in our structure an intermediate conclusion c_n somewhere between the background information and the end-product conclusion, somewhat as in Fig. 4.

Along somewhat different and more general lines, we can now also understand the role of observations in the Holmesian conception of logic and deduction. In our introductory quote above, perhaps the most interesting and most puzzling feature that may strike the reader is the strange coexistence of the notions of, on the one hand, observation and, on the other hand, reasoning, deduction, analysis, inference, and logic. Sherlock Holmes's "compleat logycien" appears at times as the perfect observer who notes the most minute revealing features of the world around him. Holmes "claimed by a momentary expression, a twitch of a muscle or a glance of an eye, to fathom a man's inmost thoughts" (STUD). At other times, we seem to be presented with a complete reasoner who can in his mind run so swiftly through a long series of intermediate steps, following all the rules of deduction, that he himself need not be immediately conscious of them.

VI. QUESTION-ANSWER SEQUENCES AS GAMES AGAINST NATURE

From the perspective we have reached, one can now see what the connecting link between the two conceptions is. The missing link is questioning. Both the teasing out of previously unattended-to premises, which is what Sherlock Holmes calls deduction, and observation can be conceptualized as question-answer processes. Later, we will see that this similarity between observation and deduction can be pushed still further.

How precisely are we to study the uses of questions and answers for the (Sherlock Holmesian) purposes we are here interested in? The first and foremost problem confronting a logician here is to spell out the question-answer relationship. Somewhat surprisingly, we do not find a satisfactory answer in the earlier literature on the logic, semantics, grammar, or pragmatics of questions. (This surprise can be lessened somewhat by realizing what is involved in such an answer to the question of answerhood, namely, to spell out the logical and semantical relation of utterances made by two different speakers with different collateral information. This background knowledge has to be brought in, which logicians and linguists alike have refused to do.) Jaakko Hintikka has analyzed the question-answer relationship in a number of earlier works (See especially Hintikka 1976). Here we shall simply take the results of those earlier analyses for granted, including the crucial distinction between full and partial answers (replies) to a given question. Likewise, the important notion of presupposition is explained in those earlier writings.

How is the process of information-gathering through questioning and deduction to be conceptualized? We shall present a formalization which looks somewhat different from the one sketched above but which nevertheless embodies the ideas presented earlier. We can think of the process as a game against nature, which may alternately be thought of as the store of my own tacit information. The reason for using the concepts of game theory is that this theory is the best existing framework for studying any questions of strategy. In the present case, the relevant strategies would involve both strategems of questioning and interconnected with them strategems of deduction.

The game in question can be explained as follows:

There are two players, myself and nature. Speaking intuitively and tentatively, my aim is to prove a certain conclusion. C_0. Initially, I have at my disposal an initial premise C_1 (which may be vacuous). The different sentences which come up during the game may be thought of as being expressed in some fixed first-order language which is extended only so that questions can be asked in the extended language. (Some extensions will be explained later.) The course of the game can be described by reference to a scorekeeping device which is not unlike Beth's (1955) semantical *tableaux*. The differences will be explained later. At this point all that needs to be noted is that we shall call this scoresheet a tableau and that we can use about them the same terminology as about Beth's *tableaux*. In particular, we shall use the notion of closure, the notions of the left column and the right column, and the notion of *subtableau* in the same way as Beth. The different *subtableaux* of a given tableau are related in the same way as in Beth, that is disjunctively. They all have to be closed for the *tableau* itself to be closed.

Our use of Beth's *tableaux* is in keeping with the best traditions of Sherlock Holmes, who speaks in connection with his "Science of Deduction" of *analysis*. As Beth pointed out in his very first paper on the subject, the *tableau* method is an excellent reconstruction of the old idea of analytical method. Beth's reconstruction of the traditional method is applicable only in the realm of deduction, however. What we are doing here can be thought of as an extension of Beth's "Science of Deduction and Analysis" beyond its narrowly deductive applications.

Initially, the *tableau* contains C_0 in its right column and C_1 in its left column. There are moves of three different kinds: (1) deductive moves; (2) interrogative moves; (3) definitory moves.

(1) The rules for making deductive moves are the same as in any usual formulation of the *tableau* method.

As Jaakko Hintikka has argued elsewhere (1979), there nevertheless are reasons to modify all the *tableau* rules in the same way as some of them are modified in the transition from classical to intuitionistic logic and to allow only one sentence at any one time in the right column of any one *subtableau*.

The instantiation rules of *tableau* construction can extend our initially given language by introducing dummy names (indefinite individuals). We assume that this is possible only when an existential sentence is instantiated in the left column or a universally quantified sentence is instantiated in the right column of a *subtableau*.

(2) An interrogative move is relative to a *subtableau* σ_j. It consists of a question addressed by me to nature. The presupposition of the question must occur in the left column of the *subtableau*. Nature must provide a full answer. Let this answer be A_i. Then A_i is added to the left column of σ_j.

For simplicity, we shall assume that a full answer can always be given, in the sense of a substitution-instance of the matrix of the question which together with certain supplementary information provided by the answerer is a full answer. This supplementary information will be introduced into the left column of σ_j together with the rest of the answer.

Substituting terms must be individual constants (in the case of wh-questions).

The fullness of nature's reply is to be judged in the basis of my background knowledge plus the assumption that I know the truth of all the sentences in the left column of σ_j. (This is what makes the question relative to σ_j.)

(3) A definitory move is also relative to a *subtableau* σ_j. It consists in the introduction of a new predicate symbol, say P(x). It is introduced by means of an explicit definition, that is, by adding to the left column of σ_j either.

(x) (P(x)⟷∫(x))

or

(x) (P(x) (x=a₁ v x=a₂ v . . . v x=a_k))

where ∫ is an expression in the vocabulary that has been used in σ_j and has one free variable, and where $a_1, a_2, \ldots , a_k$ are individual constants.

VII. PAYOFFS AND STRATEGIES

As the case usually is in game theory, players' strategic considerations are determined essentially by the payoffs. We shall not try to specify them fully here. The following general principles are nevertheless important.

(1) An interrogative move involving a wh-question is the more expensive the more layers of quantifiers there are in the question, including the quantifiers masquerading as wh-words (with the exception of the outmost layer of such quantifiers). We can tentatively think of the "price" of a question being equal to the same number of units as there are layers of quantifiers in the question. Here quantifiers occurring outside the question proper do not count.

(2) A definitory move is the more expensive the more layers of quantifiers there are in the definiens ∫. Again, each additional layer can be thought of as costing a unit.

(3) Of deductive moves, each of those introducing new dummy names costs a unit.

What these principles amount to in intuitive terms is that a move is the more expensive the more it complicates the configurations of individuals one is considering in the deduction (in the sense of introducing new individuals into the argument). This "cost" of adding new individuals to our deductive argument (whether they are actual individuals or "arbitrary individuals" represented by dummy names) reflects the importance of such moves for successful deduction. The selection of the new individuals to be introduced is the crucial strategic consideration in our games.

This is again reflected by what we find in actual Sherlock Holmes-type arguments. Take the example closest at hand: the curious episode of the dog in the night. What happens in it is that three individuals are for the first time related to each other by Holmes: the unknown thief, the dog, and the trainer. (We may perhaps say that the dog is introduced into the argument and the other two are related to each other by its means.) The surprise of Holmes's "deduction" is not in the relation of the three individuals (two of which turn out to be identical) but in asking for the first time what their relation is. And this was made possible by the introduction of one of them.

VIII. DEDUCTIONS SOMETIMES REPLACEABLE BY QUESTIONS AND ANSWERS

The closer examination of the payoffs and different strategies would take us too far. Suffice it to mention here one interesting fact. Most of the deductive moves—including some of the most interesting ones—can be replaced by a suitable question, assuming that an answer to it is forthcoming.

For instance, assume that $(F_1 \text{ v } F_2)$ occurs in the left column of some *subtableaux* σ_j. A deductive move might involve splitting σ_j in two, with F_1 and F_2, respectively, added to their left columns. However, instead of doing so one could ask "Is it the case that F_1 or is it the case that F_2?" This can be done because the presupposition of this question is $(F_1 \text{ v } F_2)$. Whichever the answer is, one is saved the trouble of continuing the construction of one of the two *subtableaux* into which the deductive move would have split σ_j.

Likewise, suppose that $(Ex) F(x)$ occurs in the left column of σ_j. Then a deductive move might involve the introduction of a new dummy name "α" whereupon "$F(\alpha)$" is inserted into the left column of σ_j. Instead of doing this, one might ask: "Who or what (call that individual x) is such that $F(x)$?" One can do so because the presupposition of this question is (Ex) $F(x)$. If the answer is "b," then one can insert "$F(b)$" into the left column of σ_j instead of "$F(\alpha)$." Since "b" is a real name, dealing with it can only facilitate the deduction as compared with the deductive move. (Notice that we presupposed here the existential-quantifier reading of the desideratum of the question.)

Furthermore, a definitory move can often be replaced likewise by a question-answer move. For instance, a definitory move might involve the introduction of the sentence

(*) $(x) (P(x) \longleftrightarrow \int(x))$

into the left column of some subtableaux σ_j. Instead of this, one might ask: "Who or what (call one of them x) are such that $\int (x)$?", presupposing the universal-quantifier reading of the desideratum. The answer will then be a sentence of the same form, except that the new primitive predicate "P" is replaced by some previously used predicate. Once again, the deductive task can only be enhanced by the change.

This extensive interchangeability of deductive and interrogative moves (as well as definitory and interrogative moves) can be taken to be a vindication of the idea that the art of deduction is essentially tantamount to the art of asking questions. This idea is perhaps the most central ingredient in the Sherlock Holmes conception of logic, deduction, and inference.

CHAPTER EIGHT

Jaakko Hintikka

Sherlock Holmes Formalized

1. PREAMBLE

In an earlier Article (Hintikka 1978), I argued that the best way of conceptualizing what often passes as deductions or inferences in ordinary discourse is to treat them as answers to tacit questions. The element of skill and ingenuity which makes "deductions" in this wide sense nontrivial comes in through the choice of these questions. A paradigmatic case in point is constituted by the "deductions" of a brilliant detective, whether real or fictional. Hence the name of such a person in the title of this chapter.

The idea is obviously suggestive, but it remains to be carried out in explicit detail. The purpose of this chapter is to make a beginning in an explicit, formal treatment of what Sherlock Holmes called "The Science of Deduction and Analysis" (STUD, especially Ch. 2). In doing so, I face a few important choices as to what conceptual frameworks I should use. It seems to me that these choices nevertheless are not very hard to make.

On the basis of our general idea, it is clear that a brilliant applied reasoner's skill is largely a strategic one. It consists in asking the strategically right questions, that is, the questions whose answers are likely to be most informative and to open up further lines of successful questioning. Now the best general tool for strategic considerations available at the present time is the branch of studies which is somewhat misleadingly known as the mathematical theory of games. In fact, it might more appropriately be called strategy theory.[1] Hence it is appropriate to construe the question-answer sequences we want to consider as games (in the precise sense of the theory of games) between the questioner and an answerer. The latter can often be thought of as Nature, and we shall call her that, while the questioner will be referred to in the sequel as "I" or "myself."

The second main choice concerns the bookkeeping method for these *questioning games* against Nature, as we shall call them. The system must allow me to carry out and record logical inferences in the narrow technical sense in which twentieth-century philosophers are wont to use the term. At the same time the scorekeeping system must allow the players to record Nature's answers in an appropriate way.

It seems to me that by far the best bookkeeping system of this kind is offered by the familiar method of the so-called semantical *tableaux* introduced by E.W. Beth (1955). The rules of a questioning game against Nature can be formulated by reference to such a tableau called the game tableau. I shall use about the game tableau the usual terminology, which is assumed to be familiar to the reader.

In the simple games considered in this chapter, it is assumed that I am trying to prove a certain given conclusion C using as my premises a given initial assumption T plus answers to questions which I put to Nature one by one. Accordingly, in its initial state the game tableau contains C in its right column and T in its left column, but nothing else.

The game rules are extremely simple. They can be formulated by reference to the game tableau. There are three kinds of moves: (i) Deductive moves; (ii) Interrogative moves; (iii) Definitory moves.

(i) In a deductive move, one of the usual rules of tableau construction is applied to the game tableau.

(ii) In an interrogative move, I address a question to Nature who will give to it as conclusive (full) an answer as possible. This answer is entered into the left column of the game tableau.

(iii) In a definitory move, I introduce a new concept by means of an explicit definition inserted into the left column of the game tableau. Explicit definitions are in the first place sentences of one of the following two forms:

$$(1) \quad (z_1) (z_2) \ldots (z_i) (x) [P(x, z_1, z_2, \ldots, z_i)$$
$$\longleftrightarrow S[x, z_1, z_2, \ldots, z_i]]$$

$$(2) \quad (z_1) (z_2) \ldots (z_i) (x) [(f(z_1, z_2, \ldots z_i) = x)$$
$$\longleftrightarrow S[x, z_1, z_2, \ldots, z_i]]$$

In (1), P is the new symbol, and in (2) f is one.

These rules require several comments and further explanations. First, I have to specify the language I am presupposing here. To begin with, I shall assume that I am using some interpreted finite first-order language L with identity and with function symbols. I shall normally be dealing with certain extensions of L. This choice of language means that no intentional notions are allowed to occur in the questions and answers. The only element in the game which is not readily expressible in such a language are the questions addressed to Nature. However, the questions are not entered into the tableau, only the answers. Hence, this restriction does not matter here.

For the time being, the extensions of L which we shall allow are twofold: (a) extensions involving new predicate functions, or individual constants introduced by a definitory move; (b) extensions involving special constants called proper symbols (for the entities of different logical types in the intended model). They include proper names of individuals in the intended domain, proper predicates, and proper functions. What the intended interpretation of these symbols is can only be explained by reference to semantics of our questioning games. Intuitively speaking, they may be thought of as (logically) proper names of different types of entities in one's domain of discourse.

(i) The tableau rules used in deductive moves can be any of the usual ones. However, it may be appropriate for many purposes to modify the usual tableau construction rules so as to become the Beth counterparts to Craig's (1957) rules of linear deduction (which Craig explained in terms of sequents rather than tableaux).

(ii) An indispensable prerequisite to our enterprise is the analysis I have offered elsewhere of the question-answer relationship (Hintikka 1976, especially Chs. 2–3). I cannot reproduce the analysis here, and hence I must assume familiarity on the part of my readers of its outcome. Suffice it to say that by an answer in an interrogative move I mean in the case of propositional questions a direct answer. In the case of wh-questions an answer is a substitution instance of the matrix of the question with respect to some term. This term must of course belong to L or to an admissible extension of L explained above. As far as symbols are concerned which occur in the answer after having been introduced by definitory moves, they must have been introduced earlier in the same subtableau.

It is a precondition of an interrogative move that the presupposition of the question occurs in the left column of the game tableau. In a certain sense which again requires semantical concepts for its (formulation, an answer can be required to be as full as is possible in the given situation.

I shall make each interrogative move relative to a subtableau. The presupposition of the question need only to occur in the left column of that subtableau, and the answer is inserted only into the left column of that subtableau. The requirements on answers to wh-questions will pertain to that subtableau only.

It was originally assumed in (ii) that the *desideratum* of the question is given an existential-quantifier reading. It may nevertheless be given (at my pleasure) a universal-quantifier reading (Hintikka 1976, Ch. 4). Then an answer will be a sentence of the form

(3) $(x) [M[x] \longleftrightarrow S[x]]$

where $M[x]$ is the matrix of the question and $S[x]$ an expression satisfying the following conditions:

(a) The nonlogical vocabulary of $S[x]$ consists of that of L and of that of the admissible extensions of L described above.

(b) $S[x]$ contains x as its only free individual variable; x does not occur bound in $S[x]$.

More generally, the question asked in an interrogative move can be a parametrized one, that is, a question with free variables (bound to outside universal quantifiers). Then the answer will be, on the existential interpretation of the question, of the form

(4) $(z_1) (z_2) \ldots (z_i) M[t[z_1, z_2, \ldots z_i],$
$z_1, z_2, \ldots z_i]$

where $M[x, z_1, z_2, \ldots, z_i]$ is the matrix of the question (with $z_1, z_2, \ldots, z_i$ as its free variables) and $t(z_1, z_2, \ldots, z_i)$ is a term which contains

(a) $z_1, z_2, \ldots, z_i$ (or some of them) as its only free individual variables;

(b) function symbols from L and/or from its admissible extensions.

When a free-variable question is interpreted universally, we have as an answer, in analogy to (4) and as a generalization of (3),

(5) $(z_1) (z_2) \ldots (z_i) (x) [M[x, z_1, z_2, \ldots, z_i]$
$\longleftrightarrow S[x, z_1, z_2, \ldots, z_i]]$

Here S is an expression which contains x, $z_1, z_2, \ldots, z_i$ as its only free individual variables and contains, as its nonlogical constants symbols from L and from the admissible extensions of L. Once again, the constants introduced by definitions must have been introduced in the same subtableau.

The presupposition of an existentially interpreted wh-question with free variables has to occur in the left column of the relevant subtableau before the question may be asked. For the question whose answer can be of the form (4) the presupposition is

(6) $(z_1) (z_2) \ldots (z_i) (\exists x) M[x, z_1, z_2, \ldots, z_i]$

The presupposition of a universally interpreted wh-question is the same as that of the corresponding existentially interpreted one.

Free-variable questions may also be asked relative to a predicate. We can use as an example a one-place predicate $P(z)$. Let the matrix of the question be $M[z,x]$. Then, on the existential interpretation the wh-question, the analogues to (4) and (6) (i.e., to an answer and to the presupposition) are

(7) $(z)[P(z) \supset M[t[z],x]]$

and

(8) $(z) [P(z) \supset (\exists x) M[x,z]]$,

respectively.

The analogue to answer (5) to universally interpreted wh-questions with free variables is

(9) $(z) [P(z) \supset (x) (M[x, z] \longleftrightarrow [x, z])]$

(iii) Definitory moves, like interrogative ones, will be relative to a subtableau of the game tableau. The definition (1) of (2) is entered only into the left column of the subtableau.

The symbols introduced by definitory moves must not occur earlier in the same subtableau. In other words, in a definitory move, as defined above, P is a predicate symbol and f a function symbol which does not occur in the subtableau in question nor in L. Furthermore, $S[x, z_1, z_2, \ldots, z_i]$ must contain as its only free individual variables of $x, z_1, z_2, \ldots,$ and z_i. In (2) the following sentences must occur in the left column of the same subtableau:

(10) $(z_1) (z_2) \ldots (z_i) (\exists x) S[x, z_1, z_2 \ldots , z_i]$

(11) $(z_1) (z_2) \ldots (z_i) (x) (y) [(S[x, z_1, z_2,$
    $\ldots , z_i] \& S[y, z_1, z_2, \ldots ,z_i])$
        $\supset (x = y)]$

As a special case of (2), (10), and (11), we shall treat sentences of the following kind

(12) $(x) [(a = x) \longleftrightarrow S[x]]$
(13) $(\exists x) S[x]$
(14) $(x)(y)[(S[x] \& S[y]) \supset (x = y)]$

Here a is an individual constant which does not occur earlier in the subtableau. Admitting (12)–(14) as special cases of (2) and (10)–(11) means allowing the definitory introduction of individual symbols on a par with defined predicates and functions.

2. Examples

This suffices to explain the syntactical appearance of a questioning game against Nature. This still leaves the semantics of the game and its payoff structure to be explained. Especially the latter is crucially important to my strategic considerations in the game. In order to sharpen our perceptions, it may nevertheless be useful at this stage to consider a couple of simple examples of questioning games against Nature. They are either taken from natural-language differences or can easily be given a formulation in terms of plain ordinary English. My success in reconstructing these ordinary-discourse "deductions" in terms of the questioning games vividly shows that I am on the right track.

My first examples of an information-seeking dialogue is an amplification of a part of Sherlock Holmes's reasoning in the story SILV, representing his deductions from the curious incident of the dog in the night. (" 'The dog did nothing in the night-time.' 'That was the curious incident,' remarked Sherlock Holmes.") The verbal formulations of the different moves are given first.

(1) Was there a watchdog in the stable? Yes.
(2) Did any watchdog in the stable bark at anyone? No.
(3) Hence, no watchdog in the stable barked at the thief.
(4) Who doesn't a watchdog bark at? Its master.
(5) Consider one of the watchdogs in the stable, say, d.
(6) d did not bark at the thief.
(7) Whoever d does not bark at is d's master.
(8) Hence, d's master is the thief.

A couple of explanations may be in order here. In the story, answers (1)–(2) are among the known facts of the case presented earlier. The deductive moves (3), (5)–(8) are all straightforward. In (4), the answer is trivial as soon as the question is asked. Sherlock Holmes's ingenuity thus consists in effect of bringing in the right extra premise by asking the right question, precisely as was indicated above.

Note that the question in (4) is one containing a free variable. Moreover, it is asked with respect to the predicate "watchdog."

A tableau formulation of Sherlock Holmes's reasoning might run as follows. Only the left column of the game tableau is written out.

(1) $(\exists x)(W(x) \ \& \ S(x))$
(2) $(y)(x)[(W(x) \ \& \ S(x)) \ \supset \ \sim B(x,y)]$
(3) $(x)[(W(x) \ \& \ S(x)) \ \supset \ \sim B(x,th)]$
(4) $(x)[(W(x) \ \supset \ (y)(\sim B(x,y) \ \supset \ (y = m(x)))]$
(5) $W(d) \ \& \ S(d)$

(5a)   W(d)

(6)   (W(d) & S(d)) $\supset$ ~B(d,th)

(6a)   ~B(d,th)

(7)   W(d) $\supset$ (y) (~B(d,y) $\supset$ (y = m(d))

(7a)   (y) [~B(d,y) $\supset$ (y = m(d))]

(8)   ~B(d,th) $\supset$ (th = m(d))

8a)   th = m(d)

Key: W(x) = x is a watchdog

        S(x) = x was in the stable

        B(x, y) = x barked at y

        m(x) = the master of x

        th = the thief

In the second example, I begin with the tableau representation and only afterwards explain the tableau entries and give a verbal example having the same structure.

Game Tableau

(1)	(x)($\exists$y) R(x,y)	($\exists$u)(z) R(z,u)	(2)
(3)	(x)[T(x) $\longleftrightarrow$	(z) R(z,c)	(10)
	(($\exists$y) R(x,y) $\supset$ (z)R(z,x))]		
(4)	($\exists$x) T(x)		
(5)	T(c)		
(6)	T(c) $\longleftrightarrow$		
	(($\exists$y) R(c,y) $\supset$ (z) R(z,c))		
(7)	($\exists$y) R(c,y) $\supset$ (z) R(z,c)		
(8)	($\exists$y) R(c,y)		
(9)	(z) R(z,c)		

Explanations of the dialogue

(1) is the given premise

(2) is the desired conclusion

(3) results as the answer to the question: Who are all the individuals x such that (($\exists$y) R(x,y) $\supset$ (z) R(z,x))?

(4) results as an answer to the question: Are there individuals x such that T(x)?

(5) results as an answer to the question: Who (say x) is (among others) such that T(x)?

(6) results from (3) by L-universal instantiation with respect to c.

(7) results from (5) and (4) by the derived tableau rule of equivalence substitution.

(8) results from (1) by L-universal instantiation.

(9) results from (7) and (8) by a suitable tableau version of *modus ponens*.

(10) results from (2) by R-existential instantiation.

Verbal formulations
(with questions included)
  Key: R(x,y) = x betrays y
       T(x) = x is a terrorist
       c = Carlos
  (1) Everybody betrays someone. (Premise.)
  (3) Who are such that everyone betrays them if they betray anyone? (Universally interpreted wh-question).
  The terrorists (answer).
  (4) Are there terrorists? (Yes or no question.)
  Yes (answer).
  (5) Who is a terrorist? (Existentially interpreted wh-question whose presupposition has been established in (4).)
  (6) Carlos is a terrorist if and only if everyone betrays him if he betrays anyone. (From (3) by universal instantiation.)
  (7) Everyone betrays Carlos if he betrays anyone. (From (5) and (6).)
  (8) Carlos betrays someone. (From (1) by instantiation.)
  (9) Everyone betrays Carlos. (From (7) and (8) by *modus ponens*.)
  (2) Someone is betrayed by everybody. (The conclusion to be proved; follows from (9) by existential generalization.)

Alternative explanations
  Some of the moves in the sample dialogue can be replaced by different but essentially (in this case) equivalent moves. Here is another way of carrying out essentially the same dialogue. In this particular example, I need to change only the explanations of the different moves.

  (1)–(2) as before
  (3) definitory move introducing the new predicate T(x)
  (4) as before
  (5) from (4) by L-existential instantiation
  (6) – (10) as before

  This illustrates the fact that different kinds of moves are often exchangeable. Frequently one interrogative move can replace a deductive move, or vice versa. This shows how natural the wider sense of the concepts of deduction and inference is which we have been trying to capture in this chapter: logical inferences in the narrow technical sense are often profitably exchanged for answers to suitable questions, which is what I am taking "deductions" in the wider sense ("Sherlock Holmes's sense") to be.

NOTE

1. For instance, the term "game theory" suggests a theory of conflicts, even though there are strategies of cooperation as well as strategies of conflicts and both kinds of strategies can be—and are—treated in game theory.

CHAPTER NINE

Nancy Harrowitz

The Body of the Detective Model

CHARLES S. PEIRCE AND EDGAR ALLAN POE

EDGAR ALLAN POE is considered by most detective fiction historians to be the founding father of the detective story, and his "Murders in the Rue Morgue" the world's first detective story. Such an auspicious beginning staked out for any literary genre should always be suspect, and the suspects in this case are the detective historians themselves. Howard Haycraft, probably the most renowned of this group, divides detective fiction historians into two schools: the majority, including Haycraft himself, who maintain that the detective genre was born with Poe; and a minority, who hold that elements of the detective story were present in literature as early as the Bible and thus strictly speaking Poe was not the inventor of the type but rather its chief proponent.

Haycraft, in his book *Murder For Pleasure: Life and Times of the Detective Story* (1941:6), discusses at length the fundamental arguments of these two camps. The former is based on a phenomenological approach which claims that in order to have detective stories—to be distinguished of course from mysteries—you must have police forces and detectives. These did not exist per se before the early part of the nineteenth century, when criminal investigation departments began to burgeon in Paris and London. As the final word, Haycraft quotes the English bibliophile George Bates's view on the matter: "The cause of Chaucer's silence on the subject of airplanes was because he had never seen one. You cannot write about policemen before policemen exist to be written of." The detective method is therefore viewed as less essential to the genre by these historians than the plot/structure elements.

The minor trend of detective historiography places more emphasis on the detective method than on the presence of a detective and a crime.

179

Julian Symons, in his *Bloody Murder; From the Detective Story to the Crime Novel: A History* (1972), categorizes the two trends and like Haycraft belongs to the mainstream school. His criticism of the minor trend brings to light a crucial yet largely ignored point, as we shall see:

> Historians of the detective story are divided between those who say that there could be no detective stories until organized police and detective forces existed, and those who find examples of rational deduction in sources as various as the Bible and Voltaire, and suggest that these were early puzzles in detection . . . The decisive point is that we should be talking about crime literature, but that those who search for fragments of detection in the Bible and Herodotus are looking only for puzzles. The puzzle is vital to the detective story but is not a detective story in itself, and its place in crime literature generally is comparatively small . . . (an) interesting exercise is in Voltaire's "Zadig" (1747). Without seeing the Queen's bitch or the King's horse, both of which have disappeared, Zadig is able to say that the bitch recently had puppies, limps in the left foreleg and has long ears . . . when he insists that he has never seen the animals, Zadig is sentenced to be flogged. His explanation, made after the animals are found, is a piece of true deduction. In the case of the bitch, hanging dugs and earmarks traced in the sand, with one paw more deeply impressed than the others, provided the clues. (Symons, 1972:24–25)

Symons's calling Zadig's method of clue analysis "a piece of true deduction" signals an underlying problem within the attempt to define the detective story genre and its origins, a problem which permeates both this kind of historical genre criticism and criticism of Poe's work itself.[1] Without specifying precisely what the detective method consists of, and how and why the method is essential to the detective story, it is difficult at best to justify either a genealogical approach to the origins of the genre or a narrowly historical one which would claim that the detective story was born in Philadelphia, Pennsylvania, in April 1841, with the appearance of Poe's "Murders in the Rue Morgue" in *Graham's Magazine*.

On the one hand, there is the unfortunate tendency to lump logical categories together under the generic "rational deduction." On the other hand, there is a nearsighted reduction of the importance of the detective method itself. The task of this particular research will not be one which would analyze the literary beginnings of the detective method in a rigorous fashion, although that work is certainly needed. The focus here will be twofold: First, an empirical attempt to be precise about the nature of the detective method in the detective fiction of Poe, texts which are primal in that they were the first examples of abductive inquiry within the detective-crime formula framework. Second, an effort will be made to situate the abductive detective model, to define its parameters within a semiotic and epistemological context.

"ABDUCTION IS, AFTER ALL, NOTHING BUT GUESSING." —CHARLES SANDERS PEIRCE (7:219)

C. S. Peirce, in his *Collected Papers* (1965–1966) and elsewhere in his manuscripts, discusses a concept which at varying moments he calls "abduction," "retroduction," "hypothesis," "presumption," and "originary argument." Looking at a collage of Peirce's remarks on abduction is perhaps the fastest way to arrive at a working definition:

> . . . a retroductive conclusion is only justified by its explaining an observed fact. An explanation is a syllogism of which the major premiss, or rule, is a known law or rule of nature or other general truth; the minor premiss, or case, is the hypothesis or retroductive conclusion, and the conclusion, or result, is the observed (or otherwise established) fact. (1:89)

> *Presumption,* or more precisely *abduction*, furnishes the reasoner with the problematic theory which induction verifies. Upon finding himself confronted with a phenomenon unlike what he would have expected under the circumstances he looks over its features and notices some remarkable character or relation among them, which he at once recognizes as being characteristic of some conception with which his mind is already stored, so that a theory is suggested which would *explain* (that is, render necessary) that which is surprising in the phenomenon. (2:776)

> Every step in the development of primitive notions into modern science was in the first instance mere guess-work, or at least mere conjecture. But the stimulus to guessing, the hint of the conjecture, was derived from experience. The order of the march of suggestion in retroduction is from experience to hypothesis. (2:755)

> Abduction is the process of forming an explanatory hypothesis. It is the only logical operation which introduces a new idea; for induction does nothing but determine a value, and deduction merely evolves the necessary consequences of a pure hypothesis.

> Deduction proves that something *must* be; Induction shows that something *actually is* operative; Abduction merely suggests that something *may be*. (5:171)

> A man must be downright crazy to deny that science has made many true discoveries. But every single item of scientific theory which stands established today has been due to Abduction. (5:172)

Peirce's construction of abduction essentially describes a process in which the subject is confronted with an observed fact which needs explaining and which seems important. In order to explain the observed fact, he/she needs to come up with a "known law or rule of nature or other general truth" which will both explain the fact retroactively and hopefully reveal its relevance as well. Abduction is the step in between a fact and its origin; the instinctive, perceptual jump which allows the subject to guess an origin which can then be tested out to prove or disprove the hypothesis. Abduction is a theory developed to explain a preexisting fact. Peirce says, "Deduction shows that something *must* be" (5:172), and induction "ascertains the value of a ratio" (1:67). Abduction is distinguished from these two other categories, deduction and induction, in Peirce's schema (2:623–625), as follows:

Deduction

Rule   All the beans from this bag are white.
Case   These beans are from this bag.
∴·*Result* These beans are white.

Induction

Case   These beans are from this bag.
Result   These beans are white.
∴·*Rule*   All the beans from this bag are white.

Abduction

Rule   All the beans from this bag are white.
Result   These beans are white.
∴·*Case*   These beans are from this bag.

It is important to remember that Peirce also uses the terms "law of nature, general truth" and "experience" to indicate what in the abductive category above is called "rule." Accordingly, "observed fact" is the same as "result," and "abductive conclusion" (or abduction, retroduction, presumption, hypothesis, originary argument) is the equivalent of "case." In the categories of deduction and induction, "rule" and "case" both can indicate an observed fact. This leads us to another problem. Obviously, the chronology of information-obtaining is important here, but does not necessarily come across in these diagrams. If you were to walk into the bean-and-bag-filled room assumed here, it would appear that the process by which you arrived at a conclusion about beans and bags would depend on what you looked at first. There is somehow an implication in these diagrams that all the information is equally available. This implication, together with the confusion of terms, is no doubt due to the excessive simplicity of the beanbag model which is used to describe a reasonably complicated set of principles.

A diagram for abduction that may prove to be somewhat more accurate would look like this:

Result(observed fact)   These beans are white.

abductive process begins here . . . .
Rule   All the beans from this bag
                                     are white.   :
∴ Case(result of abducting)   These beans are from this bag.

Putting the diagram into words: you observe a fact (these beans are white). In order to explain and understand this, you cast about in your mind for some glimmering of theory, explanation, flash, and so forth. The process of abduction takes place between the result and the rule, and concludes with the positing of a hopefully satisfactory hypothesis. Now all that remains to be done, Peirce tells us, is to test the new hypothesis.

THE CONJECTURAL MODEL

Carlo Ginzburg, in his "Morelli, Freud and Sherlock Holmes: Clues and Scientific Method" (1980b; Ch. 4), discusses a concept he calls the "conjectural model, for the construction of knowledge. The conjectural model, Ginzburg says, "quietly emerged towards the end of the nineteenth century in the sphere of social sciences, and has still not received the attention it deserves." Ginzburg maintains that the concept of utilizing obscure or remote clues in a speculative manner to build an epistemological model has been an essential—if largely unrecognized—component in our cultural heritage. Ginzburg poses as examples of this paradigm the work of three great "detectives," Giovanni Morelli, Sigmund Freud, and Sherlock Holmes.

Giovanni Morelli, a nineteenth-century art historian, was known for indexing famous painters by the way in which they habitually characterized small "insignificant" details of the body, such as ears, fingernails, and toes. Concentrating on an encyclopedic familiarity with these details, Morelli was able to easily spot imitations and incorrect attributions, since imitators in particular would have been more interested in the larger, conventionally stylized characteristics of a particular school or artist. Morelli during his career made many new attributions in the major art galleries of Europe. His method was later discredited and largely forgotten. Much later the art historian Edgar Wind (quoted in Ginzburg) revived Morelli's methods, and made these comments about them:

> Morelli's books look different from those of any other writer on art. They are sprinkled with illustrations of fingers and ears, careful records of the characteristic trifles by which an artist gives himself away, as a criminal might be spotted by a fingerprint . . . any art gallery studied by Morelli begins to resemble a rogues' gallery. . . .

Ginzburg then goes on to draw a parallel between Morelli's methods, Freud's interest in the "little details" which reveal psychological realities, and Sherlock Holmes's crime solving through clue reading. All three methods "provide the key to a deeper reality—a reality which, like a disease in the body, cannot be "seen except through its symptoms. The activities of primitive humanity are evoked as the origin of the conjectural model:

> For thousands of years mankind lived by hunting. In the course of endless pursuits, hunters learned to reconstruct the appearance and movements of an unseen quarry through its tracks—prints in soft ground, snapped twigs, droppings, snagged hairs or feathers, smells, puddles, threads of saliva. They learned to sniff, to observe, to give meaning and context to the slightest trace. . . .
> Successive generations of hunters enriched and passed on this inheritance of knowledge. . . . Its characteristic feature was that it permitted the leap from apparently insignificant facts, which could be observed, to a complex reality which—directly at least—could not. And these facts would be ordered by the observer in such a way as to provide a narrative sequence—at its simplest, "someone passed this way."

The importance of the conjectural model is not found in the notion of reading coded signs such as imprints, but rather in the fact that the systems which Ginzburg discusses were developed and invested with meaning through a process much like abduction. The rules were postulated to explain the observed facts until a causality was proved, the hypothesis tested. As in abduction, a cultural or experiential knowledge is required to codify a system. Abduction is literally the groundwork necessary before a sign is codified. As Peirce tells us, abduction creates a new idea.

Peirce's category of rule is an enormously broad and vague one. It incorporates all kinds of knowledge from the cultural to the personal. He calls rule "law or rule of Nature or other general truth," in other words any information which is common to all. Yet the category of rule also includes "experience," and experience can be either public or private. It is the kind of "guessing" in abduction—loose, as we can see from the vastness of rule—and the far-reaching, almost generic implications of Ginzburg's model which create the beauty and the beast of this method. This will be more fully discussed when we have finished examining the text of abduction itself, Poe's tales.

RATIOCINATION AND POE

The narrative fiction of Edgar Allan Poe is characterized by constructions of the hyperreal, glimpses or entire explorations into a wholly internal fantastic reality whose parameters are set only by the limits of a vastly imaginative mind. In his fiction Poe relies heavily on a concept he calls "ratiocination," an unfortunately ambiguous term. "Ratiocination," according to the Oxford English Dictionary, means "to reason, to carry on a process of reasoning, the process of reasoning." The emphasis on process is interesting since it points to the "how" of reasoning, which is of course our concern here. Other than this one indication, the term is quite vague and we must turn directly to Poe's tales in order to understand what is meant by it.

In many of Poe's tales, including some of those which are not detective stories per se, ratiocination is a state of mind of the narrator, and abductions are the acts which are made possible through the existence of this state of mind. Abductive acts are a mediating term between the world of the mind of the narrator and the physical world which he inhabits. Ratiocination and abduction are part and parcel of the same phenomenon. They serve to give order—at least a semblance thereof—to the otherwise overwhelming chaos of the hyperreal in Poe, as we can see in "A Descent into a Maelstrom."

The narrator in this story, telling his terrifying adventure of being caught in an enormous whirlpool, recounts how he saved himself by analyzing the kinds of physical shapes of objects floating around him. The whirlpool had battered these objects by first sucking them up and then throwing them back to the surface of the sea. He abducts that a cylindrical shape object is last to be drawn under, and so he saves himself by clinging to a cask until the maelstrom has passed into its calm stage:

> "It was not a new terror that thus affected me, but the dawn of a more exciting *hope*. This hope arose partly from memory, and partly from present observation. I called to mind the great variety of buoyant matter that

strewed the coast of Lofoden, having been absorbed and then thrown forth by the Moskoe-strom. By far the greater number of the articles were shattered in the most extraordinary way . . . but then I distinctly recollected that there were some of them which were not disfigured at all. . . . I made, also, three important observations. The first was that as a general rule, the larger the bodies were, the more rapid their descent—the second, that, between two masses of equal extent, the one spherical, and the other of any other shape, the superiority in speed of descent was with the sphere—the third, that, between two masses of equal size, the one cylindrical, and the other of any other shape, the cylinder was absorbed the more slowly. . . . There was one startling circumstance which went a great way in enforcing these observations, and rendering me anxious to turn them to account, and this was that, at every revolution, we passed something like a barrel, or else the yard or the mast of a vessel, while many of these things, which had been on our level when I first opened my eyes upon the wonders of the whirlpool, were now high above us, and seemed to have moved little from their original station." (Poe 1927:565)

The ratiocinative workings of the narrator's mind allow the calm, soothing voice of reason to reign over a scene of terror, the howling, heaving, boiling sea, the shrieking winds, the narrator's fear of death. He has specific scientific knowledge gained through previous observation and a keen power of observation in the face of death which allow him to make conjectures about the objects in the sea around him. He then postulates a rule which would explain certain physical facts about these objects. He arrives at the abduction, "cylindrical objects which are also small are the last shape and size to be drawn into the maelstrom, if drawn in at all." He then saves himself by hanging on to a cylindrical cask, which indeed is never drawn into the whirlpool. The narrator escapes unscathed (except that from terror his hair has turned white) and we have learned a lesson about the importance of reason, in other words, abduction.

Abductive acts abound in tales such as "The Black Cat," "The Purloined Letter," "Thou Art the Man," "The Gold Bug." In some cases ratiocination and its expressed form, abduction, furnish the means by which the narrator fends off a continually lurking insanity. But before digging Poe any deeper into this abductive grave, let us examine what he has to say on what he calls "analysis," from the first pages of "The Murders in the Rue Morgue":

The faculty of re-solution is possibly much invigorated by mathematical study, and especially by that highest branch of it which, unjustly, and merely on account of its retrograde operations, has been called, as if par excellence, analysis. Yet to calculate is not in itself to analyze. (Poe 1927:78)

Poe goes on to sketch out the differences between calculation and analysis. Calculation depends on inductive and deductive operations, as Poe makes clear from his example of the game of chess. Analysis, however, is a much more complex skill:

> But it is in matters beyond the limits of mere rule that the skill of the analyst is evinced. He makes, in silence, a host of observations and inferences. So, perhaps, do his companions; and the difference in the extent of information obtained; lies not so much in the validity of the inference as in the quality of the observation. The necessary knowledge is that of *what* to observe. Our player confines himself not at all; nor, because the game is the object, does he reject deductions from things external to the game. He examines the countenance of his partner, comparing it carefully with that of each of his opponents. He considers the mode of assorting the cards in each hand; often counting trump by trump, and honor by honor, through the glances bestowed by their holders upon each. He notes every variation of face as the play progresses, gathering a fund of thought from the differences in the expression of certainty, of surprise, of triumph, or chagrin. From the manner of gathering up a trick he judges whether the person taking it, can make another in the suit. He recognizes what is played through feint, by the manner with which it is thrown upon the table. (Poe 1927:79)

Poe the semiotician is running the gamut of possibilities here—inferences, reasoning backwards, visual, sensual and aural signs, reading faces. Playing cards with the man would have been an interesting experience. The above passage is not only a manifesto for absolute success at cards, but a game plan for abduction as well. As Poe informs us, the results of analysis, "brought about by the very soul and essence of method, have, in truth, the whole air of intuition" (Poe 1927:78).

The first narrative of abductive reasoning in "The Murders in the Rue Morgue" comes just after the definition of analysis that Poe gives us, and serves as an illustration of the method. The narrator is describing his life in Paris with a certain C. Auguste Dupin. The two are taking a walk one evening. A silence had been maintained for at least fifteen minutes, when Dupin breaks it by remarking, "He is a very little fellow, that's true, and would do better for the Théâtre des Variétes." The narrator replies, "There can be no doubt of that," and then is startled beyond comprehension and insists on hearing how Dupin knew he had at that moment been thinking of the actor Chantilly. Dupin retraces his steps in this passage:

"We had been talking of horses, if I remember aright, just before leaving the Rue C____. This was the last subject we discussed. As we crossed into this street, a fruiterer, with a large basket upon his head, brushing quickly past us, thrust you upon a pile of paving-stones collected at a spot where the causeway is undergoing repair. You stepped upon one of the loose fragments, slipped, slightly strained your ankle, appeared vexed or sulky, muttered a few words, turned to look at the pile, and then proceeded in silence. I was not particularly attentive to what you did; but observation has become with me, of late, a species of necessity.

"You kept your eyes upon the ground—glancing, with a petulant expression, at the holes and ruts in the pavement, (so that I saw you were still thinking of the stones) until we reached the little alley called Lamartine, which has been paved, by way of experiment, with the overlapping and riveted blocks. Here your countenance brightened up, and, perceiving your lips move, I could not doubt that you murmured the word 'stereotomy,' a term very affectedly applied to this species of pavement. I knew that you could not say to yourself 'stereotomy' without being brought to think of atomies, and thus of the theories of Epicurus; and since, when we discussed this subject not very long ago, I mentioned to you how singularly, yet with how little notice, the vague guesses of that noble Greek had met with confirmation in the late nebular cosmogony, I felt that you could not avoid casting your eyes upward to the great nebula in Orion, and I certainly expected that you would do so. You did look up; and I was now assured that I had correctly followed your steps. But in that bitter tirade upon Chantilly, which appeared in yesterday's 'Musee,' the satirist, making some disgraceful allusions to the cobbler's change of name upon assuming the buskin, quoted a Latin line about which we have often conversed. I mean the line, 'Perdidit antiquum litera prima sonum.' I had told you that this was in reference to Orion, formerly written Urion; and, from certain pungencies connected with this explanation, I was aware that you could not have forgotten it. It was clear, therefore, that you would not fail to combine the two ideas of Orion and Chantilly. That you did combine them I saw by the character of the smile which passed over your lips. You thought of the poor cobbler's immolation. So far, you had been stooping in your gait; but now I saw you draw yourself up to your full height. I was then sure that you reflected upon the diminutive figure of Chantilly. At this point I interrupted your meditations to remark that as, in fact, he was a very little fellow—that Chantilly—he would do better at the Théâtre des Variétes." (Poe 1972:82–83)

The first paragraph of this passage details the actual physical events of the scene, namely, the collision with the fruiterer which generates the sequence of events to follow, the reactions of the narrator to the collision. The second paragraph, however, signals a shift in the narrative as it is a description of how the ensuing events are read by Dupin. The following diagram will demonstrate an attempt to fit Peirce's categories of observed fact, rule, and case to Dupin's reading in order to see if and how the notion of abduction is operant in Dupin's analysis.

Observed Fact	*Rule*	*Case*
1. N. kept eyes on ground.	If you're looking at something you're thinking about it.	N. is thinking about ground.
2. N. glances at holes and ruts.	Holes and ruts are to be found where road repair is taking place.	N. fell on stones that were for road repair, so tie holes/ruts/stone is made; so if he's looking at holes, ruts, he's thinking of stones (rule 1).
3. a. Lips moved; b. Countenance brightened.	a. Lips moving indicate saying a word to yourself; b. Facial expression reflects thought or emotion. c. There is the word "stereotomy" which is affectedly applied to kind of stones N. is looking at.	Case 2 + rules 3a + b + c = Case 3: N. is thinking of stereotomy.
4. Cases 2 + 3.	If you think of stereotomy you must think of atomy.	N. must be thinking of Epicurus' theories.
5.	Past discussion by N. and Dupine re Epicurus and nebula in Orion.	N. must be making the connection re Epicurus and nebula.
6. N. looked up.	(Confirmation of cases 3 and 4).	

Observed Fact	Rule	Case
7.	In tirade against Chantilly, satirist quoted Latin line. In previous conversation N. and Dupin, connection made line-Orion.	Orion leads to Chantilly; narrator must be thinking of Chantilly.
8. Smile of a certain character by N.	(Confirmation of case 7) based on assumption that case 7 would produce smile.	
9.	Chantilly is infamous for his lack of height; if N. is thinking of Chantilly he is also thinking of his height.	N. is thinking of Chantilly's height.
10. N. draws himself up.	(Confirmation of case 9) based on physical expression reflects thought; if you straighten up you are thinking of height.	N. is thinking of Chantilly's height.

Chronologically the process of the abduction and the relationship of the process to the observed fact and the case is problematic. The process works not only "backwards" (as implied in Peirce's term retroduction) but "forwards" as well. Noticing the observed fact is the first step. A rule then suggests itself to explain the origin of the observed fact. The observed fact is consequently read through the hypothetically posited rule and the case is abducted. The rule, then, generates the intelligibility of the observed fact, and the observed fact is read through the rule. There is a reciprocal play here which is important to the nature of the model:

1. OF ....>rule
2. OF < .... rule
   ↓   ↓
3. ....>case

The observed facts, and later the cases, especially if the hypotheses are tested, serve to demonstrate the veracity and efficacity of the rules in some situations.

Some rules are more hypothetical and problematic than others, as we can see from the first diagram. As we have already noted, however, Peirce's conceptualization of rule is a vast one and easily embraces the kind of information with which Dupin arrives at his conclusions.

Looking at the first diagram, we can see that the first two abductions are fairly straightforward: there is an observed fact, a rule which explains it, and a conclusion. From abduction number three on, however, the game changes. In number three the two observed facts are considered together because of their simultaneous appearance in the narrative and their seemingly contiguous nature. The kind of observed facts remains the same for the present; what changes is the kind of rule in operation. Rules 3a and 3b are similar to rules 1 and 2, rules which are based on a very general knowledge of human behavior, thought processes, and environmental information. Rule 3c starts to bring us into a different realm and category of rules as it is based on a specific, localized familiarity with a particular kind of pavement and a particular nomenclature for that pavement used possibly only in that neighborhood or city. It could be assumed that the information contained in rule 3c may not be accessible either to a nonlocal reader or a nonlocal detective. This of course would be important if Dupin had not retraced his steps for us and if this were a crime-solving situation instead of an illustration of the abductive method outside of a crime-solving context.

Rule 3c begins a process in which the cases of 2 and 3 take the place of an observed fact in number 4. An observed fact is lacking in abduction number 5 as well. The chronology of the narration is crucial here. Dupin informs us that he arrived at cases 4 and 5 before the narrator looked up. The looking up is a hypothetical confirmation of these cases. It is not a testing of the cases 4 and 5 because it is not a conclusive confirmation based on either deduction or induction, as Peirce would claim the testing of a hypothesis must be. When you test an abduction with another abduction, you still have abduction.

The absence of truly exterior observed facts after abduction 3 is indicative of the movement from the public world of observable, identifiable phenomena to the interior private world of the mind which only Dupin and the narrator share: ". . . the rather fantastic gloom of our common temper . . . our seclusion was perfect. We admitted no visitors . . . we existed within ourselves alone" (Poe 1927:81).

Rule 5 is particularly indicative of the movement mentioned above as it is based entirely on previous conversations which Dupin and the narrator have shared regarding Epicurus and the nebula in Orion. Rule 4, on the other hand, demonstrates a particular quirk in the linguistic philosophy of Dupin that he then tries to attribute to the narrator: "I knew that you could not say to yourself 'stereotomy' without being brought to think of atomies." The assumption underlying rule 4 is that language is both metonymical and paranomasiac. Stereotomy contains -tomy, its suffix. Dupin asserts that -tomy makes you think of atomy. It is interesting that the word stereotomy, which means stonecutting, would cut itself out and leave its barest part, -tomy, which happens to be the part of the word that signifies cutting. At the same time, this word which is cutting itself down to the part which means cutting, is acquiring a prefix which enables it to signify atom, the smallest part of all. And all of this is a process which Dupin assumes the narrator to make as a matter of course.

It should be clear by now that Dupin is doing a certain amount of projecting here, going over the associations that he would have made in a like situation and attributing them to the narrator. The observed facts are few and far between in this passage and assumptions are running rampant. Yet this is still abduction and Dupin's explanation is somewhat feasible, although farfetched in spots due to the nature of some of the rules. It is important to keep in mind that the goal of this abduction is to read what the narrator is thinking, not to solve a crime committed by a stranger. There is obviously a vast difference in ends between these two kinds of purposes, and the means show this difference.

Overall this abductive passage is characterized by a general lack of codification of the clues (although the rules attempt to provide codes), a determinate interference of language evident in the stereotomy example as well as in the Latin line which is quoted, and the fact that many of the rules are taken from a private store of experience. This is not yet a fully realized detective problem-solving method, since there is no crime. This passage furnishes a methodological backdrop upon which the real story begins, immediately thereafter. As Poe informs us, "the narrative which follows will appear to the reader somewhat in the light of a commentary upon the propositions just advanced" (Poe 1927:80). Poe's exposition of the analytic method is a three-step one: first, a definition of analysis; second, an example of analysis in a non-detective context; third, the solving of the murders in the Rue Morgue.

A woman and her daughter are found dead, brutally murdered, in their apartment. There are several aspects to the case which completely baffle the police. The two women were mangled, one shoved up a chimney—a feat which would have required incredible strength. There was no apparent way in which the murderer could have entered or exited the premises, since the doors were found barred and the windows locked after the crime had taken place. The earshot witnesses all claim that the voice they had heard coming from the apartment just before the murders was the voice of a foreigner.

Dupin, in solving this his first crime, sets up a distinct methodology and philosophy of crime detection which became famous and is still used today in crime fiction. In fact, most of the principles of Dupin's method were lifted outright by Conan Doyle and immortalized in his creation of Sherlock Holmes.

The basis of these principles is, of course, the abductive method. The rest of the principles are in a sense a refinement of abduction, a master plan to the most fruitful use of the notion. Here are Dupin's comments on his method, remarks which reveal his modus operandi:

> "The Parisian police, so much extolled for acumen, are cunning, but no more. There is no method in their proceedings, beyond the method of the moment. They make a vast parade of measures; but, not infrequently, these are so ill-adapted to the objects proposed, as to put us in mind of Monsieur Jourdain's calling for his 'robe-de-chambre—pour mieux entendre la musique.' " (Poe 1927:88)

> "Vidocq, for example, was a good guesser, and a persevering man. But, without educated thought, he erred continually by the very intensity at his investigations. He impaired his vision by holding the object too close. He might see, perhaps, one or two points with unusual clearness, but in doing so he, necessarily, lost sight of the matter as a whole." (Poe 1927:89)

> ". . . all apparent impossibilities must be proved to be not such in reality." (Poe 1927:93)

In short, Dupin's principles are these: never assume anything, the nature of the object under scrutiny must dictate the nature of the inquiry, it is necessary to keep sight of the matter as a whole, one must prove that crucial "apparent impossibilities" are possible (if, indeed, they are so).

Using these principles, Dupin is able to solve the crime while the police are quite unsuccessful. Their myopic vision and insistence upon preconceived notions and assumptions limit them here, as it does in "The Purloined Letter," where the scope of their search is not broad enough to see the object directly in front of them. The problem of assumptions comes out clearly in this riddle: You walk into an apartment. Harry and Joan are lying on the floor, dead. There is broken glass on the floor beside them. There is a cat on the couch staring at them with her back arched. The doors and windows were all locked. There is no one else in the apartment. Question: How did the murderer escape? Answer: The murderer has not yet escaped. Harry and Joan are goldfish.

In "The Murders in the Rue Morgue" the police could not go beyond their assumption that the murderer was a human being. They were thus unable to understand any of the clues, or even realize what the clues were. The problem of what to look for, how to direct the inquiry, which clues are important and which are irrelevant, what "truth" is being sought after—all of these are problems with which both Poe and Peirce are concerned. The relevance of this kind of questioning—and the hypothetical positing of the kind of mind equipped to deal with it—is an important part of abduction.

THE RATIOCINATIVE/ABDUCTIVE MIND: POE AND PEIRCE

As Dupin and the narrator both inform us, it takes a special kind of mind to solve these kinds of puzzles. Aside from the general rubric of "ratiocination," Poe calls this mental bent the "bi-part soul" and the "poet-mathematician." The subject, when contemplating a puzzle which requires "a posteriori thinking," as Dupin puts it, goes into a reverie: "His manner at these moments was frigid and abstract; his eyes were vacant in expression; while his voice, usually a rich tenor, rose into a treble which would have sounded petulantly but for the deliberateness and entire distinctness of the expression" (Poe 1927:81).[2]

Daniel Hoffman, an interesting and imaginative contemporary critic of Poe's work, discusses the broader implications of ratiocination in his book *Poe Poe Poe Poe Poe Poe Poe Poe:*

> . . . Dupin's mind works by association. His method is a finer thing, a seemingly more supersensual mechanism, than the ordinary processes of rational reckoning. It partakes of the irrational, and is therefore the highest kind of ratiocination, since it is not the captive of its own premises. What Dupin is so adept at looks to me very much like what "analysts" in our own day call the *preconscious mind.* Dupin can summon and surrender to the associative linkages of preconscious thought, that wonderworking network of similes which the rest of us have papered o'er with the sickly cast of conscious, rational thinking. Therefore he is that much more sophisticated than we, in his conundrum-disentangling, because he is just so much closer to the origins of our being. His mind, working by metaphoric analogies, combines poetic intuition with mathematical exactitude. (Hoffman 1973:107–108)

What is interesting here is not so much the mystical tone which Hoffman lends to ratiocination, a tone which in this case could lead to a denial of its systematic nature. What is crucial is the idea that ratiocination is an operative which can cut through various levels of reality, a creative reverie which transcends positivistic reason and assumptions. This brings us directly back to Peirce, to a concept of his he calls the "Play of Musement":

> Since, then, it is reasonable to assume, in regard to any given problem, that it would get rightly solved by man, if a sufficiency of time and attention were devoted to it. Moreover, those problems that at first blush appear utterly insoluble receive, in that very circumstance, as Edgar Poe remarked in his "Murders in the Rue Morgue," their smoothly fitting keys. This particularly adapts them to the Play of Musement. [Poe's remark: "It appears to me that this mystery is considered insoluble for the very reason which should cause it to be regarded as easy of solution. I mean the outré character of its features."]
>
> Forty or fifty minutes of vigorous and unslackened analytic thought bestowed upon one of them usually suffices to educe from it all there is to educe, its general solution. . . . Enter your skiff of Musement, push off into the lake of thought, and leave the breath of heaven to swell your sail. With your eyes open, awake to what is about within you, and open conversation with yourself; for such is all meditation. (6.460–461)

The parallels between Peirce's abduction and the play of musement and Poe's ratiocination are clear. What is not so clear is the degree to which Poe was an influence on Peirce, yet this is a question that needs to be asked. That Peirce was a reader of Poe—even an attentive and enthusiastic reader—is without a doubt. Poe is mentioned several times in Peirce's *Collected Papers* and in his manuscripts. In fact, one of the manuscripts is called "Art Chirography" and is an attempt to convey through style of script information about the first verses of Poe's "The Raven." Clearly this was not the act of a casual or indifferent reader (Peirce n.d.: Ms. 1539).

The "degree of influence" question is never an easy one to answer, and can too easily fall into the realm of the reductive. It will be deemed sufficient here to make mention of the attentive readership, and point out the similar preoccupations which Poe and Peirce shared. As a final example of the above, Peirce's ms. 475 is the text of a Lowell lecture delivered in Cambridge, Massachusetts, in 1903 entitled "Abduction." In the lecture Peirce discusses the origins of abduction, which he attributes to chapter twenty-five of Aristotle's *Prior Analytics*. Peirce hypothesizes that poor transcription caused the loss of the word meaning "abduction" and that there was a consequent filling in of a word meaning reduction. Peirce retranslates the passage, substituting abduction for reduction. The sense of the passage changes considerably with this substitution and the concept that Aristotle is discussing sounds very much like Peirce's abduction. The rest of the lecture is dedicated to an epistemological speculation on the implications of abduction:

> How is it that man ever came by any correct theories about nature? We know by induction that man has correct theories, for they produce predictions that are fulfilled. But by what process or thought were they ever brought to his mind? (Peirce n.d.: Ms. 475)

Peirce points out that various factors such as prophetic dreams used to be taken into account in the accumulation of knowledge. He estimates that there are "trillions" of theories in existence, and says, "Every little chicken that is hatched has to rummage through all possible theories until it lights upon the good idea of picking up something and eating it?" (ibid.). The counterargument would be your saying that the chicken has innate ideas or instinct about what to do with itself. Peirce replies that "every poor chicken endowed with an innate tendency toward a positive truth? Should you think that to man alone this gift is denied?" (ibid.).

He limits the range of abduction by stating that believing in the next life is going too far. Peirce ends this lecture with speculation of a more tautological nature: "The question is what theories and conceptions we *ought* to entertain" (ibid.).

CONCLUSION: A SYSTEMATIZATION OF THE HYPERREAL?

In sum, there is a set of similar concerns in the thought of Poe and Peirce. Roughly speaking, these are inquiries into the method of the mind, the definition of reason, what lies beyond reason, the topology of the edges of instinct, how new knowledge is acquired, the relationship of intuition to reason.

Poe and Peirce share as well an interesting double attitude toward these questions and the abductive method which was structured to confront them. On the one hand, there is an empirically grounded systematic approach toward the model. This is particularly evident in Peirce, and in Poe to a somewhat lesser degree. The detective model is a good example of this double attitude as it is operant strictly from the laws and experience of this world. Yet, as Peirce and Poe show us, it relies heavily on intuition.

This brings us to the other hand. There is a rather direct movement toward the mystical implicit in the sorts of questions that Poe and

Peirce ask. When prophetic dreams and intuition are included in the realm of experience from which new knowledge is generated, we are talking about epistemological possibilities which have a range far broader than the usual. Ginzburg might say that this is a meeting place of the rational and the irrational. The point would be that double nature, in the light of this discussion, becomes double face.

The implications of abduction and the questions that the abductive method generates are seemingly without parameters. Ginzburg, Hoffman, Poe, and Peirce all hint at this. They bring into play such major preoccupations as the nature of the scientific and cultural knowledge we possess, by what process that knowledge was acquired, how we know what we want to and need to know.

What does all this have to do with detective fiction? you may ask impatiently at this point. The answer would be the following. Detective fiction has been and still is today the literary form which is devoted to the expression of abduction. The legacy of Poe, one special detective with a special method (and perhaps a sidekick) has been handed down through generation after generation of detective fiction for over one hundred years, from Conan Doyle to Dashiell Hammett to Raymond Chandler to Ross MacDonald. The fact that Poe's abductive method has been preserved almost to the letter is obvious when reading detective works by any of these major figures of the genre. Detective fiction has become enormously popular and widely diffused. The detective method has a far-reaching appeal to be understood perhaps through its poetic and scientific nature, its double face.

NOTES

1. For a semiotic analysis of this chapter in *Zadig* that reveals type distinctions in clues and discusses the role of abduction, see Eco, in Ch. 10.

2. It should be noted here that Conan Doyle's creation, Sherlock Holmes, goes into a similar reverie when mulling over a case; see Ch. 2.

CHAPTER TEN

Umberto Eco

Horns, Hooves, Insteps

SOME HYPOTHESES ON THREE TYPES OF ABDUCTION

I. HORNS

I.1 Aristotle on Ruminants

In *Posterior Analytics* (II, 98a 15ff.) Aristotle, discussing the problem of the kind of division required in order to formulate a correct definition, gives a curious example:

> We are now using the traditional class names, but we must not confine ourselves to these in our inquiry; we must collect any other observed common characteristic, and then consider with what species it is connected, and what properties it entails. For example, in the case of horned animals, the possession of a third stomach and a single row of teeth. Since these animals clearly possess these attributes because they have horns, the question is: "what species of animals have the property of possessing horns?"

To define something means, for Aristotle, to provide a genus and a differentia specifica, genus plus differentia circumscribing the species. A definition is different from a syllogism: those who define do not prove the existence of the definiendum (*Post. An.* II, 92b 20), since a definition only tells *what* a thing is and not *that* a thing is. However, to tell what a thing is also means to tell *why* it is so, that is, to know the *cause* of its being so-and-so (ibid., 93a 5ff.). This cause will act as the middle term in further deduction, able to infer the existence of the thing defined (ibid., 93a 4–5ff.).

Suppose a given species S is defined as M (genus plus differentia): M should be the reason why S also possesses the characteristics of being P.

It is unclear whether Aristotle is thinking in terms of classification (that is, of an embedding from species to upper genera) or in terms of cluster of many properties, more or less accidental. In the first case he would say that S, being defined as M, belongs to the upper genus P; in the second case he would say that S, insofar as it is M, in some way implies the property P (for instance, a man, insofar as he is a mortal rational animal, also is capable of laughing). It is controversial whether Aristotle believed that animals could be classified according to a unique and "global" Porphyrian Tree, or was eager to accept many complementary and "local" divisions. In *Posterior Analytics* he seems to encourage the first supposition, but in *Parts of Animals* (as well as in *History of Animals*) he (a) criticizes the dichotomic division as ineffective (what does not exclude the possibility of another non-dichotomic kind of division), and (b) he blatantly does not succeed in outlining a complete and coherent classification.

As Balme (1975) has persuasively shown, most of his group names do not denote genera but diagnostic characters. He "selects just those differentiae which appear relevant at the moment, as offering a clue to the problem under discussion. . . . It makes no difference whether he speaks of "ovipara among quadrupeds" . . . or "quadrupeds among ovipara". . . . He constantly groups and regroups (the differentiae) to focus on particular problems," and he does so because he understands that differentiae cannot form a hierarchical system, since they cross-divide and "much overlapping occurs between kinds."

But all this does not jeopardize what he is assuming in *Posterior Analytics* (II, 93a 4ff), namely, that a good definition (no matter whether obtained by dichotomic division or not), while saying *what* something is, also explains the reason *why* this something is so-and-so. Thus from the definition of S as M a good demonstrative syllogism can be outlined, namely:

(1) all M are P
all S are M
all S are P

which represents a correct instance of Barbara and a paramount example of deduction. Using the deductive schema as a previsional device, one is in the position of ascertaining whether the deduced consequences did in fact occur.

Thus, definition and syllogism, although radically different, are in some way connected. The definition cannot be demonstrated as the conclusion of a syllogism (since it is merely postulated), yet it is a further syllogism that can enable one to see whether there is a corresponding relation among *facts*.

Aristotle has then to provide a good definition for horned animals. He knows many things about this problem, to which he devotes two long discussions in *Parts of Animals*. The evidence he collects are the following:

(2) All horned animals have a single row of teeth, that is, they lack upper incisors (663b–664a).

(3) Animals without horns have some other means of defense (663a–664a). This holds for animals with teeth or fangs, but also for the camel (which, as we will see, has many features in common with horned animals), protected by its large body.

(4) All horned animals have four stomachs (674a,b).

(5) Not every animal with four stomachs is horned, see camels and does (ibid.).

(6) All animals with four stomachs lack upper incisors (674a).

These are undoubtedly "surprising facts" and Aristotle wants to decide whether there is a cause that can play the role of a middle term in a possible syllogism, and which corresponds to the definition of horned animals. He thus looks for an hypothesis able "to substitute for a great series of predicates, forming no unity in themselves, a single one which involves all of them" (Peirce 1965–1966:5.276).

In *Parts of Animals* Aristotle puts forth some explanations: in animals needing protection, the extra earthly (hard) material for horns is secured at the cost of the upper incisors. Aristotle suggests that in biological evolution, among the famous four causes (formal, material, efficient, and final) the final one plays a privileged role and horns are the goal that nature has in view; so nature deflects to the top of the head the hard matter forming the upper jaw to produce horns. Horns are thus the final cause of the lack of upper incisors. Thus, we can say that horns cause the absence of teeth (663b 31ff.).

Aristotle seems more ambiguous apropos of the cause/effect relation between lacking upper incisors and having a third stomach. He could have said either that the absence of upper incisors has produced the formation of a third stomach, so that these animals could ruminate what they do not chew enough; or that the growth of a third stomach has freed the upper teeth of any function, thus producing their extinction.

A possible answer is suggested by the discussion about birds (674aff.), where Aristotle says that nature compensates with more activity and heat in the stomach the deficiencies of the beak. It then seems that because of mouth deficiencies the bird's stomach grows up.

So far, we can say that for Aristotle the need for protection is the cause of horns, horns the cause of the deflection of hard material from mouth to head, deflection the cause of the lack of teeth, and this last deficiency the cause of the growth of more stomachs. Aristotle also says that camels, which have no horns because they are protected by their size, save the hard material and transform it into a hard cartilage in the upper jaw, since they must eat thorny food.

With these ideas in mind Aristotle should be able to try a definition of horned animals (a definition that in *Post.An.* is only proposed and not elaborated). But to define means to isolate the middle term (the cause) and to choose the middle term means to decide what has to be explained.

Let us suppose that Aristotle must explain first of all why horned animals lack upper incisors. He must figure out a Rule so that, if the Result he wants to explain was a Case of this Rule, the Result would no longer be surprising. Therefore he guesses that probably the hard material has been deflected from the mouth in order to form horns. Let us suppose that

(7)   M = deflecting animals (that is, animals which have deflected the hard matter from mouth to head)
      P = animals lacking upper incisors
      S = horned animals

If "hypothesis is where we find some very curious circumstances, which will be explained by the supposition that it was the case of a certain general rule and thereupon adopt that supposition" (Peirce 1965–1966:2.624), then Aristotle can try the following syllogism:

(8)   *Rule*   All deflecting animals lack upper incisors.
     Case   All horned animals have deflected.
 ·.*Result*   All horned animals lack upper incisors.

This syllogism meets the requirement of the model (1).

The result is explained as the case of a rule, and the cause of the result is the middle term of the syllogism resulting from a tentative definition: "horned animals are those animals (genus) which have deflected the hard matter from mouth to head (differentia)"; this essential nature makes them belong to the wider genus of those animals lacking upper incisors; or, this essential nature makes them possess the further property of lacking upper incisors—a genus which also encompasses (or a property that also belongs to) non-horned animals like camels. If by chance, in the course of further observations, it happens that one finds an S which is not a P (that is, an animal with horns and with upper incisors) the hypothesis represented by the definition will be falsified. As for the phenomenon of four stomachs, such a character seems to be linked to the absence of upper incisors, as already suggested, so that probably, given a kind of animals that have grown up a special digestive apparatus (comprehending not only ruminants but also birds) some of them did so because they lack upper incisors. The definition will then be: ruminants are those animals with a special digestive apparatus because they lack upper incisors. On such a basis, the following syllogism can be elaborated:

(9)   *Rule*   All animals lacking upper incisors have a special diges-
              tive apparatus.
      Case   All ruminants lack upper incisors.
∴ *Result*   All ruminants have a special digestive apparatus.

It must be told that Aristotle is rather embarrassed when he tries to explain the peculiar situation of camels, and this proves how difficult it is to outline the "good" division underlying a global system of correlated definitions (as it appears clearly from *Parts of Animals* 642b 20–644a 10). But for the purposes of the present argument we can disregard this point.

I.2 Peirce on Beans

It is evident that the above inferences (8) and (9), all regulated by the model (1) are similar to the well-known problem of white beans proposed by Peirce (2.623). Facing the surprising fact represented by some white beans, Peirce in fact defines then as "the white beans coming from this bag." *Coming from this bag* is the middle term, the same that works in the proposed law and in the following syllogism:

(10) *Rule*   All the beans from this bag are white.
      Case   These beans are from this bag.
∴ *Result*   These beans are white.

There is no difference between what Peirce called Hypothesis or Abduction and the effort by which, according to Aristotle, one figures out a definition, saying *what* a thing is, by explaining tentatively *why* this is such as it is, so displaying all the elements able to set out a deduction according to which, if the Rule was right, every Result will prove *that* this thing is.

An interesting problem is why Aristotle devotes some observation to *apagōgē*, as the inference that one makes "when it is obvious that the first term applies to the middle, but that the middle applies to the last term is not obvious, yet nevertheless is more probable, or not less probable than the conclusion" (*Prior Analytics* II, 69a 20), but he does not apparently identify *apagōgē* with the defining activity.

It is true that he was thinking of a definition as a scientific procedure aiming at expressing an irrefutable truth, where the *definiens* was fully reciprocable with the *definiendum;* nevertheless, he was conscious of the fact that many definitions of the same phenomenon can be outlined according to different causes (*Post.An.* II, 99b), depending on the kind of question which is asked, that is, according to the identification (or choice) of the *most surprising* fact. If Aristotle had explicitly acknowledged the consequences of this admission, the tentative and abductional character of *every* scientific definition would have become absolutely clear to him.

Peirce had no doubts. He not only identified Abduction with *apagōgē,* but he also maintained that Abduction rules every form of knowledge, even perception (5.181) and memory (2.625).

It is clear, however, that for Aristotle to define surprising facts (see the cases of eclipses or of thunder) means to figure out a hierarchy of causal links through a sort of hypothesis that can be validated only when it gives rise to a deductive syllogism which acts as a forecast for further tests.

From the above remarks, Peircean definition of Abduction should be reconsidered. Peirce says (2.623) that, while Induction is the inference of the Rule from a Case and a Result, Hypothesis is the inference of the Case from a Rule and a Result. According to Thagard (1978), there is a difference between Hypothesis as *inference to a Case,* and Abduction as inference to a Rule. We shall better see this point in 1.4 below, but for now it is important to stress that the real problem is not whether to find first the Case or the Rule, but rather how to figure out both the Rule and the Case *at the same time,* since they are inversely related, tied together by a sort of chiasmus—where the middle term is the keystone of all inferential movement.

The middle term is the triggering device of the whole process. Peirce could have decided that the crucial element was not where those beans came from, but—let us say—who brought them there; or that the source of the beans were more presumably a drawer or a pot not far from the bag. In the same vein Aristotle could have decided that the relevant elements, in his problem, were not the deflection of hard matter (a very sophisticated explanation, indeed) or the need for protection, but some other cause. The invention of a good middle term, that was the ingenious idea.

There are obviously rules which are so evident that they suggest immediately how to look for the middle term. Suppose that in a room there are only a table, a handful of white beans, and a bag. The identification of "coming from that bag" as the crucial element would be a rather easy matter. If I find upon a table a dish with some canned tuna fish and at a reasonable distance a can of tuna fish, the consequent hypothesis is *quasi*-automatic: but it is the *quasi* that still makes a hypothesis of this automatic reasoning.

So, even in cases in which the rule is evident, and the inference concerns only the case, a hypothesis is never a matter of certitude. Peirce (2.265) suggests that when we find fossil remains of fish far in the interior of the country, we can suppose that the sea once washed this land. A whole previous paleontological tradition seems to encourage such an abduction. But why not privilege some other explanations, for instance, that some alien monsters have provoked all this after a picnic, or that a movie director has prepared this *mise-en-scène* for filming *The Neanderthal Man Strikes Again?*

Coeteris paribus (if there are not actors and other movie people around, if the newspapers have not recently reported similar mysterious phenomena due to the probable action of alien invaders, and so on), the general paleontological explanation would seem the most economic one. But there were many false scientific explanations, which seemed very economic (for instance, geocentrical paradigm, phlogiston and so on), that had nevertheless to be substituted by something apparently less "regular" or less "normal."

I.3 Laws and Facts

However paradoxical, that last series of questions makes us think about two different kinds of abduction: the former starts from one or more surprising particular facts and ends at the hypothesis of a general law (this seems to be the case of all scientific discoveries), while the latter starts from one or more surprising particular facts and ends at the hypothesis of another particular fact which is supposed to be the cause of the former (this seems to be the case of criminal detection). In the above example, are the fossils the case of a general law or the effect of a particular vicious cause (which as a matter of fact could be defined as a violation of current norms)?

One can say that the first type concerns the nature of *universes* and the second one concerns the nature of *texts*. I mean by "universes," intuitively, worlds such as the one which scientists use to explain the laws, by "text" a coherent series of propositions, linked together by a common topic or theme (see Eco 1979). In this sense even the sequence of events investigated by a detective can be defined as a text. Not only because it can be reduced to a sequence of propositions (a detective novel or the official report on a true investigation is nothing other than this), but also because verbal and pictorial texts, as well as criminal cases, require, in order to be recognized as a coherent and self-explaining whole, an "idiolectal rule," a code of their own, an explanation that can work for and inside them and that cannot be transplanted into other texts.

This distinction, however, is hardly convincing. If abduction is a general principle ruling the whole of human knowledge, there should be no substantial differences between these two sorts of abduction. In order to explain a text we frequently use intertextual rules: not only genre rules in literary texts, but also common norms, rhetorical *endoxa* (such as the rule *cherchez la femme,* when dealing with a criminal case). Likewise, in order to explain universes we frequently turn to laws that work only for a specific portion of that universe, without being ad hoc, as in the case of the complementarity principle in physics.

I think that the general mechanism of abduction can be made clear only if we assume that we deal with universes as if they were texts and with texts as if they were universes. In this perspective the difference between the two sorts of abduction disappears. When a single fact is taken as the explanatory hypothesis for another single fact, the former works (within a given textual universe) as the general law explaining the latter. General laws, insofar as they are open to falsification and potential conflict with alternative laws which could explain equally well the same facts, should be taken as facts of a particular nature, or as the general models of certain facts which cause the facts to be explained. Moreover, in scientific discovery one figures out laws through the mediating discovery of many further facts; and in text interpretation one identifies new relevant facts by presupposing certain general (intertextual) laws.

Much contemporary research has identified abduction with the conjectural procedures of physicians and of historians (see the essay by Ginzburg, Ch. 4, in this book). Now a doctor looks both for general laws and for specific and idiosyncratic causes, and a historian works to identify both historical laws and particular causes of particular events. In either case historians and physicians are conjecturing about the textual quality of a series of apparently disconnected elements. They are operating a *reductio ad unum* of a plurality. Scientific discoveries, medical and criminal detections, historical reconstructions, philological interpretations of literary texts (attribution to a certain author on the grounds of stylistical keys, "fair guesses" about lost sentences or words) are all cases of *conjectural thinking.*

That is the reason why, I believe, analyzing the conjectural procedures in criminal detection can throw a new light upon the conjectural procedures in science, and describing the conjectural procedures in philology can throw a new light upon medical diagnoses. And that is the reason why the papers of this book, even though dealing with the relationship of Peirce—Poe—Conan Doyle, work for a more general epistemological endeavor.

I.4 Hypothesis, Abduction, Meta-abduction

As it was suggested in 1.2 (cf. the important remarks of Thagard 1978), Peirce probably thought of two kinds of inferential reasoning: *hypothesis,* which is the isolation of an already coded rule, to which a case is correlated by inference; and *abduction,* which is the provisional entertainment of an explanatory inference, for the sake of further testing, and which aims at isolating, along with the case, also the rule. Maybe it is better (irrespective of the terms that Peirce uses to name them) to isolate three types of abduction. I'll follow some suggestions given by Bonfantini and Proni (Ch. 5 in this book), many of Thagard's proposals, and I shall add to the list the new concept of meta-abduction.

(a) *Hypothesis or overcoded abduction.* The law is given automatically or semiautomatically. Let us call this kind of law a *coded* law. It is very important to assume that even interpreting through codes presupposes an abductional effort, however minimal. Supposing that I know that /man/ in English means "human adult male" (a perfect case of linguistic coding), and supposing that I *believe* that I hear the utterance /man/, in order to understand it in its meaning, I must first assume that it is the utterance (token) of a type of English word. It seems that usually we do this kind of interpretive labor automatically, but if by chance one is living in an international milieu in which people are supposed to speak different languages one realizes that the choice is not radically automatic. To recognize a given phenomenon as the token of a given type presupposes some hypothesis about the context of utterance and the discursive co-text. Thagard suggests that this type (corresponding for him to hypothesis) is close to my notion of *overcoding* (see Eco 1976:2.14) as the case-inference to the best explanation.

(b) *Undercoded abduction.* The rule must be selected from a series of equiprobable rules put at our disposal by the current world knowledge (or semiotic encyclopedia, see Eco 1979). In this sense we have undoubtedly an inference to a rule, that Thagard calls "abduction" *stricto sensu* (note that Thagard's notion of abduction will cover also my third type of abduction). Since the rule is selected as the more plausible among many, but it is not certain whether it is the "correct" one or not, the explanation is only *entertained,* waiting for further tests. When

Kepler discovered the ellipticity of the orbit of Mars, he met a surprising fact (the initial positions of the planet), then he had to choose between various geometrical curves, whose number was not infinite, however. Some previous assumptions about the regularity of the universe suggested to him that he had to look only for closed not transcendental curves (planets do not make random jumps and do not proceed by spirals or sine waves). The same experience had happened to Aristotle: not only his finalistic mind but a lot of established opinions convinced him that self-protection was one of the most plausible final causes of biological evolution.

(c) *Creative abduction.* The law must be *invented ex novo.* To invent a law is not so difficult, provided our mind is "creative" enough. As we will see in 3.1., this creativity involves also aesthetic aspects. In any case this kind of invention obliges one to make (more than in cases of overcoded or undercoded abductions) a meta-abduction. Examples of creative abductions are found in these "revolutionary" discoveries that change an established scientific paradigm (Kuhn 1962).

(d) *Meta-abduction.* It consists in deciding as to whether the possible universe outlined by our first-level abductions is the same as the universe of our experience. In over- and undercoded abductions, this meta-level of inference is not compulsory, since we get the law from a storage of already checked actual world experience. In other words, we are entitled by common world knowledge to think that, provided the law is the suitable one, it already holds in the world of our experience. In creative abductions we do not have this kind of certainty. We are making a complete "fair guess" not only about the nature of the result (its cause) but also about the nature of the encyclopedia (so that, if the new law results in being verified, our discovery leads to a change of paradigm). As we shall see, meta-abduction is not only crucial in "revolutionary" scientific discoveries but also (and normally) in criminal detection.

The above hypotheses shall now be verified by a text which, according to a large bibliography, displays many analogies with the methods of Sherlock Holmes and which, at the same time, represents a perfect example (or an allegorical model) of scientific inquiry. I mean the third chapter of Voltaire's *Zadig.*

II. HOOVES

II.1 Voltaire's text

Zadig found that the first moon of marriage, even as it is written in the book of Zend, is of honey, and the second of wormwood. After a time he had to get rid of Azora, who had become too difficult to live with, and he tried to find his happiness in the study of nature. "No one is happier," said he, "than a philosopher who reads in this great book that God has placed before our eyes. The truths he discovers belong to him. He nourishes and ennobles his soul. He lives in peace, fearing nothing from men, and his dear wife does not come to cut off his nose."

Filled with these ideas, he retired to a house in the country on the banks of the Euphrates. There he did not pass his time calculating how many inches of water flow in one second under the arches of a bridge, or if a cubic line more rain fell in the month of the mouse than in the month of the sheep. He did not contrive to make silk from spiders' webs, or porcelain from broken bottles; but he studied above all the characteristics of animals and plants, and soon acquired a perspicacity which showed him a thousand differences where other men see only uniformity.

While walking one day near a little wood he saw one of the queen's eunuchs hastening toward him, followed by several officers, who seemed to be greatly troubled, and ran hither and thither like distracted men seeking something very precious they have lost.

"Young man," cried the Chief Eunuch, "you haven't seen the queen's dog, have you?"

"It's not a dog," answered Zadig modestly, "it's a bitch."

"That's so," said the Chief Eunuch.

"It's a very small spaniel," added Zadig, "which has had puppies recently; her left forefoot is lame, and she has very long ears."

"You have seen her then?" said the Eunuch, quite out of breath.

"Oh, no!" answered Zadig. "I have not seen the animal, and I never knew the queen had a bitch."

Just at this moment, by one of the usual freaks of fortune, the finest horse in the king's stables escaped from a groom's hands and fled into the plains of Babylon. The Master of the King's Hounds and all the other officials rushed after it with as much anxiety as the Chief Eunuch after the bitch. The Master of the King's Hounds came up to Zadig and asked if he had not seen the king's horse pass by.

"The horse you are looking for is the best galloper in the stable," answered Zadig. "It is fifteen hands high, and has a very small hoof. Its tail is three and a half feet long. The studs on its bit are of twenty-three carat gold, and its shoes of eleven scruple silver."

"Which road did it take?" asked the Master of the King's Hounds. "Where is it?"

"I have not seen the horse," answered Zadig, "and I have never heard speak of it."

The Master of the King's Hounds and the Chief Eunuch had no doubt but that Zadig had stolen the king's horse and the queen's bitch, and they had him taken before the Grand Destur, who condemned him to the knout and afterwards to spend the rest of his days in Siberia. Hardly had judgment been pronounced than the horse and the bitch were found. The judges were in the sad necessity of having to rescind their judgment, but they condemned Zadig to pay four hundred ounces of gold for having denied seeing what he had seen. Only after the fine had been paid was Zadig allowed to plead his cause, which he did in the following terms.

"Stars of Justice," he said, "Unfathomable Wells of Knowledge, Mirrors of Truth, that have the solidity of lead, the hardness of iron, the radiance of the diamond, and much affinity with gold, since I am permitted to speak before this august assembly, I swear to you by Ormuzd that I have never seen the queen's honorable bitch or the king of kings' sacred horse. Let me tell you what happened.

"I was walking toward the little wood where I met later the venerable Chief Eunuch and the very illustrious Master of the King's Hounds. I saw an animal's tracks on the sand and I judged without difficulty they were the tracks of a small dog. The long, shallow furrows printed on the little ridges of sand between the tracks of the paws informed me that the animal was a bitch with pendent dugs, who hence had had puppies recently. Other tracks in a different direction, which seemed all the time to have scraped the surface of the sand beside the fore-paws, gave me the idea that the bitch had very long ears; and as I remarked that the sand was always less hollowed by one paw than by the three others, I concluded that our august queen's bitch was somewhat lame, if I dare say so.

"As regards the king of kings' horse, you may know that as I walked along the road in this wood I saw the marks of horse-shoes, all equal distances apart. That horse, said I, gallops perfectly. The dust on the trees in this narrow road only seven feet wide was raised a little right and left, three and a half feet from the middle of the road. This horse, said I, has a tail three and a half feet long, and its movement right and left has swept up this dust. I saw beneath the trees, which made a cradle five feet high, some leaves newly fallen from the branches, and I recognized that this horse had touched there and was hence fifteen hands high. As regards his bit, it must be of twenty-three carat gold, for he rubbed the studs against a stone which I knew to be a touchstone and tested. From the marks his hoofs made on certain pebbles I knew the horse was shod with eleven scruple silver."

All the judges admired Zadig's profound and subtle perspicacity, news of which came to the ears of the king and queen. In the ante-rooms, the throne-room, and the closet Zadig was the sole topic of conversation, and although several of the Magi thought he should be burned as a sorcerer, the king ordered the fine of four hundred ounces of gold to which he had been condemned to be returned to him. The clerk of the court, the ushers, the attorneys called on him with great pomp to bring him these four hundred ounces. They retained only three hundred and ninety-eight for judicial costs, and their lackeys demanded largess.

Zadig saw how dangerous it was sometimes to be too knowing, and promised himself, on the first occasion that offered, not to say what he had seen.

The occasion soon presented itself. A state prisoner escaped, and passed beneath the window of Zadig's house. Zadig was questioned, and made no reply. But it was proved he had looked out of his window. For this crime he was condemned to five hundred ounces of gold, and, as is the custom in Babylon, he thanked his judges for their indulgence.

"Good God!" he said to himself. "A man who walks in a wood where the queen's bitch or the king's horse has passed is to be pitied! How dangerous it is to look out of the window! How difficult it is to be happy in this life!" (Voltaire 1931).

II.2 Overcoded Abductions

It is not by chance that Zadig calls Nature a "great book"; he is concerned with Nature as a system of coded signs. He does not pass his time in calculating how many inches of water flow under a bridge (an activity that would have pleased both Peirce and Holmes), and he does not try to make porcelain from broken bottles (an activity for which Peirce would have tried to acquire the right *habit*). Zadig studies "the characteristics of animals and plants"; he looks for general relations of signification (he wants to know whether any S is a P) and he does not seem too concerned with the extensional verification of his knowledge. When Zadig sees animal tracks on the sand, he recognizes them as the tracks of a dog and of a horse. Both cases (dog and horse) display the same semiotic mechanism, but the case of the horse is more complex, and it will be more fruitful to analyze carefully the way Zadig recognizes the imprints of a horse. To be able to isolate tracks as the occurrence (token) of a type-track, thus recognizing them as signifying a certain class of animals, means to share a precise (coded) competence about imprints (cf. Eco 1976:3.6).

Imprints represent the most elementary case of sign-production since the expression, correlated to a given content, is not usually produced as a sign (there can also be imprints of natural events, like the traces of an avalanche, and in the case of the king's horse, the animal had no intention of producing a sign) until the moment one recognizes it and decides to assume it is a sign. To interpret an imprint means to correlate it to a possible physical cause. Such a physical cause does not need to be actual: it can be a merely *possible* one, since one can recognize an imprint even in the pages of a Boy Scouts handbook: a previous experience has produced a habit according to which a given type-shape refers back to the class of its possible causes. In this type-to-type semiotic relationship, concrete individuals are not yet concerned.

One can teach a computer to recognize the imprint of a glass of red wine upon a table by giving it precise instructions, namely, that the imprint must be circular, that the diameter of the circle must be two to three inches, and that this circle is made with a liquid red substance of which the chemical formula may be provided along with spectral data on the required shade of red. A type-expression is nothing else than this set of instructions. Notice that this way of defining the type-expression corresponds to the kind of definition as precept provided by Peirce apropos of /lithium/ (2.330). Once fed with such a definition of the type-expression, the computer must be fed with instructions concerning the correlated type-content, and at this point it will be in the position to recognize all the imprints of this type.

However, a code of imprints involves synecdochical inferences, since the imprint of a glass does not visually reproduce the form of the glass but at most the shape of its bottom; likewise a hoof mark reproduces the form of the bottom of the hoof and can be correlated to the class of horses only by a further link. Moreover, the code can list imprints at different levels of pertinence, that is, an imprint can be correlated either to a genus or to a species. Zadig, for instance, does not only recognize "dog" but also "spaniel," and not only "horse" but also (due to an inference about the distance between the marks) "stallion."

But Zadig also discovers other semiotic features, namely, symptoms and clues. (cf. Eco 1976:3.6.2.). In symptoms the type-expression is a class of ready-made physical events that refer back to the class of their possible causes (red spots on the face mean measles): but are different from imprints insofar as the shape of an imprint is a projection from the pertinent features of the type-shape of the possible imprinters, whereas there is no point-to-point correspondence between a symptom and its cause. The cause of a symptom is not a feature of the shape of its type-expression but a feature of its type-content (the cause is a marker of the compositional analysis of the meaning of a given symptom-expression). Zadig recognizes symptoms when he detects that the dust on the trees was raised right and left, three and a half feet from the middle of the road. The position of the dust is the symptom that something caused its disposition. The same happens with the leaves fallen from the branches. According to the code, Zadig knows that both phenomena are symptoms of an external force which has acted upon a resistant matter, but the code does not provide him with any information concerning the nature of the cause.

Clues, on the other hand, are objects left by an external agent in the spot where it did something, and are somehow recognized as physically linked to that agent, so that from their actual or possible presence the actual or possible past presence of the agent can be detected.

The difference between symptoms and clues is due to the fact that with symptoms the encyclopedia records a *necessary* present or past contiguity between the effect and the cause, and the presence of the effect sends one back to the necessary presence of the cause; whereas with clues the encyclopedia records only a *possible* past contiguity between the owner and the owned and the presence of the owned sends one back to the possible presence of the owner. In a way clues are complex symptoms, since one must first detect the necessary presence of an indeterminate causing agent and then take this symptom as the clue referring back to a possibly more determined agent—conventionally recognized as the most probable owner of the object left on the spot. That is why a criminal novel is usually more intriguing than the detection of pneumonia.

Zadig recognizes clues when he detects, from the gold on the stone and the silver on the pebbles, that the bit of the horse was of twenty-three carat gold and the shoes were shod with scruple silver. However, the code only tells Zadig that if gold and silver were on the stones, then it should have been some owner of gold and silver which left them, but no encyclopedic information can make him sure that that owner was a horse, namely, the one signified by the imprints. Therefore, at first glance, gold and silver are still acting as symptoms and not yet as clues: at most, the encyclopedia tells him that even horses, among many other possible agents, may be the bearers of gold and silver paraphernalia. Up to this point Zadig knows, however, only the rules he had previously known, that is, that certain imprints, symptoms, and clues refer to a certain class of causes. He is still bound to overcoded abductions.

Nevertheless, having discovered these tracks in *that* wood and at *that* precise moment he can take them as the concrete occurrence of the indexical statement "a horse was here." Passing again from type to token, Zadig shifts from the universe of intensions to the universe of extensions. Even in this case we are still witnessing an overcoded abductional effort: to decide, when an indexical statement is produced, that it is produced in order to mention states of the world of our experience, is still a matter of pragmatic convention.

Once all these decoding abductions are made successfully, Zadig knows, however, only disconnected surprising facts, namely:

—an x which is a horse has passed in that place;
—a y (unidentified) has broken the branches;
—a k (unidentified) has rubbed something golden against a stone;
—a j (unidentified) has left silver clues on certain pebbles;
—a z (unidentified) has swept the dust on the trees.

II.3 Undercoded Abductions

The various visual statements Zadig is dealing with can represent either a disconnected *series* or a coherent *sequence*, that is, a text. To recognize a series as a textual sequence means to find out a textual topic, or that "aboutness" of the text which establishes a coherent relationship between different and still disconnected textual data. The identification of a textual topic is a case of undercoded abductive effort.

Frequently one does not know whether the topic one has discovered is the "good" one or not, and the activity of textual interpretation can end at different and conflicting semantic actualizations. This proves that every text-interpreter makes abductions among many possible readings of a text. So does Zadig.

Once a series of general coded intertextual conventions or *frames* have been supposed, according to which (a) horses usually sweep the dust with their tail, (b) horses bear golden bits and silver horseshoes, (c) usually stones retain small fragments of malleable metal bodies that violently collide with them, and so on, at this point (even though several other phenomena could have produced the same effects) Zadig is able to try his textual reconstruction.

A general coherent picture takes shape: a story with *only one* subject, co-referred to by different symptoms and clues, is definitely outlined. Zadig could have tried a totally different reconstruction. For instance, that a knight, with golden armor and silver spear, unsaddled by his horse, had broken the branches and had struck with his paraphernalia against the stones. . . . Zadig has not certainly chosen the "correct" interpretation because of a mysterious "guessing instinct." First of all, there were reasons of economy: a horse alone was more economical than a horse plus a knight. Moreover, Zadig knew many analogous intertextual frames (canonical stories of horses escaped from their stable), and thus by an undercoded abduction he has selected, among many possible intertextual laws, the most verisimilar one.

But this was not sufficient. Voltaire is not explicit on this point, but let us suppose that Zadig has turned over in his mind many alternative hypotheses and has definitely chosen the final one only when he has met the men of the Court looking for a horse. Only at this point has Zadig dared to try his final meta-abduction, as we shall see below. It goes without saying that everything that has been said about the horse also holds for the bitch.

As a final comment, it seems that the whole picture has been realized by undercoded abductional efforts without making recourse to creative abductions. Zadig, after all, figures out a "normal" story.

II.4 On the Threshold of Meta-abduction

Zadig does not possess the scientific certainty that his textual hypothesis is *true:* it is only *textually verisimilar.* Zadig pronounces, so to speak, a *teleological* judgment. He decides to interpret the data he had assembled as if they were harmoniously interrelated.

He *knew* before that there was a horse and that there were four other unidentified agents. He *knew* that these five agents were individuals of the actual world of his own experience. Now he also *believes* that there was a horse with a long tail, fifteen hands high, with a golden bit and a silver hoof. But such a horse does not necessarily belong to the actual world of Zadig's experience. It belongs to the textual possible world Zadig has built up, to the world of Zadig's strongly motivated beliefs, to the world of Zadig's propositional attitudes. Undercoded abductions—not to speak of the creative ones—are world-creating devices. It is important to recognize the modal nature of Zadig's textual abduction to understand what will happen later.

The Master of King's Hounds and the Chief Eunuch do not have much semiotic subtlety. They are only interested in the two individuals they know and they *mention* them through pseudo-definite descriptions (or "degenerate proper names") such as "the queen's dog" and "the king's horse." Since they are looking for two precise individuals, they correctly use definite articles: "*the* dog, *the* horse."

To answer their questions, Zadig has two alternatives. He may accept the extensional game: dealing with people interested in singling out given individuals, he can try a meta-abduction, that is, he is in a position to make a "fair guess" according to which both the horse and the dog of *his own* textual world are the same as those known by the officers. This kind of abduction is the one usually made by a detective: "The possible individual I have outlined as an inhabitant of the world of *my beliefs* is the same as the individual of *the actual world* someone is looking for." Such is the procedure usually implemented by Sherlock Holmes. But Holmes and his congeners are interested precisely in what Zadig was not; to know how many inches of water flow under a bridge, and how to make porcelain from broken bottles.

Devoted only to the study of the book of nature, Zadig should take a second alternative. He might answer: "According to the world of *my* hypotheses I strongly *believe* that *a* horse and *a* dog were here; I do not *know* whether they are indentical with *the* individuals *you* are referring to."

Zadig starts with the first alternative. As a good Sherlock Holmes, he bluffs: "*Your* dog is a bitch and *your* horse is the best galloper in the stable. . . ." Acting as Doctor Watson, the officers are flabbergasted: "That's so!"

The detection has been crowned with success. Zadig could proudly enjoy his triumph. But when the officers take for granted that Zadig knows their own animals and, not unreasonably, ask where they are, then Zadig says that he has never seen them and has never heard of them. He withdraws from his meta-abduction at the very moment he is sure it was correct.

Probably he is so proud of his ability in setting up textual worlds that he does not want to commit himself to a merely extensional game. He feels himself divided between his immense power in creating possible worlds and his practical success. He wishes to be honored as master of the abductions, not as a bearer of empirical truths. In other words, he is more interested in a *theory* of abduction than in scientific *discovery*. Obviously neither the officers nor the judges can understand this interesting case of epistemological schizophrenia. So they condemn Zadig "for having denied seeing what he had [undoubtedly] seen." What a splendid model for a dialogue between a man of good intensions and some men of limited extensions.

However, Zadig does not understand that he has agreed to play the game of his opponents when he has accepted the linguistic game of definite articles and pronouns as identity operators (during his conversation with the officers he constantly referred to the animals by means of definite shifters: "*It*'s a bitch . . . *she* has very long ears . . . *its* tail . . . *The* horse. . . ." These indices were referring (for him) to his possible world, for the officers to their "actual" world. Zadig, oppressed by his schizophrenia, was not clever enough in maneuvering language. Unable to accept his fate as a Sherlock Holmes, Zadig was frightened by meta-abduction.

III. INSTEPS

III.1 Creative Abductions

Many of the so-called "deductions" of Sherlock Holmes are instances of creative abduction. Holmes, in CARD, detects what Watson was mumbling to himself, reading his train of thought through his features, and especially through his eyes. The fact that the train of thought Holmes imagined coincided perfectly with Watson's actual one is the proof that Holmes invented "well" (or in accordance with a certain "natural" course). Notwithstanding this, he did *invent*.

Etymologically, "invention" is the act of finding out what already existed somewhere and Holmes invented in the sense meant by Michelangelo when he says that the sculptor uncovers in the stone the statue that the matter already circumscribed and that was concealed by the stone's surplus (*soverchio*).

Watson threw down his paper and then fixed the picture of the General Gordon. This was undoubtedly *a fact*. That afterward he looked to another (unframed) portrait was another *fact*. That he could have thought of the relation between these two portraits can be a case of undercoded abduction, based on Holmes's knowledge of Watson's interest in interior decoration. But that, from this point on, Watson thought of the incidents of Beecher's career was undoubtedly a creative abduction. Watson could have started from an episode of the American Civil War to compare the gallantry of that war with the horrors of slavery. Or he could have thought of the horrors of the Afghanistan war, then smiled because he realized that his wound was, in conclusion, an acceptable toll to pay for surviving.

Notice that, in the universe of that story—ruled by a sort of complicity between the author of his characters—Watson could not have thought but what he actually did think, so that we have the impression that Holmes isolated the only possible features of Watson's stream of consciousness. But if the story's world were the "real" world, Watson's stream of consciousness could have taken many other directions. Holmes is certainly trying to imitate the way Watson should have thought (*ars imitatur naturam in sua operatione!*) but he was obliged to choose, among many of Watson's possible mental courses (that he probably figured out all together at the same time), the one which displayed more aesthetic coherence, or more "elegance." Holmes invented a story. It simply happened that that possible story was analogous to the actual one.

The same aesthetic criteria ruled Copernican intuition of heliocentrism in *De revolutionibus orbium coelestium*. Copernicus felt that the Ptolemaic system was inelegant, lacking harmony, like a painting in which the painter reproduced all the members without composing them into a unique body. Then the sun *ought to be*, for Copernicus, at the center of the universe, because only in this way could the admirable symmetry of the created world have been manifested. Copernicus did not observe positions of planets like Galileo or Kepler. He figured out a possible world whose guarantee was its being well structured, "gestaltically" elegant.

Let us now follow the train of thought that leads Holmes (SIGN) to infer that Watson went to the Wigmore Street Post Office to dispatch a telegram. The only surprising fact was that Watson had a little reddish mould adhering to his instep. As a matter of fact, in nineteenth-century London, not paved for motor cars, this fact was not so surprising. Holmes focused his attention upon Watson's shoes because he already had some idea in his mind. However, let us trust Conan Doyle and let us admit that this fact was in itself surprising enough.

The first abduction is an overcoded one: people with mud adhering to their instep have been in an unpaved place, and so on. The second abduction is an undercoded one: why Wigmore Street? Because its earth is of this particular tint. But why not suppose that Watson can have taken a cab thus going beyond the neighborhood? Because the selection of the closest street meets reasonable criteria of economy. Elementary. But these two abductions (which in the Doyle-Holmes jargon are called mere "observation") do not say yet that Watson has visited the Post Office.

Notice that, if it is true that Holmes was, on the grounds of his world knowledge, in the position of thinking of the Post Office as the more probable goal for Watson, every evidence was *against* this supposition: Holmes knew that Watson did not need a stamp or postcard. In order to think of the last probability (telegram), Holmes had to have already decided that Watson wanted to dispatch a cable! Holmes makes us think of a judge who, having acquired strong evidence that a given defendant was not present at the right time at the scene of a crime, concludes that therefore this person was committing at the same time another crime in another place. Since Watson lacked 93 percent of reason for going to the Post Office, Holmes (instead of concluding that therefore this hypothesis was implausible) decided that therefore Watson went there for the remaining 7 percent of reasons. A curious hallucinatory 7 percent solution, indeed. To trust as plausible such a weak probability Holmes must have assumed that Watson is in any case a regular Post Office patron. Only under this condition can the presence of stamps and postcards be taken as the evidence that Watson sent a cable. Holmes thus is not selecting, among reasonable probabilities, what would represent a case of undercoded abduction. On the contrary, he is betting against all odds, he is inventing only for the sake of elegance.

III.2 Meta-abductions

To shift from a creative abduction to meta-abduction is typical of a rationalistic mind, in the vein of seventeenth- and eighteenth-century rationalism. In order to reason as Holmes does, one must be strongly convinced that *ordo et connexio idearum idem est ac ordo et connexio rerum* (Spinoza, *Ethica* II,7) and that the validity of a complex concept consists in the possibility of analyzing it into its simplest parts, each of which must appear as rationally *possible:* a labor of free configuration of concepts that Leibniz called "intuition" (*Noveaux essais sur l'entendement humain* IV,1,1; cf. Gerhardt 1875–1890: V,347). For Leibniz the expression can be *similar* to the expressed thing if a certain analogy between their respective structures is observed, since God, being the author of both things and minds, has engraved in our soul a thinking faculty that can operate in accordance with the laws of nature (*Quid sit idea,* Gerhardt 1875–1890: VII,263) "Definitio realis est ex qua constat definitum esse possibile nec implicare contradictionem. . . . Ideas quoque rerum non cogitamus, nisi quatenus earum possibilitatem intuemur" (*Specimen inventorum de admirandis naturae generalis arcanis,* Gerhardt 1875–1890: VII,310).

Holmes can try his meta-abduction only because he thinks that his creative abductions are justified by a strong link between mind and external world. Probably it is his rationalistic background which explains why he insists so much in calling "deduction" his kind of reasoning. In a universe ruled by an innate parallelism between *res extensa* and *res cogitans* (or by a preestablished harmony) the complete concept of an individual substance implies all its past and future predicates (Leibniz, *Primae veritates,* Couturat 1903:518–523).

Peirce speaks of symbols as a law or a regularity of indefinite future (2.293) and says that every proposition is a rudimentary argument (2.344); in many circumstances he shows a certain confidence in the existence of a *"lume naturale"* as an affinity between mind and nature (1.630; 2.753 ff.; 5.604; 5.591; 6.604). But even when asserting that "general principles are really operative in nature" (5.501), he means to make a (Scotist) "realistic" statement, and in many places he is rather critical of Leibnizian rationalism (see, for instance, 2.370).

Peirce holds that conjectures are valid forms of inference insofar as they are nourished by previous observation, even though they *may* anticipate all their remote illative consequences. Peirce's confidence in such an accord between mind and course of events is more evolutionistic than rationalistic (Fann 1970:2.3). The certitude offered by abduction does not exclude *fallibilism,* which dominates every scientific inquiry (1.9), "for fallibilism is the doctrine that our knowledge is never absolute but always swims, as it were, in a continuum of uncertainty and undeterminacy" (1.171).

Holmes, on the contrary, never goes wrong. Unlike Zadig, Holmes has no doubts in meta-betting that the possible world he has outlined is the same as the "real" one. Just as he has the privilege of living in a world built by Conan Doyle to fit his egocentric need, so he does not lack immediate proofs of his perspicacity. Watson (narratively) exists just to verify his hypotheses: "What is this, Holmes? This is beyond anything I could have imagined!" (CARD) "Right! But I confess that I don't see how you arrived at it. . . ." (SIGN). Watson represents the unquestionable guarantee that Holmes's hypotheses cannot be any longer falsified.

It is a privilege Karl Popper does not have, though this lack of privilege gave him the chance to elaborate a logic of scientific discovery. Whereas in criminal stories an omnipotent God verifies the hypotheses forever, in "real" scientific inquiries (as well as in real criminal, medical, or philological detection) meta-abductions are a frightening matter. *Zadig* is not a detection story but a philosophical tale because its deep subject is exactly the vertigo of meta-abduction. To escape such a vertigo, Peirce linked strictly the phase of abduction with the phase of deduction:

> Retroduction does not afford security. The hypothesis must be tested. This testing, to be logically valid, must honestly start, not as retroduction starts, with scrutiny of the phenomena, but with the examination of hypothesis, and a muster of all sorts of conditional experiential consequences which would follow from its truth. This constitutes the second state of inquiry. (6.470)

This clear consciousness of what a severe scientific inquiry should be does not exclude Peirce himself in many circumstances from playing the meta-abductive game. We are compelled to make abductions in everyday life, at any moment, and we frequently cannot wait for further tests. Consider for instance, the case of the man under a canopy:

> I once landed at a seaport in a Turkish province; and as I was walking up to the house which I was to visit, I met a man upon horseback, surrounded by four horsemen holding a canopy over his head. As the governor of the province was the only personage I could think of who would be so greatly honored, I inferred that this was he. This was an hypothesis. (2.265)

As a matter of fact Peirce made two inferences. The first one was a hypothesis or an overcoded abduction: he knew the general rule according to which a man with a canopy over his head, in Turkey, could not be anybody but an authority, and imagined that the man he met represented a case of that unquestionable rule. The second one was an undercoded abduction: among the various authorities that could have been in that place (why not a visiting minister from Istanbul?), the governor of the province was the more plausible. I think that from this point on Peirce entertained his second abduction as if it were the case, and behaved consequently.

In the story analyzed in this book (Ch. 2) by Sebeok and Umiker-Sebeok (apropos of the stolen lever watch), there is a series of daring creative abductions that Peirce trusted without further testing, acting as if they were the case until the very end. Peirce meta-abduction consisted in betting on the final result without waiting for intermediate tests.

Probably the true difference between abductions from fact to laws and abduction from facts to facts, lies in the meta-abductional flexibility, that is, in the courage of challenging without further tests the basic fallibilism that governs human knowledge. That is why in "real" life detectives commit more frequent (or more frequently visible) errors than scientists. Detectives are rewarded by society for their impudence in betting by meta-abduction, whereas scientists are socially rewarded for their patience in testing their abductions. Naturally, in order to have the intellectual and moral force to test, and to ask for new tests, and to entertain stubbornly an abduction before it has been definitely tested, scientists also need meta-abduction. Their difference from detectives stands in their refusal to impose their beliefs as a dogma, in their firmness not to repudiate their motivated conjectures. Bertolt Brecht's *Leben des Galilei* is the story of the difficulty of entertaining such a conjecture against everybody else's abductions (as well as the story of the continuous temptation to give up such an "unfair" guess).

In fictional possible worlds things go better. Nero Wolfe invents elegant solutions for inextricable situations, then gathers all the suspects in his room and spells his story out *as if* it were the case. Rex Stout is so kind to him as to make the "real" culprit to react, thus confessing his own guilt and acknowledging Wolfe's mental superiority. Neither Galileo nor Peirce was as socially successful in his life, and there should be also an epistemological reason for such misadventures. Thus, whereas the story of insteps was a tale of infallibility and whereas the story of hooves was a tale of anxiety in face of the vertigo of infallibility, the story of horns and beans was and still is the tale of human fallibility. There is at least one point on which Peirce and Conan Doyle (via Voltaire) do not tell the same story.

REFERENCES

Agamben, G.
  1975 "Aby Warburg e la scienza senza nome." *Prospettive Settanta* (July–September).
Alpher, Ralph A., Hans Bethe, and George Gamow
  1948 "The Origin of Chemical Elements." *Physical Review* 73(7): 803–804.
Anderson, Sir Robert
  1903 "Sherlock Holmes, Detective, as Seen by Scotland Yard." *T.P.'s Weekly* 2 (October 2):557–558.
Anonymous
  1959 *Sir Arthur Conan Doyle Centenary 1859–1959.* London: John Murray.
Argan, Giulio C., and Maurizio Fagiolo
  1974 *Guida alla storia dell'arte.* Florence: Sansoni.
Aristotle
  1938 *Categories, On Interpretation, Prior Analytics,* trans. by H.P. Cooke and Hugh Tredennick. Cambridge, Mass.: Harvard University Press.
  1960 *Posterior Analytics,* trans. by Hugh Tredennick. Cambridge, Mass.: Harvard University Press.
Ashton-Wolfe, H.
  1932 "The Debt of the Police to Detective Fiction." *The Illustrated London News,* February 27:320–328.
Averlino, A. (pseud. Filarete)
  1972 *Trattato di architettura,* ed. by A.M. Finoli and L. Grassi. Vol. I. Milan.
Ayim, Maryann
  1974 "Retroduction: The Rational Instinct." *Transactions of the Charles S. Peirce Society* 10:34–43.
Baldi, Camillo
  1625 *Trattato.* Milan: G.B. Bidelli.
Baldinucci, Filippo
  1681 *Lettera . . . nella quale risponde ad alcuni quesiti in materie di pittura.* Rome: Tinassi.
Ball, John
  1958 "The Twenty-Three Deductions." *The Baker Street Journal,* n.s., 8 (October):234–237.
Baring-Gould, William S.
  1955 *The Chronological Holmes.* New York: Privately printed.
  1962 *Sherlock Holmes of Baker Street: A Life of the World's First Consulting Detective.* New York: Clarkson N. Potter.
  1967 (ed.) *The Annotated Sherlock Holmes.* 2 vols. New York: Clarkson N. Potter.
Bell, Harold W.
  1932 *Sherlock Holmes and Dr. Watson: The Chronology of Their Adventures.* London: Constable.
  1934 *Baker Street Studies.* London: Constable.

Bell, Joseph
    1893 "Mr. Sherlock Holmes." Introduction to the Fourth Edition of *A Study in Scarlet*. London: Ward, Lock & Bowden. (Previously published in the *Bookman* [London].)
Bell, Whitfield J., Jr.
    1947 "Holmes and History." *The Baker Street Journal*, o.s., 2 (October):447–456.
Benjamin, Walter
    1955 *Angelus novus: ausegwählte Schriften*, 2. Frankfurt: Suhrkamp, 1966.
    1969 "The Work of Art in the Age of Mechanical Reproduction." In *Illuminations*. New York: Schocken Books.
Berg, Stanton O.
    1970 "Sherlock Holmes: Father of Scientific Crime Detection." *Journal of Criminal Law, Criminology, and Police Science* 61:446–452.
Bernoulli, Jacques
    1713 *Ars Conjectandi*. Basil: Impensis Thurnisiorum.
Bernstein, Richard J.
    1964 (ed.) *Perspectives on Peirce*. New Haven, Conn.: Yale University Press.
Bertillon, Alphonse
    1883 *L'identité des récidivistes et la loi de relégation*. Paris: G. Masson.
    1893a *Album*. Melun.
    1893b *Identification anthropométrique; instructions signalétique*. Melun.
Beth, E.W.
    1955 "Semantic Entailment and Formal Derivability." *Mededilingen van de Koninklijke Nederlandse Akademie van Wetenschappen, Afd. Letterkunde*, N.R., 18 (13):309–342.
Bigelow, S. Tupper
    1959 *An Irregular Anglo-American Glossary of More or Less Familiar Words, Terms and Phrases in the Sherlock Holmes Saga*. Toronto: Castalotte and Zamba.
Bignami-Odier, Jeanne
    1973 *La Bibliothèque vaticane de Sixte IV à Pie XI*. Vatican: Biblioteca Apostolica Vaticana.
Black, Max
    1967 "Induction." In *The Encyclopedia of Philosophy*, ed. by Paul Edwards et al., 4:169–181. New York: Macmillan and Free Press.
Blakeney, Thomas S.
    1932 *Sherlock Holmes: Fact or Fiction?* London: John Murray.
Bloch, Marc L.B.
    1953 *The Historian's Craft*. New York: Knopf.
    1973 *The Royal Touch: Sacred Monarchy and Scrofula in England and France*. London: Routledge & Kegan Paul.
Bonfantini, Massimo A., and Marco Macciò
    1977 *La neutralità impossibile*. Milan: Mazzotta.
Bottéro, I.
    1974 "Symptômes, signes, écritures." In *Divination et Rationalité*, ed. by J. P. Vernant et al. Paris: Seuil.
Bozza, Tommaso
    1949 *Scrittori politici italiani dal 1550 al 1650*. Rome.
Bremer, R.
    1976 "Freud and Michelangelo's Moses." *American Image* 33.

Brend, Gavin
1951 *My Dear Holmes, A Study in Sherlock.* London: Allen and Unwin.
Brown, Francis C.
1969 "The Case of the Man Who Was Wanted." *The Vermissa Herald: A Journal of Sherlockian Affairs* 3 (April):12. (Published by the Scowrers, San Francisco, Calif.)
Buchler, Justus
1955 (ed.) *Philosophical Writings of Peirce.* New York: Dover. (First published in 1940 as *The Philosophy of Peirce: Selected Writings.*)
Butler, Christopher
1970 *Number Symbolism.* New York: Barnes & Noble.
Cabanis, Pierre Jean Georges.
1823 *Oeuvres Complètes.* Paris: Thurot. *An Essay on the Certainty of Medicine,* trans. by R. LaRoche. Philadelphia: R. Desilver. (Original title: *Du degré de certitude en médicine.*)
Caldera, A
1924 *L'indicazione dei connotati nei documenti papiracei dell'Egitto greco-romano.* Milan.
Campana, A.
1967 "Paleografia oggi. Rapporti, problemi e prospettive de una 'coraggiosa disciplina." In *Studi urbinati* 41, n.s. B, Studi in onore de Arturo Massolo. Vol. II.
Campbell, Maurice
1935 *Sherlock Holmes and Dr. Watson: A Medical Digression.* London: Ash.
Canini, G.
1625 *Aforismi politici cavati dall'Historia d'Italia di Francesco Guicciardini.* Venice.
Carr, John Dickson
1949 *The Life of Sir Arthur Conan Doyle.* New York: Harper & Bros.
Casamassima, Emanuele
1964 "Per una storia delle dottrine paleografiche dall'Umanesimo a Jean Mabillon." In *Studi medievali* s. III, no. 9.
Castañeda Calderón, Héctor Neri
1978 "Philosophical Method and the Theory of Predication and Identity." *Nous* 12:189–210.
Castelnuovo, Enrico
1968 "Attribution." In *Encylcopaedia Universalis* II.
Cavina, A. Ottani
1976 "On the theme of landscape II: Elsheimer and Galileo. *The Burlington Magazine.*
Cawelti, John G.
1976 *Adventure, Mystery, and Romance: Formula Stories as Art and Popular Culture.* Chicago, Ill.: University of Chicago Press.
Cazade, E., and Ch. Thomas
1977 "Alfabeto." In *Enciclopedia* I. Turin: Einaudi.
Cerulli, E.
1975 "Una raccolta persiana di novelle tradotte a Venezia nel 1557." In *Atti dell'Academia Nazionale dei Lincei* 372. Memorie della classe di scienze morali . . . , s. VIII, Vol. XVIII, no. 4.

Chomsky, Noam
1979 *Language and Responsibility*. New York: Pantheon Books.
Christ, Jay Finley
1947a *An Irregular Chronology of Sherlock Holmes of Baker Street*. Ann Arbor, Mich.: Fanlight House.
1947b *An Irregular Guide to Sherlock Holmes of Baker Street*. New York: The Pamphlet House and Argus Books.
Christie, Winifred M.
1955 "Sherlock Holmes and Graphology." *The Sherlock Holmes Journal* 2:28–31.
Cohen, Morris R.
1949 (ed.) *Chance, Love and Logic* by Charles Sanders Peirce. Magnolia, Mass.: Peter Smith. (First Published in 1923.)
Contini, Gianfranco
1972 "Longhi prosatore." In *Altri esercizi (1942–1971)*. Turin: Einaudi.
Cooper, Peter
1976 "Holmesian Chemistry." In *Beyond Baker Street: A Sherlockian Anthology*, ed. by Michael Harrison, 67–73. Indianapolis, Ind.: Bobbs-Merrill.
Copi, Irving M.
1953 *Introduction to Logic*. New York: Macmillan.
Couturat, Louis
1903 *Opuscules et fragments inédits de Leibniz* Paris: Alcan.
Craig, William
1957 "Linear Reasoning: A New Form of the Herbrand-Gentzen Theorem." *Journal of Symbolic Logic* 22:250–285.
Cresci, G. F.
1622 *L'Idea*. Milan: Naua.
Croce, Benedetto
1946 *La critica e la storia delle arti figurative; questioni di metodo*. Bari: Laterza.
Crocker, Stephen F.
1964 "Sherlock Holmes Recommends Winwood Reade." *The Baker Street Journal*, n.s., 14 (September): 142–144.
Damisch, Hubert
1970 "La partie et le tout." *Revue d'esthétique* 2.
1977 "Le gardien de l'interprétation." *Tel Quel* 44 (Winter).
De Giustino, David
1975 *Conquest of Mind: Phrenology and Victorian Social Thought*. London: Croom Helm.
Derrida, Jacques
1975 "Le facteur de la vérité." *Poétique* 21:96–147.
De Sanctis, Francesco
1938 *Lettere dall'esilio 1853–1860*, ed. by Benedetto Croce. Bari: Laterza.
Detienne, Marcel, and Jean Pierre Vernant
1978 *Cunning Intelligence in Greek Culture and Society*, trans. by J. Lloyd. Atlantic Highlands, N.J.: Humanities Press. (Original title: *Les ruses de l'intelligence. La mètis des grecs*. Paris, 1974.)
Diaconis, Persi
1978 "Statistical Problems in ESP Research." *Science* 201:131–136.
Dickens, Charles
1843 *A Christmas Carol*. London: Chapman & Hall.

Diller, H.
  1932 *Hermes* 67:14–42.
Doyle, Adrian M. Conan
  1945 *The True Conan Doyle.* London: John Murray.
Doyle, Adrian M. Conan, and John Dickson Carr
  1954 *The Exploits of Sherlock Holmes.* New York: Random House.
Doyle, Sir Arthur Conan
  1924 *Memories and Adventures.* Boston: Little, Brown. (Doubleday, Doran,
  Crowborough edition, 1930.)
  1948 "The Case of the Man Who Was Wanted." *Cosmopolitan* 125 (August):
  48–51. 92–99.
  1952 *The Complete Sherlock Holmes.* 1-vol. edition (2-vol. edition, 1953.) Garden City, N.Y.: Doubleday.
  1968 *The Sherlockian Doyle.* Culver City, Calif.: Luther Norris.
Dubos, Jean Baptiste
  1733 *Réflexions critiques sur la poésie et sur le peinture.* Vol. II. Paris: Mariette.
Eco, Umberto
  1976 *A Theory of Semiotics.* Bloomington: Indiana University Press.
  1979 *The Role of the Reader.* Bloomington: Indiana University Press.
  1980 "Il cane e il cavallo: un testo visivo e alcuni equivoci verbali." *Versus* 25.
Eisele, Carolyn
  1976 (ed.) *The New Elements of Mathematics by Charles S. Peirce.* 4 vols. The
  Hague: Mouton.
Eritreo, J. N. (Gian Vittorio Rossi)
  1692 *Pinacotheca imaginum illustrium.* Vol. II. Lipsiae: Gleditschi.
Esposito, Joseph L.
  1980 *Evolutionary Metaphysics.* Athens, Ohio: Ohio University Press.
Étiemble, René
  1973 *L'écriture.* Paris: Gallimard.
Fann, K. T.
  1970 *Peirce's Theory of Abduction.* The Hague: Martinus Nijhoff.
Feibleman, James
  1946 *An Introduction to Peirce's Philosophy, Interpreted as a System.* New York:
  Harper & Bros.
Ferriani, M.
  1978 "Storia e 'priestoria' del concetto di probabilita nell'età moderna."
  Rivista di filosofia 10 (February).
Feyerabend, Paul K.
  1971 *I problemi dell'empirismo.* Milan.
  1975 *Against Method.* London: NLB.
Fisch, Max H.
  1964 "Was There a Metaphysical Club in Cambridge?" In *Studies in the Philosophy of Charles Sanders Peirce,* 2nd series, ed. by Edward C. Moore and
  Richard S. Robin, 3–32. Amherst: University of Massachusetts Press.
  1982 "The Range of Peirce's Relevance." *The Monist* 65(2):124–141.
Folsom, Henry T.
  1964 *Through the Years at Baker Street: A Chronology of Sherlock Holmes.* Washington, N.J.: Privately printed.
Foucault, Michel
  1973 *Birth of the Clinic.* New York: Pantheon.

1977a *Discipline and Punish: The Birth of the Prison.* New York: Pantheon.
1977b *Microfisica del potere. Interventi politici.* Turin: Einaudi.
Freud, Sigmund
1961 [1923] *The Ego and the Id.* Vol. 19. *The Standard Edition of the Complete Psychological Works of Sigmund Freud.* London: Hogarth Press and The Institute of Psycho-Analysis, 1953–1974.
1965 [1914] "The Moses of Michelangelo," in *Totem and Taboo and Other Works.* Vol. 13. *The Standard Edition of the Complete Psychological Works of Sigmund Freud.*
1953 *The Interpretation of Dreams I,* and *The Interpretation of Dreams II and On Dreams.* Vols. 4, 5. *The Standard Edition of the Complete Psychological Works of Sigmund Freud.*
Gaboriau, Émile
1869 *Monsieur Lecoq.* Vol. I, *L'Enquête.* Paris: Fayard.
Galilei, Galileo
1935 *Opere.* Vol. XIII. Florence.
1965 *Il Saggiatore,* edited by Libero Sosio. Milan: Feltrinelli.
Galton, Sir Francis
1892 *Finger Prints.* London and New York: Macmillan.
Gamow, George
1947 *One, Two, Three . . . Infinity: Facts & Speculations of Science.* New York: The New American Library.
Gardiner, Muriel
1971 (ed.) *The Wolf-Man.* New York: Basic Books.
Gardner, Martin
1957 *Fads and Fallacies in the Name of Science.* New York: Dover. (Original title: *In the Name of Science.*)
1976 "The Irrelevance of Conan Doyle." In *Beyond Baker Street: A Sherlockian Anthology,* ed. by Michael Harrison, 123–135. Indianapolis, Ind.: Bobbs-Merrill.
1978 *Encyclopedia of Impromptu Magic.* Chicago, Ill.: Magic, Inc.
1981 *Science: Good, Bad, and Bogus.* Buffalo, N.Y.: Prometheus Books.
Garin, Eugenio
1961 "La nuova scienze e il simbolismo del 'libro'." In *La Cultura filosofica del Rinascimento italiano: richerche e documenti.* Florence: Sansoni.
Gerhardt, Karl Immanuel
1875–1890 *Die philosophischen Schriften von G. W. Leibniz.* 7 vols. Berlin.
Gilson, Étienne
1958 *Peinture et réalité.* Paris: Vrin.
Ginoulhiac, M.
1940 "Giovanni Morelli. La Vita." *Bergomum* 34.
Ginzburg, Carlo
1979 "Spie. Radici di un paradigma indiziario." In *Crisi della ragione,* ed. by Aldo Gargani, 57–106. Turin: Einaudi.
1980a *The Cheese and the Worms.* Baltimore, Md.: Johns Hopkins University Press. (Original title: *Il formaggio e i vermi.* Turin: Einaudi, 1976.)
1980b "Morelli, Freud and Sherlock Holmes: Clues and Scientific Method." *History Workshop* 9:7–36.
Giuntini, Francesco
1573 *Speculum astrologiae.* Lugduni: Tinghi.

Gombrich, E. H.
1966 "Freud's Aesthetics." *Encounter* 26.
1969 "The Evidence of Images." In *Interpretation: Theory and Practice,* ed. by Charles S. Singleton. Baltimore, Md.: Johns Hopkins University Press.
Goody, Jack
1977 *The Domestication of the Savage Mind.* Cambridge: Cambridge University Press.
Goody, J., and I. Watt
1962–1963 *"The Consequences of Literacy."* In *Comparative Studies in Society and History* 5.
Goudge, Thomas A.
1950 *The Thought of C. S. Peirce.* Toronto: University of Toronto Press.
Gould, Stephen Jay
1978 "Morton's Ranking of Races by Cranial Capacity." *Science* 200:503–509.
Granger, Gilles G.
1960 *Pensée formelle et sciences de l'homme.* Paris: Montaigne.
Grenet, Jacques
1963 "La Chine: aspects et fonctions psychologiques de l'écriture." In *L'Écriture et la psychologie des peuples.* Paris.
1974 "Petits écarts et grands écarts." In *Divination et Rationalité,* edited by J.P. Vernant et al. Paris: Seuil.
Hacking, Ian
1975 *The Emergence of Probability: A Philosophical Study of Early Ideas about Probability, Induction and Statistical Inference.* London and New York: Cambridge University Press.
Hall, Trevor H.
1978 *Sherlock Holmes and His Creator.* London: Duckworth.
Hammett, Dashiell
1930 *The Maltese Falcon.* New York: Knopf.
1934 *The Thin Man.* New York: Knopf.
Hardwick, Charles S.
1977 (ed.) *Semiotic and Significs: The Correspondence between Charles S. Peirce and Victoria Lady Welby.* Bloomington: Indiana University Press.
Hardwick, Michael, and Mollie Hardwick
1962 *The Sherlock Holmes Companion.* London: John Murray.
1964 *The Man Who Was Sherlock Holmes.* London: John Murray.
Harrison, Michael
1958 *In the Footsteps of Sherlock Holmes.* London: Cassell.
1971 "A Study in Surmise." *Ellery Queen's Mystery Magazine* 57 (February):60–79.
Hart, Archibald
1948 "The Effects of Trades Upon Hands." *The Baker Street Journal,* o.s., 3 (October):418–420.
Haskell, Francis
1963 *Patrons and Painters: A Study in the Relations between Italian Art and Society in the Age of the Baroque.* New York: Knopf.
Hauser, Arnold
1959 *The Philosophy of Art History.* New York: Knopf.
Havelock, Eric A.
1973 *Cultura orale e civiltà della scrittura. Da Omera a Platone.* Bari: Laterza.

Haycraft, Howard
1941 *Murder for Pleasure: The Life and Times of the Detective Story.* New York: D. Appleton-Century.
1946 (ed.) *The Art of the Mystery Story: A Collection of Critical Essays.* New York: Simon and Schuster.
Heckscher, William S.
1967 "Genesis of Iconology." In *Stil und Ueberlieferung.* Vol. III. Berlin.
1974 "Petites Perceptions: An Account of Sortes Warburgianae." *The Journal of Mediaeval and Renaissance Studies* 4.
Hess, J.
1968 "Note Manciniane." In *Münchener Jahrbuch der bildenden Kunst,* 3rd series. Vol. XIX.
Hilton, George W.
1968 *The Night Boat.* Berkeley, Calif.: Howell-North Books.
Hintikka, Jaakko
1976 "The Semantics of Questions and the Questions of Semantics." *Acta Philosophica Fennica.* Vol. 28(4). Amsterdam: North-Holland.
1979 "Information-Seeking Dialogue: Some of Their Logical Properties." *Studia Logica* 32:355–363.
Forthcoming. "Sherlock Holmes Meets Modern Logic: Toward a Theory of Information-Seeking through Questioning." In *Proceedings of the 1978 Groningen Colloquium.*
Hitchings, J. L.
1946 "Sherlock Holmes the Logician." *The Baker Street Journal,* o.s., 1(2):113–117.
Hoffman, Daniel
1972 *Poe Poe Poe Poe Poe Poe Poe.* New York: Doubleday.
Hogan, John C., and Mortimer D. Schwartz
1964 "The Manly Art of Observation and Deduction." *Journal of Criminal Law, Criminology and Police Science* 55:157–164.
Holroyd, James Edward
1967 *Seventeen Steps to 221B.* London: George Allen and Unwin.
Horan, James D.
1967 *The Pinkertons: The Detective Dynasty that Made History.* New York: Crown.
How, Harry
1892 "A Day with Dr. Conan Doyle." *Strand Magazine* (August).
Huxley, Thomas
1881 "On the Method of Zadig: Retrospective Prophecy as a Function of Science." In *Science and Culture.* London: Macmillan.
Ingram, David
1978 "Typology and Universals of Personal Pronouns." In *Universals of Human Language,* ed. by Joseph H. Greenberg, 3:213–247. Stanford, Calif.: Stanford University Press.
Jakobson, Roman, and Morris Halle
1956 *Fundamentals of Language.* The Hague: Mouton.
Jakobson, Roman, and Linda R. Waugh
1979 *The Sound Shape of Language.* Bloomington: Indiana University Press.
James, William
1907 *Pragmatism.* New York: Longmans, Green.

Johnson, Barbara
1980 *The Critical Difference: Essays in the Contemporary Rhetoric of Reading.* Baltimore, Md.: The Johns Hopkins University Press.
Jones, Ernest
1953–1960 *The Life and Work of Sigmund Freud.* New York: Basic Books.
Kejci-Graf, Karl
1967 "Sherlock Holmes, Scientist, Including Some Unpopular Opinions." *The Sherlock Holmes Journal* 8(3):72–78.
Kenney, E.J.
1974 *The Classical Text: Aspects of Editing in the Age of Printed Books.* Berkeley: University of California Press.
Ketner, Kenneth L., and James E. Cook
1975 (eds.) *Charles Sanders Peirce: Contributions to* The Nation. *Part One: 1869–1893.* (Graduate Studies, Texas Tech University, No. 10.) Lubbock: Texas Tech Press.
Kloesel, Christian J.W.
1979 "Charles Peirce and the Secret of the Harvard O.K." *The New England Quarterly* 52(1).
Kofman, Sarah
1975 *L'enfance de l'art. Une interpretation de l'esthétique freudienne.* Paris: Payot.
Koselleck, Reinhart
1969 *Kritik und Krise; ein Beitrag zur Pathogenese der bürgerlichen Welt.* Freiberg: K. Alber.
Kuhn, Thomas S.
1962 *The Structure of Scientific Revolutions.* Chicago, Ill.: University of Chicago Press.
1974 "Postscript 1969." In *The Structure of Scientific Revolutions.* (2nd enlarged edition.) Chicago, Ill.: University of Chicago Press.
1975 "Tradition mathématique et tradition expérimentale dans le développement de la physique." *Annales ESC* 30:975–998.
Lacan, Jacques
1966 *Écrits.* Paris: Seuil.
Lacassagne, Alexandre
1914 *Alphonse Bertillon: L'homme, le savant, la pensée philosophique.* Lyon: A. Rey.
Lacassin, Francis
1974 *Mythologie du roman policier.* Vol. I. Paris: Union Générale d'éditions.
Lamond, John
1931 *Arthur Conan Doyle: A Memoir.* London: John Murray.
Lanzi, Luigi A.
1968 *Storia pittorica dell'Italia,* ed. by Martino Capucci. Vol. I. Florence: Sansoni.
Larsen, Svend Erik
1980 "La structure productrice du mot d'ésprit et de la semiosis. Essai sur Freud et Peirce." *Degrés* 8(21):d1–18.
Leavitt, R.K.
1940 "Nummi in Arca or The Fiscal Holmes." In *221B: Studies in Sherlock Holmes,* ed. by Vincent Starrett, 16–36. New York: Macmillan.

Lermolieff, Ivan (pseud. of Giovanni Morelli)
    1880 *Die Werke italienischer Meister in den Galerien von München, Dresden und Berlin. Ein kritischer Versuch.* Leipzig: Seemann.
Levinson, Boris M.
    1966 "Some Observations on the Use of Pets in Psychodiagnosis." *Pediatrics Digest* 8:81–85.
Lévi-Strauss, Claude, et al.
    1977 *L'Identité, Seminaire interdisciplinaire dirigé par Claude Lévi-Strauss.* Paris.
Locard, Edmond
    1909 *L'identification des récidivistes.* Paris: A. Maloine.
    1914 "L'Oeuvre" *Alphonse Bertillon.* Lyon: A. Rey.
Locke, Harold
    1928 *A Bibliographical Catalogue of the Writings of Sir Arthur Conan Doyle, M.D., LL.D., 1879–1928.* Tunbridge Wells: D. Webster.
Locke, John
    1975 *An Essay Concerning Human Understanding,* ed. by Peter H. Nidditch. Oxford: Clarendon Press.
Longhi, Roberto
    1967 *Saggi e ricerche: 1925–1928.* Florence: Sansoni.
Lotz, János
    1976 "A személy, szám, viszonyítás és tárgyhatározottság kategóriái a magyarban." In *Szonettkoszorú a nyelvről.* Budapest: Gondolat.
Lotz, John
    1962 "Thoughts on Phonology as Applied to the Turkish Vowels." In *American Studies on Altaic Linguistics,* ed. by Nicholas Poppe, 13:343–351. Bloomington: Indiana University.
Lynceo, Ioanne Terrentio (Francisco Hernandez)
    1651 *Rerum medicarum Novae Hispaniae Thesaurus.* Rome: Vitalis Mascardi.
Mackenzie, J.B.
    1956 "Sherlock Holmes' Plots and Strategies." In *Baker Street Journal Christmas Annual,* 56–61.
Mahon, Denis
    1947 *Studies in Seicento Art and Theory.* London: London University-Warburg Institute.
Mancini, Giulio
    1956–1957 *Considerazioni sulla pittura,* ed. by A. Marucchi. 2 vols. Rome: Accademia Nazionale dei Lincei.
Marcus, Steven
    1976 "Introduction." *The Adventures of Sherlock Holmes.* New York: Schocken Books.
Martinez, J.A.
    1974 "Galileo on Primary and Secondary Qualities." *Journal of the History of Behavioral Sciences* 10:160–169.
Marx, Karl
    1872 *Das Kapital: Kritik der politischen oekonomie.* Hamburg: O. Meisner.
May, Luke S.
    1936 *Crime's Nemesis.* New York: Macmillan.

Meyer, Nicholas
1974 *The Seven Percent Solution: Being a Reprint from the Reminiscences of John Watson, M.D.* New York: Dutton.
Melandri, Enzo
1968 *La linea e il circolo. Studio logico-filosofico sull'analogia.* Bologna: Mulino.
Mercati, Giovanni, Cardinal
1952 *Note per la storia di alcune biblioteche romane nei secoli.* xvi–xix. Vatican.
Merton, Robert K.
1957 *Social Theory and Social Structure.* Glencoe, Ill.: Free Press. (First published in 1949.)
Messac, Régis
1929 *La "Détective Novel" et l'influence de la pensée scientifique.* Paris: Librairie Ancienne Honoré Champion.
Millar, Kenneth (pseud. Ross MacDonald)
1969 *The Goodbye Look.* New York: Knopf.
Momigliano, Arnaldo
1975 "Storiographica greca." *Rivista storica italiana* 87.
Morelli, Giovanni
1897 *Della pittura italiana: Studii storico critici –Le gallerie Borghese e Doria Pamphili in Roma.* Milan: Treves.
Morris, Charles W.
1971 *Writings on the General Theory of Signs.* The Hague: Mouton.
Mourad, Youssef
1939 (ed. and trans.) *La physionomie arabe et le Kitāb alf-Firāsa de Fakhr al-Din al-Razi.* Paris: P. Geuthner.
Murch, Alma Elizabeth
1958 *The Development of the Detective Novel.* London: Peter Owen.
Nelson, Benjamin N.
1958 (ed.) *Freud and the Twentieth Century.* Gloucester, Mass.: Peter Smith.
Nolen, William A.
1974 *Healing: A Doctor in Search of a Miracle.* New York: Random House. (Greenwich, Conn.: Fawcett, 1975.)
Nordon, Pierre
1966 *Conan Doyle.* London: John Murray.
1967 *Conan Doyle: A Biography,* trans. by Frances Partridge. New York: Holt, Rinehart and Winston.
Pagels, Heinz R.
1982 *The Cosmic Code: Quantum Physics as the Language of Nature.* New York: Simon and Schuster.
Park, Orlando
1962 *Sherlock Holmes, Esq., and John H. Watson, M.D.: An Encyclopedia of Their Affairs.* Evanston, Ill.: Northwestern University Press.
Pearson, Hesketh
1943 *Conan Doyle, His Life and Art.* London: Methuen.
Peirce, Charles Sanders
1923 *Chance, Love, and Logic.* New York: Harcourt, Brace.
1929 "Guessing." *The Hound and Horn* 2:267–282.
1955 "Abduction and Induction." In *Philosophical Writings of Peirce,* ed. by Justus Buchler. New York: Dover.

232 REFERENCES

1956 "Deduction, Induction, and Hypothesis." In *Chance, Love, and Logic.* New York: Braziller.
1935–1966 *Collected Papers of Charles Sanders Peirce,* ed. by Charles Hartshorne, Paul Weiss, and Arthur W. Burks. 8 vols. Cambridge, Mass.: Harvard University Press.
1982 *Writings of Charles S. Peirce: A Chronological Edition. Vol. I: 1857–1866,* ed. by Max H. Fisch, et al. Bloomington: Indiana University Press.
Pelc, Jerzy
1977 "On the Prospects of Research in the History of Semiotics." *Semiotic Scene* 1(3):1–12.
Perrot, M.
1975 "Délinquance et systéme pénitentiare en France au XIXᵉ siècle." *Annales ESC* 30:67–91.
Peterson, Svend
1956 *A Sherlock Holmes Almanac.* Washington, D.C.: Privately printed.
Pintard, René
1943 *Le libertinage-érudit dans la premiere moitié du XVIIᵉ siècle.* Vol. I. Paris: Boivin.
Poe, Edgar Allan
1927 "A Descent into a Maelstrom." In *Collected Works.* New York: Walter J. Black.
Pomian, Krzysztof
1975 "L'histoire des sciences et l'histoire de l'histoire." *Annales ESC* 30:935–952.
Popper, Karl R.
1962 *Conjectures and Refutations: The Growth of Scientific Knowledge.* New York: Basic Books.
1979 *Objective Knowledge: An Evolutionary Approach.* Oxford: Clarendon Press.
Potter, Vincent G.
1967 *Charles S. Peirce on Norms & Ideals.* Amherst: University of Massachusetts Press.
Pratt, Fletcher
1955 "Very Little Murder." *The Baker Street Journal,* n.s., 2 (April):69–76.
Previtali, Giovanni
1978 "À propos de Morelli." *Revue de l'Art* 42.
Propp, Vladimir I.
1946 *Istoričeskie Korni Volšebnoi Skazki.* Leningrad: State University.
Purkyné, Jan E.
1948 *Opera Selecta.* Prague: Spolek Českých Lékařu.
Queen, Ellery
1944 (ed.) *Misadventures of Sherlock Holmes.* Boston, Mass.: Little, Brown.
Raimondi, E.
1974 *Il romanzo senza idillio. Saggio sui Promessi Sposi.* Turin: Einaudi.
Ransdell, Joseph
1977 "Some Leading Ideas of Peirce's Semiotic." *Semiotica* 19:157–158.
Reed, John Shelton
1970 "The Other Side." Unpublished ms., Department of Sociology, University of North Carolina at Chapel Hill.
Reik, Theodor
1931 *Ritual; Psychoanalytic Studies.* London: Hogarth Press.

Remer, Theodore G.
1965 (ed.) *Serendipity and the Three Princes: From the Peregrinaggio of 1557.* Norman: University of Oklahoma Press.

Revzin, Isaak I.
1964 "K semiotičiskomu analizu detektivov (na primere romanov Agaty Kristi)." *Programma i tezisy dokladov v letnej škole po vtoričnym modelirujuščim sistemam.* 16–26 avg., 38–40. Tartu.

Richter, Jean Paul
1960 *Italienische Malerei der Renaissance in Briefwechsel von Giovanni* Morelli *und Jean Paul Richter—1876–1891.* Baden-Baden: Grimm.

Robert, Marthe
1966 *The Psychoanalytic Revolution: Sigmund Freud's Life and Achievement.* New York: Harcourt, Brace & World.

Roberts, Sir Sydney C.
1931 *Doctor Watson: Prolegomena to the Study of a Biographical Problem.* London: Faber and Faber.

Robin, Richard S.
1967 *Annotated Catalogue of the Papers of Charles S. Peirce.* Amherst: University of Massachusetts Press.

Rossi, Paolo
1977 *Immagini della scienza.* Rome: Editori riuniti.

Scalzini, Marcello
1585 *Il secretario.* Venice: D. Nicolini.

Scheglov, Yuri K.
1975 [1968] "Toward a Description of Detective Story Structure." *Russian Poetics in Translation* 1:51–77.

Scheibe, Karl E.
1978 "The Psychologist's Advantage and Its Nullification: Limits of Human Predictability." *American Psychologist* 33:869–881.
1979 *Mirrors, Masks, Lies, and Secrets: The Limits of Human Predictability.* New York: Praeger.

Schenck, Remsen Ten Eyck
1948 *Occupation Marks.* New York: Grune and Stratton.
1953 "The Effect of Trades upon the Body." *The Baker Street Journal,* n.s., 3 (January):31–36.

Schlosser Magnino, Julius
1924 *Die Kunstliteratur.* Wien: Schroll.

Schoenau, Walter
1968 *Sigmund Freuds Prosa. Literarische Elemente seines Stils.* Stuttgart: Metzler.

Schorske, Carl E.
1980 "Politics and Parricides in Freud's Interpretation of Dreams." In *Fin-de-Siècle Vienna: Politics and Culture.* New York: Knopf.

Sebeok, Thomas A.
1951 "Aymara 'Little Riding Hood' with Morphological Analysis." *Archivum Linguisticum* 3:53–69.
1976 *Contributions to the Doctrine of Signs.* Lisse: Peter de Ridder Press.
1977 (ed.) *A Perfusion of Signs.* Bloomington: Indiana University Press.
1979 *The Sign & Its Masters.* Austin: University of Texas Press.
1981 *The Play of Musement.* Bloomington: Indiana University Press.

1984 "The Role of the Observer." In *I Think I Am A Verb*, Ch. 10. New York: Plenum.
Forthcoming. "Symptom." *Zeitschrift für Semiotik* 5 *(Semiotik und Medizin)*.
Sebeok, Thomas A., and Jean Umiker-Sebeok
 1979 "You Know My Method: A Juxtaposition of Charles S. Peirce and Sherlock Holmes." *Semiotica* 26(2/3):203–250.
Segre, E.
 1975 "La gerarchia dei segni." In *Psicanalisi e semiotica,* ed. by A. Verdiglione. Milan: Feltrinelli.
Seppilli, Anita
 1971 *Poesia e magia.* Turin: Einaudi.
Shklovskii, Viktor B.
 1925 *O Teorii prozy.* Moskva: Federacija.
Smith, Edgar W.
 1940 *Baker Street and Beyond: A Sherlockian Gazeteer.* New York: Pamphlet House.
 1944 *Profile by Gaslight: An Irregular Reader about the Private Life of Sherlock Holmes.* New York: Simon and Schuster.
Spector, J.J.
 1969 "Les méthodes de la critique de l'art et la psychanalyse freudienne." *Diogenes* 66.
Spini, Giorgio
 1956 *Risorgimento e protestanti.* Naples: Edizioni Scientifiche Italiane.
Spinoza, Benedictus de [Baruch]
 1924–1925 "Ethica ordine geometrico demonstrata." In *Opera,* ed. by C. Gebhardt. 4 vols. Auftrag der Heidelberger Akademie der Wissenschaften. Heidelberg: Universitätsbuchhandlung.
Spitzer, Leo
 1910 *Die Wortbildung als stilistisches Mittel exemplifiziert an Rabelais.* Halle: Neimeyer.
Starrett, Vincent
 1940 *221B: Studies in Sherlock Holmes.* New York: Macmillan.
 1971 [1934] *The Private Life of Sherlock Holmes.* New York: Haskell House.
Stendhal
 1948 *Souvenirs d'égotisme,* ed. by H. Martineau. Paris.
Steward-Gordon, James
 1961 "Real-Life Sherlock Holmes." *Reader's Digest* 79 (November):281–288.
Stone, Gregory P., and Harvey A. Farberman
 1970 (eds.) *Social Psychology through Symbolic Interaction.* Waltham, Mass.: Ginn-Blaisdell.
Stout, Rex
 1938 *Too Many Cooks.* London: Collins.
Swanson, Martin J.
 1962 "Graphologists in the Canon." *The Baker Street Journal,* n.s., 12 (June):73–80.
Symons, Julian
 1972 *Bloody Murder; From the Detective Story to the Crime Novel: A History.* London: Faber & Faber.
 1978 *The Tell-Tale Heart: The Life and Works of Edgar Allan Poe.* New York: Harper & Row.

Thagard, Paul R.
 1978 "Semiosis and Hypothetic Inference in Ch. S. Peirce." *Versus* 19–20.
Thom, René
 1972 *Stabilité structurelle et morphogénèse.* Reading, Mass.: W.A. Benjamin.
 (*Structural Stability and Morphogenesis: An Outline of a General Theory of Models.* Reading: W.A. Benjamin, 1975.)
 1980 *Modèles mathématiques de la morphogenèse.* Paris: Christian Bourgois.
Thomas, Lewis
 1983 *The Youngest Science: Notes of a Medicine-Watcher.* New York: The Viking Press.
Thompson, E.P.
 1975 *Whigs and Hunters: The Origin of the Black Act.* London: Allen Lane.
Timpanaro, Sebastiano
 1963 *La genesi del metodo del Lachmann.* Florence: F. Le Monnier.
 1976 *The Freudian Slip.* London: NLB.
Timpanaro Cardini, Maria
 1958 (ed.) *Pitagorici: Testimonianze e frammenti.* Vol. I. Florence: "La Nuova Italia."
Tracy, Jack
 1977 (ed.) *The Encyclopedia Sherlockiana, or A Universal Dictionary of the State of Knowledge of Sherlock Holmes and His Biographer, John H. Watson, M.D.* Garden City, N.Y.: Doubleday.
Traube, L.
 1965 "Geschichte der Palaeographie." In *Zur Palaeographie und Handschriftenkunde,* ed. by P. Lehmann. Munich.
Tronti, M.
 1963 "Baldi." In *Dizionario biografico degli italiani.* Vol. 5, 465–467. Rome.
Truzzi, Marcello
 1973 "Sherlock Holmes: Applied Social Psychologist." In *The Humanities as Sociology, An Introductory Reader,* ed. by Marcello Truzzi, 93–126. Columbus, Ohio: Charles E. Merrill.
Vandermeersch, L.
 1974 "De la tortue à l'Achilée." *Divination et Rationalité,* ed. by J. P. Vernant et al. Paris: Seuil.
Vegetti, Mario
 1965 (ed.) "Introduction." *Opere di Ippocrate.* Turin: U.T.E.T.
 1978 *Il coltello e lo stilo.* Milan: Il Saggiatore.
Vernant, Jean Pierre
 1974 "Paroles et signes muets." In *Divination et Rationalité,* ed. by J.P. Vernant et al. Paris: Seuil.
Vesselofsky, A.
 1886 "Eine Märchengruppe." In *Archiv für slavische Philologie* 9.
Victorius, K.
 1956 "Der 'Moses des Michelangelo' von Sigmund Freud." In *Entfaltung der Psychoanalyse,* ed. by Alexander Mitscherlich. Stuttgart: E. Klett.
Voltaire
 1926 *Zadig and Other Romances,* trans. by H.I. Woolf and W.S. Jackson. New York: Dodd, Mead.
 1961 "Zadig ou la destinée." In *Contes et Romans,* ed. by R. Pomeau. Florence: Sansoni.

Walsh, F. Michael
1972 "Review of Fann (1970)." *Philosophy* 47:377–379.
Warburg, Aby
1932 *Gesammelte Schriften.* Leipzig: Teubner.
Webb, Eugene J.
1966 (et al.) *Unobtrusive Measures: Non-Reactive Research in the Social Sciences.* Chicago: Rand McNally.
Winch, R.F.
1955 "The Theory of Complementary Needs in Mate Selection: Final Results on the Test of the General Hypothesis." *American Sociological Review* 20:552–555.
Winckelmann, J.J.
1952–1954 *Briefe,* ed. by H. Diepolder and W. Rehm. 2 vols. Berlin: W. de Gruyter.
Wind, Edgar
1964 *Art and Anarchy.* New York: Knopf.
Wolff, Julian
1952 *The Sherlockian Atlas.* New York: Privately printed.
1955 *Practical Handbook of Sherlockian Heraldry.* New York: Privately printed.
Wollheim, Richard
1973 "Freud and the Understanding of Art." In *On Art and the Mind.* London: Allen Lane.
Yellen, Sherman
1965 "Sir Arthur Conan Doyle: Sherlock Holmes in Spiritland." *International Journal of Parapsychology* 7:33–57.
Zeisler, Ernest B.
1953 *Baker Street Chronology: Commentaries on the Sacred Writings of Dr. John H. Watson.* Chicago, Ill.: Alexander J. Isaacs.
Zerner, H.
1978 "Giovanni Morelli et la science de l'art." *Revue de l'Art,* 40–41.